BURN

Book 3 of the Apex Society Trilogy

Rhone Atleshen

LONE SPIRE PUBLISHING

SERIES LIST

APEX SOCIETY

Gaslight

Matchstrike

Burn ←you have arrived

BURN

RHONE ATLESHEN

Published by Lone Spire Publishing
www.LoneSpirePublishing.com

ISBN:
eBook: 979-8-9934362-3-4
Paperback: 979-8-9934362-4-1
Hardcover: 979-8-9934362-5-8

Cover design by Candlelight Creative LLC
Interior design by Lone Spire Publishing

Library of Congress Control Number: 2025924206

Printed in the United States of America

First Edition: December 2025
10 9 8 7 6 5 4 3 2 1

DEDICATION

Dedication

For every woman who turned her ruin into reckoning—rise, my Queen.
Their ashes; your rebirth.

Content Advisory

Before you begin...

I write thrillers designed for emotional intensity. The characters and events in these pages aren't real — but the stakes are meant to feel real. My villains do bad things. My heroes are flawed, layered, and not always altruistic.

I hope you enjoy the ride, but your mental and emotional health matter more. In these stories, you'll encounter adult language, violence, and at times sexual content.
If you need to step away–*please do so.*
My characters will still be here when you're ready.

For a list of potential triggers, visit the book's page at www.rhoneatleshen.com before you dive in.
Protect yourself.
Never stop reading.

CONTENTS

PROLOGUE

GIA: 4 MONTHS AGO

THE GILDED BARS OF my childhood were forged in the iron-clad law of unquestioning obedience. From birth, I was taught to heed my father's word as gospel—to be silent, devoted—the perfect daughter who would someday become the perfect wife. I was a prize for someone else's climb up the ladder of destiny.

As such, I was afforded every luxury except freedom.

Freedom was the carrot dangled in front of any rebellion. Someday, my husband might grant me privileges—if I pleased him. I was dressed in the finest clothes, taught by the finest minds, and surrounded by a curated opulence that would've made any Regency-era princess look common.

It was all I knew.

My mother died when I was a baby. I was never told how, but it must have been tragic based on the way my father fretted. He sheltered me so close I had no friends beyond passing acquaintances of my all-girls boarding school and the occasionally generous but short-lived college tutors. All bought and paid for by my father's success; Provisions that came with a political ladder of starched men currying his favor with displays of grandeur and groveling, doled out in equal measure.

I was raised by people on my father's payroll, silently watching polished men adorned by beautifully vague women who offered pitying side glances I couldn't understand. My unremarkable life slipped through obedient fingers, and they averted their eyes from the truth in my bruises.

The week of my 21st birthday, my father had a business trip that lasted longer than expected. Even before I received his text that he'd miss our planned birthday dinner, I knew he'd be late. The household was on edge, silent in its acknowledgement; unplanned changes made him irritable. His role in the political world demanded tight control over everything, and his temper showed in full force when plans went awry. Knowing my role, I ensured the staff had the house spotless, everything in its place, and his favorite meal prepared in case he came home in time.

When dinner passed and he'd not arrived, I tidied his office and waited with a drink.

Three nights of dinners wasted and drinks sat sweating as I held my breath for his explosive arrival. Three nights of me pacing the house, checking the lights, locks, and windows before slipping into bed and praying I wouldn't wake up to the whole house in terror.

On the fourth night, my father's harsh stomping echoed like thunder. Bellowing so loudly I could hear him all the way from my perch on his office Chesterfield, I rose to meet him, hoping his favorite scotch and a smiling daughter might soothe the anger he spewed at whoever was on the other end of his phone call. Instead, I was thrown off course when I met him in the hallway and found him holding a baby.

"What the..."

My father ended his call, already two steps past me, before he stopped and glowered over his shoulder like I'd thrown rocks at his back. Turning, he shoved the baby into my arms, grabbing the scotch from me, assuming my reflexes wouldn't let the helpless child drop to the ground. Heart thumping, I clutched the tiny dark-haired bundle, still miraculously sleeping despite my father's noise and jostling; I was shocked at how tiny and new it appeared.

"This can be your responsibility until I can secure a nanny." He ran his hand through his tousled, slicked-back hair, slugging the scotch in a gulp before straightening his tie and smoothing down the front of his charcoal suit jacket.

Unable to fully comprehend his command, words flew from my mouth before I had time to think.

"Whose baby is this?" I asked, knowing I was on thin ice. "How old is - "

"Don't question me, Gia." He cut me short and stalked to his office. I followed behind him, waiting for more information about why an entire little life was thrust into my hands. I wanted him to tell me how this happened and if this was why his travel plans were so disrupted. I needed to know what he meant by this being my responsibility. Foolishly, I pressed harder, desperate to hear that this baby wasn't proof of things I had long feared, that his darker dealings had shifted lower than drugs and weapons.

"Where is this baby's mother?" I blame my shock for my harsh tone; I was pushing too hard.

My father ignored me as he methodically poured a 2nd drink, the clinking ice resonating between us. A subtle shifting I should have recognized for what it was slipped into the air between us—the calm before the storm.

"You know, maybe I don't need a Nanny." He didn't face me as he spoke, but I felt his anger in as surely as if he'd spit in my face. "Perhaps you need a little more responsibility if you think you're old enough to question me, now." The words crashed over me like a bucket of cold water as my brain pieced together the pieces of clues I hadn't yet seen.

A trip elongated.

A baby with no mother.

Plans to keep it long enough to need a nanny.

"Is this baby...yours?" I knew, with a clarity only earned through past failures, that I had taken a step too far. Still, I couldn't stop myself in the face of this helpless life, stirring in my arms and grasping my finger as if begging me to find answers.

My father's response was nearly inaudible.

"I'll tell you this, and no more. The baby stays, and you will care for it until I find a suitable place for it. This is your duty as my daughter," he half smirked as a huff of laughter slipped out. "Consider it practice for the babies you'll soon have."

"Soon?" My heart stuttered in my chest at the weight of his words.

Duty. Practice. Soon. It.

My father never bluffed. His every word was drenched in absolute truth, and it was something his enemies never learned fast enough.

But I did. I knew.

My time was limited, and in the wake of that clarity, I spoke carelessly.

"I don't know how to take care of a—"

My face jolted to the side so fast that I barely registered the change in my field of vision as the world flew hard to the right. The pain didn't register fully until the cold marble floor jumped up to meet me, my wrist twinging as I caught myself from falling onto the startled baby, jolted awake in my arms with wide eyes staring into mine.

"He's your responsibility! Understood!?" My father's voice was unhinged screams between spittle and red-faced fury as his glass went careening across the marble, shattering around me in a glittering spray of violence and light against the black floor.

I'd been on the receiving end of his discipline, or as he called them, corrections, before. But never was his voice louder than a growl, and never had he hit my face. As the numb detachment curled around me, I looked down at the crying, red-faced baby and its little trembling hand, and my heart broke.

I didn't know if the baby was a boy or a girl; did they have a name or a mother?

Gripping my fingertip again, the tiny thing rooted towards my hand, slipping the tip of my pinky into its mouth with a suckling motion that seemed to soothe, and my heart seized with pain that in this moment...I was the only comfort this baby had. I was shelter for that tiny soul. Me. Nothing else mattered. Only when I saw a small drop of blood fall onto its cheek did I realize Father had struck me with such force that he split my lip, shattering something irreparably within me.

"You will not question me again." His black dress shoes slipped into my field of vision, their gleaming shine set against the black marble floor and the shimmering shards of discarded anger. He stepped so close I could feel his rage boring a hole into the top of my head.

The stance brooked no argument.

He expected compliance.

The baby needed it.

"Yes...Papa," I whispered as I focused on the tear-filled blue eyes begging me to protect him.

Satisfied by my answer, the man who'd raised me walked away as I knelt in a bleeding heap, clutching some stranger's child; my obedience now its cloak of protection.

I didn't know it then, but that distant shattering of glass was the sound of my cage breaking.

1

TROY

Sentinel Alert: Fire alarm event logged at 211 E. Pineview Ln at 4:37 PM ET.

Alarm cancelled onsite.

Reply 1 to request local dispatch.

Reply 2 to confirm receipt and close this notification.

For assistance, call Sentinel Monitoring at 1-800-555-0199.

"WHAT'S UP?" CHASE PULLED my focus back to the room full of family watching me.

"Text about a rental property." I set my coffee mug in the sink like I wasn't already halfway out the door. Sam leaned forward, reading me like a book.

"You're heading over there?" His concern was touching, if not grating. The ping on my phone was routine—likely a false alarm. I'd upgraded every damn alarm system we owned after Chase's fire. This notification was a matter of protocol, and my brothers need not worry.

"Likely nothing," I tried to wave them off.

I should've dismissed it. But I hadn't rejected a routine text since I'd put these systems in place, and my brothers had no idea. I'd added trackers to vehicles, safety nets, and redundancies galore, in the name of family defense, and it was my honor. But the growing pressure, 'one missed signal and it'll fall apart,' had my skin crawling. I'd learned the hard way how fast nothing turned into catastrophe—Chase's fire, Sam's shooting, the scars we carried from both. Still, my brothers were immensely, deservingly, happy. The last thing they needed was a ride along as I wrestled the voice taunting me, 'but it's never nothing, is it?

"Our Pineview rental detected a fire alarm." I smoothed my tie and pocketed my clenched fists. "It was cancelled onsite. I was texted as a point of procedure." My family gathered closer, reading what I wasn't saying and ruining my attempts to salvage their happy brunch.

"Your face says you'd like to check it out." Moira chirped, the only one in the room still carrying a semblance of a smile as was her way. I could have argued further, but I gave up the ghost when even Lila shot me that narrowed stare of scrutiny.

"So, we'll go." Chase handed his daughter, River, to his wife. "Sam can come too in case they need first aid." Sam glanced at his new bride for approval before disappearing to his room.

"A check in would be prudent," I turned my gaze to Lila, merely hours home from her honeymoon and losing her husband to nothing more than a false alarm. "But only if new sister doesn't mind me stealing away her husband."

"As long as you promise never to call me 'new sister' again...we're good." Lila gave her sing-song response while waving the chubby hand of baby Blue at me. "We can girl-talk about you all while you're gone."

I didn't miss the wistful glance my brothers gave the rearview as we piled into Sam's SUV. My brother's happiness brought me happiness, and I was always, only, ever in their court when it came to making sure their lives were whole and fulfilling. A role our Nonna entrusted me with before she died, her frail hand in mine as she commanded, 'Troy, you are such an old soul. Lead your brothers in happiness.' I wasn't entirely sure what that meant then, but seeing their smiles now—the women they loved by their sides—I supposed it was a task well done, even if the stress of their journey to bliss had a gnawing darkness growling inside of me.

Too much darkness had touched the people I loved lately.

We arrived at the rental to find the front door slightly ajar, and all the lights in the house on, though the blinds were closed. Walking up the two small steps, I could hear a woman's voice inside, repetitive sounds mimicking the soothing of a child. This caught my attention since the rental agreement never mentioned a child, and I wondered if there were possibly others inside that weren't planned. The closer we got to the door, the more I could hear pacing footsteps and even intermixed shushing sounds.

"Ma'am," I called out, perched a few steps back from the door so as not to startle the woman inside. "I don't want to alarm you. I am Sgt. Troy Wilder of the local Police Department." The steps halted. "This is a courtesy visit regarding the fire alarm. I am here to make sure everything is okay." I waited a heartbeat, staring into the cracked door and willing it to open. A heartbeat later, a forcefully light and airy voice called out.

"I told the company that called...it was a false alarm." The woman spoke clearly enough, but the hesitation had me clenching. "There is no fire. I lost track of my dinner. That's all." A baby began to fuss again, and shuffling footsteps sounded until the woman's voice murmured until the cries subsided.

My brothers and I exchanged a quick look; we all sensed something was off. I nodded towards Chase to step forward.

"Ma'am, I'm Lt. Chase Wilder with the Fire Department. I'm glad it's a false alarm. But since I'm here, I could double-check the stove and oven; make sure everything is working correctly."

I strained to hear any noises that might give probable cause to enter the premises, my anxiety growing at being held on the outside of a cracked door. I jerked my chin at Sam, who took his turn.

"And I'm Sam...a local EMT. If that false alarm caused any scrapes or burns, I'm happy to patch you up. Free of charge, and we can be out of your hair in no time."

Relieved as I was to pull up and not see smoke, the open door and disembodied voice had that protective urge inside me clawing to the surface. A woman was inside with a baby, and something triggered the fire alarm. If it was nothing, why hide from us?

"No one is in trouble," I added. "But I need to lay eyes on you before I can go."

It was a slip, far more personal than intended, but accurate. I needed to see both the woman and the child safe and unharmed. I couldn't leave without it.

"Do you have a badge?" She was closer now, and I looked up to find her peeking around the door's edge. Her face was partially hidden, but I inventoried what I could.

Jet-black hair.

Ice-blue eyes.

Lilting voice.

And smart...insisting on a badge from three strangers at her door.

"This place isn't mine. I'm just renting it. I don't want to get in trouble with the owner by having people over without permission."

"Good girl." The praise fell from my lips carelessly, but it fit my pride that she'd taken control of her safety in that small way. Praying that my brothers had missed the faux pas, I handed over my badge, clocking the bloodied dish towel wrapped around her outstretched hand. "I'm the property owner. The alarm triggered a courtesy alert—no authorities were called."

I pointed to my business card, gently sliding it free to show her the NB Realty logo, my name, and title, which matched the name on my license and badge. Then we waited as she scrutinized my documents before pulling the door open enough for a full view of her.

She was tall and willowy, with a flawless, fair complexion that stood in stark contrast to the dark hair framing her breathtaking face. She clutched my badge and ID with one hand, but in the other, she held an infant swaddled in a blue blanket. Wrapped as he was, I could only see the shock of dark hair that matched hers, tufting out from under his small hat.

"That has the makings of a mighty fine gash." Sam's voice floated around me, but the woman hardly took her eyes off me. "I brought a small first aid kit, and I could clean it up for you." She briefly flicked her gaze to Chase and Sam before settling her gaze back to me.

That's when I noticed the dissociated cast that looked too war-weary to belong to a carefree young mother. She had a wide glance, a thousand yards long, seeing everything and nothing with pure adrenaline-laced fatigue fringing the edges of what seemed to be complete and utter terror. I'd seen it before, and I burned to make it all go away. Taking in her predicament again, clearly wanting to keep us all out and seemingly needing to find some semblance of control, I offered a compromise.

"If you would feel more comfortable, we are happy to see you on the porch, out in the open, though I would advise an extra blanket for your child."

She tugged the baby closer, as if afraid I might take him from her, and I hated that I had become part of her fear. She needed to trust me if she was going to let me help her. I needed her to trust me if I was going to walk away with any peace of mind.

"And I can call the police department to verify your badge number?" Her chin raised in beautiful defiance as she ignored her fear, and I felt a small measure of relief that she wasn't so beaten down as to cower in the face of three large men on her porch.

"I encourage it." I smiled. "Officer Kramer should be answering tonight if I recall the duty roster. She is easy to speak with. I can provide the direct number for you if you like, or you can use my phone to - "

"Okay." She tucked my badge and ID into her pocket with a wince, drawing my eyes again to her bloodied hand. I had no grounds to enter the premises forcibly. Still, all my instincts were telling me that this woman needed help, and I wasn't leaving until I had answers.

"My hand does hurt." Stepping back, she opened the door in invitation even while hugging the infant closer to her. "But afterwards, you can all go."

I nodded, but I knew better.

This wasn't over.

Not by a long shot.

2

TROY

THE SIMPLE ONE-BEDROOM COTTAGE was in an odd state of disarray, though it lacked the hallmark aroma of charred food. From the glance my brother cast my way, I could tell Chase also noticed the empty stovetop and lack of burned food. In fact, the kitchen looked hardly used, except for the floor around the small table, where a vase had shattered, leaving puddles of glass and broken flower stems strewn across the floor. Sam nodded towards the small drops of blood near the back door, and the woman followed his eyeline.

"I was in a rush...from the smoke alarm...and knocked it to the floor." She held her bandaged hand with an awkward shrug, "I hadn't had a chance to clean it up yet with all the phone calls and drop-in visitors."

The pointed note of irritation in her voice rang false, and that grated on my inner desire to see her safe and unharmed. I needed her open honesty if I was going to feel secure about leaving her here, even though all my alarm bells told me she was hiding something big.

"As I mentioned, my name is Sam. And you are?" Sam lowered himself into a chair at the small table, opening his medic kit and gesturing to the seat across from him with casual ease.

"I'm J–" Her name stuttered in the air between us, and she cleared her throat, adjusting the pacifier for the baby in her arms.

Another lie.

"Jane." My eyes scanned past the unpacked suitcase in the living room, noting how Sam made space to work by sliding aside partially full grocery bags of diapers, infant formula, and toiletries–all in their original packaging. Jane noticed my eyeline, too.

"I just checked in yesterday. Hadn't had a chance to unpack fully to find my things."

Too many things didn't add up—the empty stovetop, the fresh bags, the blood drops leading to the back door. This wasn't just a tenant fumbling dinner. This was a woman on the run.

"If you are like me," Sam gave the baby a jovial smile, "There's no point in unpacking when you just have to repack later, ammiright?" I appreciated his casual assertion that he, too, could see she planned to be temporary, even as he gingerly unwrapped Jane's hand for cleaning.

She never flinched, not at the cleaning, nor the antiseptic spray he applied. Instead, her eyes followed all our movements with an impressive display of focused dissonance.

Hyper vigilant, never eased, seated as if perched to run.

"I hope you are otherwise settling in well?" Sam continued, noting Jane's nod of affirmation even as I felt her eyes on me. I made for the laundry room, knowing there would be a broom and dustpan, and used the time to visually survey the rest of the house, noting the lack of a travel crib or bassinet for her child.

"The place has been great. Very comfortable." A thin smile accompanied her shallow compliment.

"It's a jagged cut, but not deep. You won't need stitches, but derma glue would help hold it closed while it heals." Sam applied his skills effortlessly, and I found myself grateful that she wasn't in any pain under his care. "I can bandage it and give you the address to the local urgent care clinic in case you see signs of–"

"I'm leaving tomorrow." Jane half-shouted the response, jerking her eyes back towards her hand as if she'd just remembered Sam was in the room. He froze, body stilled by her sudden rise in reaction, but I didn't miss the swift glance he cast my way, both of us noting her forced smile when she added. "I'm sure it'll be fine...thank you."

"So soon?" Chase asked, returning from the back room with a subtle head shake. No fire source found. "You've only just arrived."

"Yeah. I have had a change of plans." She watched as I slowly began tidying the broken glass into a pile. "I'll get on the road early and head to my final destination."

I bent to grab some large pieces of glass, uncovering a florist card hidden in the debris. Flipping it to read the note, I felt my jaw lock tight as my vision narrowed down to the small, typed letters.

"Your flowers," my voice was a symphony of practiced calm. "They were a delivery?"

"A gift...from a friend." Jane's voice grew distant as I took in the pile of broken red flags still sitting at my feet. Tiny lies, discarded to the ground in defense of what? "It was clumsy of me to knock them over...I feel bad."

Chase moved to my side, noting the atmospheric shift, and I casually snapped a pic and sent it to the family group chat. I held the card out for Sam to read, seeing afresh the pile of broken white roses, with a ticking time bomb in my hand, inscribed,

Courtesy of

The Apex Society.

Apex.

Again.

Jane's lies all reframed in the light of this new, damning revelation, and the beast I long kept hidden from my family began snarling, demanding I drag the truth from her if only to haul her from this house and into my own to keep her and her baby safe.

My brothers, having no doubt read the text messages flooding in from their wives, made polite excuses and stepped outside, leaving me Sam's vacated chair in front of Jane.

"Jane." She was watching my brothers leave and didn't so much as blink at the mention of her name.

False or not, I needed her to answer me. I needed her to hear me and see me as safe so that I could shield her from whatever vile thing Apex had planned. Apex, the albatross that had plagued my town and my family for far too long, and one that had eluded my grip and nearly cost me everything.

"Jane," I snapped, softly but firm enough that her wide, round eyes came back to me. I had her attention; now I had to keep it. "I have concerns about your situation here."

She was shaking her head even before I finished speaking.

"I appreciate your visit, but as you can see, there is no fire." She snuggled her baby like a shield, readying to stand, and all my protective instincts screamed to stop her.

If she left, I'd lose track of her. Whoever was after her could find her again, and she'd have no protection. I couldn't let her be hurt, be killed, because I couldn't keep her safe.

"I'll clear out tomorrow, and you can rent the space out to another– "

"Please, do not mistake my concern as that of a landlord." I lifted my hand in petition, noting her ramrod posture —rigid and straight, but frozen, no longer trying to stand. "I do not care about the house, only its occupant." I surveyed her face for every nuanced expression I could find in an effort to read her, aching to make her feel secure, and hating that I didn't know how. "I can't protect you if you run."

Jane's breathing grew shallow, and her eyes blinked rapidly in an attempt to dam the tears I saw glistening at the edges of those ebony lashes.

"I...I don't..." A battle was waging behind those hypnotic blue eyes of hers, and whatever two sides warred for dominance, they both had a hold on her so tight she could barely speak. If Apex was after her, and she was running with a baby, her situation had to have been more dire than we'd encountered as yet. I wanted, needed, to protect her, but first I needed to shut down the onslaught in her head so she could hear me and trust that I meant her no harm.

"Jane." I let my hand fall gently on top of hers and the babe she folded around. Not gripping, not pulling—just a warm weight.

Steady. Unmovable.

That's what I meant to be for her.

Enough for her to lean on if she chose.

At my touch, she glanced down at my hand, her tears winning out as they fell on my hand, and at last she exhaled a long, slow breath.

"I will not hurt you or your baby. I *will* keep you safe. But I need to know what happened here."

She lifted her gaze back to me, measuring my words against whatever conflict still consumed her, and I steadied my whole body, preparing to wait as long as she needed to find me honorable enough to shield her.

"I know trust is the last thing you've got left to give. Please, give me just a little and I'll prove to you I'm worth it."

3

JANE

H E PROMISED HE WAS worthy, and in my moment of blind, exhausted, drained despair, my whole body screamed to give up. Hand over every decision in my life if for no other reason than to have a reprieve from the stress of being in the constant hot seat of choices with unknown consequences.

But what were the promises of strangers when I couldn't trust the word of the man who'd raised me? The same man who'd sent one of his henchmen to attack me with flowers, sitting shattered around my feet.

"You can call the police on the number I gave you earlier. Verify my name and badge number." Sgt. Wilder repeated his proof of his identity. I wanted that to be enough, but I scanned the room still, as if someone might jump out from behind a chair. "Or I could call a unit out here to assist us further–"

No. Ben. They'll take Ben!

"I don't need to go to a police station!" My head pounded as I fought to remain as calm as possible under the weight of a thousand ways my world was unraveling. I'd taken Ben with me, but my father clearly hadn't reported me missing, not when he had his own reasons for wanting me back. So did that make me Ben's kidnapper...or was I a caretaker? If police came, with questions, would they see me as a loving mother, or would they be the pin pulled in my grenade of lies that would send us both hurtling back into my father's clutches?

"Ben and I are just going to rest tonight and then we'll..."

Sgt. Wilder's face spread into a warm smile that caught me off guard.

"His name is Ben?" He smiled at Ben, not reaching for him or touching him, but admiring him while his hand gently guided me back down to my seat. "A good, strong name. Is it short for Benjamin?"

"Benji, actually," offering more information out of sheer trained obedience, then instantly hating my Pavlovian response. I should have given them a false name for him, too, or else they might report us, and my father would find–

"And you?" His question took me aback, and he must have seen it in my expression as he removed his hand, sitting back into a position of casual repose. "Do you have a last name, Jane?"

A last name. Suddenly, my brain went empty for want of a last name. Holding my mask steady, pure panic choked off my words as I realized I was not keeping track of the lies I'd already told and the litany of ones I would no doubt need to draft. Luckily, as if the universe knew I needed a reprieve from the scrutiny, Ben began to squirm and grunt.

"Oh no. I forgot. I was getting his bottle ready when—" I stopped, my contradiction glaring at me as I surveyed the clean kitchen, free of all dishes, and shopping bags filled with no food. The lie about ruining my dinner burned its way to the surface, and panic gripped my chest.

"If he's like my nieces, you are now precariously short on time before he erupts like Mt. Vesuvius." Sgt. Wilder somehow, blessedly, missed my flub. "Stay seated and rest. I'll prepare his bottle."

There was that word again, rest. My body was tired on a cellular level. His offer of assistance on such a simple task felt like a drop of water in a vast desert of exhaustion.

"How many ounces does he take?"

"I, uh..." I had to clear the emotion from my throat before I could talk him through the bottle-making process, and it all felt easier to do it myself as I was accustomed to. "I can do it."

I stood, but Troy offered only a simple raised eyebrow, his body relaxed and steady and unyielding as he awaited me to slowly sit back into my chair.

Why did I do that?

"It's no trouble, Jane. And I'll be just here, where you can see that I do it correctly."

I could blame his looming presence. I was 5'8", and slim if not athletic. But Sgt. Wilder was easily over 6 feet tall and carried a bevy of well-defined muscles that showed in every movement. The ropes of strength in his neck disappeared into his fully buttoned dress shirt, even as it pulled across his broad shoulders. His biceps strained when he crossed his arms, and his thighs pulled his slacks taut when he sat. He wore a badge, a holster for guns that I was relieved to see were missing, and a slick-shaved scalp with a pin-tight goatee. For all intents and purposes, he should have been terrifying. But he wasn't. He moved with an ease, so different from the chaotic machismo I was raised around. Sitting back down, I watched as he prepared Ben's bottle, saying nothing until his phone vibrated an alert in his pocket. He glanced at the screen and then returned to me, shaking Ben's bottle.

"I have information." He handed me the bottle and stepped several steps back to lean against the kitchen counter. "I invited my sisters to meet you. They will arrive soon. I didn't want you to be alarmed when they pulled up, but I believe they can help."

I was pivoting Ben around to rest in my bandaged arm, but halted as his words registered.

"Why would you invite...your sisters? I don't understand." Sgt. Wilder remained in the kitchen, well away from me, as if trying to be less intimidating. Still, the idea of more people coming at me had me scanning the windows. More people meant more questions, and I was so beyond terrified that any wrong answer could have dire consequences.

"If you will trust me," His voice was smooth and even, no placating frustration lacing his words. "I have information that might be better received from the fairer side of my family. I apologize for the extra stress, and I want to remind you again that my goal is only to keep you and young Ben safe. I promise it will make sense."

"Information?" I looked at the baby in my arms and remembered the other two huge men who, no doubt, lingered outside, and I felt suddenly vulnerable. I couldn't have outrun three men before, but now more people were coming, and I was entirely at their mercy. "I have no options here."

Sgt. Wilder winced at the words I didn't realize I had whispered aloud.

"Please, Jane. I will not let anyone harm you...Or Ben. Please," He pleaded, his face nearly stricken as he lifted a hand to the door. "Moira, she's blonde and bubbly. She is a new mother, and I know she would love to meet young Ben. Lila, my other sister, is a bit more sardonic. She is newly pregnant and would also be honored to meet you. I share these details so you won't feel so disadvantaged when they arrive, and to try again and be as transparent with you as I can. Above all, they wish to help you understand more about your situation, as do I, so that we can help you."

"Understand what?" Panic climbed up my spine as my phone vibrated in my pocket, indicating a text I couldn't read.

I'd received more than one message since Sgt. Wilder arrived, and each notification felt like a noose around my throat. The last message I'd read came moments before the flowers, which, still, sat mockingly at my feet.

> Papa: I'll be seeing you...

My father never said anything idly, and his threat proved nearly true when the not-delivery man shoved his way in behind a vase of flowers, grabbing my hair and pulling me to the door. I felt helpless until I saw Ben, asleep still, where I'd laid him carefully on the couch. That burst of adrenaline made the vase an easy weapon, and the man's face an easy target. Blood fell into his eye from the fresh gash across his forehead, and it was enough of a distraction for me to lunge at the alarm panel on the wall, and God, how I wished any of that energy sustained me now as I tried to shake off the memory and reclaim my footing.

"There is no situation here." I made one more effort to appear fine, still hoping to make a hasty escape if only I could get the man to leave so I could pause to think things through. "I keep telling you I am fine, and Ben and I will just be - "

"Those white roses weren't a gift." His voice cut sharply through my panic as he pushed on, "They were a warning."

4

JANE

E VERY NERVE ENDING IN my body went simultaneously numb and raw.

My father's affinity for the white roses as a harbinger of doom was commonplace to me, but hearing this officer of the law, a man all but begging me to trust him, recognize their menace settled into my bones. Was this the man I was searching for? Who might help me?

Not that I had much time to contemplate it before a tap at the door scared me to death.

"The girls are here." The EMT, Sam, hooked a thumb over his shoulder from the open doorway. "Is it okay if we let them in?"

He held a peaceful expression, free from any urgency or pressure that I expected and, I realized, I had grown far too used to. I wondered if Sam knew what the flowers meant. The silence lingering, I looked to Sgt. Wilder for his response, only to find him watching me with an expression of patient resignation. He, too, wasn't ruffled or anxious but calm despite the utter storm raging in my chest. That's when I realized Sam's request for permission wasn't directed at the officer...but to me. They were waiting for me to approve or deny their offer, and they both seemed perfectly at ease waiting for me to answer in my time. Surprise tossed its hat into the flurry of emotions I now wrestled.

"Chase and I can come in or wait outside. It's your call, Jane." Sam's added line, 'it's your call,' only reinforced their desire to give me choices, and I was dumbfounded.

Sgt. Wilder made it clear he wanted these women to come, to help, but they weren't forcing me. The EMT, the Cop, and presumably the Firefighter, too, were giving me a choice. Exhilarating as it could have been on another day, in another life, today it was simply too much. I began considering all my angles, then following each to its end reaction to try to foresee any permutation I might need to be prepared for. It was easier with my father; he wanted blind obedience and otherwise my silence, but these men were new. This situation was different. I had Ben, and little else, and I felt like I might drown in the decision-making, if not for a woman's voice floating over their head.

"Of course, you all need to wait outside." A smack resounded as the EMT smirked over his shoulder. "She definitely doesn't need a giant wall of muscle freaking her out right now." The two men parted to let a blonde woman pass through. Her golden hair bounced around her shoulders, and her pink cheeks had a little glow of what could be described as effervescent.

"We got this, guys." Another second woman's voice, with a definitive New York accent, entered boldly, accompanied by a curvaceous woman with wild, golden-brown locks. She hooked a thumb over her shoulder to the porch as she took a seat at the table across from me. "You too, Troy. Muscle on the porch, if you please."

Sgt. Wilder's eyes never left mine, and in the flickering second that passed between us, I think I begged him to stay.

"I'm not leaving her." He uncrossed his arms, pocketing his hands in a move that felt casual but restrained still as he exhaled in time with my own. Nodding his chin at me, he reaffirmed the earlier message. "Take a moment if you need to. We won't begin until you are ready."

Another choice to make, and if I chose poorly, there would be a hidden consequence. Who would pay the consequences this time? Ben? My phone vibrated another text alert in my pocket, and it might as well have been an electric cattle prod for the way it jolted me to speak.

"I'm not even sure what's happening," I stalled. "Who are you people?" I folded around Ben, gazing down at his contented expression and trying desperately to lose myself in his beautiful eyes for just a moment. He trusted me so freely, and I had to be strong, to be smart, for him.

Another text message set my teeth on edge, and with it came a wave of frustration that I'd ever answered the phone for the alarm company. I should have ignored the call and fled, but I didn't, and now here I sat, surrounded by a growing crowd of people who seemed kind and terrifying, while losing precious time to outrun whoever else my father may have sent to collect me.

"We will tell you everything about who we are and answer all your questions." The blonde began.

"But whoever sent those flowers is still out there." The dark-haired woman added pragmatically. "We're on borrowed time." Tallying my dwindling list of options, the staggering accuracy of her words hit like a ton of bricks. I didn't have time to navigate my ever-growing sea of worries and doubts. I had spun wildly off track of my one goal, and the longer we lingered here, the closer I came to my father finding me yet again. I was on borrowed time, as was Ben, and that spurred my frustration to rise above all the fear, all the doubt, until it spilled out in a flurry of decisive anger.

"Then give me the highlights!" My raised voice startled Ben, who fussed around his bottle, and his agitation steeled my indignant spark. "And talk fast; I'm a good listener, but for god's sake, get on with it." My patience was shot, but looking at Ben now, resettled and again drinking his bottle, I told myself I could be brave for him. I could show him what not-cowering looked like. "You have until this bottle is gone to say whatever you need." I pulled out my phone, dialed a nine and then a one, and set it on the table in front of me, my finger poised over the one in clear threat to my intention to call the cavalry if need be. "And Ben's a fast eater. So, I suggest you explain what you know about those flowers quickly."

"Oh, I like her so much," The blonde smiled at Sgt. Wilder, before turning to the dark-haired New Yorker. "Reader's Digest version?"

"I'm Lila." The brunette began. "I was a cop in Manhattan before coming out here. I'm married to that one." She pointed to the EMT, still standing outside but leaning on the doorjamb. "I got my roses from a sleazy uptown attorney who ruined my career, murdered my family, and tried to kill me for what I knew." I kept my face trained on her, as calm as possible, while my stomach roiled at the familiar violence of her straightforward words. "These guys all found me, hid me, helped me, and ultimately saved my life."

I knew that sleazy attorney…too well. Not that I spoke, as the blonde picked up the story.

"I'm Moira." She smiled and waved, sympathy in her eyes despite her chipper tone. "I'm married to the big guy." The hulk of a firefighter lifted a hand in salute. "I was catfished out here by a creep who sent white roses like there was a fire sale at the florist. Then he set my apartment on fire and tried to kidnap me." It was hard to fathom how they could deliver the details without so much as a tremble in their voices. "These three found and protected me and ultimately saved us both." She gave a waving gesture towards Lila before smiling at Ben. "I have twin girls who look about the age of your little guy. Ben is his name?"

"Benji." Sgt. Wilder answered for me, moving to stand next to the other men. "And it's worth noting, these two are my sisters because they married my brothers." I took them all in, seeing absolutely no family resemblance between the giant blonde fireman, the swarthy EMT, and the strikingly handsome officer whose warm brown skin and smooth voice had somehow become the only thing keeping me from bolting from the room.

"We're triplets." The EMT said, smiling as his eyes lit with playful excitement.

"Adopted," the fireman clarified, with an eyeroll at his brother. "No resemblance except the stubborn streak."

"We thought maybe we were past the worst of all this when my bad guy and her bad guy both..." Moira let her words trail off when I jerked at another notification vibrating in my pocket.

A text fired like a bullet straight through my chest.

A reality settling in the hole it left behind. The longer I sat, the closer my father got.

"Jane." Sgt. Wilder crouched in front of me until we were eye to eye. "The cut on your hand didn't come from spilling a vase. No burned dinner set off the alarm. You aren't here on vacation." In a breath, he'd stripped me bare of almost every lie I'd told him. "You need to be safe. You need to be hidden. I can provide a place where you and your baby can rest. You can tell us your story when you feel stronger."

Rest. Safety. I could hardly believe those things still existed. Yet, my whole being screamed to wrap my arms around the man in thanks because, for some inexplicable reason, I believed him.

"Please," Moira said, leaning forward and reaching across the table, not quite touching me. "Let us help you the way they helped us."

"You aren't doing this alone," Lila added. "But you gotta take a leap here."

"We won't force you." The EMT added.

"But if you choose to stay here, we'll need to gather camping supplies." The fireman gave a small smile, a hint of a dimple showing. "'Cause no way you're going it alone."

Their blunt delivery came with the ring of truth. They didn't shelter me from the harshness of their stories. They hadn't pressured me, hadn't tried to bend to their will, either. I hadn't been cajoled or coddled or shamed into action or inaction.

I could go with them.

I could stay.

Either way, they would try to protect me.

As my eyes went back to the officer in front of me, his hand slowly lifted to brush a thumb across my cheek, wiping away a tear I hadn't realized had fallen. His warm, dark eyes and chiseled jaw were a study in confident peace, and his whole countenance called to me like a burning fire on a cold night. A fire that called out to all the parts of me hidden away, begging me to rest in him.

A variety of scenarios played out in my head. I could refuse, go my own way, and last how long? How long could I run when I was out of cash, using a car registered to my father, owning nothing of my own, and dragging a baby along with me, searching for some unknown help? I was using a fake name that I'd only now considered, and I was bone-weary tired. Even if I tried to push on alone, I was already making mistakes...and what if the next person who found me wasn't so easy to scare away?

Would my next time come with a group of people begging to help me?

Would the next time even be survivable, and if not, what would happen to Ben?

That was the final thought that entered my mind as I looked into Sgt. Wilder's dark, umber eyes, then down at Ben. How much longer could I fight the whole damn world with a baby in tow?

Breathing in slowly, I held my breath as if preparing to leap off a cliff into oblivion on a wing and a prayer that I was making the right choice.

"Okay."

5

TROY

J ANE'S HESITATION WAS BORN of fear; that much was plain. Still, the lies she'd told grated against my desire to know everything I needed to know to help her. And the way she held little Ben so protectively, clutching him as if she feared I would snatch him right out of her arms. Had someone tried to take her baby? I shuddered to think of what she may have already endured. Her striking blue eyes had pupils blown wide the entire time we were there, and that fear was the hook I hung my theories on. Resolved as I was to earn her trust, seeing her dried blood along the edges of that last shard of glass had the beast in me wanting someone to pay, and it was unsettling. In all my years on the force, all I'd seen as a cop, my anger had never been a consideration.

Something in *her* drove this.

My sisters helped Jane gather her belongings, while Sam and I walked the perimeter. The anger I felt at finding nothing of use was palpable, but the walkabout did my temper good. Chase stayed behind, spending that time tidying the rental. He did a serviceable job, but I was compelled to scrutinize every room, ensuring no trace of Jane and little Ben remained.

Loading Jane's things into the car, I found my brothers conversing in hushed tones on the porch. A pang of guilt stabbed into me. With Jensen and Brinks gone, they had just begun to settle into the domestic bliss they deserved. My haphazard text to their wives, knowing they would rally, left my brothers no way to side-step this mess. My instinct to provide Jane with a sense of security clashed with my role as patriarch. Approaching them now, I prepared for their well-deserved frustration. I was ready to apologize, then push forward alone, for her.

"Whatever you are thinking right now, the answer is no," Chase began with a stern look.

"No?"

"That somehow you've failed to shield us from something." Chase mimicked my arms-crossed stance and continued. "That you need to take all this on, alone, protecting us like when we were kids."

Speechless.

Sam cocked a thumb at Chase and gave a wry grin.

"What he said." He crossed his arms, too, the three of us standing as we often did when conferring on something. "We walked into this at the same time. You didn't do anything we wouldn't have done." I marveled at their support, even as they had new lives to think of beyond themselves; they read me like a book. "We know that look."

"You 100% had my back when Moira showed up. Especially when the shit hit the fan." Chase lifted a fist, and Sam knocked his against it.

"And don't think I didn't see you engage Lila's cop instincts, drawing her out little by little." Their words squeezed into my chest as Sam motioned to the space between him and Chase. "We're good now."

"We've got you." Chase finalized with a nod.

I opened my mouth to argue, but Sam cut me off.

"Just so we're clear, Apex is still a problem, right?" Sam's question was aimed at Chase, who hauled up a last bag of trash.

"So it would seem." Chase glanced over his shoulder at me. "We assume you'll be using that new cabin - on the other side of Sam and Lila?"

No hint of frustration at my rash actions, nor any hesitation in rallying Jane's aid. I had to swallow hard around my pride in them both.

"Uh-oh," Sam teased. "Grandpa's speechless."

"Does this make us the big brothers now?" Chase puffed his chest, beating on it like a caveman.

"Who knows what might go off the rails?" Sam and Chase laughed, slapping my shoulders and tugging me back into the house.

Stumbling after them, I swear I felt the beast in me unfurl a little bit, like a bear stretching after a long hibernation, ready to launch into the world.

6

TROY

WHEN WE ENTERED, THE girls had Jane and Ben packed, and my brothers began loading the final items into the car. Jane sat in the same chair, still holding Ben, who appeared to be alert but calm, as Moira spoke gently to them both. Lila sidled up next to me, her voice hushed.

"I have yet to link Apex to anything nefarious." She thumbed the florist card we'd found. "I've checked tax records, news, and media sources, and more. Their footprint is pristine."

"But you have a theory?"

"We only know about Apex because of Brinks and Jensen." She narrowed her eyes on the card. "Maybe Apex stays clean. It's the members who get their hands dirty." She tipped her chin towards Jane. "So maybe *her* story starts with a guy, too."

Lila's hypothesis rammed into me like a Mack truck. I'd nearly lost both my sisters and my brothers to Apex men. I loathed to imagine what Jane had endured, running with an infant in tow.

"And that cut," Sam whispered, draping an arm over her shoulders like the world couldn't touch them. "She slammed that vase into something hard. Based on the amount of blood on the floor, I'm guessing someone's face."

New details fleshed out my imagination, and I had to pocket my fists to hide their clenching, as Jane watched my every move. I couldn't open an official file when she herself hadn't reported an assault. Without a report, I couldn't run DNA or prints. Jane's wall of mistrust was maddening—but understandable. It'd take time to take it down, brick by brick, if I had to. For now, I had to get her to safety, and she hadn't made a move from the chair she and Ben were planted in. She looked shell-shocked, exhausted, despite her mask of calm. She needed grounding, and I could provide it. Inhaling deeply, I centered myself and crossed to sit in the chair in front of her.

"Are you ready to go?" I nodded towards the empty car seat perched on the tabletop. "I can have my sisters join us for the drive or–

"No. I think just one person in the car...is better." Her harried interruption gave way quickly to stutters of doubt.

"A wise choice. It would make for a quieter ride for Ben as well." That at least seemed to soften her face as she peered down at the boy, gently securing his pacifier. "Do you need assistance placing him in his car seat?"

My mistake was immediate.

Her hands were clutching Ben to her, protecting him...from me.

Loath as I was to admit it, I envied Sam's innate ability to soothe patients on his rig. Still, I wasn't without a training of sorts of my own. Trying to consider things from her perspective, I took a different tack.

"Actually, I'm all thumbs with these contraptions." I waved a hand over Ben's car seat. "You pack him up while I warm up the vehicle?"

Not waiting for her to respond, I walked out.

I started the car and then walked around to the passenger side to wait, considering all the options available to me. A veritable laundry list of things I couldn't do that barely touched the surface of the mounting stuff I wanted to do. It took all my control not to physically pace the length of my car, knowing she needed to take this first step of trust before I could take her the rest of the way. The wait was brutal.

I wanted her safe and away from this house.

I wanted to secure Jane and Ben in my cabin.

I wanted her trust.

And God help me; I needed her in the goddamn car.

I was half a breath from cave-manning her into the SUV when she emerged, Ben's carrier hanging from the crook of her elbow. She only nodded in acknowledgement as I held open the rear door. Her hands trembled as she secured Ben's seat, tightening his straps. Once complete, she sat upright, giving that same defiant look I'd glimpsed earlier, as she grabbed her seatbelt and clicked it into place.

She would not be riding up front with me.

The drive was silent as the grave. I contemplated pointing out things around town to help pull her from her thoughts, but she remained glued to my phone's GPS screen as I navigated up the mountain. Stealing glances in my rearview, I watched her care for Ben, always watching out for him, but never did her eyes meet mine. It grated against something in me I didn't want to admit—a longing to connect with her that I hadn't earned yet.

Pulling into the cabin, I parked next to my family's cars, noting Jane's already parked around the side of the cabin. Holding open the door for her, I pocketed my other hand, stifling the urge to lift Ben free. She wasn't ready for me to take such a hands-on approach. Once inside, I showed her the room where her stuff was, then gave her a moment of privacy, as much to unclench my jaw as to give her some breathing room.

"Did she say anything?" Moira asked, opening pizza boxes and plating up slices. "On the drive?"

"Not a word."

"Whatever she's running from," Lila sighed, "It's big."

"We tried at first to get her talking while you guys cleaned up the rental," Lila answered. "But she only asked about you."

"Me?" This caught my attention since she'd shown no interest in me beyond answering my direction questions.

"She asked if you'd always been a cop." Lila tilted her hand back and forth in consideration. "My gut says she was fishing to see if you were dirty. Not unreasonable, all things considered."

The familiar dread of shadow-boxing an unseen villain gnawed at the pit of my stomach. If she had a fear of dirty cops, who was I hunting now?

"She's completely shut down," Moira said with a sigh. "She looks exhausted. And based solely on how her stomach growled, she's likely starving too." She offered a plate. "Hence, we grabbed pizza."

I snagged a bottle of water and returned to the bedroom.

"Jane. It's Troy." I tapped lightly on her bedroom door. "I've brought some dinner for you. May I come in?" After a moment, Jane's voice granted me entrance.

Scanning the room, I noted her things piled on the floor next to the bed, and Jane in the furthest corner of the room, perched in an overstuffed recliner, feet curled under her, and Ben in her arms.

"My sisters ordered pizza." I set the plate on the dresser near her, the bottle of water next to it. "It's been a long and stressful day. You should eat, so you have energy to care for young Ben."

"Put the oxygen mask on yourself," Jane mumbled down at the baby, her curtain of dark hair hiding her face. I desperately wanted to tug it back so I could see her eyes.

"Oxygen mask?"

"Oh, it's a..." She gracefully tucked her hair behind her ear. "It's a concept I've read about in mommy blogs." I nodded encouragingly at her pause, hoping this moment of sharing would help her open up about other things. "About taking care of your needs so you have the energy to take care of the baby." She looked down at Ben, sleeping in her arms. "Of course, they never quite explain how exactly that works when the little man refuses to sleep unless he's in my arms."

The corner of her mouth tipped into a small, genuine smile, and it was stunning.

"Perhaps you start by accepting a meal." I lifted the plate from the dresser, handing it to her as she stared up at me with a quizzical look.

"I could hold Ben for you...for a moment...so that you can eat."

I lifted my hand in offering, catching a glimpse of myself in the window's reflection, too late. Chase may have held the family record, but I was still larger than average. My reflection showed me looming over the chair, with the badge and gun on full display, reaching for her child.

A regrettable power dynamic that needed swift correction.

"After I get myself situated, of course."

Slowly, I removed my badge and gun, depositing them as far away from her as I could on the far end of the dresser. Then, I walked to her other side, positioning myself against the wall and thus clearing her path to the door should she need it. Jane watched me move about, silent but studying, as I settled myself cross-legged on the floor. Curiosity, then worry, maybe even a trace of amusement, flickered across her face all the while.

I lifted my hands, not all the way to her, but halfway, then held her gaze and waited.

This trust had to come from her, and I would not force it.

"If you are sure..." She gently leaned forward, gifting me Ben. "I'll eat fast."

7

JANE

THE PLATE OF PIZZA may as well have been a Michelin-star meal for the way my mouth watered at the smell of it. I was starving, having gone without food all day. A conscious choice born of necessity as I pushed to gain as much distance as possible, only stopping at whatever roadside pull-out would allow me to address Ben's need for a bottle, a diaper, or a cuddle. I had a routine of waiting to chug water and inhale vending machine food only after I got the two of us situated for the evening. Then I'd crash for a night of fitful sleep, promising myself I would do better, only to rise and be gripped by the overwhelming sense of being watched. A fear well-founded, considering the text messages awaiting me once I had a moment of privacy to look at my phone.

Unknown: You bitch, you'll pay for that.

> **Unknown:** You think those guys are gonna protect you?

> **Unknown:** I can't go back without you…might as well get rid of them and make this easier on yourself.

> **Unknown:** You won't get away that easily.

> **Unknown:** I found you once. I'll find you again.

I clung to the last message as proof that, at least for now, I was hidden enough to pause and consider my next move. Out of cash, tired, and starving, I had been running headlong to this town in the hopes I could find someone who might offer me sanctuary. All I had to go on was a name mentioned in passing from a man I knew to be pure evil.

Was Sgt. Wilder, who would help me?

Considering that, I thought back to the night the rug was yanked out from under me and the starting pistol of my great escape was fired.

My father's summoning text found him seated behind his large wooden desk, surrounded by laptops and ledgers, like a captain of industry perched on his mighty throne. A scene so familiar and nefariously laced. I had no hints of what this meeting was for. I never knew, when I entered his lair, what I was there for, and it made me an excellent improv artist.

"You called for me?" I left off his preferred moniker, 'Papa.' The narrowing in his eyes told me he hadn't missed my omission.

"There's a dinner planned for next week. Several gentlemen are attending that you will meet." He slid a folder across his desk, oblivious to my shock at his discussing business with me like the previous two months hadn't transpired. "Inside, you'll find a dossier for each man to research ahead of time. After the dinner, you can decide who you'll wed."

Time stopped, my vision tunneling to the manila file folder, as the reverberating gong of my father's words clanged through my head.

Who will I wed?

"I've booked the Plaza for a month from now, which should give us enough time for media work and planning. I'll hire a coordinator, and you will, of course, accommodate whatever family traditions the groom has - "

"I don't understand." I interrupted, scowling at the papers to avoid my father's disapproving gaze. "You called me for...my opinion...on an arranged marriage?"

My father was a shipping magnate turned political powerhouse with a litany of increasingly influential titles, and he had never once asked me for my opinion. Furthermore, while he'd encouraged me to be prepared to be a good wife, an arranged marriage had never been discussed.

"Of course, Gia." His tone was flat, and I looked up to find him leaning back, steepling his fingers together in a move I'd seen him make during negotiations when he held the entire upper hand.

I was the lamb being led to slaughter.

"Consider this my apology for our last...conversation. I was, perhaps, too curt with you."

"Curt?" Anger I hardly knew I carried bubbled up at the casual mention of such a pivotal, violent moment. "Curt!" My temper overrode my better judgment, and I couldn't contain my mouth from shouting all the things I'd been left to stew on in my father's stilted silence. "At our last 'conversation,' you shoved a baby into my arms and hit me so hard I saw stars for days! You have since ignored me completely, and now you summon me to a pile of prospective husbands and announce I'll be married in a month!?" I tossed the file across the desk, a defiant move I felt sure would spell my doom, but I barely cared. "And I'm to be grateful for the mea culpa?"

The bastard smirked at the file as it slid to a stop before him.

"One of these men *will* be your husband. I am allowing you to have a say in who I select." He reached for the folder. "I've placed my favorites on top, but any you choose will serve my purposes, and as such, I will give you what you want." My father stood, rounding the desk and extending the folder to me again with a smile that didn't reach his eyes. "Of course, I will happily make the selection without your insights. As always, the choice is yours, mia caro."

My darling. The nickname he'd used for me since I was a child, and only when he played Doting Father for diplomats. It turned my stomach, and mea culpa be damned, his threat was clear. You have no choice; this is your future.

"What about Ben?"

"Ben?" His confusion was a lit match to the indignation I couldn't contain.

"Yes. Ben. The baby you gave me to raise." Fury filled me that he'd forgotten Ben.

My Ben.

"Ah, yes. Of course." My father leaned against his desk, tucking the folder under his arm and waving his hands as if shooing an invisible gnat. "Please, my Gia, tell me all about your brother."

Buckets and buckets of icy water fell around the memory of my father's madman's smile, even as I sat in a cabin full of strangers, hanging my every hope on the large police officer perched on the floor in front of me and offering assistance so I could simply eat something hot.

It was surreal.

"Thank you, Sgt. Wilder." I swallowed the emotion trying to flood my senses.

"Call me Troy," he answered with a small smile. "And do take your time. Holding a little boy for a change will do me good." There was a shift in his voice, and I realized that he was talking to Ben. "All I've held so far is River and Blue." Ben stared intently back at Troy, having come awake during the transfer of arms. "That's my two nieces. Their names have sentimental intention as I under - "

His words were cut short by the long, pornographic moan that somehow slipped out around the stuffed full bite of hot mozzarella I was luxuriating over. I'd never tasted anything so good in my life, and for a moment, all of time and space hung on the promise of pepperoni. Before the bite was entirely swallowed, I took another, wolfing down a third and fourth bite. Reaching the crust too soon, I nearly cried in want of more.

Only the soft ticking haptics from Troy's phone tugged me back into my body.

"Just making sure there's another slice saved for you." Summoned on cue, a smiling Moira walked in carrying two fresh slices of pizza and a second bottle of water, cocking an eyebrow down at Troy before leaving us alone again.

"That look?" I asked, finally slowing down enough to make human words.

"If I had to venture a guess?" Troy nodded to the door. "I'll be the subject of much humor in the living room. Siblings...and all. Do you have any siblings?"

His question was innocent enough, but impossible to answer. Technically, I was raised as an only child, but there sat the man holding my baby brother. But I'd been Ben's caretaker from before his umbilical stump had fallen off, so that made me what, the de facto mother? Or worse, was I a kidnapper? Had my father reported me as his missing daughter or as a fugitive who fled with an infant? Would this cop, Troy, take Ben from me?

"What happens now?" Ignoring his questions, I set the half-eaten second slice aside.

"I would like to discuss a little of a case I've been working on; it connects to Moira and Lila's stories...and I suspect yours." He looked down at Ben, his voice returning to the dulcet tones from earlier. "But it will wait until you both have rested well." My heart stuttered in relief, knowing I had more time, but Troy continued. "I realize we have no place for Ben to sleep, but - "

"That's okay. I've had him co-sleeping with me since we..." Cutting that sentence short, I mentally kicked myself. "He sleeps better when he's with me." I quickly lifted Ben back into my arms, using the move to shield me from Troy's soul-piercing gaze. "I'll just get him changed into a clean onesie."

Maybe it was the food, the lack of gnawing hunger abated, that pulled back the last of my resolve, but emotion rushed to my cheeks. My eyes stinging as I willed tears not to fall, turning my back on the man who'd done nothing more than hold Ben for me.

"I'll help." Troy stood but made no move to gather his gun or badge. "Shall I find his clothes in your bag or hold him a moment longer so you can shower?"

His simple offer of help, a hot meal, and a shower might as well have been bombs lobbed straight at my stiff-upper-lip as I felt my resolve crumble.

"I don't...I can handle..." No one had helped me care for Ben; even my father's staff avoided us whenever possible. I'd been doing it all alone for so long.

Hot tears spilled forward, undeterred by my rapid blinking as they spilled onto my cheeks and dripped onto Ben's blanket. I rushed to wipe them away, to clear them off of Ben, but it was useless. The crushing wave of undammed emotions wrenched the air from my lungs as my sobs came so fast I nearly doubled over in physical pain.

"Jane." Troy's reached for Ben again, and I let him as the pain of my whole world narrowed to the desperate wish that Troy's gentle voice would have said my real name.

Turning, Troy handed Ben to Moira, who I hadn't heard come in. Swiping at her own tears, she gently gathered Ben into her arms as Troy gathered me into his. This embrace, built in the arms of a man who'd done nothing more than check on my well-being, secure me a place to sleep, and feed me, was enough to unmake me. He caressed my hair, murmuring soft words and stroking my back. Between my heaves, I caught only passing phrases, 'Let the tears come,' and 'They'll heal you.' Exhaustion lanced the festering pain in my chest, and for the first time, I was allowed to breathe.

"I've got you," Troy spoke that phrase again and again. "I've got you."

"I've just," The truth came unbidden. "I'm so very tired of being alone." Pulling back, I look up into Troy's face, noticing up close how his warm brown skin seemed to glow even as his dark eyes anchored me to him.

I stood because he held me to stand.

"I can't imagine what you've been through." Using the tip of his finger, he slipped a strand of hair away from my cheek. "You've shown incredible bravery, caring for Ben all alone." His words called forth fresh tears. "But you are very much not alone now. I will stay by your side as long as it takes for you to believe that." His warm hands spread along my lower back, calling me to melt into him. My whole body screamed to let him take it all away.

But then the air shifted. He stiffened and pulled back. Only then did I notice my white-knuckle grip on his shirt, splotched with stains from my soaking tears. I looked back at his face and saw something unnamed flicker in his eyes—some unknowable consequence that felt like looming doom.

What had I done?

"I...I'm sorry...about your shirt." I tried wiping away the wrinkles and wet stains, imagining his anger at my carelessness, but my efforts were futile. Embarrassment warmed my cheeks as I rambled a feeble apology. "I'd like to repay the dry cleaning but–"

"All is well." He held my hands still, stepping back again until he was fully separated from me. His face was calm, but pained, and I ached to think that instead of anger, I had disappointed him. "I'll gather Ben and give you a moment." Grabbing his gun and badge from the dresser, he turned towards the door. Seeing him go, not knowing what misstep I'd made, a final, panicked question tumbled out of me before I could stop it.

"But you'll come back?"

Troy halted at the door, never turning to face me.

"Without a doubt."

8

TROY

Closing the door behind me, I leaned forward, hands on my knees, as my brain slowly imploded. I walked into that room hoping to get her to eat, and ended up with that stunning creature in my arms, tears soaking my chest as I stroked her hair. Her fear and exhaustion became my calling...my honor to shoulder.

She needed me.

Her words, 'I'm so tired of being alone,' rendered me incapable of coherent thought as she clung to me, with a desperation that called to me like a siren on the waves. I was helpless against her pull. Unaware until it was too late, I barely managed to pull my unexpected hard-on back before I sent her a thousand wrong signals and...

Breathe in... breathe out.

"Dude." Sam's voice pulled me upright. "Are you good?"

"Yes." Running my hands down my shirt, lingering at the stain from her tears, I secured my gun and badge. "I am fine."

"She broke?" Lila halted her pacing, blunt as ever.

"Indeed." I nodded, unsurprised that my family had been listening.

"She was due," Moira added, snuggling little Ben close.

"So it seemed." Keeping my words short, I smoothed my tie and gathered my composure. "She needs rest. We can reconvene in the morning."

"You've got the girls." Lila cocked her chin at Moira. "I can sleep here."

Their pre-determined arrangement hit the room like a bomb. I opened my mouth to protest, but Sam's rebuttal came faster.

"The fuck you can," Sam scowled, an argument already forming on his wife's lips that he swiftly cut off. "We just got home, and you need rest before that morning sickness kicks you in the teeth. No way you are sleeping anywhere but in my bed, where I can hold your hair back if my baby decides you need to lose dinner."

Not wanting this to escalate further, I stepped forward.

"I am staying." Every eye in the room shifted to me. "I have the weekend off work. I have no children to look after."

"Troy." Moira began, "She's been through - "

"I will sleep in the room across the hall." I sidestepped my sister's well-intentioned intervention gently, but I would not yield. "Tomorrow I'll assess her state and determine next steps. I have her."

"So...we're swimming this river now?" Chase leveled me with a knowing look. "Where you pretend this woman hasn't gotten under your skin."

"That's not what..." My argument floundered in Chase's huff of smirking laughter.

"And we're all expected to accept the 'I'm in charge, do my bidding, I'm the big brother' bullshit while you ignore how affected you are?" His incredulity rippled throughout the room, as everyone's eyes followed his logic straight back to me.

"Denial's kinda magical, ain't it?" Sam nudged me as he walked his wife towards the door. He turned back with a sigh. "What can we bring you from the house tomorrow? Clothes? toiletries?"

"Everything you own?" Moira teased.

"You are all adolescents." Reaching for Ben, I held him to my shoulder, suddenly understanding his capacity as a shield. "The woman has been traumatized. I'm here to help. That is all."

"Clothes and?" Lila's penetrating brown eyes bore into me with a look that could have rattled the bones.

They all stared at me, holding a baby and shunning them all, so I could stand watch? Who was I kidding? I was affected deeply, and without shame. I wasn't leaving Jane or Ben, and ignoring that fact wouldn't do either of them any good.

"Perhaps some food basics would be useful." Glancing around the cabin, I recognized we had woefully little to accommodate an infant. "And a list of baby things Ben will need would help."

Moira nodded understanding as they all filed out, and I slipped the deadbolt closed. Walking through the cabin, shutting off the lights, I glanced at my reflection in the kitchen window; holding a baby I knew nothing about, helping his mother I knew nothing about, thus breaking all of my routines in what had to be the most disorganized rescue I'd ever taken part in.

"Your family... they seem nice." I turned to find Jane crossing the living room in thick, slouchy socks, an oversized sweater that slipped off one shoulder, and a pair of shorts that let every inch of her creamy white legs waltz on display, to my side. "I wasn't trying to eavesdrop. I just came out as they were leaving." She reached for Ben, a hint of irritation lining her words. "I've got him."

"The cabin is locked tight. Alarm secure." Following her back towards the hall, I felt the urge to reassure her of her safety again.

"And you will be across the hall." Jane offered... a statement rather than a question, and again that hint of irritability in her tone grated. "I heard."

"Indeed," My head was a mix of conflicting urges. I wanted to know why she seemed both irritated and distant. I wanted to offer to help with Ben. I wanted to explain my earlier abrupt departure, but I couldn't when I hardly understood things myself. "Should you need me..." I let my words trail off. Jane, mercifully, cut me loose.

"I'll know where to find you." When her blue eyes met mine, the Beast in me screamed a vow to end whoever had chased her to breaking.

And as I stood, dumbfounded, unsure how I had gotten here, I began to feel a familiar, unsettling tension in my chest. One I hadn't wrestled in years and one that felt eerily familiar.

Thus, my watch began.

Pacing the cabin, checking the perimeter, slugging coffee, and remembering the first time my Beast yawned its gaping jaws to life. Remembering another woman I'd been pulled to help.

My commanding officer often used my brothers and me on small surgical strikes; our convenient shorthand made us efficient tools. This job was expected to be a simple recon, and my brothers were both exhausted, so I volunteered to go it solo–confirming chatter that the arms dealer we'd been hunting was in the area.

My orders were to observe, verify, and withdraw.

Two hours of watching trucks come and go gave me no match for my target until a blacked-out, armor-plated Hummer rolled in.

"Possible target," I whispered into my comms mic.

'Copy.' My CO responded. *'Verify and pull back.'*

The back door opened, and the man I hunted stepped out, dressed in a head-to-toe black-on-black suit. I had evidence — photographed and ready — to pack up when he turned, reaching into the vehicle behind him and dragging out a woman by her hair.

"He's got a hostage. Female. ID Unknown." She was already battered—split lip, black eye, torn clothes. She tried to fight even as he backhanded her to the dirt. My crosshairs hovered over his skull. "Permission to engage."

'Negative. Stay on mission.'

"Sir, she's—"

'Pull back, Wilder. That's an order.'

I couldn't make out the target's words, but his intent was clear. He was furious — she was begging. Whoever this woman was, she'd been reduced to a punching bag, and my anger grew to peak performance as I readied my long-range.

"He's beating her!" I barked into the mic. "Permission to waste the bastard."

'Negative.' The denial grated against my urge to spare the woman from being slapped towards his compound. *'Pull Back.'*

"Sir. The woman–" I protested again, gripping the butt of my weapon as a distant voice in my head roared to take the shot.

'Stay on mission, Wilder. Stand down.' I could only watch as the target buried his face in her hair, whispering words that drained the fight out of her. In a moment, he'd stilled her, wrapping an arm around her waist and dragging her into the compound. *'That's an order, Wilder!'*

"Fuck!" I shouted. "Copy. Reporting to base." My shot lost, I packed it in, storming into the base and all but demanding an immediate return and rescue. Never had I gone against orders, but I was prepared to do so if I hadn't been given leave to return the next night for extraction.

Too late.

Our target, gone.

The woman, slain and left behind.

Her eyes were fixed in that thousand-yard stare, and the silence of that failure detonated something inside me. My Beast was born in that crack between what I'd been ordered to do and what I'd wanted to do. The memory haunted me for months after, driving me into a space of rigid control and diligence until I could feel confident I'd never let someone die from my failure again.

The Beast prowled in me again now, picturing Jane behind that door—hoping she was resting well as I paced the cabin, checked the perimeter, and stood sentry.

I would not fail her, too.

9

TROY

KNOWING JANE SLEPT SILENTLY through the night felt good, but when her footsteps didn't come with the sunrise, my frustration built into something darker.

My brother came and went with groceries and an overnight bag, but she remained. I showered, changed, and paced, but she remained. I wanted to respect her privacy, but didn't want her to feel confined to that room, and I had no idea how to do either.

I wasn't built for waiting.

I paced, drank coffee, checked the perimeter...again. Each hour she stayed behind that door, my agitation grew. By mid-afternoon, my stomach was growling, and the Beast echoed my need to feed Jane.

"Jane." I tapped on her door, keeping my voice as gentle as I could, despite my heart beating in my chest. "You need to eat." Stifling silence was my answer, but I pushed on. "I will prepare lunch." Shuffling footfalls approached, but she didn't open the door. "Perhaps you'd like to come out to eat and stretch your legs a bit?"

"Only...if it's no trouble." After nearly 18 hours of silence, her voice was oxygen; soft, but not frightened, and clear as a bell. Closing my eyes, I let my forehead rest against the door. "When would it be ready?"

"Ten minutes."

Unsure what she liked, and with only basics on hand, I opted for a simple fare of sandwiches with lots of vegetables and fresh fruit. The simplicity of my task uncoiled the knot in my chest, and she emerged from her fortress of solitude just as I plated her meal.

Her close-lipped smile was a message; she wanted quiet.

Placing our plates on the table, I gestured for Jane to take a seat. She surveyed the sandwich, which required two hands, and gave her bandaged hand a weary glance.

"I am happy to hold him so you can eat." I let the offer hang, careful not to reach for Ben prematurely, knowing last night's willingness to accept my help could have been fleeting. "I can move my plate to the floor, if you would like." It was a poor attempt at a joke, but it worked. Jane's beautiful smile made its first appearance. It was small, her pink pout closed tight, but at the corners just the slightest upturn as her nose scrunched into the most adorable light I'd seen in days.

I could be this for her.

"No floor required, Sergeant Wilder. But maybe you can eat first, before I hand over Ben. He's quite wiggly today."

"Call me Troy. I insist." I reached for Ben immediately, needing to see her eat first.

Happy she let me help with Ben, the stilted silence hung thick in the air, Jane offering nothing to my cordial questions about their sleep.

The perfunctory meal was neither satisfying nor productive, but she remained until she finished.

Returning to her room, anxiety gnawed at me. Pacing the cage of this cabin, waiting around for her to share my air was a torture I wasn't equipped to endure. Deciding to use the meal as an anchor, I let her know dinner would be ready at 6:30.

Her nod of agreement had me planning a feast.

I all but applauded when she came to the dinner table at 6:30 sharp. I tried to engage Jane in small ways, but it was forced. I needed more information about the flowers and whoever she was running from. The Beast couldn't hunt what we couldn't name. The tears from the night before never made a reappearance, but neither did any other emotion. My anxiety about floating a one-sided conversation nearly spilled over when Jane finally engaged.

"You've outdone yourself," She waved her hand over the spread of roasted chicken, garlic mashed potatoes, broccoli rabe with a hollandaise sauce, and Parker House rolls with honey butter. "That was all really amazing."

"I enjoy cooking." I latched onto her sliver of interest like the life preserver it was. "Cooking for one is rather dull." She didn't comment further and only allowed me to hold Ben as long as it took her to eat. Immediately reclaiming him, which bothered me more than I liked.

How could I get her to trust me further?

"If you have a favorite recipe, please pass it along. Desserts too. Tonight I made a chocolate torte, but tomorrow I could..." An expression slipped across her face, fleeting pain, then gone. "Is everything alright?"

"Can I..." She eyed my hand, still frozen mid-air in my reach for the dessert plates. "Well... never mind." She shook her head, placing her napkin on her lap around Ben. Her posture was as prim and rigid as I'd seen it.

This was a landmine, and I was tripping over it.

"Finish that question." The 'Please' was lost in my commanding tone.

"I don't want to seem ungrateful." Her eyes locked on her plate. "It's just that..." Again, her words trailed off, her bottom lip slipping between her teeth in worry.

"There is nothing you could ask that would offend or anger me." I sat back in my chair and crossed my arms. Inside, I was roaring for her to open that sweet mouth of hers to start talking, and waning patience was all I had to hold it back.

"Nothing?" Jane cut her eyes from underneath her lashes, her furrowed brows questioning.

"Give me just...a...little." Using the exact words that got through to her the night before might have been high-handed, but it worked. With a slight tilt of her head, her gaze softened, and the air between us cracked around the shared memory.

Still, she waited.

I could wait longer, watching as she again battled some internal foe, preparing myself for anything and everything, steeling my nerves and schooling my face into a mask of calm.

"I'm...full." She sighed out the two words that took an embarrassingly long minute for me to register.

"You're full?"

"Yes. Stuffed, actually." She gestured to the table. "You are an amazing cook, and everything was delicious. Maybe it's the days of eating nothing but gas station beef jerky, but last night's three pizza slices were still here when I sat down to that behemoth sandwich you made earlier."

She said, and at last a smile emerged as she continued. "I don't want to be rude or decline your Michelin-rated food. But I might bust if I put even one bite of that torte in my mouth."

Fucking...finally. It took a full day and a demolished kitchen, but Jane, at last, delivered the most honest lines–spoken more words in a single moment–and did it with a genuine smile that lit up her face and sparkled into laughter at the end. I wanted confessions and all her truths, but this small win made me feel like a soldier standing at attention while the war ended behind me; valiant and victorious.

"Say no more," I gestured to the two bottles of wine on the table. "May I at least offer you something to drink?" It was a reach, but I couldn't allow her to retreat to the room. I needed to keep her here, anchored with me, and talking.

"Having anything fizzy...like seltzer?"

A request...yes!

"How about we move our drinks to the living room?" I stepped into the kitchen for a drink. "And give you something other than those four walls to stare at." Even thinking of her retiring for the night had me itching to sledgehammer that damn door.

"I appreciate the meal, but I think tonight—" I met her half-lift from her chair, with my outstretched hand, palm up in invitation. "I don't want to be a—"

Cutting her off again, I cupped her elbow, tugging her to her feet. She obeyed my silent request, and moreover, her face held curiosity, not worry or anxiety. I hung my next move on that feeling. Squaring my posture in front of her, I slowly reached for Ben. To my great relief, she handed him to me without hesitation. The trust was everything, and I spoke with confidence knowing she'd receive my command without fear.

"You are welcome in this cabin, Jane. The whole cabin. I expect you to treat it as your own for as long as you are here. You and Ben are not to be relegated to that small room. I expect you to make yourself at home here." One second, then two, Jane considered my words before nodding her acceptance. "Thank you. Now, how about we try and find a movie to watch while Ben gets in some pre-bedtime wiggles."

WILDER FAMILY GROUP CHAT

-1-

> Me: I need an assist.

Sam: We're listening…

> Me: I have to head into the station for an hour.

Chase: Everything okay?

> Me: Just some last-minute PTO paperwork.

Sam: Ahhhhh that old chestnut

Moira: Need me to stay with Jane?

Me: I hoped you might offer.

Moira: Lila, too?! We can make it a girl's day!

Sam: Lila might need to sit this one out.

Moira: Still barfing?

Sam: Exorcist level.

Moira: Remind her it will pass...1st trimester is the worst.

Chase: How was the weekend?

Me: Quiet.

Me: I'll grab some things for Ben on my way back.

Moira: What are you getting!?

Me: I used your list as a guide, plus a few supplies and a grocery list.

Sam: When did you have time for all the lists?

Me: Sleep has been...intermittent.

Sam: Sure, Grandpa. Okay.

Chase: Need any help?

Me: Assembly would go faster when I return.

Chase: Send me the list. I'll meet you after the station.

Sam: I'm in too. Shift ends at noon.

Moira: Assembly?

10

JANE

I T TOOK NEARLY TWO full days before I stopped panicking at the sound of Troy's movements around the cabin. The freedom to pace the cabin with Ben during night feeds on Sunday, beneath peaceful skies and brilliant stars, was such a far cry from the restless nights sequestered in the opulent childhood bedroom.

My phone's continual pings plagued me. Silencing the alerts only served to feed my anxiety. Not knowing what was coming was somehow worse than constant threats. I did manage to muffle the vibrations at the bottom of my bag — under a pile of towels, shoved under the bathroom sink — but morbid curiosity got the better of me Monday morning.

> Unknown: Do you know how much fucking worse you are making things?

> Unknown: It's only a matter of time before I find your ass again.

> Unknown: Come quietly, and it'll go easier for you.

> Unknown: I'll talk to him if you are worried about the baby. I'm on your side here.

> Unknown: He just wants to talk.

Any comfort that my would-be abductor hadn't found me evaporated with the shift in his message, from crude and threatening to syrupy and predatory. My father's fingerprints were all over it. The idea that I'd trust a man who tried to bodily drag me to his car by my hair was comical. The last line, 'he just wants to talk,' held the most venom. I knew who he meant, and talking was never an option. My only protection right now, Ben's security, was this cabin and the leverage of what I'd stolen from my father.

I'd retreated to my room after my father informed me I could 'choose a husband' from his pre-selected list. I paced until after dark, sifting through a million things I'd seen and heard but never questioned; it all now felt dirty.

I felt dirty.

I'd gone from priceless art, to be displayed but never touched, to a bargaining chip. And if I could be so callously discarded, what would happen to Ben? That driving question moved me to action, leading me to retrieve the file from my father's office in the hopes that one of the men would let me bring Ben.

I tiptoed through the darkened penthouse into my father's empty office. Grabbing the folder and turning to leave, I heard voices approaching. Any confidence that I retained my father's good graces was long gone, and I was certain that if he found me here now, a split lip would be the least of my worries. Seeing nowhere safe, I dove under my father's desk, tucked my feet up under me, and prayed I could remain hidden as my father's voice filled the space.

"Have you secured our connections at the Canadian border?"

"Not yet, but I have a plan." I recognized Brinks' arrogant inflections, and my stomach turned. The man was a polished bottom-feeder if ever I'd met one. Circling my father, doing his bidding like a lapdog begging for his next meal. "My admittance into IA is all but secure. The leverage will kill two birds with one stone."

"Rivera?" My father's question was punctuated by the ice clinking in his glass—no doubt pouring scotch that said I could be stuck here awhile.

"Jensen, too. The fool landed on the wrong side of an officer in Lake Placid who could prove a nuisance—a tedious rule-follower." Brink's pacing steps halted as he continued. "I have it in hand, though we should temporarily halt all shipments." I didn't recognize the names Rivera or Jensen and wondered if they were men in the file folder I clutched to my chest. "May I ask... what is the plan with your daughter?"

"Gia's marriage will secure the final support I need for my campaign, especially with her purity intact." My stomach turned at the way my father discussed me as easily as choosing his suit for the day, my virginity the flower in his lapel.

"If I may, Michael," Brinks's simpering was so close he had to be standing directly in front of the desk; I held a hand over my mouth, sure the pounding of my heart would echo across the room. "Your leniency with her might have become your Achilles heel. And lovely as she is —"

"She'll do as she's told." My father's tone brooked no insolence, but my fear-addled brain wondered what Marcus considered lenient with how I'd been treated.

"For you, I have no doubt." Brinks slipped into syrupy placation. "But what of the man she marries? Will her obedience carry forward to another's house? She's been privy to so much here, and her new husband might not hold with the same...guidance that you've provided."

The word 'guidance' held a tone of violence, and I immediately knew that Marcus was fully aware of my father's proclivities for disciplinary direction. The file suddenly felt ominous—would all of these men control me with an iron fist?

"It's late, Marcus, and I'm tired." Father's glass hit the bar top with finality. "Make your point."

"She could become a liability if emboldened by the false bravado of a new surname. Another man might try to use what she knows against you. Let me take her."

Bile...pure and sour...rose in my throat.

"I could keep her in line and use my IA leverage to encourage the votes you need from a sitting judge, perhaps."

"Never took you for the marrying type." Ice clinked again as a second glass was poured. "Your proclivities run a bit south of the traditional marital bed."

"You do know me well." The desk vibrated with Marcus's laughter. "But there comes a time in a man's life when settling down grows appealing. The comfortable familiarity of ..."

"A set of virgin thighs cradling you to bed each night?" My father finished the crude sentiment with a laugh, and my stomach lurched into my throat as hot tears spilled down my cheeks.

"You always could turn a phrase, Michael." Glass clinked against glass. A toast? "I would ensure she was given every luxury she's accustomed to. Any good father would want everything for his darling princess while she propagates a legacy."

"You know my Gia takes after her mother." A comparison that once meant something—it was filthy now.

"Nothing a firm hand and a solid pair of handcuffs can't train out of her if I recall your marital days." The two men clinked glasses again.

Toasting. Toasting!

"Even your wife's fleeing turned to your favor." The last of my heart shattered into tiny, tiny pieces. "Her death garnered so much sympathy."

"Speaking of...I have a family for the boy. We'll make arrangements tomorrow."

"Ah, yes, the surprise bundle on your doorstep." Brinks hissed. "That is a rather large nuisance."

"Was. A governor and his wife have been unable to conceive. I convinced him that the public sentiment of adoption was preferable to a divorce and remarriage. The boy is perfect." The breath in my lungs burned as I choked back a scream. "In exchange for the infant, he'll guarantee me PAC funds via one of his offshore businesses."

"Not to mention the leverage of planting your offspring under his roof. Only you can turn such a bucket of shit into a bed of roses...masterfully twisted, Michael."

I don't know how I hadn't blacked out under the pressure of my hand clamping down on the sucking need to sob uncontrollably at the horror filling my ears. The space under the desk began to suffocate under the weight of becoming Mrs. Marcus Brinks, and, worse, of knowing Ben would be farmed out for money or votes, and that I was powerless to stop it all.

"I'll consider your proposal for my daughter and let you know."

The two spoke awhile longer, but I didn't dare move until their business concluded and my father's retreating steps vanished. Only then did I crawl, painstakingly slow, from under my father's desk on aching knees, demanding I pause for feeling to return to my feet. My head was spinning from all I'd learned–the men in the file, my father's plans for me...and Ben.

My only option crystallized on the race back to my room. Cramming items into backpacks and duffels, I slipped down the servant's elevator to the garage, shoving everything into my backseat—grateful for Ben's deep sleep as I clicked his carrier into place. Only then, thinking of how long I had before he'd need to eat, did I realize I needed cash.

I had no bank account, but my father had a safe in his office.

Insane with fear and in my adrenaline haze, I grabbed a backpack and snuck into my father's office once more. A voice in my head screamed to get out, but fear told me I needed the leverage of whatever those ledgers contained. My hands moved without thinking, snatching ledgers and a thumb drive—anything that felt important. Then, opening the drawer safe in his desk with a code I'd known since childhood, I swiped out a stack of cash.

Thus began my journey with Ben.

From the office to my car, I never look behind me, and I didn't pause for a second to let my brain talk me out of my haphazard plan.

I was a crazed animal kept too long in the dark, flinging myself into the blinding light of day and hoping anywhere was safer than here. Searching for the one person on the right side of whatever vile thing my father was planning, I ran to find the tedious rule-follower that might hold the key to Ben's and my safety, with nothing to go on about, save his town's name.

I headed for Lake Placid.

11

JANE

T HE ADORABLE GRUNTS OF a squirming Ben pulled me from my memories as he stretched his tiny arms, banishing the shadows with his toothless grin, and I discarded my phone and its nefarious messages to the floor behind me.

"Good morning, little man." He curled his chubby fingers around my hair, tugging with all his might. "Slept soundly, did you?" Ben latched onto my finger, dragging it to his mouth. "I know I slept better than I have in ages. Perhaps we both needed a little mountain air." I stretched out, rolling the ache from my shoulders after another night curled around Ben's makeshift bassinet of towels and pillows.

"I've often found that nights up here bring the best sleep." Jumping to my feet, a startled yelp broke the peaceful wake-up before I registered Troy's voice. "I apologize. I heard you speaking to Ben." He gestured to the door and then back to me. "I didn't want to knock for fear of startling you, and now I've... well... startled you."

Relief flooded my senses.

"I uh...needed to get moving anyway. Ben likes a tight morning routine. If I don't get his bottle ready in under ten minutes, I'll have a cranky baby on my hands." Lifting Ben from the bed, I grabbed his diaper bag and turned the dresser into a makeshift changing table.

"I respect a man with a plan." Troy crossed to us, standing at my side and gently stroking the top of Ben's head, whose eyes tracked to Troy's face. "Let me take him. I can give you a moment to get ready." Troy's soft voice mesmerized Ben and, to my surprise, soothed me too.

"I think Ben would enjoy that more than lying in a pillow fortress while I brush my teeth."

"I am happy to help, Jane." Troy captured my gaze, his deep brown eyes feeding the desire to hear his velvety voice speak my real name. He stood so close I could have leaned into him and been snuggled into his chest as easily as Ben. Instead, I nodded in agreement and fished a clean bottle and the baby formula from Ben's bag.

Watching them leave, I admired how Troy's broad shoulders stretched his dress shirt tight and how his slacks moved as he walked. Embarrassment flushed my cheeks as my mind veered into a boxers-or-briefs debate. Shaking my head, I admonished my imagination and hustled to get ready quickly, emerging to find Troy and Ben in the kitchen, deep in conversation,

"Now, many police officers will tell you black is best." Troy then made a face as if to brag. "I mean, they aren't wrong, my boy. But black coffee is only preferable to subpar powdered creamers and artificial sweeteners." I marveled at this new side of Troy. "If you have quality coffee and quality ingredients, the proper way to prepare coffee is with freshly whisked half and half and raw turbinado sugar."

Gone was the stern, controlled man who spoke in short sentences and kept an arms-crossed stance; this giant, buttoned-up man swayed and danced, gathering mugs and spoons with one hand as if he'd been doing it all of Ben's life. And Ben, comfortable as ever, somehow sensed that Troy had him safe in hand as he gurgled and yanked at Troy's tie, unbothered by the amount of drool he left deposited in his wake. My chest squeezed at the scene, but knowing I was on a clock before Ben's hunger got the better of us all, I announced myself.

"I'm not sure how much he'll remember by the time he's old enough to make himself a cup." Troy straightened, smoothing damp wrinkles from his tie.

"Babies learn how to communicate by watching and listening. I figured a narrative experience would be more engaging." Troy handed over a cup of coffee before stroking his finger along Ben's chin. "The least I could do, since I'm slower at bottle-making than Mommy."

The word 'mommy' felt like a caress as Troy spoke it over Ben. I had long felt more like a mother than a sister to him, but claiming the title felt undeserved. When Troy said it in that deep timbre of his, the label felt right.

"It's working for me." I gulped down the delicious morning glory of Troy's coffee, only realizing my Freudian slip after my third gulp. "I mean, the coffee... is working for me... because I'm tired, and it's caffeine and -"

"I understood your meaning." Troy took a long drag of his own coffee, his eyes drilling into me over the edge of his cup. "Is it not the best cup you've ever had?"

"It is a good cup of coffee." I agreed, loving the smile my answer put on Troy's face. Lifting his cup again, I noticed the holster and gun, his badge clipped at his waist, and my body went on high alert.

Troy's eyes followed the line of my gaze and sighed.

"I must go to the station today. Only an hour or so...for paper-work." He paused, waiting for his words to sink in. "I have only a few administrative duties to attend to before I take some time off, and my sister, Moira, has offered to stay with you. She would like to bring her daughters to play with Ben." The crunch of tires on gravel drew our attention to the front of the cabin. "That must be her now."

He handed Ben off to me, and his fingers briefly slid up my arm in the transfer. I might have thought the move accidental, had there not been another second of his dark eyes boring into mine at the exact moment. The heat that rushed my cheeks couldn't have gone unnoticed, but he said nothing as he stepped back and away, off to help his sister while I tried to figure out how his simple touch sent lightning through my core.

Moira and the girls were unloaded within minutes, and as Troy's truck pulled away, Moira had the living room converted into a makeshift baby gym. A playpen, two bouncy seats, and a blanket-cov-ered floor turned the living room into a wonderland for wiggly babies.

"Welcome to the Wilder Brothers' Protection Services," Moira announced when she was done. "I'll be your companion for the day. I come bearing babies and snacks!" Her smile was effortless and magical.

"Wilder Brothers'... what, now?"

Moira laughed as she pulled out food containers in the kitchen.

"When I first met Chase, he was *so* worried about me that he barely left my side." She grabbed a slice of bread, her smile faltering for a beat. "But then, after the kidnapping... when my job burned down? He went over the top." Turning to me, she offered an empty plate as nonchalantly as if we were discussing the weather and not kidnapping and a fire. "Breakfast?"

76

Looking down, I saw that she'd seamlessly arranged an entire buffet of Cheese, fruit, nuts, deli meats, and even soft bread and butter.

"Is this for Ben?" She lifted his bottle, which I hadn't realized Troy had left prepared and waiting for me.

"Oh... um." Baffled at how quickly she worked, I struggled to make words around my mouth, which grew drier by the second. "Yes. Thank you." I took the bottle, settling Ben into his breakfast in the crook of my elbow. "That all sounds... intense."

"You don't know the half of it." She huffed, filled her plate, and continued. "Sam moved Lila into his cabin, built her a war room, and cut his hours down by over 50%, all so he could pull her out of her head, feed her, and bathe her...."

Her words trailed off, drowned by the questions in my mind. Another brother, another cabin, another work leave — similar to Troy and our arrangement here — and I wondered where my story would lead. I only realized she was waiting for me to speak when her face floated into my line of sight, her kind eyes pinched in question even as she held a tentative smile.

"Did you say war room?"

"Oh, Lila was *obsessed* with catching the guy responsible for the death of her family. He got her fired from her job at the NYPD, too, and... Yeah... for a while, she had a whole room set up like a mad scientist lab with files and papers and computers strung everywhere. She was dead-set on finding Marcus Brinks, and it left her a little manic. Sam was the only one who could pull her out of it."

Lila mentioned a Manhattan attorney from before, and I suspected it was Marcus, but hearing his name sent fear skittering down my spine. For the first time, I wondered where he was now. Was he the one sending the madman with flowers? Was he the author of the text messages still buried beneath the bathroom sink?

"Oh, whoa, I'm sorry. I didn't mean to scare you." Rushing to my side, Moira slid a chair behind me, guiding me to sit as she brushed her hands up and down my arms. "I should have been more careful. I know you've been through something terrible and... recent." She paused, looking at my face with compassion before starting again. "God, you are so pale. I'm so sorry. I wanted to help you see how Troy's leave from work... and asking me to be here with you wasn't so weird, given the protective family, and now I've stepped in it."

"But he's... coming back?" The question came unbidden, revealing a source of anxiety I hadn't had time to name yet, with the flurry of feelings overwhelming me.

"Yes. Sweetie. Oh my gosh." She wrapped her arms around me, and time halted.

I couldn't remember the last time I'd received a hug.

Had I ever been hugged?

Surely a nanny, or my father, but no.

"I'm so sorry. I was so excited to come and spend time with you and Ben and to help you the way they helped me....I should've slowed down." Resting her hands on my shoulders, she held me at arm's length and took me in. "I promise, Troy is returning. He's taken some time off work to be here full-time... for you. And if he can't be here, one of us will stay with you." I could feel my pulse slowing as if my body instantly believed every word she said. "Lila couldn't make it this morning, but she wants to join us a little later... if that is okay with you. Hopefully, between the two of us, we can help you feel at ease being here. However, please know that we understand if it takes time to accept the help. Especially if you haven't had much of it before now."

A tear fell down my cheek, and I could hardly tell if it was the stress over Troy being gone, the hug from Moira, or her ability to capture soul-deep fears in so few words.

"I'm sorry... I'm not..." Brushing the tear away, I glanced at Ben, who smiled around the bottle he half drank, half gnawed on.

"Don't you dare apologize! It's my job to keep you company today, including hugs in the face of worry." Her phone texted an alert in her back pocket. "It's Lila. She's done puking for the day and wants to come over." She started typing a response but paused before sending it. "Would her being here be helpful, or too much? There is no wrong answer, and I promise no one will think less of you, no matter what you choose."

Again, I was given choices, not ultimatums.

Back at the rental, Troy and his brothers waited for permission to enter. They let me decide to come here. Choices, not commands. A distinction I kept reminding myself of, though—none of my choices had yielded anything other than more support, more protection, and even more promises of companionship and even...friendship?

Choosing to trust this next step, I nodded in agreement as Moira happily texted away.

12

JANE

We passed the time nibbling on food and making small talk. Moira's enthusiasm for her girls was a perfect buffer to avoid any discussion about me or Ben, and I was grateful for it. I even enjoyed the few crossover moments when we shared experiences that let us commiserate. Apparently, Ben's capacity for spitting up down the entire back of my shirt was a skill shared by both River and Blue. Time flew by until the mid-morning nap collided with Lila's arrival.

"I brought lunch," she announced, wincing as Moira and I mimed shushing over the sleeping babies. Whispering, she continued. "And not a word about my outfit." At that, we both took in her comically oversized button-down flannel sitting atop dark leggings and sneakers. "Sam hid all my heels 'cause he's afraid I'll trip and fall, and I haven't had time to do any laundry since we got back, hence..." she ran a hand down her body with a sarcastic smile. "Lumberjack couture."

"You're playdate chic." Moira hugged her sister, snatching the bakery bag from her. "Leggings are my entire wardrobe these days. The fourth trimester is for real!" Peering inside the bag, Moira smiled and handed it to me. "I take it Fetal Wilder has a craving?"

The bag was filled with cookies.

"Anything else risks making a repeat appearance," Lila lamented.

Reaching inside, I pulled out a peanut butter blossom and passed the bag back, each of them selecting a treat.

"Did you have morning sickness?" I thought Lila's question was odd. She and Moira seemed so close. Why wouldn't she know about Moira's morning sickness? Then I realized they were staring at me.

"Oh... me?!" I mumbled around the mouthful of cookie, threatening to choke the life out of me. I took the precious seconds given to chew, swallow, and consider my words carefully.

"My stomach wasn't too bad with the girls, but I couldn't handle food smells." Moira chimed in on the wait as she grabbed a few water bottles, joining Lila and me at the kitchen table. "Poor Chase made his coffee on the back deck, chugged it, and then ran in to brush his teeth so I wouldn't vomit." Endearing as her story was, I mentally chastised myself for not being more prepared for such questions. "I promise it gets better!" She leaned across to Lila and squeezed her hand in solidarity as the poor woman went a little green.

"I swear this kid has an alarm clock. At 5 AM every day, mommy gets a quick jog to the porcelain throne for a little technicolor screaming." Sipping her water, she pointed directly at me. "Don't tell me you were one of those lucky women with no morning sickness, or I might have to hate you."

My cheeks heated as I grasped at the tenuous thread of truth I could cling to since I was, in fact, a woman who hadn't had morning sickness.

"Guilty as charged," I said with an apologetic shrug.

"Ugh, you're the worst," Lila smirked before tipping her chin towards the bedrooms. "How'd you sleep? Everything go okay last night?"

"Yes." I relaxed back into my chair, grateful for the pivot. "The bed is comfy. Ben and I both slept well with such a quiet space."

"Ben's a good sleeper, that's great!" Moira cast a loving glance at her girls. "I don't think I'll ever sleep again. Blue currently wants to cluster feed all night."

"Ya'll are freaking me out," Lila waved her hand around her baggy shirt-covered belly. "I'm so not ready for all this."

"Don't mind her." Moira swatted at her sister with good-humored dismissiveness. "Motherhood kinda snuck up on her."

"Do you know if it's a boy or a girl?" I hoped to keep the conversation focused on them.

"Oh, it's way too early," Lila said. "But Sam wants to keep it a secret."

"Hey, Jane?" Moira's brows pinched together. "How old is Ben?"

"About 4 months," I answered, grateful for my time researching umbilical stump care. "And the girls?"

"3 months next week," Moira answered quickly, plowing into another question. "And how are you feeling?" I cocked my head back in surprise, but hardly had time to come up with a lie as she barreled forward. "It's just...forgive me if this is too personal...with you and Ben on the run...did you get any post-natal care?"

My stomach sank, and a cold sweat crept across my skin. I had no idea what post-natal care looked like since I, myself, was never actually post-anything.

"Giving birth is hard work, and recovery can be tough." Moira continued, unaware that my breathing had grown shallow. "There are hormones to balance and nursing issues," she said, resting a hand on my arm in kind consideration while I tried to stop my galloping heart. "I know Ben uses formula, but drying up can be painful too; there's mastitis risks, and... "

Her questions came one after another, and each seemed to be my swan song. My one lie —letting them believe Ben was mine —was about to unravel everything if I couldn't find a way to pivot the chat back into safer territory, and God help me, I didn't know how. If I confessed I hadn't given birth to him, they could turn me in for kidnapping and take him from me, and that would only deliver him and me both back into the hands of the man we were currently running from.

"Ben should have had at least 3 or 4 peds visits by now. And - "

My lungs felt tight as I did mental gymnastics, crafting a creative way to address her reasonable questions without losing my son. I hadn't had any post-natal visits, nor had I ever nursed, or struggled with whatever a 4th trimester was. I'd spent the entirety of my time learning to care for Ben, as he came to me, and that oversight was now going to ruin everything.

"Of course, there are the vaccine schedules. "

I began considering contingencies. My car was here, and Troy was not. I could make a polite excuse about being tired, using my naptime to load up Ben and be gone before Troy returned. My car should have well over half a tank of gas, so I'd get some reasonable distance before I'd have to figure out what to do for cash. And if I were fast enough, we could make it to -

"Take a beat." Lila's voice cut through the pounding in my head as she calmly eyed me from her slouched position across the table. "She needs a minute."

Following the line of Lila's tipped water bottle, Moira finally saw me, her eyes going wide.

"Oh, Jane! No, no, no." She squeezed my hand, and only then did I recognize how fast I was breathing. "I shouldn't have hit you with so much. Forgive me." Leaning forward, Moira wrapped me in another hug, lingering around me as I worked to pull in air. "I sometimes get ahead of myself. I wasn't trying to pry or push you. I'm so sorry."

"I'm okay," I wondered when I started crying as I wiped away a stray tear. "Your questions are normal. You didn't do anything wrong. I don't know–"

"You don't have to tell us anything." Moira sat back in her chair, still holding onto my hand. "I didn't mean to overwhelm you."

"She's all heart, that one," Lila added, nudging Moira's leg with her foot. "But her enthusiasm can take some getting used to."

The two shared a silent, sisterly smile before Moira came back to me.

"I only asked all those things because, if you need a pediatrician visit or a gyno for a check-up, I have great ones." The relief that washed over me stripped the last of my nerves down to the nub, fresh tears falling in its wake.

They weren't trying to catch a kidnapper; they were caring for a young mother.

"We could get you in discreetly, too," Lila added. "So don't let that worry you."

"Thanks," I swallowed my guilt that survival mode had excluded pediatric visits and focused on steadying my shaking hands.

Ben took that moment to grunt, squirming free from his swaddling and giving me the perfect out to step away for a moment to gather my resolve. I lifted him to my shoulder, apologizing with all my heart as I whispered in his ear. 'I promise I'll do better.'

The remaining few hours were spent listening to stories of the brothers, their epic spaghetti dinners, and even a few funny pregnancy and baby-related moments. Mercifully, they didn't ask me anything else about my past.

"I told her about the Wilder Brothers' Protection Services." Moira elbowed me as she smirked. "I don't think she believes me."

"Where's Troy again?" Lila glanced at her phone, her smile mimicking Moira's. "Oh yeah...WBPS is coming."

"What am I missing?" I tried to peer at Lila's phone, but she pocketed it with a wink. "What's coming?"

"Oh, you know," Moira sing-songed while playing peek-a-boo with River. "When he won't just tell you he's smitten, but he buys you a laptop, a wardrobe, and a car."

"Or he shifts his entire career around," Lila mimicked the melodious voice for baby Blue, happily gnawing a squeaky giraffe. "All so he can make you three gourmets a day, buy you office furniture, and obsess over knocking you up so much he dick's you into oblivion." I gaped openly at her last statement, but Lila waved me off with a smile. "Eh, I tease him about it, but honestly..." Her contented gaze as she rubbed her belly revealed a peace I envied. "I'm so in love with this little parasite. Even if he or she makes Mommy scream at the porcelain every morning."

The sound of tires on gravel drew our attention.

"That must be Troy?" I rose to peek out the window. "Oh, and he's got Sam...and Chase?" Moira and Lila flanked me at the window, smirking like the cats that ate the canary.

"Wilder Brothers' Protection Services is in full swing," Moira knowingly high-fived Lila as we watched Troy lower the tailgate on his truck full of boxes.

13

TROY

LEAVING THE CABIN WAS torture. I'd bypassed the goodbye I wanted, an embrace promising swift return, because my emotions were unraveling faster than I'd had the good sense to contain. I had to regain some self-control, so I let Moira's arrival be my excuse for a hasty, cowardly exit.

Jane's sleep-heavy voice tugged at me like a siren call, her sweet words murmured to Ben, and I sneaked a peek into her room just as she began to stretch. Her lithe body arched in a graceful stretch, sweater sliding high enough to steal my breath. But when that beautiful boy smiled up at me, flailing his grasp at my finger, I felt something splinter in me. Or rather, something already splintered, slipped into place, and I found myself craving the very thing my brothers found.

Family.

A whole family where a father loved his wife, and together, they loved their children, and the role I played was no longer built on the duty of shoes too big to wear, but on a connection to a soul put on this earth solely...for me. I'd never wanted something for myself, and the enormity of it was heady. I imagined my desires mirrored in Jane's eyes seconds before she spotted my badge and gun. Reality's slap was timely as she stiffened, the innuendo in her words doused under the icy reality that she needed my protection–free from unearned advances. I held all the power here, and I'd be damned before I'd wield it in any way beyond her security and peace. I would not fail them.

I used the ride into the station to focus on my conversation with my captain. Having never used emergency PTO before, I expected questions. I didn't want to lie, but I desperately didn't want Jane's name to come up. Weaving through the sea of desks colloquially called 'the pit,' I waved at my fellow officers, pausing at my captain's office with a brisk rap against the windowed door. Captain Phil Newton, on the force as long as I could remember, was a firm but fair supervisor. Even allowing me the leeway to delve into Moira's arson case off the books for a time, turning a blind eye to the conflict of interest given the family connection.

"This is unexpected." He peered over the rim of his readers and gestured for me to have a seat. "Don't you normally hit the gym this early?"

"Indeed." Taking a seat, I smoothed a hand down my tie as I began. "I apologize for the short notice, but I require time off." My captain leaned back in his chair and interlocked his fingers behind his head. "Starting today."

"No notice? Is everything okay?" I was prepared for this question.

"All is well; I simply wish to de-stress from the past months' tension." I left my answer vague, banking on him filling in the blanks in a way that would benefit me. "Gain some...equilibrium, if you will." I settled into the pregnant pause stretching between us, my patience rewarded when he rubbed both hands over his face with a resigned sigh.

"Can't say as I blame you. Your family has been through the wringer. I know how close you all are." Not wanting to miss the opportunity to capitalize on his sympathies, I tossed in another point.

"You've hit the nail on the head. I've hardly had time to bond with my nieces or sisters-in-law."

"Lord knows you've banked a little stop-and-smell-the-roses, Wilder. Your family's really been through it." He handed over a set of blank forms. "Get these to me before you go." I stood, but the captain held a hand up. "PTO starts today, you say?"

"I trust that won't be a problem." Having nearly made a quick exit, I held my breath at the added question. I needed to get back to Jane and Ben.

"I'll approve the time, but the mayor has another bigwig coming for a little dog and pony at the new library re-opening. He wants a big show."

This I was not prepared for, though it was as common a nuisance as a rock in my shoe of late.

"Surely a few uniformed officers would make a better showing than - "Captain held up a hand, silencing me with a glare.

"He requested you by name, Wilder." I inhaled, holding my breath for a silent three-count before resigning myself to another task by the town development team I had been voluntold for. A community outreach program I had more time for before my world expanded by five, no six, people. I needed to clear the decks to focus all my energy on Jane, but I couldn't share this with my boss. That meant I'd take what I could get and make the most of it.

"How much time can I have?"

"I can give you two weeks," he huffed, shaking his head. "I'd give you more if I could."

Two weeks didn't feel like enough time—not by half—but I opted to leave in good standing rather than risk more questions by pushing. Lila's story had already shown that Apex could, in some fashion, ingratiate itself into Internal Affairs. There could be more, and the last thing I needed was my abnormal behavior leading some unknown mole straight to Jane.

"I appreciate the time." I turned to the door, jaw clenched as my Captain called out behind me.

"And I can't guarantee I won't call if the mayor gets his underwear in a twist!"

I finished the paperwork in a matter of minutes, relieved to walk away from the thing that had identified my outer control ever since I'd exited the military; shaken from what I'd witnessed and in need of something to channel my protective instincts into. The badge grew into my life, seconded only by my family. But now I had a greater pull. I longed to protect Jane. I wanted her to feel safe enough to open up and share everything with me, so I could burn Apex to the ground. The pressure of a two-week countdown drove me to immerse myself in her space, and I was grateful I'd spent time pre-ordering what Ben needed so I could stay with her from here on out.

As I pulled up to the loading bay at our local box store, I found everything piled and ready to be loaded. I was thankful for the store's efficiency as I drove back up the two-lane blacktop towards the cabin, every minute ratcheting my anxiety.

How were Jane and Ben doing?

Was she able to relax with my sisters?

Was she eating enough?

Unable to ask her these things, I swung into my cell phone provider and purchased a new phone. I needed to be able to reach her if we were apart. I needed her to be able to reach me.

Sam and Chase pulled into the cabin's gravel driveway behind me. I began unloading boxes, filling my arms with the smaller items before rushing ahead of the two idiots competing to see who could carry the most bags in one trip. Stepping inside, I found Jane holding Ben at the front window. When her eyes met mine, the tension left my body, as the held breath left hers. Chase and Sam also paused, Moira and Lila having flanked Jane, each carrying one of the twins.

"Well, isn't that a picture?" Sam whispered, stalking his wife for a kiss before dropping bags on the kitchen table.

"If ever I saw one," Chase finished, nodding to Moira to join him in the kitchen. Closing the door behind them, I fought the urge to wrap Jane in an embrace. Longing for a measure of the peace my brothers had found, and watching it blink back at me from icy blue eyes that searched me with a tentative look of curiosity.

"Need a hand?" Jane eyed the stack of boxes in my hands.

"Grab the box on top." I lowered the stack so she could reach the cell phone.

"You got a new phone?" She followed me to the living room, where I began staging boxes against the wall.

"I'm guessing that's yours, now," Lila interjected with a rye smirk that made me wonder what they'd discussed while I was gone.

"I acquired that for you so you can reach me if we're apart," I lifted the lid and presented her with the latest iPhone. "I've preprogrammed it with my family's contact info, as well as the number to the station, the local pediatric urgent care clinic, our Fire Chief, and his wife Carol, who you haven't met yet but are just as trusted as any family friend could be."

"Oh...wow." Jane gave the phone a wide-eyed once-over. "You didn't have to do that, I have...." She halted, a beautiful flush of pink soaring up her neck and cheeks.

"I'm aware you have a phone of your own," I reassured, needing her to know I wanted this for safety, not control. "This one would be untraceable. You'll have a secure way to reach any of us without your existing number linking you to my family." I left off the note about being able to track her phone through my account, knowing we had legions of discussions still ahead of us and not wanting to overwhelm her now.

"Score one for the WBPS," Moira nudged Jane's shoulder.

I blinked at my sister, inquiring silently about an inside joke they seemed to be sharing, but couldn't speak to it as Lila interjected.

"Wanna bet he's got a phone case, protective glass cover, and all the accessories too." Lila's eyes focused on the small bag in my hand.

"Of course, there's a case, a charger for every room, and earbuds." I agreed, hanging endlessly on Jane's deepening blush. "In case you wish to listen to music without waking Ben." Her flushed cheeks were beautiful, and I couldn't help but smile when I opened the bag, producing the items listed and sending Lila and Moira into peals of laughter.

They had developed some inside joke, Jane's blush notwithstanding, and it warmed my heart to see the camaraderie growing between the three. I'd not anticipated them growing close, and I loved the outlet it would give Jane. I also hoped it meant she'd open up more to me, too.

As the women said their goodbyes, my brothers finished unloading the last of the boxes.

"Troy, this is all..." Jane waved an arm across the boxes and bags filling the living room. "You didn't have to do all of this."

"You will be stuck here for a time, and I wish you to be comfortable." I closed the space between us, sensing a rise in her anxiety by the way she slipped her bottom lip between her teeth. "Purchasing Ben a proper bed and a few comfort items might help both of you get better sleep."

"Speaking of, want this in the master bedroom?" Sam inquired, holding one end of the crib box.

"I'll be in momentarily to help assemble it." I nodded, turning back to Jane. I sensed she needed more reassurance that I wanted this all for her comfort as much as Ben's. "I am happy to do this for you." I reached out, pleased that she didn't retract from my fingers grazing down her arm. "You've been uprooted for a time, but even before you ran, I suspect your life wasn't known for comfort. I want to give you that now. Comfort, here, with me." The words seemed to cascade down her face; eyes softening, a smile teasing the corners of her lips, and her shoulders sagging ever so slightly as she leaned into my palm.

It was a start.

"Assembly should be quick. You and Ben can rest a bit, and I'll make us some dinner after."

"Or...I could make dinner?" Her request was a pleasant surprise. "It might not be fancy, but it's the least I can do, seeing as you've spent the day robbing a furniture store." The huff of laughter revealed the joke as she flickered her gaze again to the new influx of bags, boxes, and more.

Jane...joked.

I didn't fight my smile, leaning into the levity she invited.

"I may have gone a tad overboard." A lock of hair drifted in front of Jane's eyes, and my hands found my pockets in their resistance to tuck it behind her ear. "If you need anything more, I–"

"I believe an expensive new phone and a nursery of furniture earns you a pass at any potential oversight." She turned to the kitchen, navigating the maze of boxes like she belonged here with Ben tucked in close, and a little more of that peace settled in my chest.

14

JANE

THE DAY WITH MOIRA and Lila felt like a gift. They happily regaled me with stories about Troy, Chase, and Sam; an endearing family dynamic so far removed from the cold existence I endured. Then again, maybe my life wasn't the norm but the exception. Even the guys, all orphaned in some fashion, were given a fantastic home by their adopted mother. Their bond clearly included their wives and children; their roles of brother and uncle as fluid as any. It was a vast ocean of love and acceptance compared to my life drifting along shallow shores, dragging an anchor of lies.

My guilt at navigating conversational topics to avoid getting caught in a lie was suffocating. I nearly shouted my truth to the sky just to be free of it. Especially given their welcoming kindness and grace. Girlfriends were a luxury my father's privilege never bought. Moira's enthusiasm for playdates and Lila strolling in like we were old friends—it felt so new and amazing, and I felt woefully incapable of reciprocating when my words were continually measured and stunted. To their credit, if Lila and Moira noticed my pivots and hesitations, they didn't show it—small mercy given the text messages vibrating away in my pocket.

> Unknown: I know you are still in Lake Placid. I will find you.

> Unknown: Did you stay with one of those men? Maybe I'll check them out.

> Unknown: Maybe I'll tell dear old dad you hooked up with three guys.

> Unknown: He might even come here personally to hunt for you.

There was no longer any question of whether I wanted to share everything with Troy. His departure this morning made my chest ache, and the way my body relaxed when he stepped into the cabin could hardly be described. I'd never felt so safe. I wanted to tell him everything, to be free from the burden of secrets and the guilt and shame they brought, including this looming threat that my father's henchman was actively searching for me still and might now be looking at them.

But how to begin?

Troy had to be the officer Marcus Brinks talked about that night in my father's office. If his stalwart behavior hadn't shown it, the stories shared by Moira and Lila of Troy's rule-following nature did. So I knew I could trust Troy to keep Ben and me safe, to protect us from dangerous criminals, and to provide a safe harbor as we restarted our lives, but what would he think about Ben's parentage?

Therein was the rub.

If my father lied, who were Ben's real parents? Were they looking for him, me complicit in his kidnapping? Then again, if Ben were my half-brother, would that make me a legal guardian? Would I be allowed to adopt him fully and raise him as the son I already felt he was? Was I even qualified, being unemployed, homeless, and on the run? Would any of that be possible without birth records, which then required my father's involvement, and so the cycle continued.

This was where my mind stayed as I rummaged through the fridge, setting out ingredients for the only meal I knew I could make with one hand while still holding Ben, who'd been clingier than usual all afternoon. Chase and Sam finished their tasks, said their goodbyes, and left just as I plated scrambled eggs and skillet-fried toast.

"It smells amazing," Troy said, sliding into a chair.

Still in his work attire, he'd rolled his sleeves up his forearms, revealing impressive muscles I hadn't seen yet. He'd even loosened his tie and unbuttoned the top few buttons of his shirt, relaxing in a way that helped me feel more at ease. Then, I noted the ratty clothes I'd been wearing for days and made a note to try to wash them this evening after bedtime.

"I was in such a rush to get everything done on my list that I failed to eat breakfast or lunch, and I am famished." He held out my chair to join him.

"The toast is a little darker than intended," I shrugged. "But Bon Appétit."

"If I may." He lifted both hands, gesturing for Ben. "You deserve to eat your meal while it's hot." He scooped the snoozing bundle from my arms, settling Ben on his shoulder as if he'd been holding my world his whole life. "How was your day?"

Then, as if he'd said the words on an exhale, he began eating while I peppered in tidbits from my time with Moira and Lila, carefully dancing around the parts I was still unsure of. He never stopped watching me, shoveling in his food, nodding and humming along to the conversation until he slid his plate back at his last bite and declared, 'Perfection.'

"Are you often too busy to eat?" I asked, impressed that he'd not spilled so much as a crumb, finishing his meal before I'd gotten through half of mine.

"Small towns offer their own excitement. Last week alone, I visited a woman 3 times who refused to accept that squirrels, not vandals, were in her attic." Troy's voice was soft for Ben, but he looked only at me as he spoke. "Paperwork is always riveting."

"Sounds like you should deputize a cat," I teased, enjoying the smile it won me.

"Her house is near an old playground, though." He looked down at Ben. "Maybe we can take this sleepyhead there when he is older."

My heart fluttered at the unspoken meaning behind his words. He wanted us...when Ben was older. But if I was wrong, and he was compelled to return Ben to my father...but surely not. My head swam, and I swallowed hard around emotions I couldn't voice. The weight of that small sentence gripped my guilt by the throat, throttling me into spilling my guts before the man got too attached to a problem his law-abiding instincts might well have to cast back into shark-infested waters.

"Jane?" His voice pulled me from my thoughts, and I had to shake away the sadness and fear that held me.

"That sleepyhead has been snoozing off and on all day. I think he's teething, maybe." I stood and prepared a bottle, grateful to escape Troy's scrutiny. "His naps today were more interrupted, and he didn't want to lie down much. Hence, your one-handed dinner with slightly burnt toast." I reached for Ben, but Troy took the bottle from me instead, his eyes locking on mine, and I swear I felt something fall away...a heaviness I longed to be free of, momentarily slipped into oblivion.

"Allow me," Troy draped a burp cloth over his shoulder. "A growing boy needs his dinner." He gently dragged the bottle tip across Ben's little lips, and my heart skipped a beat. Troy was so natural with Ben, surely he'd never send us away. "Anything else of note today?"

"Moira and Lila shared stories about weddings, and one about you avoiding diaper duty by ducking behind furniture?"

"All Lies." Troy smiled.

"Is it true that Chase married Moira first for insurance, then proposed a second time?"

"That much is true." Troy lifted Ben for a small burp before resuming his bottle. "Though Sam and I both saw the first wedding for what it was. A stepping stone towards forever." The turn of phrase was beautifully descriptive.

"Are all Wilders so poetic?"

"Chase was hooked the first night he saw her." Troy set the empty bottle on the table and propped Ben back on his shoulder. "His ruse to get her to a justice of the peace was earnest, but the man was utterly gone over her." Troy's eyes smiled when he spoke of his brothers.

"Did Lila and Sam have a similar insta-connection?"

"Oh my, that was an entirely different story that involved shenanigans that would have sent our dear Nonna rolling in her grave." He laughed. "I'll let Lila share the details, but yes. Sam was immediately hooked, his reluctance to admit it notwithstanding." Troy spoke fondly of his family. Never a shift in posture or hidden intent beneath his words. Every syllable felt genuine, and his family's love seemed impossibly true. A pang of envy pierced my heart.

"You are incredibly lucky to have found one another."

"And now we've found you." If my heart had all but stopped before, this five-word sentence would have jolted me back to life, carving through my defenses and settling somewhere fragile and dangerous beneath my ribs. He had found me...and I so wanted to be found in him.

Thankfully, Troy never saw my jaw unhinge before he leaned to hand Ben to me.

"If you don't mind, I'll grab a shower and then clean up dinner." I began to offer to clean things myself, but his simple raised brow stopped me. "Nonna's rules. You cooked. I clean." He lowered Ben into my arms and then dropped his voice into a low timbre that rattled my very bones. "I expect you to relax and wait for me."

A command. A request. An inviting.

"I suppose I can..." My words trailed off as my cheek brushed against Ben's downy hair, noting a wave of heat. Quickly unwrapping the blanket from around his legs, I removed it to find his damp onesie clinging to his sweaty little body. "Oh god!" Standing, I held my cheek to his; the heat radiated. "He's burning up!"

"A fever?" Troy cupped Ben's head. "Let's get him stripped."

I crossed to the couch, laying him down to gently strip Ben of his clothes. The sudden burst of cold air sent him into a series of frustrated grunts. Troy dug around in a shopping bag and fished out a thermometer from a first-aid kit. Ripping it open, he administered it to Ben, and we waited.

"101." The number slammed into me. "That's too high—he's too little..." My mind raced through everything I'd read about babies and fevers. "Teething, maybe...he's so young. What if it's something bad?"

"Grab his bag." Troy wrapped Ben in a clean blanket, grabbed his cell, and led me to the door. "We're going to the pediatric urgent care clinic."

Wilder Family Group Chat

-2-

> Me: APB

Chase: What's up?

> Me: Ben spiked a fever, 101.

Moira: Oh no!

Sam: I can be there in 15.

> Me: Already en route to the pediatric after-hours,

Lila: What can we do?

Me: Nothing yet. I just wanted you to know.

Chase: We're here.

Sam: Lemme know what they say.

Moira: Tell Jane to text me updates.

Lila: Us...I'll start a chick-chat.

15

JANE

ETERNITY WAS DEFINED ON that drive. Every minute, another slip into spiraling doubt. When had the fever started? Was this avoidable if I'd gotten him basic pediatric care sooner? Moira's kind offers from earlier were now a haunting reminder of where I had failed Ben.

Troy was equally worried, as evidenced by his tight grip on the steering wheel. When we parked, I had Ben unbuckled and in my arms before Troy opened my door. The brightly lit clinic was empty, save a reception desk staffed by a solitary chipper woman with grey wisps framing kind eyes that crinkled at the edges when she welcomed us.

"Good evening," she cooed. "Who do we have here?"

"This is Ben." My panic had me near-yelling. "He seemed sleepy today but fine until just after his dinner bottle, and then he was warm, and we took his temperature, and it was 101!" The woman stood and addressed me with a soft tilt of her head.

"Okay, mama. Deep breath. You've brought him to the right place." She handed Troy a clipboard of papers and offered me a soft smile. "I'll tell the doctor you're here, and we'll get you back right away."

As she disappeared behind closed doors, I began pacing, debating the merits of keeping Ben wrapped and cozy, then worrying that he was too warm. Troy, ever the pillar of calm, thumped the clipboard with his free hand.

"I might need help with some of this." He spoke in an odd whisper I had no time to analyze.

"Right," I closed my eyes and sighed. "Sorry. Pacing doesn't help Ben, but - "

"It helps, Mama." Troy's hand anchored my lower back as he led me to a colorful plastic chair. "Let's try to knock out the big stuff." He was being as gentle with me as he was the night we met, a sign I looked as frantic as I felt.

Fighting tears, I lowered myself to the chair he pointed to.

"He doesn't have any allergies." I began, not waiting for Troy to ask. "He had a normal delivery. Full-term. No complications." A smooth lie delivered courtesy of mommy blogs that discussed such things. I rattled off a birth date and was prepared to offer more when a voice called out.

"Ben?" A young doctor scanned the room, finding us on the far side.

"That's us!" I jumped to my feet, feeling Troy right behind me.

"First door on the right." The doctor gestured past him to the room and waved a hand over the exam table, which was prepared with a little nest of rolled-up blankets. "Let's get this little guy undressed while you tell me what happened?"

"I'm not sure when it happened." I gently laid Ben down, hating the flush in his fevered cheeks. "He seemed fine this morning, maybe a little clingier than usual. I thought it was a growth spurt or teething."

"That's a great guess, Mom." The doctor spoke to me but never took his eyes off Ben as he quickly warmed up his stethoscope to listen to Ben's heart and lungs. "Both of those things can cause a clingy boy."

"After his dinner bottle, I held him and realized he was warm. I don't know how long - " Ben grunted in frustration at the doctor's cold hands.

"I was feeding him," Troy added, his hand again on my back. "He drank normally. Burped like a champ."

"Dads love good burps, don't they, Ben?" The doctor missed the look that passed between Troy and me as he carried Ben to a scale. Ben cried the second he was laid onto the paper-covered scale. "I know, big guy, no one likes the mean ol' scale." Writing down the information, he nodded to Troy. "You can grab him, Dad. Warm him up while I check his sinuses."

Troy scooped Ben up, snuggling him with low shushing sounds as the doctor took a teeny, lighted tool and peeked inside Ben's nose and ears; the latter, an instant source of discomfort.

"Whoa there." Troy slid a hand between Ben and the doctor, his voice quiet but edged. "That seemed like it hurt."

To his credit, the doctor was unflappable.

"Sorry, Dad, but I believe we've found our culprit." He settled the tool back in its wall holder. "You can go ahead and dress him." He continued talking as he measured out a purple liquid into a dropper. "Ben has fluid in his ears. I'm guessing he's fighting Rhinovirus, which is making the rounds right now."

"My nieces just recovered from it." Troy offered. "Perhaps he caught it from them?"

"It's common, and it's everywhere. He could just as easily have caught it from a grocery store run. The good news is, little Ben's ear infection is mild. It'll clear up in a day or two. His sinuses are clogged, which would explain his clinginess." The doctor gave me a reassuring smile as he continued. "Lying down can cause pressure, so they like to be held more. You had good instincts keeping him upright today." The compliment to my instincts was barely a blip in the deep sea of guilt I was drowning in. "With permission, I would like to give a low-dose antibiotic. And this," He held the dropper of purple liquid, "Motrin will knock that fever down to a manageable burn and help him be more comfortable tonight so he can rest. May I?"

He gestured with the dropper, spinning its companion bottle with the medicine's label around so we could read it while he waited for permission to administer it.

"Yes, please," I answered, my voice cracking.

"These things are hard to detect in the littlest patients. They can't communicate their feelings in words." The doctor tucked the dropper into Ben's cheek pocket, squirting the liquid in even as I wondered what signs I'd missed. Resting his hand on my arm, he continued. "This was not caused by anything you did or didn't do. Babies have underdeveloped sinus cavities. Ear infections can crop up within hours of a virus coming home to roost."

"Will the antibiotics be hard on his stomach?" Troy stepped closer to me, sliding his arm around my waist with a tug he hadn't used before. The doctor removed his hand from me, though his smile never wavered.

"You noted no allergies. I'm assuming he hasn't had antibiotics before?" I shook my head. "Great. We'll start with a low-dose, broad-spectrum antibiotic for just 5 days. The most significant risk will be diaper rash as his body processes everything out." The doctor scanned the paperwork, noticing Troy's badge. "Where are you stationed, Officer?"

"Lake Placid." Troy's voice held that same low edge to it from earlier, but the doctor seemed not to notice.

"Cute town! I've done a few rotations in their ER." The doctor flipped through the paperwork again. "You left the vaccine records blank." He looked up at me, and panic set in.

Vaccines. Vaccines! How could I forget vaccines?

"My wife and I opted for a modified approach, giving Ben time to grow bigger before introducing the standard vaccines." His lie was smooth, seamless even, with zero hesitation. "We're taking social distancing precautions to mitigate his exposure risk. Our pediatrician knows our plan." As easy as breathing, Troy answered with a thorough, detailed response. Lying to this fellow essential worker as if the words were the gods-honest truth. I willed my face to a measured calm but could practically taste the shock and relief.

"Sounds like a plan. Call your pediatrician in the morning and tell them about tonight. They'll want to follow up in a few days." He tapped something into his tablet before heading towards the door. "Officer," he reached out to Troy, who accepted the handshake, "Mrs. Wilder." He didn't offer me a handshake, just a polite nod of his head, and I was grateful for the excuse not to speak or move as I reeled first from Troy's effortless lie, and then again from that name–Mrs. Wilder.

It felt dangerously close to something I wanted.

"I'll have your discharge papers up front. They'll detail the prescription antibiotic and dosing for Motrin. There is a 24-hour pharmacy at the five points on your way home that should be able to fill this for you."

"Thank you, Doctor." I said, "Is it safe for me to swaddle him now?"

"Absolutely. He'll feel clammy and chilly while he wrestles the fever. Keep him covered loosely until it breaks." The doctor looked at Troy then. "Kangaroo cuddles work great. Avoid a bath 'til morning to avoid any unnecessary chill."

Troy nodded his understanding, taking Ben's bag and the clipboard, and then tucking me into his arm to again guide me back to the front desk. The kind woman offered another sympathetic smile along with a lyrical round of 'Coos'..

"And all's right with the world." She smiled with grandmotherly affection.

"Yes," I said, remembering how frantic I'd been when I came in. "I'm sorry I was so panicked. It's just an ear infection."

"I'll tell you a secret." The woman gave a playful whisper. "Only the best moms give a good panic when their babies are sick." She winked at Troy as she retrieved the clipboard he offered. "Isn't that right, Dad?"

"Indeed, it is." Troy's hand returned to my back, and without thinking, I leaned into him. "What do we owe you?"

"I don't have your insurance card on file, Officer Wilder." The woman glanced at the incomplete paperwork, then back at us. "I can upload that now."

"I'm afraid my time with my son has flown by. I've been derelict in completing the paperwork with HR to add him to my insurance." Another lie delivered flawlessly, protecting Ben and me from the cold, hard consequences of our lives. "I'll pay cash. And I'll put my credit card on file for any future visits my wife might need." Troy never looked my way, but I swear his fingers flexed when he called me his wife.

As we walked out, my mind swirled with a new eddy of sensations and emotions. Worry for Ben layered shades of shock and awe, even a tinge of want, as I replayed how smoothly Troy had covered for us. Troy's intimate touch on my back, like I belonged to him, and when he took Ben to load into the truck, I reshaped all our interactions in this new light. Surely, I could trust him to protect the truth of who I was... and who Ben was to me.

16

TROY

I F EVER I HAD doubts about Jane's identity, they were all but ce-
mented tonight.

The drive home from the after-hours pediatric office was quiet,
with Jane in the backseat, wholly focused on Ben. Knuckles white on
the wheel, I forced my breathing steady as I sorted through what I knew.

She rattled off his allergy and birth history before I asked, as if
memorized by rote, including his full-term status and lack of complications, which weren't even on the form. That might have gone
unnoticed if not for how she went ghostly pale when the doctor asked
about vaccinations. A question she was not expecting and for which
she had no solid answer. I stepped in before the doctor noticed, giving
a response I'd heard while listening to an infant care audiobook earlier
in the day. But her reaction confirmed my suspicions that her earlier
answers were rehearsed.

A good cop can always spot a lie.

Still, Jane's connection to Ben felt authentic, and that dichotomy was what I couldn't wrap my head around. Pulling into the pharmacy, I leaned on my training as I let the mask of calm level me.

"I'll run in and grab the meds. It might be best if you wait in the truck, so we don't expose Ben to more germs." Jane nodded and held her cell phone aloft.

"I texted Moira. She suggested a bottle of Pedialyte to mix in his formula in case he gets dehydrated." I nodded my understanding, a whole new feeling mixing in. Knowing my family was already texting Jane brought warmth into the picture, prompting me to use my time waiting for the script to call my sister.

"How's Ben?" Moira answered on the first ring.

"The doctor says it's likely rhinovirus. I'm at the pharmacy now."

"Ugh, I feel awful. The girls had that a week ago. I hope I didn't bring it to Ben."

"As I understand it, it's going around."

"Grab one of those nose-sucker tools. It'll help to clear the gunk."

"Will do," I found the bulbous torture device and tossed it into the basket. "May I ask how everything seemed today?"

"It was good." Her chipper answer was oddly soothing. "Ben is such a happy baby. I'm sure tonight was scary, but everything will feel better tomorrow."

"And...Jane?" I pressed.

"Jane is a doting mother. She'll do great with whatever Ben needs to run this little earache out the door." Then she paused for a single second before adding. "But...that's not what you want to ask me, is it?"

My sigh came from deep inside me.

"You have questions about Jane." A statement...not a question.

"Yes."

"And her real identity." That halted my steps.

"What did she tell you?"

"Nothing... outright." Moira began. "But there were things." Moira's voice went a little softer, as if the words felt heavy to hold, and she was glad to be free of them. "I don't think she and Ben have *ever* been in a safe space. I don't think Ben ever had a bed or bassinet, and I don't think Jane has had a single post-natal check-up."

"By now, she should have had several, yes?" I was alarmed to realize I hadn't even considered Jane's healthcare in all this. She appeared well enough, if not tired, but with Ben's age, I should have thought of Jane's care.

"Ben should've had two check-ups at least," Moira answered. "And Jane should've had a 6-week post-natal exam at a minimum, if not additional visits, depending on the birth." Moira then sighed. "But Troy, I got... a vibe."

"A vibe?" I asked, worry taunting the beast to lift its head.

"Jane is running from something, and it's bad...and it's old." My sister's worldly observation hit harder than any evidence I could find on paper. "I can only compare it to mine and Lila's situations. Both raw, but both relatively new. The way she's reacted when I hugged her...I think Ben and Jane were in survival mode from the moment he was born. I think she was alone even before that. And I think she's stuck there, at least mentally."

I hummed an acknowledgment as I set the basket on the counter, but inside my heart was shattering. The potential scenarios Jane could be running from, with an infant and zero provisions, grew more horrific by the second.

"How can I help you at this point?" Ever the dutiful sister...offering to help despite having her own children to care for.

"Kiss my nieces...and update the family so Sam and Lila don't worry." I loved her offer of assistance, but it was never far from my mind that they needed their peace. Moira and Lila, my brothers, had run their race. Their battle with Apex was done, and they were no longer in danger; both Jensen and Brinks were dead. I was now off work, and for a time, I could focus my energy and time entirely on providing such security for Jane and Ben.

My family didn't need to worry about it.

Heading back to the truck, I remembered the night I found Jane in my rental, eyes wide with adrenaline, and my blood began to boil. If Jane was important enough for Apex to send someone to attack her and a baby, then what did she know... and how long before they tried again? The pressure to get her to open up dialed even higher, along with an awareness that I was on borrowed time. For the first time, I felt pulled to both wield my badge and to cast it aside and let the beast loose.

"Everything okay?" Jane asked as I entered the truck, shaking my head to clear my anger.

"Moira suggested a few extra things for Ben." I handed the bag back to her. "Some bulbous, nasal, thing. And I grabbed a diaper rash cream just in case."

"Oh, good," Jane sighed. "Moira is so free with her knowledge. It's nice having someone to lean on with this." As I turned to back out, Jane's eye popped wide as she hastily added, "Not that you aren't amazing in every way. I'm so sorry! I didn't mean to say you hadn't been helpful...you have been–"

"Whoa, whoa, whoa." I slid the truck into park and turned to face Jane, unnerved at her burst of insecure rambling. "Please, never apologize for being happy that my family is helping you." If she clammed up now, if she pulled away because I'd failed to be enough, we were screwed.

"I'm new to baby things, too. If ever the phrase 'blind leading the blind' were applicable, this night might fit." Her shoulders sagged as I reached for her hand, and she met me halfway, lacing our fingers together with an ease that I leaned into. "But Jane, you can tell me anything. You can lean on me for everything. I will not fail you...even if we flounder through new territory together. I want to be everything you need."

17

JANE

You can tell me anything.

You can lean on me for everything.

I will not fail you.

I want to be everything you need.

Troy's earnest expression as he spoke almost unraveled me. He pleaded for me to be open with him, and God, I wanted to be. I wanted to be free of the isolating secrets my father had planted so deeply within me.

Hadn't Troy shown I could uproot them with him?

Sam greeted us at the cabin door, medic bag in hand, and swooped in to check over Ben again. He asked about the doctor's exam and nodded his approval over Troy's pharmacy selection. Their bond as brothers seemed so easy and foreign. He and Troy discussed a baby book that Troy apparently had already been reading. Worried as I was over Ben, I didn't say much, but my curiosity got the better of me when Sam left and Ben was asleep in clean, dry clothes.

"Did you say you were listening to a baby book?" Troy's lips tipped at the edges as he turned off the porch light.

"An audiobook on baby care. I like to be prepared. I wanted to anticipate what Ben might need." He tipped his head towards the mountain of boxes still edging the living room. "It helped fill out the shopping list, as well."

I glanced at the boxes, then back to him and his arms-crossed stance. His eyes pleaded for something, and again his words echoed in memory. *You can tell me anything.*

"It's an incredible gesture." I waved an arm around the space. "All of this has been an incredibly kind and thoughtful gesture." I crossed to him then, debating with every step how to bridge the divide between what he knew and what I needed to share. "But tonight was... more. More than I could've asked. More than I can repay. Just...." I let my hand rest on his forearm, and I could feel the flicker of tension ripple through him. "'Thanks' feels woefully lacking after what you did for Ben tonight, but it's all I have to give."

"It was nothing - "

"It was everything!" I stopped whatever polite deflection he planned, needing to say this before I lost my nerve under the dark intensity of his eyes. Fear, uncertainty, flooded me with memories that I pushed through, trusting that he wasn't like my father. "The way you rushed us to the clinic, comforted Ben, and me, and - "

"Jane, truly, it was nothing." He lifted his hands in surrender, backing a step away as if afraid to touch me. It might have hurt if not for the way he held my waist at the clinic, and God help me, all I wanted was his hand back around my waist again. "I was happy to– "

"Gia!" My name blurted forth like the first painful breath after too long underwater. "My name... is Gia."

Troy froze, stalwart and still; only the flex of his neck muscles showed any reaction at all, and that left me wanting and waiting, wondering what to say next—if I should wait for him to ask me questions—debating if I'd just leapt off the wrong damned cliff.

"I'm listening." That was all he said; no anger or malice, his voice was that low, rippling calm I'd felt before.

Please, I begged the universe, don't be like my father.

"The florist came, but he wasn't a florist, and he tried to take me. I ran him off and tried to leave when three ginormous hulks showed up." I gave a half-hearted smile, willing away the threatening tears. "So I gave you a false name."

He nodded his understanding but remained quiet.

"I was so scared of what was happening, of who you all were. Out of options, out of cash, and..." I squeezed my eyes shut, shaking my healed palm as if banishing the nerves that skittered down my spine. Troy's hand, large and warm, rested on my upper arm. I opened my eyes to see his uncrossed arms now reaching for me.

"I'm listening." He repeated, voice even softer. "Please...continue."

He guided me to the couch, settling Ben into a bouncy chair on the floor while I tucked my feet under me, hugging a pillow in the hopes it would muffle the butterflies thundering through me like elephants.

"I gave you a fake name because I was scared you'd send me back. I couldn't go back to him. I couldn't take Ben back to that place." Tears stung, and I took another deep breath, pinching the bridge of my nose to try and stave them off.

"So his name is Ben?" I couldn't speak or the tears would win, so I just nodded. "And are you running from his father?" I swallowed the urge to give more and nodded again. "Please, Gia..."

There. My name. My true name.

It was as if he spoke warmth across my body, settling into my bones. Troy grasped my hands, squeezing them in a silent plea, 'I will not fail you. I will not fail you. I will not fail you. I will not fail you. I will not fail you.'

Closing my eyes, I took the next step.

"Ben's father is also...*my* father. I love Ben like my son, but he is my half-brother. Our father shoved Ben into my arms when he was a newborn and told me he was my responsibility." My head was spinning, and the words just flew out. "He was given to me without name or pretense; I don't even know who his mother is, and when I questioned our father about it, I was– "

My hand lifted to shield myself from the phantom sting that raked across my cheek, but I found only stinging tears.

"I was banished to my room with a baby, left alone to figure out how to care for him, and only allowed to order things through members of my father's staff. Weeks went by like that." My fingers snapped, and my voice became otherworldly as I spoke through sobs and gasps. "No one would help. I had no sleep..." The air grew thin, and racking sobs burned my lungs. "I was so afraid I'd somehow do something wrong or hurt Ben...or that my father would take him back...but then he said..." I heaved, unable to continue through the wildfire of memories razing a path across my heart. Words stifled behind sobs, unable to see past the tears, I could only let the sadness take me under as weeks of fear and worry–months of isolation and terror–poured out.

"I can only imagine how heavy such a duty must have been." Troy's voice was soothing, and I clung to it as the darkest memories came one after another.

He rubbed his hands down my back; the connection bolted through me, unaware I had leaned into him. He cradled me to his chest, and I let the world fade away in the embrace of a man who touched me with kindness and offered me peace.

Time was lost.

Minutes to hours.

Hours to lifetimes.

Hurt. Release. Empty.

I didn't speak again until my breathing calmed, and Troy waited for me.

"The night I left, I discovered I was to be married off to his attorney, Marcus Brinks." Troy's eyes narrowed at the name, but he didn't speak. "And Ben was being sold out to strangers for future favors..." I fisted my heart to counter the fresh pain. "I didn't know what it all meant, but I couldn't fathom losing Ben to someone who was okay with taking a stranger's baby, and after hearing my 'fiancé' laugh about me in handcuffs for taming, I just..." I gasped again, feeling lightheaded from the pure adrenaline coursing through me as I relived each moment. "I ran. I had to. I couldn't let Ben fall into a home that would hurt him. Not like that... like I had been...I couldn't lose him." My words came faster and faster as I pleaded for Troy to rescue me with every fiber of my being. "I love him like he's mine, and I just...he can't... not like I lived with...So I just... took everything I could carry, and I... " Wracking sobs hit. Fear afresh, my entire body seized as I silently begged, 'Please don't take my baby.' "I ran. I ran, and I ran until I found... you."

Troy pulled me into his lap, wrapping my arms and legs around him as he pressed me so tightly into his chest that all that was left in the world was him.

"Shhh." His voice soothed, and his arms squeezed around me, securing me with his body as I released a lifetime of isolation and fear. Uncontrollable heaves, born of secrets, brought walls crashing down around me. "My god, Gia. What you have endured," My name from his lips rippled through me, and I melted into him. "The sheer courage you have shown all this time. To escape, to save Ben, and to run." He pulled back, lifting my face with his palms on my cheeks until I looked directly into his eyes. He grazed a finger across my cheek, tucking tear-soaked hair behind my ear. "I will not let you down, Gia....I promise you."

18

TROY

THE SAME MONSTERS WHO'D taken my sisters, who'd shot Sam and almost murdered Chase, were behind this. The beast inside me crawled confidently to the surface, ready to mete out its due. Of all the scenarios I'd considered, none prepared me for the absolute fury of hearing Gia describe neglect at best, systemic abuse at worst. Witnessing her being discussed as chattel, handcuffed to a man's bed for control, was enough to make me sick. 'Not Ben...I couldn't lose him...not like I had lived with...' Whatever Gia endured was so horrific that she pushed past a lifetime of indoctrinated fear to embrace isolation and loneliness to spare Ben a single moment of that pain.

Her courage was astounding.

The beast wanted blood.

I would take away her fear, shield her from any more pain, and I would bodily ruin whoever treated this beautiful creature so abhorrently. To think that they felt Marcus Brinks was a suitable husband for her...

the thought sickened me. I pulled her face back again and took in her vibrant blue eyes, red-rimmed with tear-soaked.

This confession had been brutal for her.

I had a million questions, but they would wait. Gia needed rest, and I could provide that for her.

I stood, her still wrapped around me, and I carried her to the bedroom. Pulling back the comforter, I put her on the bed's edge and knelt to remove her shoes.

No words were required.

Her teary eyes watched as I retrieved her pajamas and returned to her. Her arms floated up in obedience to my silent command as I removed her shirt, replacing it with the sweater she slept in. I only unlatched her bra after she was covered so she could be free of it. Lying her back on the pillows, I unbuttoned her jeans and slid them past her hips, loving the way she lifted her feet for me so I could replace them with her sleep shorts. It was a dance of limbs, silent and fluid, until I could pull the covers over her, stealing only the briefest second of contact as my finger slipped past her bare thigh.

She was beautiful, but deserved rest without feeling ogled.

Looking down at her, small and broken in that bed, my whole body screamed to climb in behind her. But this was not the time for carnal urges of a beast wanting to surround her forever–his body, her shield. Her soul needed caressing first. I leaned in for a chaste forehead kiss but was tugged into an embrace as she wrapped her arms around my shoulders.

Heaven–Gia was heaven.

The beast in me purred as I inhaled her essence, sliding my hands under her back and swearing death to anyone who would take her from me.

Standing at last, I crossed to the crib and scooped up Ben's baby monitor, making sure she saw it and its meaning. I would take the first shift for the night; She would let me.

This I could do for her, now.

The door closing behind us might as well have been a vault of steel for all that it separated me from her. But gazing into Ben's flushed cheeks, he needed me too. Kangaroo cuddles were an easy internet search, and I was in my pajama pants with a naked Ben lying on my chest within minutes.

My body heat would help him regulate.

I would help Gia regulate.

In the dark silence of the living room, a rush of awareness knocked the breath out of me. Ben had only been in my life, Gia...had been in my life for a few days, and I couldn't fathom a moment where they would be taken away and cast off to strangers. How much more visceral was the pull for Gia to protect him if she'd had him from birth? The very beast in me was born in a moment of desperation for want of protecting a stranger; how much more broken would I have been to have lived that brutality on someone I loved? Gia, so much stronger than I, had no beast; Thus, I was her beast. And still, the very idea of losing her, Ben, my family, and all of the past colliding with all my new future, stung my eyes. I was in over my head. An unfamiliar feeling, strong as I had trained myself to be, and brought to a broken heap under the mythical weight of a tiny babe, lying on me with all the trust in the world, while my heart slept in the room next door. I had no words. How did I walk through this, splintered in so many pieces?

That desperation had me texting my brothers.

Me: I need you.

Sam: On my way.

Chase: Be there in 10.

They entered with their spare keys, immediately rallying around where I lay on the couch with Ben.

"Thank you for coming so quickly," I whispered.

"Dude," Chase scowled at me. "Like you wouldn't do the same for us."

"Kangarooing?" Sam said, a half-smile on his face.

"The doctor said it would help with his fever," I confirmed. "Gia needed to sleep."

"Gia?" Sam glanced at Chase as they sat, one on the couch, the other on the chair. "Not, Jane."

"There is much to share."

My brothers sat patiently as I unfolded the night, our time at the clinic, my suspicions, and Moira's insights. I ended it with Gia's jarring confessions, how she fell apart and into me, and what I learned about Ben's parentage—everything she'd said, and everything else I'd inferred.

"Jesus. They were gonna toss Ben aside." Chase whispered, his hand clenching and releasing.

"And the piece of shit that haunted my wife was gonna handcuff that poor girl to a bed and –" Sam's eyes were closed as he gritted the words through clenched teeth—a sentiment I understood.

"You see why I texted then," I said plainly. "I hardly know how to begin."

"Ben is here, and Brinks is pushing daisies... that's all good, right?" Chase lifted his arms to the room. "We're all safe now, at least."

"No one knows the laws on this more than you," Sam added, nodding towards Ben. "But she's his legal sister, so that's not an issue, right...him being here."

"But the law here isn't the problem, is it?" Chase nudged me with his elbow. "You aren't struggling with the law. You are at a loss... about Ja—"

"Gia." I corrected, my tone sharper than intended.

"Gia...Sorry." Chase huffed a laugh. "If you are sitting bare-chested cradling that baby, it's pretty clear Ben's worked his way in, too."

"In?"

"You care about 'em, you big idiot." Sam tapped my foot with a smirk, "Boyscout's right. The law isn't even on your radar."

"And your brain doesn't know how to function outside of black and white," Chase tagged on, "You like control and order, and this grey-area-chaos is really uncomfortable...ain't it, brother?"

My brothers never knew about my other...proclivities. But their observations were astute, nonetheless. My need for control was a part of all of me, in and out of the bedroom.

"How can I care for a woman whose name I only learned today?" I argued, not wanting their words to feel so right.

"How could I marry a woman I'd barely met?" Chase met my question with one of his own.

"How could my ball of sass pull me in after a few bar brawls?" Sam chimed in, thumping my foot with a grin. "The heart, man... it goes where it goes."

"And we're the lucky assholes hanging on for dear life." Chase said, bumping fists with Sam as he muttered the familiar 'Oorah.' Ben began to squirm, and I glanced at my watch.

"That's his hungry grunt." I started to get up, but Sam rested a hand on my leg.

"I need the practice. I'll get it." He walked into the darkened kitchen, careful not to turn on any more lights than necessary.

"I'm sure your wives would like you back soon," I shifted Ben to cradle in my arms for his bottle and noted the sweat that had gathered between us. "His fever seems to be breaking. I think I can handle it from here."

"Dude," Sam returned, motioning for me to hand over Ben. "You've never asked us for help in your entire life." He settled into the armchair and propped his feet on the coffee table; Ben cozied into the crook of his elbow.

"We aren't going anywhere." Chase agreed. "So, let's put our heads together and find a way to protect your woman."

"I would hardly call her my—" I started to protest, feeling foolish, but Sam cut me short.

"If she decided to date another man," Sam smirked, "And take Ben to go live with him?" The notion sent my blood boiling instantly, the beast howling for muscle and sinew.

"Or if the law decided she had to be returned to her father, and you had to watch them go back to her abuser?" Chase narrowed his eyes on my clenched fists and nodded knowingly

"I hate you both a little bit right now."

19

GIA

I AWOKE TO THE late-morning sunlight streaming through the window. Reaching to stretch, I realized my shoulder wasn't aching. Bolting upright, flipping covers back in a frantic search for Ben, a scream nearly escaped before my groggy brain reset.

Troy had Ben.

Peeking into the living room, I was gifted a glorious tableau: Three Wilder brothers, sprawled around a room that looked vaguely like a baby-supply store held a frat party. Sam slept under a baby blanket, a stuffed toy as his pillow, while Chase used a tummy-time pillow as a neck pillow. Empty bottles were everywhere. Troy lay stretched out on the couch, Ben on his bare chest, both sleeping cocooned under a blanket. A good night's sleep would have been enough to swoon, but these three rallying against the mighty rhinovirus had my heart fluttering.

Unable to resist, I texted Moira and Lila a pic as proof of life in gratitude for their sacrifice. Then, slinking into the kitchen, I started the coffee. Within minutes, Sam and Chase joined me.

"Good morning," I offered them a mug with an apologetic smile. "I didn't expect Troy to call in the cavalry."

"It was refreshing to have only one baby between us," Chase yawned.

"I hope it wasn't too rough." I peered at the back of the couch, noting Troy hadn't stirred.

"Ben's fever broke about an hour after we arrived," Sam said. "He took a few extra bottles but otherwise did great. The extra hydration helped."

"We stayed up talking mostly," Chase fist bumped Sam. "Been a minute since we did that."

"Up...talking?" I aimed for nonchalance, unsure what Troy had shared.

"Yep." Sam yawned, then continued. "We should head home, but dinner's at my place tonight." He chugged his coffee, setting the cup in the sink on his way out. "See ya tonight, Gia."

My name landed in my chest like an anvil, which must have shown on my face since Chase quickly jumped in with a nudge to my shoulder.

"We're brothers. We share each other's worries." He caught the keys that Sam tossed to him, turning towards the front door. "But we've got you, Gia."

I swallowed thickly, hearing my name with reassurance; They would keep us safe.

I stared at the front door, which snicked shut as Troy and a still-sleeping Ben shuffled over. Still in shock over hearing my name, I openly ogled his bare chest; muscled, thick, with abs rippling down to lounge pants slung low enough to display that fabled V. Only when I came back up to his beautiful but sleepy eyes did my good sense return on a wave of embarrassment.

"Did you get any sleep?" I reached for Ben and offered him my coffee.

"Adequate." He grumbled half into the mug, then hummed his approval as he downed the remains in a single gulp. Guilt at how exhausted he seemed stifled the urge to pepper him with questions.

"I'll put him in his crib," I said, sidestepping Troy to avoid drilling him for information, or drooling apparently. "You should get a nap."

Stepping into my bedroom, I collected myself and my emotions, bringing them back into a space of quiet resolve. Whatever Troy had shared with his brothers was done and couldn't be taken back. Besides, this was what I wanted, right? To be free of all the secrets.

"He was no trouble." Troy pulled me out of my head as I reentered the kitchen, accepting a fresh cup of coffee.

"So easy, you called in reinforcements?" I eyed the daycare bender that was the living room.

"I needed to share what I learned. Not to break your confidence, but to request their help. I am..." He rubbed his free hand over his head as if shaking off the last of sleep. "Struggling to find the path forward."

"The path forward?" A fearful part of my mind began lobbing questions over the wall of my earlier resolve. Troy's face was tense and weary; a combination historically reserved for my very short-fused father, and if Troy was—

"Hey." Troy's hand rested atop mine, gingerly prying my fingers off my coffee mug, setting it aside. "I don't know where you just went, but let me clarify." He tugged my hands until they gathered to rest on his chest. "You and Ben are safe here. No one is taking him. No one is taking you. No one is sending anyone away. Dinner tonight will help explain things." Troy wrapped his arms around me, pressing me into him. He was warm and firm, and as I inhaled the mix of him and Ben, I felt a hum of reassurance rumble through his chest.

I clung to it as the day passed in the busy work of organizing bags and boxes that littered the living room. We hardly spoke again, beyond discussing Ben, before Troy disappeared for a shower and a nap. That's when Moira texted me:

> Moira: Well, isn't that the cutest family pic ever
> <3 <3 <3

Her reply to my earlier pic felt precious and weighty. I instantly began replaying the previous 12 hours. Troy begged me to trust him, held me when I fell apart, gave me my first whole night's sleep in months, and so much more. But now Moira called Ben...family.

What did that make Troy and me?

Was there a Troy and me?

Why did my brain jump to Troy and me?

That was the spiral I nested in for a solid hour before slipping into my bathroom to change my hand's bandage. Reaching under the sink for a bandage, I noticed my old phone, dead and forgotten. Morbid curiosity bid me to charge it, and I cringed at the messages waiting for me:

> Unknown: Your father's furious. Be smart here...tell me where you are.

> Unknown: Surely you've run out of money ...doesn't that baby need food?

> Unknown: Bring the books back, and all will be forgiven.

Forgiven, a word I might've fallen for back when my father's sparing praise was all that sustained me. Now, its emptiness landed like a slap. I tossed the phone into my backpack, disgusted with how much I once craved that man's favor–disgusted that I was still keeping this from Troy when I truly wanted to tell him everything. But when? He had said dinner tonight would help. Did he mean for us to talk over a meal with his entire family?

The afternoon blurred as my anxiety circled tighter and tighter.

I busied myself with Ben's bag, my backpack, my hair, my clothes—anything to keep my hands occupied until we piled into the truck. I was grateful for the excuse to sit in the backseat with Ben, shielding myself from the odd silence stretching between Troy and me. I caught him watching me in the rearview, but he looked pensive, and so I retreated to focus on Ben, too full of my own questions to pose any to Troy.

Pulling into Sam's driveway, Troy quickly removed Ben's carrier from the back seat and opened my door before I could even unbuckle. He moved with an urgency that seemed out of place. Still, it was when he caged me between him and the truck, making no move to let me pass, that all the intensity swirling inside my stomach leapt up into my throat. I should have helped more last night. I should have kept quieter while he napped, or perhaps sat up front–

"Gia. This silence has me more on edge than I can accept." My mouth fell open at his directness, as I scrambled for words to soothe the intensity in his eyes. "While I am content to let you have your space, I find myself needing... clarity." He took a breath and let it out slowly. "Are you angry?"

"Angry?" I blinked in surprise, having prepared to hear he was, in fact, angry at me.

"At me, yes. Are you angry with me?" I took in his clenched jaw as mine fell open. "I asked my brothers over without thinking. I should have been more careful in sharing, perhaps. I should've asked permission before disclosing your identity. Since they left, you've hardly said two words to me and–"

"You think I'm angry... with you?" I breathed out the words on an unbidden laugh. No one had ever offered such consideration, and yet he worried I was mad. "Troy...I am..."

I trailed off, unable to find the right sentiment to convey everything swirling in my head. Then, remembering I had something better to offer, I grabbed my phone and opened the photo I snapped that morning.

"I was overwhelmed when I woke up—amazed that your brothers came to help watch over Ben. And just there," I zoomed into the portion where Ben was on Troy's chest. "I could never be angry with a man who cared so deeply for Ben and me."

My heart fluttered as the last words slipped past intention, but I could only watch Troy's expressions for every nuance of reaction to tell if I'd overstepped. Instead, Troy's shoulders relaxed on a sigh, his question answered. He lowered my phone, tension slipping away as he laced his fingers through mine, guiding us up the driveway with bold, unhurried steps.

The door to Sam and Lila's place felt like a portal to another world.

Aromatic garlic and tomatoes wafted through the air, carried on a cacophony of noise from the four adults, two babies, and background music. Chase and Sam donned aprons in the kitchen as they worked on dinner, laughing and talking with ease. In the living room, Moira and Lila held babies and laughed like old friends who'd known each other their whole lives.

"We saved this for you," Lila lifted a wine glass with a smile. "Hope you like red. You and Moira have to make up for me since my parasite is cock-blocking all the fun."

"No more grumpy Mama, remember." Moira chastised Lila's eye roll. "Tonight is for Jane, and she's stressed enough without you Hellcatting everywhere." Then she looked at me in question, handing over a glass of wine. "Oh, wait, it's Gia...right? Sorry, it might take a minute to adjust."

"So...the guys told you everything," I gulped a mouthful of wine, wishing I could dive into the glass and disappear.

"It's a Wilder thing." Lila waved her hands toward the kitchen, "There are no secrets in the family, but nothing leaves the family circle." Her assurance did little for the butterflies swarming in my stomach.

"And Hellcatting?" I tried to shift the attention away from me.

"Now that is a much funnier story," Moira flashed a gleeful smile. "Can I tell it?!"

"Please, you'll get all swoony and heart-eyes," Lila focused on me then. "Let's just say Sam and I had an...unusual start."

"More unusual than being pulled from a burning building, even." Moira mock whispered.

"Pulled from a building?" I could feel the first gulp of wine warming me from the inside.

"So you haven't shared your little masterpiece yet?" Lila jabbed a finger into Moira's side. "You first. Chase makes everyone else make sense." Moira elbowed Lila, then looked back to me as if asking permission to share.

"I'm game to hear anything about anyone that isn't me right now." I deadpanned as I finished the first glass. "Share away."

Lila topped off my glass as Moira dove into a whopper of a tale about Chase saving her from a fire, staying with her at the hospital, moving her in, and marrying her...twice! She finished with a photo of the three men gathered around her in a beautiful pink wedding gown with a baby bump lovingly held by three massive hands. Then, she snuggled in close to me, clinked our glasses together, and flourished a hand for Lila to begin.

Her tale of toe-curling one-night stands, multiple bar brawls, Sam's affinity for carrying her around caveman-style, and even a small toast as Lila raised a glass to Sam's prowess in the bedroom. I couldn't hide my blush at their mention of things I had zero knowledge of, and that was before Lila revealed that Sam tricked her into getting pregnant. I blame the wine for blurting, 'He did not!' before slapping a hand over my mouth.

"Well, I guess she knows how Lila got pregnant?" Chase elbowed Sam, sending the latter into the living room with a mischievous glint in his eyes.

"You know the deal, Lumberjack." Lila pointed in warning. "I get to give you shit until I'm allowed sushi and bourbon again!" Sam stalked to his wife with a grin, scooping her up with a squeal as he buried kisses on her cheeks.

"It's unconventional and ill-advisable, but," Moira sighed with a shrug, "they do love each other." She turned her gaze back to me. "The Wilder men are intense and tend to move quickly." My head might have spiraled into oblivion over that little nugget if I hadn't been two glasses deep.

"Ladies?" Troy's voice drifted over, his hand outstretched to the table. "Shall we?"

Everyone sat, babies in laps all around, and Troy pulled out a chair for me to sit next to him. I dropped my backpack under the seat as Sam scooped up Ben, and within minutes, platters of pasta and meat were being passed around, along with bowls of sauce and baskets of bread. Sam recommended that I start with the salad to test his new dressing recipe, and Chase rounded the table pouring wine.

The room was filled with warmth and laughter; babies were welcomed, and the women-led conversations were filled with smiles. A far cry from the stiff dinners of silent servants accompanied only by men's hushed whispers and women's disinterested stares.

Midway through the meal, the air shifted, and Troy gave a subtle nod.

"Time to hash this shit out, then." Lila was clear and direct, leaning into Sam.

The whole room waited for me, and I floundered on where to begin. From my childhood, or from the moment they found me? Did I talk about my father, or Ben? What had they already known, and what should I share tonight versus later? The enormity of questions all but held me mute, frozen in analysis paralysis under the weight of too many what-ifs.

Troy's arm gently draped across my chair, anchoring me to him like a lifeline.

"When you are ready." He whispered, grazing my jaw with his nose in a private and intimate gesture. "And only as much as you can give."

"Honestly, I'm not sure where to start," I let my gaze lift from my plate to his eyes. Two swirling dark pools that promised to hold me forever if only I let them.

"How about we start with proper introductions?" Lila's voice cut through my nerves, and I prayed some of her confidence would flow into me. "I'm Lila Wilder." She gave a cursory wave and smiled. "Sam and I met in a bar because I was hunting Marcus Brinks. He killed my father and brother, both NYPD cops, like I was before he got me fired." My stomach clenched as she described death with such practiced ease. "I was running on booze and anger, hell bent on revenge, and would've run myself into an early grave if not for this big oaf." She playfully swatted her hand against Sam, who captured it and tenderly kissed her fingers. "He gave me balance." She cocked her head at the room at large and added, "All of them did. They wrapped around me and gave me a new family."

"I'm Moira Wilder." Then she smiled at the babies in their arms, "The arsonist who set the fire Chase pulled me from was my ex-boyfriend, Dean Jensen. A Grade A psycho hoping to be king-misogynist in the Fire Department."

"Jensen was a colleague," Chase picked up the tale. "I got him fired when I found recordings he'd made of women without consent. He tried to kidnap her and eventually tried to kill us both, yet another fire." Chase's voice was calm, but anger flashed in his eyes.

"All to gain prestige for that damned Apex Society." Moira held a look of disgust, and Lila and the guys all nodded in agreement at the sentiment, as I froze.

Pieces of my life slipped into place with a near-audible click as I filtered through everything I'd seen, heard, and taken with me when I fled from my father. Troy's thumb brushed up and down my shoulder, bringing me back to the table, and I noted that everyone was waiting for me to speak, but there was only one question ringing through me.

"You know about Apex?" It was a silly question since they'd said as much, but it's all I had.

"The flowers," Moira lifted her eyebrows at Troy. "Came from Apex, right?" Troy nodded in agreement, his eyes flickering to me with a hint of regret or apology?

"I didn't....I wasn't expecting..." I stopped and inhaled the courage to push past the rising anxiety. "I never saw the card?"

"I had it here." Lila handed me the white florist card. "What can you tell us about The Apex Society?"

And there it was. The first real question, and I was woefully unprepared.

Apex, my father's pet project, started before I was born. I didn't fully understand what Apex did; only that the wealthy and elite wanted to be involved. More than once, I'd been ushered out of my father's office so they could plan some big Apex event that I assumed was politically focused. I had seen it mentioned in one of the books I'd taken the night I ran, and I mindlessly shifted my foot against the backpack under my chair.

"You are safe here," Troy murmured his reassurance in my ear, his nose grazing my cheek again, and I couldn't resist the pull to turn into him, breathing in his strength. "Perhaps start with an introduction?"

"I need Ben." I thought I whispered the words to Troy, but Sam sprang to action, placing Ben in my arms. Troy's hand slid from the back of my chair to fully wrap around my shoulders, and with Ben wrapped in me, and me in Troy, I began.

"My name is Gia. Ben is...my baby brother." I felt the words ripple silently through the space, though I didn't dare look up as I breathed in Ben's soft hair like aromatic courage. "I ran away to save myself from a forced marriage to Marcus Brinks." Lila's body stiffened at the name, barely noticeable if not for Sam's fingers pressing around her shoulders as he held her. I hated that I hurt her. "I took Ben away to save him from being farmed out to strangers for political favors. I was hiding under my father's desk when I overheard him and Marcus discussing all this, plus a cop in Lake Placid causing them problems."

No one spoke, and even the babies seemed silent, as if they knew this moment was fragile. I gulped more wine, trying to pull back the tears and memories.

"They said someone here 'needed to be handled,' And I heard the names Jensen and Rivera."

"That was me." Lila's voice was stronger than I had thought possible, given how I'd surely ripped her heart open by mentioning Brinks' name. "Rivera's my maiden name."

"If you are the 'tedious rule-following' officer causing them problems," I used a set of air quotes for words that weren't my own. "Then yes...I suppose it was you. I figured any thorn in Marcus's side was someone worth taking a risk on?"

I glanced around the table, realizing I'd found so much more than a single person...and it only added to the emotions swelling in my chest.

"You are doing so well." Troy slipped a finger down my cheek, wiping away a tear and drawing me back with his steady, unshakable, caring. "Please, Gia. We will not let you down."

"At the Cabin, I'd been attacked by a man I only know as an associate...of my father." I emptied my wine glass, never more grateful for the liquid courage as I stood on the knife's edge of a cliff. "My name is Gia Bianchi." To my doom...or to the safe arms of these people...off I flew. "My father is US Senator Michael Bianchi. Presidential hopeful and founder of the Apex Society."

20

TROY

T HE ONLY SOUND HEARD in the wake of Gia's gubernatorial bomb was the thudding of my heart in my head. Gia wasn't on the run from some deadbeat guy; she was the daughter of a sitting US Senator who was also the leader of the organization haunting my family for months. An organization that'd never let any of its members be known, infiltrating my town through community outreach and private funding in what felt like death by a thousand cuts.

"When we met," Gia stared wide-eyed at the weighted silence, pleading for something I longed to interpret for her. "I was terrified that my father's reach would demand you return me to him."

I began to sift through the timeline in my head.

"I never knew what Apex was." Gia turned to Lila, as if to explain herself. "Marcus is my father's attorney and right-hand man. He plans the events where wealthy men come and....I swear I didn't..." she swiped a stray tear. "I didn't know about your family."

"Was," Lila spoke with confidence despite the crack we all heard. "Marcus *was* your father's attorney. He's dead now." Gia visibly flinched at the revelation, and I couldn't help but lean in—my body needing to ground her.

"When...how..." Gia deserved the details, but that risked an unravelling of a different sort, so I gave Sam a subtle shake of my head.

"That story," he interjected, "will take a little more time."

"Please continue." I let my hand on her shoulder slip back to caress the back of her neck. "You left your father's home with Ben?" Gia breathed in and out, once, twice, then continued.

"I was in wildly over my head. And I would've done something...or said something if I had known." A fresh sob choked her words, but she pushed through like a goddamn war hero. "I heard your name that night when I ran, but I didn't know. I swear I didn't."

"Hey, hey, hey," Lila reached a hand across the table to Gia. "What happened to me had nothing to do with you."

"I panicked, ran, and didn't know what I took with me. But I heard about Jensen," Gia's eyes flew to Moira. "If I'd stood up to my father that night...instead of hiding under the desk...I maybe could've..." Another sob sliced through my heart. "Or if I'd agreed to marry Marcus, maybe I could've found a way to spare you both–"

Lila was on her feet, kneeling beside Gia and wrapping her arms around my girl in a hug so fierce it muffled Gia's apologies. I wanted to pull Gia into me, to take it all away, but there wasn't a breath of space between them.

"Jesus, is that what you're thinking?" Moira whispered across the table, wiping her tears. "That you could've spared Lila if you'd sold yourself to that sadistic bastard?"

Lila sat back and unwrapped her arms from Gia, only to cup her face with both hands.

"You listen to me, and you listen good." Lila's tone was stern, and her intense gaze was fierce enough to have me glance at Sam, unsure where this was going. "*Evil* men do *evil* things, do you hear me?" Lila ignored her own tears and continued. "I have enough hate in my heart for a thousand Marcus Brinks for what he took from me, and still, I wouldn't wish it on anyone else. So I don't ever again wanna hear you apologize for the shit that *evil* bastard did. Do you hear me?"

Tears brought volume, and Gia's sobbing swelled at Lila's command.

"You are *not* responsible for their actions...and what you did do *was* enough." Lila broke, tears running through her like I'd never seen. Moira crossed to them, all but pushing me out of the way as she flanked Gia.

"You worked with the knowledge you had. And the second you knew Ben was at risk, you ran like a brave little badass!" Moira cooed, and Lila nodded in agreement. "You were brave, and smart, and you found help," Moira glanced at me. "The best help there could ever be."

She looked to Chase, then, who pulled his wife back into his lap, wiping her cheeks as he murmured in her ear.

"I don't know what I can offer...to help fix things or..." Gia began, her voice trembling. "But I have documents and ledgers that talk about Apex...they don't make sense, but–"

"It's a good start." Sam agreed, tugging his wife back to wrap his arms around her. "And we have time. These cabins aren't in our names; your cell number is new and private. Everyone here is safe. We could take extra precautions, though, right, Troy?"

The room turned to face me, their resolute leader with absolute plans.

But my objectivity was shot—my voice of reason silenced by a screaming beast seeking blood. Even as Gia sat beside me, cradling Ben, and both of them searching me with angelic blue eyes, I wanted to steal them away to hide while I burned the world. But I promised not to let her down, and that started now. So I shoved my heart to the back and mentally pulled up my shield.

"If your father is as powerful as that, dumping your car would be wise," I began, puzzling over the details. "We could have it transported, possibly sending him off track. Putting together all our files and documents in light of Gia's knowledge might help us piece together enough to open an active case." I took a deep breath and slowly let it out. "You said you took files and ledgers?"

"When I left, I...I was in a hurry." Gia reached beneath her chair for her backpack, answering my earlier curiosity about why she'd brought it. "I needed cash, and I knew where he'd kept a stash hidden, so I grabbed what I could, but" She pulled a small black book from the bag along with a flash drive. "I found these. They seemed important. I don't know what it means; I've looked at the book a half-dozen times. I recognize the names...and they know Apex. I'd seen them in my father's office. But the dates..." Gia's words trailed off with a shrug while Lila began scanning its pages.

"I know some of these names," Lila ran her finger down the paper. "Brinks was their attorney." Lila looked at Gia with investigative intensity blazing in her eyes. "Did you interact with Marcus much?"

"He was at my home constantly from the time I was a child," Gia answered, her hands white-knuckling the backpack's strap. "He mostly ignored me."

"Do you know what the dates are?" Moira took the ledger from Lila and reviewed it. "Or these tally marks." Gia shook her head apologetically.

"I don't know anything, but it's important to my father." She handed a file to Lila. "He was never without that book."

"Do you know *what* Apex is?" Lila questioned as she flipped through the papers in the file.

"No." Gia shook her head again. "I mean, I was there, and I saw things, heard things, but - " She looked back at me, and I could see all the whites of her eyes. "I didn't know what it all meant. I was so used to being silent and invisible."

Lila opened her mouth, but Sam's hand rested on his wife's knee, some hidden signal between them as she eased herself back in her seat. I loved my brother for that.

"It's okay." I steadied my voice. "This is a good place to start." I reached for her hand, but she flinched when I did, as if startled by my touch.

I stilled—not backing off, not retreating.

Holding space between us, I kept her eyes locked on mine, waiting for that flicker of trust to return. When it did, when she let me in again, I moved—slow, deliberate—wrapping her hand in mine—a reminder.

I'm here.

I'm unshakable.

"We won't keep these things. They are yours. But Lila is a research whiz."

Gia's hands shook, and her speech sped up.

"This ledger sat on my father's desk for as long as I could remember. They don't make sense to me. I only took them for leverage." Her cheeks flushed, and her breathing grew shallow. "I was stupid, I thought the books would make my father listen."

"You were smart." Moira jumped in, her eyes casting a worried glance my way. "If he was doing something shady, you surely slowed him down, and that's a good thing."

"And the file...that's," Gia slid the file to me this time. "These are the men my father wanted me to choose to marry...before Brinks. He said he would give me a choice." She hesitated, taking a deep breath and releasing it slowly as the sickening reality of the file echoed through me. She wasn't a runaway daughter; she was a trafficked woman fleeing servitude. "But whoever I chose would give him some votes or favors. They must be connected."

She was unraveling, pupils wide, Ben clutched to her.

"You don't have to say anymore - " I began, but she shook her head violently.

"No!" Closing her eyes, Gia stilled. Taking another deep breath, I could almost feel her counting it down, slowing her heart rate the way I might during target practice. We all watched, helpless and awestruck, as she commanded her fear. When she finally spoke, she did so with defiance in her eyes.

"My father shoved a newborn in my arms, knocked me to the floor, then tried to cuff me to Marcus' bed as an apology." Leaning to kiss Ben's head, she murmured, "I may have been raised in a gilded cage, but I'd be damned if I let him grow up in one."

I opened the file, glancing at the cut sheets for each man, which included vitals, a photograph, and a summary rundown of their business and wealth. My face twisted in disgust as I slid the file back to Lila, tapping the circled dollar figure at the upper corner of each page.

"What's in the bag?" Lila's voice held all the authority of an interrogative cop. "Every time you flinch, you grab that thing." She held Gia's gaze, and when I looked over at Gia, the tear that slipped from her lashes and fell down her cheek might as well have held a knife in it for the way it cut me to the quick. "I know it's hard. But so are you."

Moira stacked the books and files to the side and leaned forward, reaching a hand to rest on Gia's trembling arm.

"Come on, badass. Take the poison out...get a little power back."

Gia looked to me then, a fresh sob rushing forward.

"I'm sorry. I..." She reached into the backpack and pulled out a second cell phone. "You got me a new one, and I didn't know how to tell you..." She handed it over, unlocking the screen to show me a slew of text messages. "The man who came for me, with the flowers," another sob before she could finish, "He's still looking for me and Ben."

Taking the phone, all my instincts went on high alert, and I could feel that Sam and Chase had done the same. Their eyes scanned the perimeter even as they held their wives closer.

"He knows she's in town, but hasn't located her yet," I announced, trying not to break the phone in my hand as his threats scrolled past, the last of which Gia had yet to read.

> **Unknown**: Enough is enough.

> **Unknown**: At least text me a location where I can pick up the books.

> **Unknown**: You bitch! Do you know how much heat I'm catching?

> **Unknown**: I will find you, and you will pay for this.

I was grateful to have spared her at least that last message, passing the phone to Chase and Sam. They scanned the messages and then gave me a curt nod.

"Can you do anything with this, babe?" Sam asked Lila.

"Is there any personal info, emails, photos, documents of any kind on it?" Lila asked. Gia shook her head, and then Lila shrugged. "It's a brick."

Without hesitation, Sam tossed the phone to Chase, who pulverized it, pulling the SIM card out at the end and snapping it with the end of his fork on the table.

"I should have said something sooner." Gia started, but I cut her off with a finger under her chin, tugging her until she faced me. "But Ben and—"

"You don't apologize to me." I cupped her chin, holding her gaze steady, forcing her to see the truth in my eyes. "Not for protecting yourself. Not for surviving." My thumb brushed the last tear from her cheek, the motion gentle, but my grip firm. "You bring me every truth, Gia. No hesitation. No hiding. That's the deal."

My chest eased as she sighed and melted into me, nodding in agreement and resting her head on me. I wanted words, but the nod would be enough for now. I didn't want to move away from this moment. Her leaning into me, and my arms surrounding them both, was finite.

I didn't know when she became mine. Only that she was, that she and Ben weren't just under my protection—they were carved into my soul.

"I think," Sam cleared his throat, nodding to Chase, who tipped his head in agreement, "That it's safe to say you've been courageous as a mother fucker, Gia. Coming here and trusting us to help you takes balls."

Then he looked to me with regret in his eyes. "But I gotta ask about Ben, man."

I understood where his head had gone, and it was one thing I could easily, mercifully, put to rest for everyone.

"It stands to reason that Gia's father hasn't reported her as missing, nor Ben. Not if he is sending such men as the florist after you. As Ben is your sibling, and you are an adult of legal age, having him poses no risks for kidnapping charges. If anything, you've made the case for requested asylum given the...treatment you both endured, and witnessed." Sam and Chase both nodded, but it was Gia's exhalation that settled into me.

I'd given her comfort. I'd done that.

"You've trusted the right person," Moira beamed a smile that belied the tears in her eyes. "No one could protect you better."

Grateful as I was for my family's confidence, I knew by the way her body pressed against me that Gia needed me to block the world out. She'd run so long on her own, and I would do everything in my power to make sure she never suffered another single solitary moment like the hell she'd been through. Even if I had to move heaven and earth to do it, Gia and Ben would forever be safe, protected, and, God willing, forever be with me.

"This is a good place to pause for the night." I raised a hand to halt Lila's next question as she pointed to the circled dollar figure, and went on. "A lifetime can't be shared in a single night."

My hand wrapped around Gia's wrist, firm enough to still the tremble, thumb pressing the pulse point—reminding her who held her now–who wouldn't let her fall. I tugged her closer, tucking her under my arm where she fit so damn perfectly.

Mine.

"Ben needs to be in bed." I nodded to my nieces. "River and Blue as well. It will take time to clean up and - "

"We got clean-up tonight," Sam interjected. "Least we can do." I nodded in thanks.

"There, it's settled." I leaned into the top of her head, inhaling her scent. "You've been brave, and now you've gotten me off the hook for dish duty." Gia nodded in agreement. "Let's pack up and get home."

As we stood, Gia half-turned before pausing, resting a finger on the page Lila had left showing from the file, pointing at the five-figure dollar amount circled at the top corner.

"The numbers are what they were willing to pay for me." She turned silently back towards the door, as both of my sisters held their hands over their mouths...my brothers' eyes roiling in the same anger I barely contained.

21

Troy

My truck was silent as the grave on the drive back to the cabin.

Gia was utterly drained, so I understood why she was quiet. I'd seen the tears she'd let slip and felt all the emotions she hadn't shared. Her intense anxiety had taken everything she had to tamp down. I understood when she walked into the cabin and went straight to the bedroom.

I respected her need for space.

Until I couldn't.

My brave siren did the hard work of baring her soul, and I allowed it because I needed to know what monster I was fighting. But in the end, I was as strung out as she was. Her every flinch cut to my core, and I was a barely contained storm of pure fury, my fists clenched, jaw locked, frothing in want of protecting her. She'd been mistreated, mishandled, damn near sold, and while I knew she desired the space because she was overwrought and strung out from the night, the distance from her room to mine had become cavernous. The primal need to be near her grew undeniable as I settled the cabin for the night.

I'd listened to the sounds of her and Ben readying for bed as I shut off the lights. I'd counted the seconds until her breathing grew soft and steady while locking doors and checking windows. I told myself she was safe, even as I slipped shirtless into my lounge pants, but it wasn't enough.

Not anymore.

I needed to see her, to know she was safe and present.

I slipped into her room like a ghost. I padded first to Ben's crib, letting my hand rest ever-so-gently on his back, his presence calming me; his fearless peace a testament to Gia's love for him, despite her turmoil. I hated that she'd done it alone.

I'd never let her be alone again.

Stepping to Gia's bedside, I loved that my siren was a side sleeper. Curled half into a ball, one gorgeous leg arched gracefully outside the comforter, my fingers begged to trace her ankle to hip. My jaw ached as my teeth clenched away the temptation. Instead, I admired her fingers clutched around a stray pillow, as if her body missed Ben. I imagined her splayed across my chest, hugging me instead.

My cock enjoyed the imagery.

Her raven locks sprayed out behind her in a glorious fan on the pillow, made almost blue by the moon's light. I had to lean in and inhale her scent. It soothed the beast in me just enough to pull back, admiring her half-hidden, sleepy face before lowering myself into the chair. I told myself I was making sure she slept soundly. She wouldn't know I'd been here, but she'd feel it—the safety.

And so my watch began.

I snuck out of Gia's room just as the sun rose. I'd not rested near enough, but I felt rejuvenated in my purpose, fulfilled. I showered, dressed in the worn jeans and grey Henley only ever seen on my off-duty days, and scooped Ben out of his crib.

My siren would sleep her fill while we men bonded over breakfast.

Having emptied breakfast bottles and coffee cups, Ben oversaw my work from his new bouncy chair as I tidied the cabin. The boxes and bags had been neglected for too long, and I felt grounded by making the cabin presentable. Ben's happy jabbering was my soundtrack before Gia's voice pulled me from my inner thoughts.

"Sharking?" I turned to find her padding into the kitchen, still in shorts and an oversized sweatshirt. "I do that too."

"Sharking?" She grabbed a stray glass from the living room and joined me in the kitchen.

"Sharks never sit still, right? Constantly in motion?" She set the glasses into the sink and grabbed a towel. "When my mind is full, I get this frenetic energy. I can't settle, so I move around, like a shark, and keep busy while thinking." Lifting the towel in offering, she gave me an expectant look. "Didn't you say you were glad to be out of dish duty?"

"Sharking." I smiled at the silent partnership she offered. "You'll have to share that with Moira. She adores making up new words."

"You didn't have to take Ben this morning."

"Last night was...intense. You needed to recover." I loved her by my side, I loved the domesticity of our task, and her warmth against my arm. "You slept well?"

"I don't think I've ever slept better in my life." Her answer came on a breath...and my chest swelled with pride.

"Do you all cook?" Just like that, she pivoted the conversation away from last night's emotional renting and straight into an innocuous safe space. I allowed it...knowing she needed the normalcy.

"Our Nonna taught us."

"Nonna, is your mom?"

"Was. She passed a few years back."

"Oh, I'm so sorry." Gia offered a tender smile, her eyes placating and somber. Yet another expression I cataloged away as one of the many faces I'd grown attached to.

"She came into motherhood late in life, through foster-adoptions. She insisted that we all know how to cook beyond standard man-fare."

"Man-fare?"

"I would never have known until I was in the Marines. But I suspect it only comes from a can, a box, or a microwave." Gia's laugh was effortless, and I had a mission to hear it as often as possible.

"You were a Marine?"

"My brothers and I enlisted right out of high school. Two tours and some special ops work."

"So you're Super Spy Sgt. Wilder." Gia arched a side eye with a smirk.

"Hardly." Another laugh, that was two now. "Our CO quickly realized that my brothers and I had a shorthand communication. It made us efficient. We ended up doing precision work, extractions, and the like."

"You really *were* a super spy."

"If bumbling around the desert, helping politicians get from point A to point B can be considered covert ...then I suppose." I turned towards my third laugh of the day, happy not to share the details of the other missions that shaped the breadth and whole of my darker tendencies. "None of us went career, though."

"Wanted to come home to Nonna?" Her brow rose at the question, sensing perhaps the tension in me, and I didn't want to burden her with the weight of my worries.

"And the town," I added, shifting back to a happier topic. "We loved our community and wanted to give back...make it better. Chase's fire position was locked in from high school. And Sam's medic training made EMT a natural choice for his temperament."

"He is very gentle." Gia lifted her nearly-healed hand, wiggling her fingers with ease.

I pulled her hand into mine, letting my fingers graze the sides of her healing cut and wishing beyond words I could damage the man who did this to her with fire and pain.

"The Corps gave me a leg up as an officer. Police work has been a good fit for my–"

"Desire to keep things controlled?" Gia answered, half-smiling, and my chest squeezed at the accuracy that slipped from her lips. She didn't seem unnerved, nor worried, about that side of me, simply noting it with a hint of question.

"As good a description as any." I laughed, noting that we'd completed the entire kitchen while chatting.

"Seems we've sharked away all that we could." Gia followed my gaze, leaning against the counter, her arm brushing against mine.

I looked down at her, and the close-up view of those vibrant blue eyes felt like a gift. I could make out the pale, icy middles of my kryptonite. A piece of her messy morning bun slipped free, caressing her cheek. I turned without thought, tucking it behind her ear. As I did, she lifted her hand, resting it on my forearm, and there we lingered for what might as well have been an eternity before she cut me loose.

"I should go change," and she was gone; the rest of the day spent in amiable silence with Ben her faithful shield from any deeper conversations.

I allowed her distance, again knowing she needed breathing room between yesterday's intensity and the future conversations that needed to happen. However, in truth, she appeared steadier than I felt, and by the time dinner arrived, I was nearly aching to draw closer to her. I wanted to dig into her, not about my controlling tendencies, though I hardly knew how.

Dinner came, and I placed Ben's bouncy chair on the floor between us. She watched as I buckled him safely inside, making sure he could see us and us him, before pulling out her chair and guiding her to sit. I was determined for her to eat a meal with free hands, and if she felt the move high-handed, she didn't say. I noticed she wore the same jeans, knee boots, and shirt as before, only then realizing I hadn't seen her in anything else. I tried visualizing all of her things to no avail and resolved to rummage after she went to bed.

If my girl needed clothes...I would provide.

"You make that face a lot." I blinked, my brows pinching at her words. "Yeah, that one." She sipped her wine while swirling a pointed finger at me. "Penny for your thoughts?"

"I was..." stalling like a chump to cover the fact that I planned to pillage her drawers while she slept. "I wanted to know more about you."

Her smile fell, only a fraction, then she deflected to Ben.

"What would you like to know? Ben here is ticklish and–" Her tone was light and airy, but her avoidance of my gaze was unacceptable. She'd been more than peaceful this morning as we worked together, and I ached to have that same peace with her now. Hooking my finger under her chin, I guided her back to eye contact. She closed her mouth, her eyes all but pleading with how they locked onto mine.

"There is more to you than your father's actions." Releasing her, I was pleased she didn't shy away again. "I would like to know all of you, Gia."

"No one has ever asked about me." The revelation landed like a stone in my gut, but I forced my mask in place and pushed on. Pulling a card from my sister, Moira, and her unfathomable ability to make someone laugh, even while tackling impossible subjects.

"Shall we make it a game?" Moira and Lila used this one evening around our dinner table, and it proved fruitful. If her lips tipped up in a hint of a smile, it would be any indicator that I'd chosen well. "We'll set a time for 2 minutes. I'll ask me as many questions as I can, and you answer as fast as possible."

"2 minutes?"

"The speed eliminates overthinking. It also eliminates the pressure of conversational back-and-forth. Round two, you get to question me." I nodded, sitting back and crossing my arms. "AMA style."

"AMA?" She was curious, but not nervous, and that was a win I could work.

"Ask me anything." I nodded. "The only rule is full honesty."

"Anything?" She asked once more, and I nodded, pulling out my phone. When she settled herself with an exhale, I set a timer and began with an easy question.

"How old are you?".

"22."

"Did you attend college?"

"Yes."

"Where?"

"Long-distance...from home...it was so boring." I loved that she was adding in extra tidbits.

"Major?"

"Poli sci. But I hated it."

"Why?"

"My father picked it." She didn't bristle at his mention. "I much preferred domestic things."

"Domestic?"

"Home design, decorating, and even architecture." Her eyes were alight as she expressed interest in topics I filed away.

"Favorite food?"

"Italian." Beaming...her smile was beaming.

"Why?"

"Because you make it." The timer alerted as she slapped a hand over her mouth, eyes shimmering with nervous laughter that I wanted to bask in.

She loved Italian, because I made it for her.

"I don't know why–" she began, but I would not be denied her honest slip.

"I'll make it for you every day." I leaned forward, tugging her wrist away to uncover her mouth. "I'll make it for you every night." I pulled her closer, her trembling body leaning across the table as I held her wrist firm, tugging her to me. "For the rest of your–"

A loud squawk from Ben snapped the moment in two. Both of us turned to see him flailing his hands and feet, showing clear frustration at being ignored too long.

"H-he probably needs changing." Gia snatched her hand away, and I felt the loss of her like a blade. "I should ..." She leaned over, unbuckling him from his seat.

"I'm happy to handle–"

"Thank you...for dinner." She walked away, never looking back, and the vault of her bedroom door clicked shut, leaving me in gut-wrenching agony. Her confession may have been unintentional, but the light in her eyes wasn't. And holding her wrist, I could feel the racing pulse when I pulled her towards me. She couldn't deny her feelings even if she wasn't ready to face them now. But I had to be patient, I reminded my beast that beat its chest at being denied its feast, sprawled across the table. I resisted for one hour and thirty-three minutes before giving in to the only thing that could soothe it—her.

Slipping into her room was as easy as breathing. I checked on Ben, securing his pacifier and letting his soft baby purr soften the worst of my anxious edges. Turning then, I strolled to Gia's bedside, the adorable siren again curled half-tangled in the comforter, only this time facing the window. Crouching bedside, I perched eye to sleeping eye with her. A vantage that let me bask in every detail of her moonlit face. Unencumbered by social graces that prevented a man from openly staring at a woman.

Her hair, black as sin and softer than any confession, framed her moonlit face in angelic symmetry. The softness in her eyes was a vision of peace under brows uncreased by stress or worry. Closed as they were, I was less distracted by the vibrant blue...and able to see the smattering of freckles kissing the bridge of her nose.

I counted them–Named them by their virtues and claimed each one.

Her lips were soft and pink, and as much as I loved to see her smile, this relaxed pout was a kissable temptation. I lingered there, letting all the technicolor details of a kiss play through my mind.

My cock enjoyed the imagery.

Dragging my gaze to her neck and the junction of her collarbone, I admired how her bare shoulder sat fearlessly in the open air—a testament to how safe she felt here...with me. Lower—where her loose sweater framed the curve of one breast. My teeth ached to mark her there. A secret vow, hidden from the world, but branding, nonetheless. She stirred, giving a slight hint of a whimper as she readjusted, her top arm reaching. I slid her spare pillow in place, knowing she'd reach for me one day. But the leg, Christ the leg. In her move, her thigh slipped out of the comforter completely, her knee bent towards me, and the bottom swell of her perfect ass peeked under the edge of her sleep shorts.

Those legs could bring a man to his knees—and I was already halfway there.

Ben grunted.

I was there in an instant, scooping him to my chest. My Siren needed rest. My Ben needed a diaper change. Quickly done, I snuggled him to me and perched in my chair, holding him to my chest as we watched his mama sleep.

Mine.

Here—holding Ben, guarding her—I could breathe knowing she needed me here. Her body craved my presence. She'd slept more deeply last night than ever before. She'd sleep even better tonight.

Because I was here.

Because I wouldn't leave.

My watch began.

22

GIA

W^{ARM.}

It was the first thing I noticed as birdsong called me to wake. I wasn't bolting upright to care for Ben or keep him quiet. I wasn't rising to make myself perfect and presentable; ever-ready for my father's whims. Nor was I achy from cheap motel beds or cold from being alone in the marble tomb of my childhood home. I was warm and safe, and it was as unfamiliar as it was luxurious.

Rolling to my back, I stretched long and full, letting every fiber of my body rush with movement and energy, kicking off the covers and letting the cool air drift across my abdomen as my sleep sweater lifted up and up and up. This was the second night in a row Ben had slept so soundly, giving me a whole night's rest, all thanks to Troy's provision of a crib.

Or was it just Troy?

Letting my limbs flop back to the bed, I mentally ticked off all the things Troy had done for us: the safety, the furniture, the food. I couldn't resist my smile at the memory of last night's moment. I hardly meant to say what I did about Troy's cooking, but Troy's face held a look of barely contained feral energy the moment the words fell from my mouth. Then he gripped my wrist, not hard, but not yielding either. The move felt intimate and stripping as he pulled me into his dark, smoldering eyes. My body was a live wire, and had it not been for Ben's timely interruption, I think I would have followed Troy's pull to the ends of the earth to keep that feeling. I longed for it now, my core clenching low in my belly, as I remembered his words, 'I'll make it for you every day...every night...for the rest of your–'. Was he about to say he'd cook for me for the rest of my life?

Shaking my head to focus on the day ahead, I sat up, my eyes going to Ben's crib but finding Troy. There, in the chair next to the crib, with pillows up under his arms to support him, sat a sleeping Troy with a comfortable, cuddled Ben. They had no blanket over them, and I imagined it was wholly unnecessary, remembering how Troy exuded warmth. Shirtless, head lolled to one side, and Ben hugged gently into him, Troy was a statue of masculine art: his muscles, his hands, his....erection.

I'd read about morning wood in books. Still, never having witnessed it before, I was at once scandalized and intrigued to find Troy's entire length stretched tight against the front of his thin grey pants. The silhouette hid nothing of the impressive length or girth. If I wasn't mistaken, he wasn't wearing underwear, leaving nothing to soften the rigid outline that encircled the tip. Goosebumps scattered across my skin like lightning as I imagined the finer details of his–

"Morning, Siren."

Troy's voice was sleepy, gravel-filled, and mercifully delivered from behind closed eyes–wholly unaware that I was drooling over imagined veins in his thinly veiled third leg.

"Good morning!" I chirped entirely too enthusiastically, lunging forward and scooping a sleepy Ben from his chest. "Did you sleep here all night?"

"How did you sleep?" He ignored my question, stretching his arms down at his side as he arched his back, lengthening and flexing every muscle in his beautiful torso.

"Like a rock...again." I placed Ben in his crib, knowing he'd wake at any moment. "How long were you in here?"

"You'll be happy to know Ben also slept quite well, stirring only once for a diaper change." He eased to my side, gazing down at Ben, and fitting us into a space that felt as if it had been carved just for us. He never let his eyes drift from Ben when he voiced dropped into a low timbre that resonated deep in my bones. "This was where I was needed." His answer was gentle and finite. "I'll start the coffee."

I opened my mouth to speak, to ask why he was needed here, but his hand lifted to cup my cheek—a silent answer to my unspoken question. I was why he was here. His eyes drilled through me, looking long enough to nearly have me lifting my lips to his when he stepped back.

"I'll also get Ben's bottle. Take a moment for yourself to shower." Dropping his arm, he strode out of the room, leaving me baffled and achingly un-kissed.

Half in a daze, I showered, wondering if he'd slept in my room all night and why that didn't bother me. I had slept so well, so peacefully, and I had to wonder if something in me knew he was there. Was he there the night before, too? Has he been there every night? Finishing my shower, I wrapped a towel around my body, my wet hair still strung around my shoulders, and I walked to my basket of clothes at the foot of the bed.

"He voiced regrets for sleeping in." Startled, I turned to find Troy again in the chair, now feeding Ben, who was happily wiggling and kicking as he gobbled his breakfast. "Coffee is brewing, but he couldn't wait."

Their shared smile melted me.

"You are good with him." I leaned on the edge of the bathroom door, forgetting my clothes. Ben and Troy were so at ease with each other, and vice versa. The two of them had fallen so effortlessly in step with one another, and it made my heart swell to see Ben's morning smiles now alight in Troy's warm gaze.

"You showered too quickly." Troy looked to me with half-hooded eyes. "I told you to take time for yourself."

"And I did." A sigh of relief escaped me. "I can take him from here if you'd like." I reached my arms for Ben, taking a few steps before my towel began to slip, reminding me that I was completely nude. I clasped my arms down, pinning them in place even as Troy's eyes grazed up and down my terry-cloth-clad body. Heat flooded my senses as I clenched a fist across the top of my towel.

"I will stay here," Troy's eyes held a mischievous glint as he half-smirked, his words crossing into a demand. Like someone had taken the weight off for just a second, something in his words lifted something in me. "Go, Gia. I've got you."

Grabbing the small basket, I darted back into the bathroom, near-panting with an intensity of emotion I had no words for.

With the weight of my old cell phone and its malicious messages gone, the rest of the day passed quietly. Sunlight, soft baby coos, and the click of Troy's keyboard were the only soundtrack we needed. Every so often, our eyes met, and I'd feel the air between us spark. Each moment ended with Troy looking away, and I told myself I was imagining whatever I was feeling. When evening came, Troy dove into the kitchen like a man on a mission, rebuffing all my offers of help. He worked silently until he had plated our food, and I decided to return to our previous game.

"I believe it's my turn, Sergeant Wilder." I teased his formal title, hiding my blush behind the rim of my wine glass.

"Your turn?" The edge of his lips tipped up, amused.

"I didn't get to ask you any questions last night." I tapped open the timer app on my phone and set it for two minutes, my stomach fluttering with anticipation. The questions I'd been rehearsing all day suddenly felt ridiculous, and I distracted myself by fussing needlessly over Ben's blanket in the bouncy chair between us. "Unless, of course, you'd prefer to remain a tight-lipped enigma?"

"Tight-lipped enigma?"

"You know the game will take all night if you repeat everything." I mock-whispered it to taunt him, and it paid off with a rare, broad, toothy smile that had curled warmly into my belly like a cat.

"All's fair, Siren." He wiped his mouth and tossed his napkin onto his plate before leaning back with his wine glass. "Fire away."

Taking a deep breath, I hit go on the timer.

"What's your middle name?"

"James."

"Do you have a nickname?"

"TJ and," He scowled, huffing, "Grandpa."

"Grandpa?" I was dying to uncover this little nugget.

"Sam thinks I am stodgy...boring at times. The moniker was his doing."

I was shocked to hear that his brother thought of him as stodgy and boring. I found Troy to be the exact opposite. He was calm, collected, and even, but his whole body seemed to exude this virile energy in everything he did. At times, I swear he seemed like a barely contained live wire.

"Do you love having brothers?" I had to clear my throat to focus my voice once more.

"Absolutely...sisters too now."

"Moira and Lila fit well, then?"

"Perfect matches for my brothers." He leaned forward and squinted his eyes. "You can do better than this."

He was taunting me to swing a little harder, and I couldn't resist the temptation.

"Boxers or briefs?"

"Boxer briefs."

"Do you ever regret being a cop?" The words were born of curiosity I couldn't shake. I came searching for a cop who was a rule-following troublemaker to my father. Instead, I found a man willing to lie for me, hide me, and it itched against the grain of what he showed the outside world. I loved everything I'd seen in him, but wondered if the duality was hard to carry.

"No." He offered one word, and nothing more, so I pressed.

"So, you like enforcing the law?"

"I like stopping bad people. I like protecting people." Then his gaze sharpened, his voice dropping into that low timbre that rattled across the table. "I protect what's *mine*." He'd slipped into that voice from time to time, and I was beginning to recognize it line beyond that buttoned-up shell of his.

His curtain pulled back; My peek behind the veil.

"How many women have you brought to this cabin?" Another curiosity that had been burning since his family's acceptance of my presence was already old news.

"None." He let a subtle huff escape, his brows drawing down like he was irritated. "There never will be." Another bold declaration dropped softly in that low timbre, and my pulse was racing.

'None' was simple enough, but 'there never will be' held oceans of nuance. Did it mean he was so frustrated with my situation he'd never do anything like this again? Or was it what I dared to hope for, that he was enjoying our time so much, he never wanted me to leave?

"Tick tock, Siren." Troy tapped the phone, snapping me back to the dwindling countdown.

"Right! Um....Why do you—" The timer alerted, but Troy remained frozen, his face and body a statue as I silenced the phone. "Guess I didn't get that last one out in time."

"Ask anyway." The command, that tone, made it untenable not to do as he asked.

"Why do you call me Siren?" Willing myself to wait, I begged my nerves to settle, knowing the question wasn't rehearsed and the answer may well be an atomic bomb.

"Sirens are mythic creatures of rare beauty, known to lure men to their doom with beautiful voices." I could only swallow, shocked to be compared to something so epically devastating. "And while you are a beauty like no other," Troy reached for me, pulling me across the table towards him even as he slid the plates out of the way. "It's your voice that has irrevocably altered me, Gia."

My arms fully extended, he continued pulling. Lifting me from my seat, he dragged me across the table, his face inches away from mine, as his eyes went all but black with the pupils blown wide, and God, how I wanted to drown in them.

"Your eyes pulled me in, but every word that has left those lips has utterly stitched me to you."

He shifted my hands until they were laced into one of his, the other lifting to cup my cheek, and he leaned forward until our lips nearly brushed together. Gasping, I could do nothing but wait for his next move, which my entire soul begged for.

"I would happily throw my ship against the rocks to hear you say you are happy."

Gentle, grazing at first, Troy brushed his lips across mine in an almost kiss, and I silently hated that I was already on my toes, unable to push myself closer so he could devour me whole.

"But you trust me, Gia. With your safety and Ben's," He grazed my lips again, not kissing, but taunting. I could only stay there, stretched out, helpless to do anything but receive. "That is a gift I cherish most of all, so I maintain my control in return. Watching over you."

Releasing my cheek and my hands, Troy sat back in his chair while I lay sprawled across the table like a buffet of carnal want that had my whole body clenching into a blaze of unsated lust. The man hadn't even kissed me, and my entire body was on fire.

Troy...watched.

Cataloguing my every breath as I tried to get my limbs moving again. An unbidden whimper escaped, and he cocked an eyebrow in response.

"But keep making sounds like that... and my restraint won't hold."

There, stretched beyond my sanity, drowning in a pool of feral lust, was where my phone rang.

Troy's face shifted instantly, from wolfish to watchful, his jaw tight. Then his phone chimed, too. One glance at the screen, and the heat in the room evaporated as he slid to accept the call and handed me my phone.

"Lila?" I forced out, still trying to settle my heart.

"Hey, Gia. I've been going through the files you gave me. I'm starting to piece things together, but I've got questions."

All the wind rushed out of my lungs. My stomach dropped as the world tilted back toward reality—my father, Apex, Ben's safety.

"Of course. Questions," I glanced at Troy, who repocketed his phone with a sharp nod, already withdrawing behind his stoic walls of perfectly pressed control. "Do you need me to come over, or–"

"I'll come to you. Sam's chomping to squeeze in some Ben time. Shouldn't take long."

"Okay, sure." I glanced up at Troy, who stood and began clearing the dishes.

Our moment was gone, and I wanted to cry, though I hardly understood why. Troy all but admitted he longed for me, showed it everything he'd just done, yet he said he held back. Was it duty, or desire, and which of those did I need to torch like an angry henchman to get him to pull me back across that damned table?

"How about lunch tomorrow?" Lila pulled me back to our phone call. "I'm usually done puking by then, and Sam will be home from his shift."

I murmured something that must have sounded like agreement and hung up, heart crashing somewhere between arousal and dread. Troy was already at the sink, dishes in hand, his shoulders tight with silent tension. I reached for the wine glasses, needing something to occupy my hands.

"They'll be here around—"

"Sam texted." Gone was the low timbre. In its place, the clipped finality of his self-control. Everything shut off as quickly as it had been turned on, while I drowned in the embarrassment that I'd momentarily forgotten the dire straits of my life at a simple grazing of his lips.

Depositing the wine glasses, I stepped away, scooping Ben into my arms and retreating to our room to find my own self-control. Settling Ben and changing into my pajamas were the tiny things I could focus on as my mind begged to return to the table and the time before the call. Slipping under the covers, I fought a battle of wills with myself as I tried to sleep, replaying Lila's phone call and all the myriad questions I needed to be prepared for.

I tossed and turned for an eternity.

Then the door clicked.

Then the door opened.

Then Troy's feet padded across the room.

I watched him stop by the crib, reaching down to caress Ben. I watched him turn to me, his eyes narrowing on mine, silently acknowledging that he knew I was awake. Then he stepped back and sat in the chair. It's familiar creak, the last thing I heard as I closed my eyes, feeling safer, more protected, than ever in my life.

23

TROY

T HE MEMORY OF GIA stretched across the table like a wet dream refused to leave my mind, even after Lila's bucket of ice water. I knew she was affected, could feel her pulse racing, could see the desire in her eyes. I'd heard her tossing and turning, unable to settle into sleep, and I knew we needed to have a conversation, discuss what I wanted with her, and make sure she knew what she meant to me. But when Gia watched me enter their room, tracking my path as I confirmed Ben's placement in the crib before perching in my chair, that sealed her to me. Eyes locked as I slid into place, my Siren drifted into a sleep only I could give her: Safe and protected.

The next morning, I nestled Ben into her arms with a promise to return with coffee, and my good girl didn't argue. It soothed the beast to watch her slip into this new role; mine to be cherished. My poor sleep was beginning to wear thin, and I knew another night or two of this would have me completely unraveled. I needed to settle Gia soon, so we could sleep as we were meant to, but Lila and Sam arrived earlier than anticipated.

"Lemme get you up to speed on what I got so far," Lila spoke to Gia with her all-business bravado, hands waving over a stack of files. "This is what your guy pulled on Apex's footprint here—building buys, weird charitable work, etc." Yes...I was Gia's guy. "This pile is what I had on Marcus Brinks' client roster back in Manhattan." My hand was on Gia's back when Brinks' name was uttered, and she leaned into her spot.

"Wow, this is already so much." Gia's eyes were wide as she surveyed the table. "And my father?"

Lila shook her head in response.

"That's my struggle. I believe you completely," I silently praised the reassurance given. "But the ledger you brought doesn't match anything we have. See this," Lila opened the ledger, showing the column headers to Gia and me. "The dates in the ledger don't match up with any of the movement here in town, or any of the meetings I could track between Brinks and his clients. And the names, while some of them are familiar, are unrelated to Brinks' former law firm. And this code here...this weird alphanumeric sequence." Gia watched intently as Lila began flipping pages in the ledger. "Far as I can tell, the numbers are unique, one per entry. They aren't a date or account number. I couldn't find property deeds, driver's license," Lila thumped the book with the back of her hand. "I even fucking checked library cards. Nothing matches!" I could feel the tension skitter down Gia's spine as Lila's tenacity grew bolder. But she didn't back down; her breathing remained steady, so I kept quiet. "I haven't found anything connecting to your dad, much less anything that connects Brinks and Apex with any surety."

"It's shipping." Gia's voice was calm and confident. "These," She pointed to the alphanumeric sequence Lila had struggled with. "They're container identification codes."

"Shipping containers?" Lila looked at the codes with new intensity as Gia continued.

"The first three letters are the owner code, the fourth letter is the freight type." Gia slid her finger across to the numbers. "These are serial numbers assigned, and the last digit is a sort of digital check or verification." Gia offered a triumphant smile. "My father got his start in shipping. I played on the floor of his office for years, listening to him discuss his work."

"Shipping Containers...Christ!" Lila opened a laptop, sitting amidst the pile of papers and effectively blocking out the world.

"We won't see her come up for air for a good bit." Sam placed a kiss on his wife's head, his smile unfiltered.

"I helped." Gia turned her face to me, eyes beaming.

"Without a doubt." I tugged at her waist, wanting to pull her to me just as Ben squawked proprietarily.

"He may be ready for a nap." Gia reached for Ben, and he nestled in her arms. "He'll do that better in the bedroom." I watched as she walked Ben back to the bedroom, something clenching in my chest at the sight of them leaving.

"She seems to be settling in nicely," Sam interjected with a nudge in my ribs. "I was prepared for more...hesitancy."

"I confess, I worried this would upset her more." I tipped my head towards the table strewn with papers. "Her contribution was not only helpful to Lila, but perhaps helpful to Gia as well."

"She was awesome." Lila barked, fingers flying across her laptop. "People always underestimate how much a woman hears when they think she ain't worth talking to. She's way stronger than y'all realize." The comment rippled through the room, and I filed away the well-meaning admonishment with the meaning intended. Gia wasn't as frail as I'd perhaps attributed her to be.

"You look like shit, dude." Sam cocked an eyebrow at me. "Are you even pretending to sleep or just patrolling all night?" I didn't bother answering. "I get that you walled you both into this pit for her safety—and I'm all in. But take your girl for a walk. She needs it. You need it. Hell, look at you—you're fraying like a cheap rug." Sighing, I eyed my wrinkled shirt and well-worn lounge pants as Sam slapped a hand on my shoulder. "My wife ain't going anywhere soon, and Ben's sleeping. Take your girl outside, show her why you love hiking, and maybe uh," He leaned in, whispering salaciously. "Show her the hot tub down there."

"The hot tub?"

"Trust me." Sam cocked an eyebrow and smirked once more. "You'll *both* feel better after."

He made it sound so simple, but I'd been battling a burning need to clarify things with Gia. I thought I was hiding it, but if Sam could see the fractures, then I wasn't winning this war. I needed to clear the air...before I lost control completely.

I lightly tapped the bedroom door, nudging it open to see that she'd nestled Ben into the crib.

"They are going to be here a while. Sam will listen for Ben." Gia nodded in agreement. "I want us to take in some air. There is a private trail out back that we can walk." I tried to smile, to keep my demeanor light, but inside a war waged as I watched all the feelings flit across her face as she considered my invitation. Realizing I hadn't actually asked her, I added, "It would please me greatly if you would join me. We can talk." Gia's smile was instant, spreading warmly across her face and lighting up her blue eyes.

"Okay. I'll slip on my boots and be right out."

24

TROY

L EADING GIA DOWN THE back steps and onto the narrow, winding
path eased the tension I barely realized I carried in my shoulders.
Each crunch under my feet, a stripping away of coiled-up anxiety that
needed me to stretch and breathe. Strolling in comfortable silence, I let
the sounds of early spring's birds and squirrels bring the ambiance as we
both embraced the moment of peace.

Nature, hiking specifically, was always an outlet for me. A chance
to move my body, soak in the surrounding wildness, and stretch myself
beyond the confines of my daily life. It's where I first began calling my
urges 'The Beast' because I felt nearly animal-like when I'd climb and
scale rocky terrain. A sensation not unlike when I'd get a chance to
stretch my dominant urges in the bedroom, drafting and controlling a
scene.

With all that had transpired with my family, I'd not hiked in nearly
9 months.

I'd not been with a partner to scratch any other itch in over a year.

No wonder I was practically gnawing my arm off for want of release.

Gia's hand in mine felt natural...and necessary as we traversed the relatively wide path. But when it narrowed slightly on a downward slope, I took the lead to prevent her from slipping. As I did, Gia's hands glided to the top of my shoulders. A moment of unrehearsed connection–movements so fluid you'd think we'd hiked together a dozen times. Gia followed my lead effortlessly, and this pleased all of my parts greatly.

"The trail officially stops here," I said, pointing through the trees covered in the bright green leaves of spring. "My brothers and I haven't cleared the rest yet, but if you are up for a little off-roading, I'll show you where we plan for it to go."

"Sure," Gia said with a smile, letting me again lead the way as we meandered over dirt and mossy rocks, before emerging at the edge of the wooden deck built around a hot tub covered for Winter.

"My brothers and I own three neighboring cabins that will one day have paths leading to this hot tub. Only Sam's is properly connected so far."

"This is beautiful," Gia said, rounding the deck to the stairs and stepping up to sit on the wood decking, her legs dangling over the edge. I loved the comfort with which she moved around me of late, and I held onto that, promising that our future conversation would go smoothly. "You guys own a lot of property around here?"

"Our real estate business is primarily rentals," I answered, standing at the bottom of the stairs, my chest at the height of her knees. "Mostly residential rentals. These cabins are for vacation rentals." I laughed at the last part, adding, "We normally book the cabins out during tourist season, but now we can't seem to stop living in them."

"I can see the appeal." Gia gestured to the woods around us, "Who wouldn't want to live here?"

"A hiking enthusiast?" I studied how she let her head fall back, eyes closed, as she inhaled the green, earthy scent around us. I wanted to curl her on our lap so she could sunbathe nude while I caressed her body, an urge I had to beat back, reminding the beast in me that we needed to go slow.

"I was never allowed to hike." Her eyes never opened as she spoke. "But I would have loved it if it meant getting to be in places like this." The word 'allowed' had my jaw clenching in proprietary rage.

How dare her father keep her from something so clearly meant for her... but then she leaned back, resting her weight on her palms. The sunlight dappled through the tree leaves, and I was helpless to do anything other than drink in the way her dark hair fell away from her creamy skin, exposing her long neck to the edges of her collarbones.

I would always have her hair pulled back.

"And you?" Her question pulled me back to the present. "Are you a big hiker?"

"I like all manner of outdoor pursuits. Rock climbing, camping..."

The bob of her throat as she swallowed had my blood pumping as I envisioned all the ways I could lick the sunlight from her skin. I wanted to devour her here, in the woods, like the damned animal I was, but her face turning down to me, gently smiling, put me in my place. I relaxed, crossing my arms across my chest to regain my composure.

"I like the wild and unexpected elements outdoors. Getting to tame it with my bare hands is..."

"Therapeutic?" And just like that, she'd seen through everything I'd ever said, ever done, and stripped me bare to the core of my whole being. "I can see the appeal." A hint of what could only be described as flirting gleamed in her eyes as she took me in. Still, a fleeting sadness danced there when she added, "Michael Bianchi's daughter could never be seen gallivanting around in the dirt." She shifted on her perch, her back straightening. "Michael Bianchi's daughter must be presentable, at a moment's notice, never wrinkled and never a hair out of place. Michael Bianchi's daughter should never be seen sweaty or disheveled, but only ever polished and presentable in just the right way for any occasion." She flicked an invisible speck off her jeans as her tone took an edge of beautiful anger. "Of course, these were lessons learned after I'd made some unseen misstep. His preferred parenting method was stick first...carrot never."

Her face was a symphony of anger that I could relate to...but also a hurt I couldn't bear. Betrayal flicked past with pain and finally settled into a crease of disappointment so deep it made my chest ache. The beast in me wanted to take it all away, to absolve her of any negative feelings associated with a man who didn't deserve oxygen. I yearned to turn back time and spare her all of it, but at the very least, I wouldn't let her linger in that space for a moment more.

"You don't have to share everything with me right now. But I do expect to hear it all." Gia lifted her eyes to me, brows furrowed in confusion. "I want to know exactly what you endured before you got here, so that I can know exactly what I need to do to heal every single mark...seen and unseen." She blinked, surprise clear in her eyes, but I pressed on. "And so I can know exactly what manner of retribution needs delivering as I make the bastard pay." I held her gaze, making sure my words weren't missed as my command came as gently as I was able to deliver it. "You will tell me. I will make it go away...forever."

"Troy," she breathed my name like a prayer, her eyes taking me in as she considered my words before lowering her gaze again to her hands and fidgeting with the hem of her shirt. I closed the distance between us and paused at the edge of her knees until I had her eyes again.

We'd need to work on that.

Eyes locked, I pushed until she opened her legs, giving me space to slide my body between her thighs, my hands resting on either side of her hips.

"I know I have said thank you...But it's more than gratitude." Her words trailed off, but her fingers gently glided up my forearms even as I tipped her chin once more.

Eyes on me, Siren.

"More," I repeated, sliding my free hand over her hip and around her waist, fighting the urge to dig my hands into her and yank her mouth into me.

"I hardly have words." Her voice was barely a whisper as I hooked her belt loops and tugged her gently to the edge of the deck. "To tell you how much I need you."

Need. Need. Need. Yes!

My whole body shuddered at her use of the word, and inside, I beat my chest in victory.

"Mine." My forehead leaned against hers, her hands now slung over my shoulders. We were so close I could feel her heart beating against my chest. "Say it."

The sun-warmed heat on her skin radiated as she tilted her head to the side, giving me the perfect angle to bury my nose in her raven locks.

"You are my oxygen. Tell me you're mine."

"Troy," she whispered, fingertips grazing up the back of my neck and head.

My lips grazed the side of her neck, loving the way her chest rose with a soft gasp. God, I wanted to stay there all day, smelling her, feeling her, testing how she could respond to me. Nuzzling back up her neck, I brushed my lips over hers in a gentle, barely-there kiss, and when I did, the softest little sound escaped her.

"Say it, Siren." I had to have her. My hand slid up her back, fingers threading through her hair, ready to grip—to claim— "Tell me." God, she was making this hard, and I loved and ached for it...for her. "Tell me you're mine and we'll explore every inch of these woods in whatever sweaty, dirty, disheveled manner you–"

The click of a cocked gun shattered the moment.

And the beast in me went stone cold silent, preparing to strike.

25

GIA

THE GUN CAME FIRST.

A gleam of steel shoved into Troy's temple.

Then came the voice.

"Hands off the merchandise, Romeo."

He'd found me. The man I'd smashed a glass vase into. My father's lapdog, who'd texted incessantly with placating promises.

"Oh God, please... don't hurt him."

Troy's simmering rage blurred behind the face of my father's sneering associate, who stepped between us as he nudged Troy aside.

"You were a tough one to find." The man shoved the gun deeper into Troy's temple, and his fingers brushed my knees as he shifted sideways, his eyes targeting the assailant. "It took a little detective work." The man cocked his head at Troy, oblivious to the menace facing him. "Something you should appreciate...Sergeant Wilder." The way he drew out Troy's name made my skin crawl. "And a little luck." The gunman gave a slight shrug. "I knew she was with you guys from that night at that other house. I was watching. This town ain't that big. So I figured it was just a matter of time before I got a lead."

Having successfully put himself between Troy and me, the man stretched his free hand to me, palm up, with impatient fingers that grasped at nothing—a silent demand for me to heel. I hesitated, but the gun digging a little harder into Troy had me moving.

"Then, lo and behold, if I'm not sitting at some intersection, and who do I see getting out of his truck but Goodie Wilder here. Comin' outta the pharmacy with a bag of shit for Gia and baby boy."

He yanked me off the wood decking and onto the uneven ground, causing me to stumble into Troy. I wrapped around him instinctively before I was jerked back by an arm around my middle.

"I already said, hands off the merchandise, didn't I?" He pulled me into him, my back pressed to his front, and his grizzled face pressed into my ear. "Your father is gonna be wicked pissed when he hears you've been rubbing up on this cop like a cat in heat." Lowering to an oily whisper against my ear, he added, "Of course, if that cherry is popped, I could sample you myself... who's gonna fuckin' know?"

"You won't touch her." Troy's voice was steady, but loaded with the promise of violence even from the business end of a gun. That was the only thing holding my stomach in check as it threatened to revolt at the smell of the gunman's breath in my face. "Not now. Not ever."

Troy's eyes were wild, but laser-focused, his jaw tight. His entire body seemed almost preternaturally still. I don't know how the assailant holding me couldn't see the danger, because Troy looked absolutely murderous. I swallowed the bile in my throat, locking onto Troy's eyes and knowing he meant every word...but the gun was still there. The power shift of that weapon was everything.

"Let's not pretend to be the hero when I have the hardware, eh, Loverboy?" In arrogance, he turned his gun sideways, and my mind raced to think of any way I could distract the man without putting Troy at risk of being shot.

"Troy... it's okay." I bargained, praying I could de-escalate the situation before one of them snapped. "I'll go with him. My father won't hurt me." My unspoken plea for him to care for Ben screamed through my eyes. "I'll be okay. Just let him take–"

"You aren't leaving with her." Troy ignored my words and only addressed the armed man as he stared down the barrel of the gun. "Drop the gun. Give me Gia. Only then do you walk out of here on your own power."

Ropes of muscle twisted under Troy's forearms as his hands clenched into fists, slowly bending and flexing as if preparing for battle. The knot in my stomach mirrored that action as terror painted a picture of all the ways Troy could get killed trying to protect me.

"And if I don't?" The gun-wielding idiot snarked. "The fuck you gonna do about it... Huh?" His nose slithered up my neck as he laughed. "Kinda seems like I got the upper hand here." He waved the tip of the gun, not seeing the way Troy tracked every inch of my body that was touched. It felt like Troy was calculating offenses, and his previous words came to mind. 'So I can know exactly what manner of retribution needs delivering as I make the bastard pay'.

Troy was going to make this bastard pay...I had no doubt. As much as I wanted that, I also worried he wasn't taking into account the weapon that was a flick of a finger away from ending his life.

"I'm taking that gun," Troy answered, his voice cold and hard. "I'm taking your gun, and I'm going to shoot you in the foot with it." A hint of what I could only describe as feral amusement flickered briefly across Troy's face. "Then, I'll break your nose and give you a concussion."

"The way you were putting the moves on my girl here, I don't think so." He pulled me tighter, his stench filling my nose and mouth as he stole my air. "You won't put this gorgeous piece of ass in danger."

This fool was taunting Troy, goading him, and it was his doom. For all the tightly wound control that Troy had demonstrated, I'd seen a fire under the surface. I'd seen the moments when he seemed to be staring at me through the eyes of a barely caged animal. Those eyes flashed at me now. Not the swirling pools of dark brown embrace, but the blown-wide black pupils of an animal stretching at the shackles of its confinement. I didn't know how he would pull it off...but Troy's eyes, his body, his entire being screamed the promise of violence, blood, and victory.

"This is your final warning." Troy's hands stopped flexing. Cold, icy freeze spread over his entire countenance. The very air seemed to still as if the whole of the world held its breath for a single heartbeat.

"Fuck you." The man responded.

"Noted." Troy was an eruption of violence, clean and precise. In one fluid pivot, he slammed his forearm into the gunman's wrist, wrenching the weapon free with a full-body spin that momentarily crushed me between them—Troy's back to my chest, and me pinned against the gunman.

A gunshot split the air, deafening and final as the man howled in pain.

Somehow, I hit the ground before Troy's elbow slammed into the man's nose with a sickening crunch. The blood flow was instant.

Troy never paused.

His momentum spinning again as his opposite fist collided with the side of the man's head in a brutal, skull-cracking blow that I might've worried was Troy's knuckles breaking if not for the way the gunman dropped into a bloody, screaming heap.

"Behind me!" Troy commanded. "Now!" Grabbing the gun from the ground, Troy cocked it and aimed with the stance of a man practiced at working with weapons.

I was still a half-boneless heap on the ground, my body ignoring my requests for action as I tried to detail out how quickly everything had happened.

"Gia. Get up. Get behind me."

My eyes locked on the man—his face gushing, his body curled around a foot visibly bleeding from a fresh bullet hole.

I couldn't move.

"Gia. Hear my voice," that voice, that low timbre—I could hear him. "Get. Up."

I blinked once, then twice, trying to register what was happening before scrambling to my feet and moving to Troy's back. Leaning my forehead to his back, I wrapped my hands around his waist, blocking the world as I rushed to process everything.

"That's good, Gia. Take one breath for me." He complimented my shaky efforts even as I took another second to register everything...to inhale his scent. "Now. Back right pocket. My phone. Pull it free." My hands shook, but I did as he asked. "Good girl. Dial 911 and press the speaker button."

I took a deep breath, opening my eyes to dial, but froze at the stampeding sound of some wild animal careening through leaves and sticks. Troy and I both snapped our eyes to the side just as a wild-eyed Sam barreled through the brush, gun in hand and cocked for action.

"What the mother fuck! "Sam had so much momentum that he narrowly missed landing on top of the bloodied man on the ground, his eyes quickly taking in Troy, me, and the gun before slipping his weapon into the back of his pants.

"I have no cuffs." Troy glared at the man bleeding on the ground, though he did move one hand around to rest on my hip. For his own comfort, or mine, I couldn't care. The connection was everything.

"On it," Sam said, sliding his belt free in a single fluid motion, fashioning a makeshift hand restraint.

The gunman flung curses at Sam as he rolled him on his stomach and secured his hands behind his back.

"Yours," Sam commanded, reaching an open hand to Troy, who removed his belt just as quickly for Sam to secure the man's feet. "Shot him in the foot?"

"He was warned." Troy's voice leveled only a fraction but seemed steadier now that the bloody, cursing, mess on the ground was secure.

Or it was Sam being here.

Or maybe it was because he was touching me.

"Oorah," Sam said, reaching a fist out for Troy, who relaxed enough to return the bump before handing the gun off to Sam.

When at last Troy turned to me, I could see his pupils were blown wide in an expression I could only describe as crazed.

"Did he hurt you?" His shaking hands were everywhere, inspecting my shoulders, waist, and face. "Were you hurt when you hit the ground? Are you okay?"

"I'm okay," I said, lifting my hands to his chest and hating how fast his heart was beating. I had done that. I had brought all of this. "Troy, I'm...he... I'm so–"

"You. Don't. Apologize." His words were sharp, but his eyes were pleading as he continued inspecting me. "What about when I knocked you aside? It was unavoidable, but still I -"

He slid his grasp to my palms, turning them up to inspect the dirty scrapes with a mumbled curse word at the superficial marks that he pressed achingly tender kisses on.

"I'm okay." I could sense the panic now, simmering beneath Troy's commands and his movements. He was as scared as I was, but not of the man with the gun. He was concerned only... for me. "Troy...look at me. I'm okay." His eyes finally floated up to mine, locking onto me with a desperation that would have stolen my breath if I'd had a chance to take one.

Troy pressed his lips to mine in a bruising kiss that sent shockwaves of emotion skittering through me. Lifting me off the ground, he devoured me with desperation, his tongue sliding across my lips in question. I opened to him without thought, begging him to deepen the kiss as a low animalistic growl vibrated up from his chest. His hands found the edge of my shirt. The heat from his bare palms against my back soaked into my bones, and that simple touch burned through all the chaos and fear.

I melted...and he took what he needed.

Everything and everyone around us was lost.

There was only Troy, his body, his lips, and a desperate, aching need that throbbed within me; emotion barreling through me that screamed for his body to take it all away. To take control...of me.

"If anything had happened," He whispered when he pulled back to look at my face, his absence almost painful. "Anything." His anguish was intense and damning as I tossed the last of my free will and restraint into the void for want to give him everything I had. "I don't know what I would do."

"You protected me," I wished for better words to take away the pain in his eyes. "I'm safe. You did that." I rested a hand on his chest, pressing gently so he could feel me where his heart was beating like a racehorse. "I'm okay."

The thought immediately brought Ben to my mind, and I turned to Sam.

"Ben is - "

"He's okay. I made sure the house was secure before I took off." Sam nodded to Troy, "Lila has one of your guns. We need to remedy that before you call this in?"

"I'll make the call," Troy nodded to his brother, then looked back at me. His face was pained again, torn as he glanced to the man on the ground and then to his phone. "I don't want to leave you."

"Hey," Sam's voice was steady and slow. Not unlike how he spoke that first night we met. I turned to face him, but he was watching Troy even as he slipped a hand around my arm. "I've got her, TJ. She needs to be with Ben, and you need her not to be here for what you have to do."

Troy considered Sam's words with a scowl before nodding.

"Go to the cabin with Sam, check on Ben for me. I'll be a while, but I will return to you."

He pulled me towards him, kissing my forehead before grabbing the gun once more and dialing his phone.

26

TROY

THE CREATIVE TALKING I had to do to shield Gia from the police was shockingly minimal. I called it in, and Sam led the officers down a side path, avoiding the cabin. I knew I couldn't trust the degenerate I'd shot, not to mention Gia, so I had to offer her up, though I excluded her last name on the paperwork. I kept everything as fact-based as possible to avoid stretching the credulity of those involved. She was a woman I was dating, and too shaken to give a statement. Sam correlated my story, and given my status on the force, I earned time to figure out our next move.

Telling the officers that I was dating someone was an uncomfortable lie. We weren't dating; we were more. Not that their opinions mattered when the thought of her being taken or even touched by that man was enough to have me seeing red. My omission to my fellow officers was to protect her, just as the lies at the pediatric clinic were to protect Ben. I realized I would always defend them both a lifetime ago. So doing so now was easy.

Dean Jensen was buried in the fire department. Marcus Brinks wormed his way into Internal Affairs. I had no reason to believe there weren't other Apex plants in town. People with connections to Gia's father would report her location and connection to me in exchange for a favor. Hiding her was a precarious house of cards built solely on a timetable working against me, and the asshole being hauled off to the hospital was the weakest link.

Vile images of him pressed against her flooded in as I turned back up the path, sun shifting to cast long shadows through the trees as I replayed it all. In my adrenaline-fueled haze, I'd kissed her with reckless abandon. I was so consumed with worry that when she looked into my eyes, I lost all control of myself and could only be satisfied by having her body pressed as close to mine as possible, physically shielding her from everything and drawing her into me. A moment I'll never regret, despite the fear and stress it was born from, but it barely scratched the surface of what I needed.

Kissing her wasn't enough...not by a mile. I ached to taste her. I burned to claim every inch of her, body and soul. The separation of sending her away was a fresh scream of pain, soothed only by the knowledge that she went to Ben and safety.

Climbing the steps to the deck, I worried I had been too intense for her. We hadn't talked, hadn't discussed limits or expectations. I'd recklessly shoved the cart wildly before the horse out of sheer, unadulterated panic. Still, obsessed as I was, I would never push her unwillingly forward if she weren't ready. If I'd unintentionally pressured her in that careless moment, I would break. Reaching for the cabin door, I knew one thing with pristine clarity: I would never be able to let her go.

If she needed time...she'd have it.

But I could never again be free of her siren pull.

She would never again be without the shadow of my protection.

27

GIA

A FLURRY OF ARMS greeted me as Lila and Moira rushed to hug me. My face was buried in a bed of blonde and brown locks; their strength holding me up as the first tears fell.

"Sam texted us a little. I came as soon as I could. I know you are okay, but" Moira pulled back until our eyes met. "Are you okay?" I opened my mouth to speak, but Lila's face stopped me short. Her puffy eyes were smudged with remnants of the makeup that still streaked her cheeks. She looked absolutely shattered.

"Lila?"

"Ignore me. It's hormones and - "

"Babe." Sam was already there, tugging her into his body. "We talked about this. Say the hard shit." Moira nodded in agreement, the three of us still arm in arm.

"Take the teeth out of it, right?" Moira squeezed her sister's arm.

The two had such a tight bond that they instinctively knew what needed to be said. I might have felt like an interloper in their moment had Lila's eyes not drifted back to me, as if assessing if I was okay enough to hear whatever truth she was suffocating under. I couldn't imagine what horror could take down such a formidable woman, but I nodded my encouragement, unwilling to let my fear hold someone else back.

"We heard the gunshot...and then Sam took off..." She gave a staccato inhale between sobs. "I knew he was okay, but..." Stuttering again, she exhaled an attempt to compose herself.

"You worried about Troy?" Sam offered, and she nodded.

"And you," Lila added, squeezing my arm like Moira did for her.

"She witnessed her father and brother killed in the line of duty." Moira lifted a hand to Lila's cheek, giving her sister words. "But Sam was shot a few months back by Brinks...right in front of her."

My heart sank. My world had spilled so much blood into theirs.

"He would've finished the job if not for you, Quickdraw," Lila squeezed Moira's hand before Sam tugged his wife to a private moment.

"You killed Marcus?" I asked, hardly believing the bubbly personality holding me upright could have done such a thing.

"He *so* had it coming." She squeezed my hands, leading us to the couch as we both tucked our feet under us and sat. "How are you?"

"I'm okay. Really." I assessed my hands, dirt-streaked from the fall. "Just a few scrapes, really."

"I don't mean your body, silly." Moira pulled me closer, cupping my hands in hers. "If there were even a hint of physical injury, Sam would come unhinged." She huffed a small laugh. "But...that had to be scary."

Moira peered into my eyes with a kind intensity that stripped me bare of any evasiveness I might have attempted. But, taking an honest assessment of myself, I had to admit that I was really okay.

"I've been so scared that this man would find me...find Ben. But when the moment came, all I could think of was...Troy." I glanced sheepishly up from my lap to find Moira smiling. "The man held his gun on Troy, not me, and I was beyond terrified." I slumped into the couch, trying to voice all the thoughts in my head, knowing somehow Moira wanted everything. "I'm prepared to face my father's anger; I've lived with it. I know that. But the idea of it bleeding over to - "

"A man you care about." Moira's statement might as well have sparked a gasoline can because it exploded inside my chest.

I didn't care about Troy; I loved him. I would do anything to keep him and his family safe from my father. Even the word, father, felt like bile in my mouth, knowing that the man who should have given me love had sent a man to capture me for a second time–this time under threat of a gun or rape. And all for some books and a baby he didn't want. The humiliation of that reality covered me like a dark blanket of despair.

Its weight could not be overstated.

I was worth nothing beyond the leverage I could deliver.

Temporary and disposable.

Looking up, I saw Moira's expression of utter understanding. Behind her, I saw Lila and Sam, embracing through the memory of God knows what. The question building in my mind took shape, and with it came the shame of what I really longed to understand.

"Take the teeth out of it." Moira encouraged, as if reading my mind. "Ask me," She pressed her hand against my leg again. "Anything."

"You told me your story, about you and...that guy." Moira's eyes were unflinching, so I continued. "Did you know? That he was so–"

"Sick and twisted?" She answered for me, and I nodded in agreement. "No. Not really." Then she leaned back with a sigh. "But when I look back, there were signs."

"Signs?" I asked.

"Little things I overlooked then, like him pushing my boundaries to the max. There was never any compromise. No room for me in his world, not really. I was always bending to him." Her words rang true as I thought of my childhood and how I was raised just to do my father's bidding without question. "And if Dean and Marcus were indicators, that's something Apex supports."

"No compromise?" I wondered aloud.

"Women," Moira answered softly. "Who yield."

I nodded, a lifetime of memories rushing through me filtered through this new lens. My all-girls boarding school, the denial of on-campus college, and the parade of vacant stares from disinterested women, all the same by-product of shared gilded cages. And I'd ignored it all...handing my father my virtue for his votes.

"I don't blame myself for that, ya know." Moira's voice pulled me back into the present. "There was a time I harbored a lot of guilt for not seeing the signs sooner. So ashamed, I even resisted Chase's help. The guys tried telling me it wasn't my fault, but Lila helped me most."

"Helped how?"

"Her work on my laptop. She'd found records of all the fake crap Dean laid out for me after he died...it helped me see how much effort he'd put into the con. Months of crafting a character. Weeks of research, finding the right woman to play. Months more of wooing me, spoon-feeding me what he thought I would receive the easiest. It was masterful, if I'm being honest."

"Masterfully twisted," I mumbled, remembering countless plans I'd heard Marcus and my father plotting.

"No doubt." She agreed. "I could only see it from the outside looking in. It took his death, three laptops, and months of investigative digging to piece it together. It took me, Lila, Chase, Sam, and Troy to finally fill out the real picture, and we still don't have it all yet."

"For what it's worth...I agree with them. You couldn't have known." Moira smiled at me, but her eyes cast down to her lap.

"It was easier to release the guilt when I accepted I was never really up against Dean...but all of Apex and their resources." She fidgeted with her thumbnails a moment longer and added, "I can't regret how I found my way to Chase, my girls, and this family I love." Her voice cracked, the telltale tremble of her chin betraying the scars she carried at the hands of a man my father controlled.

"I...hardly have words," I swallowed around the lump in my throat. "I'm so sorry for what you endured."

"I don't tell you this for pity." She wiped away tears, her smile returning. "But to help you see that it's okay."

"Okay?"

"It's okay if you didn't recognize the signs at first." Her words landed in the middle of my chest. "It's okay if you needed to keep your head down, or couldn't see a way out. It's okay if you remained quiet and held onto the only thing you'd ever known for as long as possible." Gripping my hand tightly, she added. "It's okay that you didn't leave sooner."

And there it was. The question I didn't know I needed answered was voiced in the wake of Moira's tears, and with it, my walls crumbled at the edges. Before I knew what I was doing, I rose to my knees, leaned forward, and hugged her.

"I am so sorry, though, for what happened to you and for what Lila lost." I couldn't stop the words once they began, the tears and apology flowing in equal measure. "I know I'm not responsible for my father's actions, but I am sorry that I wasn't strong enough to stop him."

"Not then," Moira added. "But now you have us." She squeezed me a little tighter. "You didn't just run. You found help. It makes all the difference."

Our moment was shattered as the back door banged off the wall.

We all turned to find Troy quickly scanning the room until his eyes found mine. Crossing in just a few footfalls, he scooped me into his arms, melting me on a sigh as all the world narrowed to just him and just me.

"I'm okay," I whispered, knowing he needed to hear it. "I'm okay," I said again, needing to listen to it for myself.

"Ben?" His question was loaded with an intensity of emotion I could hardly put into words. He was worried for Ben and me because he cared for us both.

Both.

Both.

"Tucked into his car seat," Sam's answer pulled me from Troy's cocoon. "Ready to spend the night with Aunt Lila and Uncle Sam." I opened my mouth to question what he meant, but Troy lowered me to the ground, resting his hand on my jaw and drawing me back to him.

"Let them take Ben for an evening." His words were a command, but his eyes were begging.

These people had done nothing but keep us all safe, right up to Sam running blindly into gunfire for us. Ben would be safe.

I nodded in agreement.

Lila shouted that she'd text updates.

The front door clicked.

Troy lifted me off my feet and carried me to the bedroom.

28

TROY

FRANTICALLY, ENTERING THE CABIN, I burned to find her. Seeing her tear-streaked face was a punch to the gut. He'd scared her, hurt her, and I had to fix it. Without conscious thought, she drew my body to hers like a magnetic pull. Effortlessly, I lifted her in my arms and inhaled her intoxicating scent like I'd never breathed before her.

Gia, the drug I never wanted to be free of.

Even as her legs wrapped around me, we weren't close enough. Kneeling at the edge of the bed, I laid her out, pressing my body on hers as my mouth explored her lips with all the restraint I could muster. My cock screamed to be inside her, and her heat responded in kind, pressing against me and begging invasion. God, I needed her naked. Every nip I took of her jaw, then her neck, drew out a whimper. Each pant and shiver, another hook my siren dug into me, and still I needed more.

"Gia...I..." My words trailed off, the earthy scent of the wood still lingering in her hair like a reminder of my failure. We should wait, talk, and plan. There were rules and things I needed her to understand.

"Yes," she sighed, blowing my restraint out of the water. "Please."

I opened my eyes to find her gazing up at me, pupils blown wide as she cupped my jaw and pulled me back to her mouth, her teeth tugging my lower lip, her tongue sending charged bolts of longing through my body. The bite wasn't hard, but it gave me leave to experiment. I fisted her hair, firmly tugging at the back of her neck in a primal gesture of dominance. A test to be sure, wanting to be careful with a creature so delicate, but her body was so responsive. A gasp left her lips as her hips lifted, grinding, and I was seconds away from coming unhinged.

"I need to taste every," I slid my mouth to her jaw. "Single," I trailed my tongue down to her collarbone, "inch," dragging my scruff across her skin, I bit gently into that place where her neck and shoulder met, "of you." I sat back on my heels, pulling her hands until she sat up with me. I removed her shirt. She slipped the clasp on her bra, let it slide down her arms into her lap, and oh, the vision. "You are exquisite."

I groaned between the cleft of her breasts, gathering them both into my hands as she lay back on the bed, and I died in the mounds of her sweet tits. Gia seemed to enjoy the attention as she dragged at the color of my shirt when I tried to pull my body lower.

"I want to feel you on me," she panted, "skin to skin."

Sitting back, I admired the way she panted. Gracefully reaching for me, her fingers whispered over each piece of art tattooed on my skin. Rivers of lust rushed through me, and I tried to be patient. I tried to give her time to explore at her leisure, but the distance it created was too much. I unbuttoned her pants with one hand as I again fisted a handful of her hair, pulling her back enough to look into my eyes.

"You can admire my ink later, Siren." Her pants undone, I quickly slipped mine open. "I need you." I pulled myself to the edge of the bed, taking her jeans and panties with me. Dropping my clothes to the floor, I knelt at her delicate ankles and drank in the sight of her.

My Siren.

My drug.

I kissed a trail up Gia's body. Back and forth, each calf, both knees. First a kiss, and a bite, followed by a lick to soothe the sting. I took small measures and gentle pressure to gauge her interest, not wanting to overwhelm her with the fire I barely contained. At each connection, she granted me a gasp or a whimper, a moan or an arch of her back. And her scent, sweet merciful God, the intoxicating smell of her sex sang my name as her symphony of want moaned me home.

"Troy...Please." Her begging sank its claws into my chest, and I glanced up, finding her beautiful neck stretched back as she arched her body closer to me. "I need you."

"Tell me who you are, Siren." I growled the command around the sensitive edges of her pussy, never breaching her folds as I nipped and licked at the tip of her thighs and across the top of her mound. "I'll give you everything."

"Please, yes," she breathed, frantic as her hips moved, seeking more contact. "Yes." Her permission was another luxurious plea for more singing from her lips. I nearly lost it. But I needed her to own her place with me.

She was mine.

She would own that.

"Who are you?" I wrapped my hands around her creamy thighs, shoving her knees wide with my shoulders and baring the whole, beautiful breadth of her to me. "Please, woman, tell me before I die from wanting you."

"Yours...God, Troy...I'm yours." The snap of my restraint was nearly audible.

I spread the full width of my tongue and dragged it from her opening straight up to her clit, earning me a gasp that might as well have been a starter pistol. I tossed her legs over my shoulders and feasted. Licking and sucking every inch of her perfect pink pussy, I explored inside every fold of my girl.

My girl.

My Siren.

Mine.

Her whimpers, my guide, I found the rhythm she needed as I circled her clit, then gently sucked it into my mouth before dragging my mouth down to tongue-fuck her entrance, then repeated it all over again. Her sounds were music to my ears. I repeated the pattern time and again, never lingering in any spot too long, but feeling her swell into a needy wet mess as each second passed.

Heaven.

My cock ached as I pressed it into the mattress, demanding to be buried inside her, but knowing she would cum first. Her pulses against my tongue spoke to me. She was close. But I didn't want her to merely cum on my face. I wanted her so saturated in pleasure that her higher brain functions would cede all control to me.

I wanted her wanton, desperate, and pliable.

"Troy...Oh god...I'm..." I could only growl an approving laugh at her inability to form sentences as I let one of my fingers graze her opening, circling the edge as I sucked at her clit and then barely penetrating her with just the tip.

So hot.

So tight.

The single finger I gave her was being squeezed as she writhed for me, even as her thighs tensed around my ears, and God, if I didn't love that moment of near suffocation as she pulled my head, dragging me into her with an abandon I yearned for.

This was it.

My first orgasm in a lifetime of moments we'd share. Gia was mine, and forever and ever I'd own all of her pleasure.

Only me.

Only mine.

I clamped down on her clit, sucking it hard into my mouth as I pushed my finger inside her, nearly seating it to the knuckle, but for....a barrier. She screamed my name, nails clawing at the sheets as she twisted and writhed through her climax, and my cock nearly spilled its load even as my brain tried to register what I felt.

My world stopped.

Her whimpers, my desire—everything we were building—collapsed beneath the weight of what I'd just felt. No mistaking it. Not with the way her body clenched around me, tugging me into the unyielding wall.

"Just now... Gia...did 1..." I pulled back, stunned, breath gone.

My voice trailed off as I stared down at her gasping, trembling form. Her thighs still shivered, and between them, her slick, pulsing center confirmed everything. But it was her face—the bloom of pink creeping from her chest to her cheeks, the hesitant shine in her eyes—that drove it home.

Grappling for every ounce of restraint I had, I forced the words out.

"Gia... are you a virgin?"

29

TROY

I WAS A FOOL.

Allowing myself to very nearly lose control without considering. Gia, my siren, was so sheltered that, of course, she'd be inexperienced. Even Ben was not her biological son. I selfishly wanted to be close to her—to claim her—but failed to consider whether she was ready for someone like me. Then I shifted back to the file of men...the money. It wasn't just for her...but her virginity.

Oh, the bile that rose, the anger, at their lecherous bids, and was I any better, conquering without first giving her voice and choice and agency.

"Yes," Gia sounded small and fractured. "But it's okay." She reached for me, but I had to pull back again. I was lost to her feel and taste, and I needed a moment to cool down before I took the one thing she'd never get back; I had to cage the beast.

I could have hurt her... badly. The thought sickened me. I'd never been so reckless before. Every partner I'd ever had began with clear communication—sometimes even formal contracts when my dominant needs demanded it. Boundaries, safewords, rules. Above all else: explicit consent was non-negotiable. And yet here I was, ready to throw all of it away for a woman, an angel, perfection in form and character, who I couldn't stop needing. I'd lost myself in the need to protect her, claiming her body like it would restore order to mine.

Without checking.

Without control.

Thus, I spiraled, pacing and schooling myself, lost in my spiral until her siren call.

"Troy, are you alright?" She sat up, reached for her shirt to cover herself.

"I...owe you an apology, Gia." I hated the flush of embarrassment in her cheeks and hated myself even more for wanting to see that flush for another reason, my cock still rock hard for her. "I should have known. You'd never–"

"Please don't apologize." A tear slipped from her lashes, and its path down her cheek might as well have held a knife for all the way it carved into my chest. "I should've spoken sooner. I didn't mean to anger you or – "

"Anger?" Everything melted away as Gia slowly covered her beautiful form, closing her legs and curling her knees up to hide or protect herself. "You could never anger me, love." I knelt in front of her. "You are perfect. I am only angry at myself for not going slower, or giving you more time." The burning need to feel connected spurred me on, and I let my hands rest on the top of her feet. "Your first time should be special, precious even. You deserve to–"

"Have a *choice*." Gia's brows drew together as the edge in her voice cut me to my core. "I *deserve* to have a choice." Her shoulders subtly rose and fell as she measured my breadth and depth with a penetrating stare. She...was angry. "I deserve to choose. My life...my path."

Her eyes shone with tears, but her voice never wavered.

This was her declaration, and I knelt at her feet in awe of her strength.

"I deserve to be loved and cherished by a man who will see me for who I am and not for what he can gain from me," Her shaky breath was the only show of emotion as she collected herself with a sigh, "I deserve the freedom to own my worth; to share that with whoever I choose." Then, as if beckoned by my desires, Gia uncurled. Slowly stretching her legs, letting her feet slide down the edge of the bed until they rested on either side of my thighs, she reached for me. She cupped my jaw, damning the tear that slipped down her cheek. "And I *choose* you, Troy."

I choose you.

Her words ripped through me, lighting my body on fire as I lifted off my heels and slid my hands around her back, forging us together.

I choose you.

The echo flooded my senses as I held her to me, climbed the mattress, dragging her beneath me: a beast, and his master. Letting my lips linger on her mouth, I nestled her into the pillows and then blissfully trailed back down her neck, her collarbone.

She chose me.

I kissed and nipped my way across her, feeling my cock throb at each gasp she released. My fingers returned to her, dripping wet, swollen, and fiery hot. One wasn't enough, and when I stretched her with a second finger, she arched her back with a lingering sigh of 'Yes.'

My joy was complete at her yielding.

She melted into my mouth, her nipples were my playthings, my bites her branding.

My siren liked the hint of pain.

My leaking cock slammed into my better judgment, and with a groan of agony, I allowed only one more interruption before my higher brain functions ceased completely.

"I don't have any condoms." I mentally prepared for a complete stop and the world's worst case of blue-balls since the dawn of man. "I am clean, and I pray to God that it's enough, cause I won't put anything between us...but if you don't want this, speak and I'll stop. No guilt. No shame."

"Don't you dare." Her breathy command had me popping my eyes wide to take her in, only to see her face flushed, eyes hooded, and lips kiss-swollen as her hair sprawled around her on the pillow in the most beautiful frame ever invented. "I want to feel all of you....in all of me....I'm yours."

My brain officially checked out.

I growled my pleasure, knowing full well the caution we threw to the wind as we skated right past the birth control checkpoint. I didn't care. I wanted her to be mine in every way possible. Stripping my underwear, I lowered into the apex of her thighs and positioned myself at her entrance.

"I will try to make this part quick." As I spoke, I rubbed the head of my cock against her, letting her arousal and mine surround my head until I was slick with our juices.

The only grace I could give was to prepare her for me.

"I trust you." Her mouth found mine again as she let her tongue explore, and I pushed forward the barest inch. "I want this."

She was my air. Pulling her into my lungs just one more way I claimed her, body and soul, even as I pushed a little more.

"I need you." Her words fell on a pant, and I was in the sweetest agony at the slow, surrendering stretch of her.

"You...are taking me so well, baby." Her body was molded to mine, and her arms wrapped around my neck. I advanced further, testing restraint not to slam to the hilt, and grateful for the caution when I reached resistance.

"Breathe for me, Siren. Relax and let me take care of you." I claimed her mouth and let my thumb circle her clit until she was whimpering in my mouth.

Wanton and starved, her arms tightened around me.

"Yes. Please. Take it. Take me." At her command, I snapped my hips, thrusting past her barrier and burying myself to the hilt as her cry branded a core memory into my brain.

I could feel her tremble slightly as I sat, unmoving, inside her.

"I'm sorry I couldn't make it - " I was unable to finish any apology as Gia moved her hips, angling back and then thrusting into me again. "Fuuuuuck." My face sank into her hair, nuzzling her neck and desperately clinging for control as the siren writhed beneath me.

"Troy....Please," I pulled back to look into her beautifully shining blue eyes. "Please don't stop." Her nails dug into my shoulder as her hips shifted again, and I finally let myself move within her. I rocked back and forth in short, even strokes. Still hoping to keep things as gentle as possible despite the intense grip my cock was sheathed in. Gia stripped my restraint with another bite of my lower lip, my kryptonite. Snapping my hips into her harder, I won the most delicious sound I've ever heard.

"More."

I drove into her in longer and longer strokes, fully slamming into her in a rhythmic dance of pure obsession. Her walls pulsed around me, and if I felt like she was tight before, the sensation of her squeezing had me clinging to the last vestiges of restraint with all I had. Needing to last longer, I slid a hand beneath her back, rolling Gia on top of me. Her eyes went momentarily wide with surprise as I grabbed her hips, surely leaving bruises as I guided her back and forth. It took only one or two passes before my girl was lost in the sensation of grinding herself against the base of my cock. Deeper than ever, the view of her body, breasts tight in the cool air, hair tossed back as she gasped to the ceiling, was the single most beautiful sight of my life.

Her hands found mine, and our fingers laced together as she took over, grinding and gyrating on my cock with wild abandon. Relishing every undulating move of her hips, Gia's moans grew more frantic, her walls tighter and wetter, and I could feel my balls tightening. Slipping a hand to where we were joined, I pressed my thumb against her hood and commanded.

"Cum for me."

With a great thrusting shutter, Gia screamed through the first wave of her orgasm. My name and her tears on her lips, I bent my knees and thrust up into that gorgeous creature, roaring my release straight into her over and over. The intensity sent her arching back as I roared my finish, sending her into another cock-milking climax. She was a vision of pure, unadulterated beauty as she wept through each cascading wave of pleasure, her body shuddering of its own volition before finally releasing her into a boneless heap against my chest.

Mine.

Waves of ragged breathing and whimpering hitches.

She trembled beneath my fingers, aftershocks pulsing against me.

"You are nothing short of perfection." I splayed my hand across her back, placing a kiss on the top of her head and wondering if I could somehow stay in this place for all of eternity.

Sweaty, spent, and still sheathed inside the goddess panting on my chest. I couldn't go back to a time when Gia wasn't in my arms. Her life was now my purpose, and Ben was now my son; together, we would forge a life and take on the world. My soul settled into a deep serenity like never before.

Then the haze of lust subsided, and I worried.

This was her first time, and as much as I wanted to take it slow and gently, in the end, I was rougher than I intended to be.

"I am sure you must be sore. I can get you some pain reliever and - "

"No." Her hands, once lying on my chest, now clung to my shoulders, her feet and legs tugging most endearingly. "Please...not yet." She turned her face to the side, and as I slid a finger across her cheek to tuck those siren tresses behind her ear, I saw the tears she'd been hiding. "This was more than I could ever have hoped for."

I loved the weight of her across my chest.

I loved the smell of our sex mixed with the sweet scent of her hair.

I loved her.

Our breathing steadied, and I could feel her relaxing into me with self-satisfaction that I knew I'd never match. Knowing that this gorgeous siren was now lazing atop me, my cock still inside her, and our juices dripping down my length.

We hadn't used a condom.

She had no reason to be on birth control.

We may have created a life and added to our family.

My family.

She needed my name.

That was the final thought that settled and soothed me as I curled my arms around her in relief from a lifetime of searching.

Gia was my home.

30

GIA

O F ALL THE WAYS I imagined losing my virginity, I never expected that.

Troy hadn't just taken me for perfunctory consummation of some arranged marriage. Nor had he lost himself to his lust and ignored my pleasure. What we shared could only be described as a claiming. He'd devoured me, worshiped me, and when the time came to take me finally, he'd done so with such passion and care. But I claimed him too. I chose him, drove him, begged and yielded to him. When I lost myself to my pleasure, he encouraged me, ensuring I orgasmed more than once before finally releasing himself with a roar like a victory cry.

When we finally moved, he carried me to the shower and worshipped my body with warm, soapy lather. Troy's hands were firm but gentle. Exploring my body, even taking time to shave my legs. I began to protest, but he leveled a look at me that brooked no argument. Oiling my skin and gliding the razor over it with a careful, steady hand, he was methodical and focused.

The act was intimate and defining.

By the time he finished, I could feel the building heat of longing in my core again. He stood, looked me in the eyes with a yearning that made me ache, and then devoured me right there in the shower.

Hard, passionate kisses.

Pinned to the tile wall.

I screamed to pieces within minutes.

Afterwards, he cleaned and dried me off, silently massaged my entire body with oil and lotion, lavishing extra time around achy hips. Troy carried me to bed and handed me a small glass of water and two Tylenol. I argued I didn't need them, but the same intent expression from the shower told me I wouldn't win this battle either. His relief when I swallowed the pills was palpable, as if he'd held anxiety he couldn't release until I gave him this.

I was so glad I could.

Satisfied at last, Troy climbed into bed behind me, pulling me against his chest until his face was buried in my hair. Molded around me, his arm acting as my pillow, I'd never felt so safe in my life. Deliciously spent as I was, I almost missed his final words.

"This is how we sleep from now on." I can only blame my post-coital high for my boldly teasing response.

"Okay, Boss Man." His low chuckle was the last sound I heard as sleep took me.

He wasn't done.

I awoke in the dark hours of the morning to Troy slipping between my thighs, spreading me open even before I was fully aware, and tasting me until I screamed his name...twice. I expected him to take me entirely, but he didn't. He merely kissed his way up my shaking body, laying the last of his affections on my mouth before pulling me against him with words of filthy praise. I might have blushed if not for the hazy, contented sleep that tugged me under.

The next time I awoke, the smell of coffee called.

Stretching, I took stock of new aches—tight hips, a tender core, legs that trembled with memory. Images of everything we'd shared flooded in, and with it came a blossoming arousal.

I wanted more.

I wanted everything.

Shuffling to the kitchen, I found a lounge-pant-clad Troy handing me a mug of coffee. He was barefoot and shirtless, with acres of dark, umber skin on display. A far cry from his work attire, buttoned up and freshly pressed. I loved seeing him this way.

"Good morning." He grabbed his phone and pulled me close to his side. "It appears my brother has enjoyed his time with Ben." He angled his phone to show a series of photos that Sam sent to his brothers: Lila feeding Ben, Sam playing on the floor at tummy time, Ben snoozing in Lila's arms on the couch, and even one with Sam's stethoscope around Ben's little ears while he gnawed on the bell at the end.

"Is it crazy that I miss him?" I pulled the phone closer to zoom in on the drooly smile I'd built my world around.

"I miss him too." Troy leaned into me, inhaling deeply from the top of my head. "Though I did love having you to myself all night." My core clenched, arousal instantly dampening my panties as if the power of his words lit my body on demand. "Are you sore?"

"Only a little," I admitted, burying my face in his chest to hide my blush. "But I like it."

"So...no regrets?" He asked, his words leaving a vagueness that I wasn't expecting.

"What?" Troy gently tugged me around, caging me against the counter as he took in my face with a worried expression.

"I know I was a little...heavy-handed." He started, his face stoic as he took in my every expression. My finger moved to trace the worried furrow on his forehead unbidden. "Careful as I wanted to be, you must've been hurt." He studied me carefully, reading every nuance of emotion for some hidden meaning. "I tried my best to make things gentle but - "

"Hey." I couldn't bear his concern in the wake of my blistering happiness. "I'm happy it was you," I noted how his lips pressed into a thin line, and considering how he commanded my body last night, I rephrased my statement with something that felt more truthful. "I'm glad it is *only* you."

The change in wording was subtle, but powerful, and the new meaning seemed to pour over him like a healing balm. His whole body exhaling with relief like an unclenched fist.

"I've never taken a woman bare before, without protection." His arms tensed, and his chest flexed as if gripping the counter around me with all his might.

It was so painfully clear that some battle was waging below the surface with him. I lifted my hand to cup his jaw. His eyes closed as he turned his face and kissed my palm before continuing.

"I wouldn't go there before, but with you... knowing my proclivities towards control," Troy took another breath then, exhaling it almost on the whisper of his words. "I won't have anything between us, but I don't want you to feel trapped by my–"

Finally, I understood his worries as I used both my hands to lift his gaze to me, forcing him to open his eyes again to look at me.

"Bossy pants tendencies?" I smiled, cocking an eyebrow to add to the playfulness I was hoping would snap him out of his brooding worry, but he just studied me in that stone-still face of his, so I kept going. "If your...proclivities...give me extra attentive showers with full body massages, and multiple orgasms, I think I got the okay end of that deal." Then, in a moment of bravery I'd never had, I opted to be utterly raw and honest in the face of the man who'd seen every inch of me stripped bare, inside and out. "If by controlling you mean feeling safer than I ever have in my entire life...that's a stepping stone I'll happily walk along."

It was a phrase I'd only heard him use once before when describing Chase and Moira, but I hoped they conveyed all the things I couldn't yet put into words. I saw a light flicker in his eyes that told me he'd caught it, but the tension in his body remained.

"Tell me," I commanded, hoping my confidence would allow him to trust me with whatever he was wrestling. "Anything...everything."

"I've always needed to feel in control. But with you, it's - " He hesitated again, still needed to say something he couldn't voice. "It's more. I need to care for you and Ben... in every way. It's...visceral."

Of course. He'd spent his whole life caring for his brothers, but as they married off and started families, he lost the outlet for what was proving to be an intensely caring nature. And here he was, anxious that he was somehow too much for me after I'd spent a lifetime being wholly neglected and ignored.

"Last night was perfection in its truest form for me. And I can't go back." His face still held a shadow I couldn't place, but one I was aching to remove for him. "I did not use a condom. I don't think I'll ever be able to."

His tone had shifted again. Subtle but there, the low timbre of a near-command. I couldn't tell whether he would be angry if I agreed with him or if I didn't. So, I kept my voice steady and calm, and again volunteered my most honest response.

"That's okay."

"Okay?" He pulled back, not far enough to release me, but enough to hook me with his intense gaze. "You've no other thoughts on the matter?"

I had oceans of thoughts on the matter, I was drowning in them, but I couldn't tell where he was going, and that ingrained training to hold my tongue and wait to gauge my situation rose to the surface.

"What are your thoughts?" A deflection I'd used countless times when my father would ask my opinion on something and I worried my answer would fall short of his expectations. I hated even going to this place with Troy; he was nothing like my father, and I knew that, but it was the only tool in my arsenal.

"I'd like to know your opinion." His face shifted away from the man who'd devoured me in the shower and back to the cop, crouched at my feet, surrounded by glass and debris, and I hated it.

He must have seen my worry, because he visibly relaxed his shoulders.

"I will never be angry with anything you share with me. I will never be disappointed or inconvenienced by your thoughts or feelings." He added, shifting his voice back into that low timbre that crawled across my bones like water. "But I won't have you feeling trapped just because I want you irrevocably tied to me in every way possible. Nor will I allow my dominance to pressure you into a place you aren't fully aware of or ready for, so before I share, you must speak your truth...now."

His command, his proclamation, settled the last of all my fears and worries that what I was feeling was somehow one-sided. He wanted me tied to him in every way possible.

"I liked feeling you...that way." I had to swallow hard around my cowardice, knowing blunt honesty was the only thing Troy wanted from me. He nodded, but said nothing more; He wanted more from me. "I liked feeling your body in me, with nothing between us." Clearing my throat, I squared my shoulders and silently thanked Lila and Moira for the sliver of confidence I was about to borrow from them. "I liked the way it felt when you came inside me. I liked that you let go like that...for me." I ignored my blush, forcing my eyes to stay locked onto his two intensely focused brown eyes, anchoring myself in the moment and forging forward. "I felt special...l-loved even." I didn't mean to stutter, but the word was so damned heavy it nearly dropped to the floor between us had Troy not caught it with the absolute elation in his eyes. "I don't want to put anything between us ever."

Laid bare, all my truths shared, I could only wait. His eyes flicked to the bob in my throat when I swallowed, as the seconds of his silent consideration felt like thunderous eons of time.

"Loved." A single word that snapped my anxiety like a rubber band. "You are so incredibly loved, Siren." He leaned in, finally releasing me from my torturous cage by brushing his lips along my neck, lighting a new fire in my soul. "There will never be anything between us. You are mine. Body and soul. Inside and out." My panties ruined, need blazed through me. "And I...am yours."

"I love you." I panted as he growled, backing me to the table, where he laid me out like a buffet and feasted like the king he was.

31

TROY

Loved.

That's how Gia said she felt when I let slip how deeply I needed to care for her.

If I could've frozen the moment—her body splayed across the table, those words sinking into the marrow of my soul—I would have. But Gia needed to shower and dress, and I used the excuse of cleaning the kitchen to give her space. I'd taken her several times, and still I wanted more. I wanted everything. There was so much exploring still to do, but I knew she had to be sore. And after that intense conversation where I all but planted a sword and swore fealty to my queen, she needed breathing room.

I needed to regain control of myself...or risk pulling us both into madness. I'd never had anyone accept the whole of me, inside and out. Yet Gia, this delicate gift from the universe, saw the outer control, witnessed my Beast with the gunman, and called me to unravel between her thighs, and felt loved.

Heading to dress, I noticed my clothes were in all the wrong places. They needed to be in the room with her—our room. Grabbing an armful, I crossed the hall and noticed her small laundry basket on the bed. I went to put the items away, only to realize these few things were all she had. Her closet was bare, save for a few empty bags. The dresser drawers only held things for Ben. I scanned back through every moment I'd seen her and realized she'd only worn the same handful of clothes, layered in different ways to give the illusion of more. Urgency roared to life. She'd never asked for anything—but it was unacceptable that she should have had to.

"Stalking outside the bathroom again, Sergeant Wilder." Her lilting voice pulled me from the clothing site I was shopping on my phone. There she stood, wrapped in a towel. Again. And again, I had to fight not to lick every inch of her bare skin. "Is this a habit, now?"

I might've enjoyed the banter more if she hadn't reached for the damn laundry basket.

"Are those the only clothes you own?"

"Oh, these?" She waved a hand dismissively over the pathetic offerings. "No! These are just the jeans I—"

"Gia." Whatever words she planned fell short of my expectations, and she knew it. Deflection was unacceptable. Her head dipped with what looked like shame–equally unacceptable.

"I washed them the day you went to work." Her wet hair curtained her face.

Unacceptable.

"The failing is mine." I crossed the room in three steps even as she opened her mouth to protest. "I made sure Ben had what he needed. I got you a phone, food, and shelter. But I failed to consider your other needs."

"Troy, you've done—"

"An oversight I won't make again." My hand found her neck, gently pulling her closer, and I loved how her body melted into mine. "You will allow me this indulgence." She searched my face, torn between acceptance and the need to push back "Do you want to choose, or simply give me your sizes?"

"I ran so fast...that night...I didn't think it through." Memory. She'd been pulled back into memory, and with it came a wave of sorrow.

"There is no shame here. No anger. This is me, also loving you." She needed to accept that my control extended beyond the bedroom, as did my affection for her. "You choose...Or I can."

Locking onto her hypnotic blue eyes, I stood unyieldingly until acceptance washed over her. I was glad this battle was easy. It would make it much easier for her to accept my other provisions.

"I'm easy. I can wear anything. I'll give you sizes... choose whatever you see fit." Then, as if in afterthought, her eyes hinted at a flirtation, and she added, "Choose whatever you want to *see* me in."

Then, taking full advantage of my imagination's temporary distraction, the siren turned out of my grasp.

I swear I smiled for half an hour as I scanned websites, selecting items I could tweak to her sizes. I didn't care what she wore—only that she didn't wear *those* clothes again. Anything that reminded her of that place needed to be destroyed. Then I remembered Sam's recommendation that we needed to get out a bit, and a plan took shape as she emerged.

"Ready to go get Ben?"

"Since we have a bit more freedom," I began, interrupted by a text from my Captain.

Captain: Paperwork on your perp ain't filling it-self out, Wilder.

Planning to get to that later, I refocused on Gia.

"I'd like to visit a local store to pick up some basics for now." I gestured at her clothes. "I'll order the rest online." Her resolve flared—mouth opened and ready to argue—but I raised a hand. "It's done." High-handed, sure. But her shoulders relaxed, and I knew I hadn't crossed the line. "First, we'll stop by my place so I can grab a few things. Then shopping. We'll pick up Ben on the way back." Knowing she'd need reassurance, I added, "We can video call Sam and Lila if it helps."

"Oh, Lila's been sending me pics." Gia sat to pull on her boots, her brow furrowed. "What did you mean by 'more freedom'?"

"The immediate threat is contained. Today is a good day to get out and let you see more of the area." Her thousand-yard stare was back; running mental calculations—planning for what could go wrong. I hated it.

I'd seen her smile, heard her scream my name in pleasure, and smelled her on my clothes and my hands and my bed. This shell-shocked version of her weighing risk versus reward was unacceptable.

I crouched at her feet, resting my face in her line of sight and my hands on hers, knowing how a soft voice and all the spoken details helped.

"I know your father is still a consideration. But it's too soon for him to know we've apprehended his associate. We have a window." Her eyes snapped to mine. Good. I had her attention. "I'll take *every* precaution. Trust me..." I squeezed her hands. "I've got you."

32

TROY

T HE LATE-SPRING CLIMATE HAD fresh buds peeking out from
the greening landscape, which seemed to delight Gia. She
pointed out each new color along the road, and seeing it all through
her eyes brought a new enjoyment to me as well. I mentally noted
that I owed Sam thanks for his insightful suggestion, as Gia held my
hand while we traveled – the sense of peace helped Gia open up.

"I can't wait to show Ben all the colors." She paused momentarily and added quietly, "My father never left me alone...even before
Ben. I was always with a nanny, a bodyguard, or a driver." She
watched the small-town shops pass by as we crossed Main Street,
her hand tightening in mine. "After Ben, it got worse. I wasn't even
allowed to get things or see a pediatrician, no matter who was with
me. Then, when I ran...well...I went from prisoner to fugitive."

"Not fugitive." I corrected. "You did nothing wrong."

She took in my comment, shaking her head as if chasing away bad memories, and returned to her commentary on our drive.

"Is that a church in the middle of the grass?"

Happy to share a good story, I used the moment to regale her with memories of Chase and Moira's wedding, hoping to balance the darkness she was battling.

"And there is the playground." I nodded my head to indicate the area where I'd seen other mothers pushing strollers. "Something we could perhaps take Ben to when he's a bit older." Her smile was the sun my beast languished in like a housecat stretching in the warmth of an errant ray. "This is my neighborhood," I announced, driving down my little street of modest houses.

I pulled into the cul-de-sac that held my home and my brothers', with the middle house nearing the end of reconstruction, a for-sale sign hanging in the yard.

"Be it ever so humble." I parked in the narrow gravel drive and entered my home, anticipating a wave of comfortable familiarity. Yet, despite all the sweet memories it contained, I longed to return to the cabin with Gia and Ben.

Turning towards her, I loved her wide-eyed expression.

"Surprised?"

"Happily so," she said on a sigh, scanning my small living room.

I watched her stroll through the space, running a long, slender finger across the furniture, throw pillows, and blankets knitted by Nonna. She paused to take in my coffee table stacked with books, lifting one to inspect the cover before bringing it to her nose to smell it. She was fascinating to watch, and I didn't dare break whatever spell was being cast to inquire about what she found so captivating.

She made her way over to the console cabinet, cluttered with photo albums and memorabilia, slowly passing by years of framed portraits, newspaper clippings, medals, trophies, and other keepsakes that Nonna had preserved. Lifting a small photo album, she glanced at me as if asking for permission, only continuing when I nodded in approval.

Everything I had was hers after all.

The album was filled with pictures of my brothers and me at boot camp, in our Marine Corps gear. She scrunched her nose and giggled, pointing at a photo of a much younger me. Lifting another album, Gia gently examined photos of us as children, laughing out loud at a picture of us knee-deep in the muck of a proper mudslide after a rainstorm. I had collected all these items as a respectful nod to my Nonna, but seeing them through Gia's eyes made my heart soar as she took in snapshots of history like they were treasures.

"That was my Nonna." I pointed to the frame of the beautiful woman whose eyes sparkled when she laughed.

"She looked happy down to her toes."

"With an infectious laugh, too. One couldn't be unhappy in her presence." I waved a hand around the room at large. "Most of these things were hers."

"You were an adorable kid." Gia nudged me with her shoulder, pointing to another Corps picture of me, clean-shaven with a high and tight fade, razor-parted. "When did you decide to flip that script?"

"The facial hair came in on its own in time." I ran a hand over my goatee. "I prefer this over the hassle of a daily clean shave or the upkeep of a full beard, but," gliding a hand over my smooth scalp, I couldn't help but grimace. "I confess this is a necessity courtesy of Mother Nature."

"Avoiding the inevitable march of time?" Gia teased with a laugh. "You carry it very well...." Her compliment resonated as she slowly turned around the small room. "There are so many things here, this cabinet, this whole room... a far cry from the museum I grew up in."

I hated the sadness that weighed down her words, so I pulled her back to me, squeezing her hips and willing away the shadows with my body.

"I rather like you snooping through my memories." Leaning down, I gave a soft kiss to the side of her neck, loving how she shivered just the barest bit when I did. "I need to grab a few things from my room. I'll be right back."

Entering my room, I could only shake my head at the stark contrast of my life from the last time I had entered this space. Compared to the cabin, which, despite all my efforts, was a chaotic landmine of baby things for Ben in every corner of the house, my small home was flawlessly organized but felt barren. Gia had called my home a living, breathing scrapbook, but the whole place was a time capsule. A bygone era before the weight of duty bore down on me, and the control I'd craved grew teeth. That feral need clawed at my insides even now—take her to the courthouse, give her my name, adopt Ben, chain them to me forever. But there were too many loose ends.

Apex.

Her father.

Truths still to uncover.

I had to wait, but I'd never let go.

Exiting my room, I watched her smile at the wall of memories, relishing the way she touched each photo as if it were a treasure. Moira and Lila had seen my brothers in these photos.

Gia saw only me—and it changed everything.

33

GIA

FOR ALL HIS BUTTONED-UP stoicism, our pivotal moment of join-ing held the lynchpin into a wellspring of connection I never had...but always wanted. Hearing him say he never wanted us to be separated by so much as a condom was intense, and still promising to be his was as natural as breathing. When he sealed his promises in bed, my whole body vibrated with the rightness of it. But then he told me I was loved, and well, everything in me melted and reformed at his side.

Troy was all-consuming in his need for me. I loved that most about him.

Seeing his home was like pulling back the curtain to see even more of who he was. And now, driving through the little town that helped shape the man beside me, I could only revel in the warmth left in our wake. His hand never left mine until we reached the store. He parked carefully, selecting his spot with practiced caution. Then, hand in hand, he guided me directly to our first section, lingering nowhere in between.

This would be a search-and-destroy mission, not a leisurely shopping excursion.

"Allow me to halt any protests before we begin." His face was stern, his posture stiff in the arms-crossed wall of muscle; his standard when that all-business tone came out. The overall stance might have been intimidating if he hadn't been standing in the middle of women's pajamas at the time. "We are here for the basics, but I expect you to get enough."

"Enough?" I stifled the laugh threatening to ruin his statue of resigned grumbling, doled out between flowery moo-moo's and bulk-pack cotton tube socks.

"No less than one week of items on every level. That's 7 days." Expecting this, I had no argument prepared.

"Aye Aye, Boss Man." As I turned, I offered a mocking salute, loving the smirk it won me.

Troy hovered nearby, face intently scanning his phone but still watching my progress until my arms were full. Then a cart appeared, procured from the ether as I never saw him leave my side, and he prodded me along. When I surmised I had enough items, I cocked my head towards the dressing room. He eyed the shallow cubicle of changing spaces and nodded in agreement. I could only smile at his wordless yet crystal-clear communication as I entered the changing room.

Stripping out of my clothes, I had a moment to notice how my body was evolving. I was always slender, almost willowy in stature. On the first night in the cabin, I saw how the stress and isolation of my life had taken their toll; my ribs were painfully visible, and my skin dry. Now, in the few short weeks I'd been with Troy, I could see the remnants of rest and good food. I was still leaner than before Ben's arrival, but the circles under my eyes were gone, my ribs barely noticeable under the harsh UV lighting.

Then, realizing I'd never had such a luxury, I let myself daydream.

I imagined a life with Troy. Where I wouldn't be paraded around social events to perform like a trick poodle, but I'd be cherished. I imagined a partnership where I had a voice and freedom to pursue the things I loved, without fear of retaliation if I made a mistake—a partnership grown in love...a marriage. Turning to the side, I couldn't resist pushing my stomach forward and imagining myself pregnant, wondering what our baby would look like: dark-skinned like him, or fair and blue-eyed like me, or perhaps some beautiful combination of the two. Would we have a boy, or maybe a tiny baby girl?

Then came doubt. I wasn't looking for this when I escaped my father. I just wanted to be safe. I wanted Ben to be safe. Everything was so new. And Troy and I were precariously new and intensely consuming. How much more would he be if a baby were involved? Would his protective instincts heighten to a space of dutiful, ever-watchful father, or would it tip into that grey area of love masking control? I had to shake away that last thought, not wanting to imagine anything of Troy resembling my father's household. Things were surely too fresh, and my emotions were rushing too fast.

I exited the dressing room with my selections, finding Troy offside on a phone call. Not wanting to interrupt him, I used the time to select a few personal items in private. Despite having had Troy's mouth on every inch of my naked body, the idea of buying bras and panties in front of him felt insanely intimate. I'd never purchased such personal things in front of a man before. Sorting through the options, I selected a variety of basics and added them to the cart.

When I stood up, my eye caught on a beautiful black nightgown in the pajama section. A simple black satin sheath, slit to the upper thigh and trimmed with lace. Next to it was a matching robe. I held the item against my body and envisioned Troy's expression if I came out wearing this instead of the standard sleep shorts and slouchy sweater I'd been in all week. I was immediately drawn into a fantasy of Troy, gorgeous and muscled, stalking me across the room the way I'd seen Sam or Chase do with their wives. Prowling at first before pouncing, he'd loosen the tie of my robe, maybe saving it to use in other ways.

The fantasy vanished when a display of adorable baby clothes called to me from the next aisle.

The cute little outfits with teeny pants and little onesies instantly enamored me. There were baby bow ties, jaunty little caps, infant-sized sport jerseys, and mini-me outfits for nearly every occupation. I could see Ben wearing one of these and looking quite dapper. Of course, each outfit needed tiny matching socks, which hung directly next to bibs, blankets, and pacifiers of every shape and size. Nearby stood a rack of books, including one on the care and feeding of infants and babies, and next to that was a book on toddler development, along with some adorable early reader books I could read to Ben each night.

The excitement was real, but so was the guilt over everything I'd never given Ben. Our isolation had surely impacted his early development, and the guilt became a ball of anxiety I had to swallow around. I didn't want to burden Troy with more cost, so I began digging through my wallet to see what was left of my father's cash when I heard Troy call me.

"Gia."

I turned the cart back towards the dressing room, but ended up in the toy section instead.

"Gia!"

Troy's voice called out again, more faintly, with a tinge of worry. I stood stock-still, spinning in place, scanning the endless racks of clothes as panic began to prick. Then, a man's voice sounded directly behind me.

"Looking for something?"

34

TROY

I DIDN'T WANT TO crowd Gia too much.

That was a lie. I wanted to exist forever in her orbit. But I knew I had to cage the beast, even as it gnawed on its restraints. My chest ached with a nagging worry each time I looked away from her, anxiety growing that we were suddenly out in the open too long. She caught me watching her no less than three times before she entered the dressing room.

The longer she was out of my line of sight, the more my anxiety grew. I scanned the dressing area, knew there were no windows or back exits, and I secured a position at the only door. My worry was baseless.

And still.

I remembered how quickly we nearly lost Lila and Moira. I could see the man in the woods, his arm around Gia, a gun in his hand. By the time she'd been gone 8 minutes, I was white-knuckling the urge to perch myself on the dressing room bench while she changed. An idea rife with as much sexual desire as it was raw panic, and she'd surely retract from my pull if I let the full-strength obsessive in me out on full display. I opted to text Sam as a distraction.

Me: We finished at the house faster than anticipated. We are at the store now.

Sam: Take your time.

Me: We should finish here soon. We'll head straight to you.

Sam: Grab some dinner if you want. I'm off shift all day.

Me: Ben is doing well?

Sam: Dude

Me: Still fever-free?

Sam: He's all good. We got this.

Me: He prefers to be burped sitting up on the leg versus on the shoulder.

Sam's face lit up my phone screen, and I instantly regretted texting him.

"What the fuck are you doing?" He barked by way of greeting

"Am I not allowed to check in?" Any hopes I'd harbored to deflect Sam's teasing were instantly put to rest when he burst into ear-splitting laughter.

"You have never checked in so many times in a single day in your goddamn life. What gives?" Pinching the bridge of my nose, I sighed in resignation.

"Nothing gives," I paced a few steps away from the dressing room, worried Gia would hear Sam's booming voice.

"This is your second text in only a few hours. Where's Gia?" His question caught me off guard enough that I answered too quickly.

"She's trying on clothes."

"And you're pacing outside the dressing room, freaking out, ammiright?" His astute observation was gratingly accurate. "Lemme guess. Last night rocked your world, and today you are all in your head trying to be both aloof and clingy at the same time, which is impossible, and you're calling me for a distraction to avoid climbing the goddamn walls."

"I didn't call," I mumbled through gritted teeth. "I texted."

Sam had always been good at reading people. A boon in his work as an EMT, certainly a plus in his role as husband and soon-to-be father. When did it extend to me?

"So...you and Gia enjoyed your evening?"

As loath as I was to share details, he was right. I was climbing out of my skin, and Sam gave me the lifeline to give Gia a little personal space. Glancing over my shoulder to see her cart in its original spot, I strolled further down the aisle to continue.

"I have no words." Was my answer. "And having her in my house was..."

"Intense?"

"In a word."

"Based on what I saw yesterday, Gia's feeling you too. Is that what scares you?"

"No." I nearly shouted the word before taking a breath to compose myself. "Nothing about Gia scares me."

"Then what's got you so twisted, man?" I opened my mouth to start, then closed it again as a flush of foolish embarrassment washed over me. I was the big brother; I was supposed to be the one guiding them. "I can't help if you can't put words to it, dude. Spit it out."

I exhaled hard, trying to find the right words to convey the emotion without sounding like a lunatic. I'd always shielded my brothers from my dominant proclivities, so how could I now describe how they were bleeding out across my life in ways that felt close to uncontrollable?

"The idea of not being near her is simply..." My words fell short, unable to convey what I barely understood.

"Remember when Lila and I met, and you found me the morning after our drunken one-nighter?"

"Reeking of booze, bruised up, and denying how much she'd crawled under your skin," I answered easily, happy to focus on anything other than myself.

"I was hooked from that first night. Couldn't get her out of my head. I couldn't focus on work, Marge's bar, nothing." Sam sighed, as if reliving it was a happy time despite the description of being driven to madness. "It wasn't until I gave up and planted myself in her space that I had any peace."

"Being in Gia's space is not my problem," I said, turning to pace back towards my dressing room post. "She's literally in the cabin with me."

"Oh, but it is. Think about when you were most at ease with Gia." He paused as I let my mind drift back to her in my arms, us in the shower, our hands clasped together in my truck. "Now think about what you are doing right now, dumbass." I stopped pacing, trying to connect the dots on Sam's train of thought. "I'm guessing all the happy places you just

thought of, you were physically connected...body to body...ammiright?"
I could only sigh at the astounding accuracy yet again. "And now you are
not only physically standing away from her, but likely mentally telling
yourself to give her even more space."

"When did you grow intuitive?" I asked, as proud as I was irritated.

"Do you think we don't know how much you've held yourself in
check with us through the years?"

"In...check?" I halted my pacing.

"Chase and I have been the sole beneficiaries of all your best inten-
tions for years, and as much as we love you, we are beyond thrilled to
see you find your match." Sam chuckled and added, "If for no other
reason than to have someone else absorb the brunt of your lovable al-
pha-dom-control-mongering."

My mouth went dry, realizing a lifetime of trying to hide who I was
had all been for nothing. My brothers had seen through me. Did Gia see
through me, too? Was I tempering myself as much as I thought, or was I
overwhelming her without realizing it?

"Shocked as I am, I admit..." I reached the edge of the dressing room
and found the shopping cart gone. Stepping inside, I found Gia's empty
room, with only a small pile of clothes. "Gia?"

I turned, hoping to find her nearby, but I did not see her.

She was right there.

I never looked away...Except I did.

Just for one goddamn moment!

"You good, dude?"

"She's gone." I scanned the nearest aisles and saw neither her nor the
cart.

"I'm sure she's nearby. Call her cell and text me when you have her."
I hung up on Sam and called out again.

"Gia." I paused, holding my breath and straining to hear her answering call. "Gia!" I called her cell; I heard it ringing behind me.

Walking towards the dressing room, I rummaged through discarded clothes to find her phone on the floor. Lifting the screen to stare at my name across the display, my blood turned to ice. Without the phone, I couldn't track her. Walking swiftly towards the front of the store, I scanned each aisle I crossed as panic clawed up my throat.

"GIA!" I started down the first aisle.

She had the cart. She wouldn't go far.

"GIA!" Second aisle. Nothing.

I barely registered the glances from nearby patrons as visions of the man in the woods clouded my judgment.

Clinging to her.

Sniffing her.

Burying his face in her hair...my hair!

"GIA!"

Images of Moira handcuffed to a chair in a burning building, and Lila broken and bleeding on the floor with Sam, who'd been shot, flooded my senses.

Gia was gone.

And where was I? Carrying her discarded cellphone, impotent to stop whatever violent act was ripping her away from me because I needed a fucking pep talk.

"GIA!" Rage whipped through like fire on dry kindling. I snagged the arm of a store employee, spinning them to face me. "Have you seen..." Realizing I had no photo to show them, I began rattling off details. "A woman, about this height. Slender, with pale skin and blue eyes."

"Sir, are you okay?" The associate placated, pulling away from my grasp. "I can call a manager for you-"

"HAVE YOU SEEN HER?" I bellowed, blood drumming in my ears even as I knew I was so monumentally screwed. How had I let this happen? "She has dark black hair, blue eyes, her name is Gia, and - "

"TROY!" Her siren call pulled at me, drawing me offside where she stood with another employee. "I'm here!"

I ran to her, hardly able to breathe until her arms were around my neck. Unable even to think straight, as I buried my face in her, breathing in her essence.

"I'm okay. I'm sorry." She spoke softly, her words trembling in my ear even as I tried to steady my breathing. "I got turned around. This man was helping me find my way back, but you were gone."

Setting her feet on the floor, I turned to see an elderly gentleman in a store uniform standing next to the discarded cart of clothes. His concerned eyes gave way to a slight head nod, and all I could do was nod in return.

"I tried to call you, but I lost my - " I held up her phone, not missing the relief in her eyes as she pocketed the thing before grasping my cheeks. "I didn't mean to worry you like that."

"I stepped away for just a second. Sam called and–"

"I didn't want to interrupt you. I was - "

"Jesus, Gia." I snapped, harsher than intended, and her faint flinch dropped me to my knees like a stone. "I thought someone took you again. I thought..."

She crouched before me, pulled my face to hers, pressing her lips into mine and instantly melting away every worry. Sliding my hands again around her waist, my fingers dug into her, needing her closer to me. I let myself linger there until the beast in me unclenched, retracting its claws.

Standing with her, I took her mouth, needing to inhale her taste as much as her scent, letting her essence sink into me and settle the vibration in my bones. We stayed pressed together, sharing breath, kissing like it was all that held us together until the elderly employee politely cleared his throat.

"I'm so sorry." Gia was apologizing, but it was I who had come unglued. "I never meant to scare you like that."

I shook my head, absolving her before the apology left her lips and hating, again, how my moment of panic brought out this robotic shift in her voice.

"The error was mine. I should've kept closer watch, and perhaps," glancing at the small crowd and her pink cheeks, I realized I'd put us both on display. "Kept a cooler head."

"Given how we met, you get a pass on a moment of overreaction." Her smile settled the last of my ruffled nerves, and I allowed my hands to release her only as far as I could lace our fingers.

As I steered the shopping cart to the checkout with one hand, she leaned against me, wrapping her free hand around my forearm and hugging me, a gesture at once endearing and soothing.

I added this day to my list of things I never wanted to endure.

And another list began—of ways to never repeat this mistake.

35

GIA

SOMETHING TANGIBLY SHIFTED IN Troy the moment he found me. I felt it in every place he touched me, from the desperate grip in the store to the way he clutched my hand on the ride out to Sam and Lila's. Even there, under the safety of his brother's roof and surrounded by his most trusted family, his body never left mine.

Fingers laced.

Hand on my waist.

Arm draped around my shoulders.

A constant tethering, conveying unspoken messages. Troy was using me to recalibrate; my presence... his grounding. Sam and Lila saw it, her questioning glance to me quickly turning into a subtle text exchange.

Lila: You good?

Me: Yes.

I was good, but also hyper-aware. Continually reminding myself that this new intensity was driven by momentary panic, and not by anger. Reminding myself that he was not like my father.

We drove home in silence, somehow managing to unload the car in a single trip. I think he would've driven the truck through the front door to avoid letting go of me. Once inside, cabin secured to his standards, he sank to his knees. Face buried in my stomach, arms vice-tight around my waist. Troy clung to me, body trembling as if nothing in the world would ever make sense, haunted him. It made me ache to return his peace, but I knew not how, and, frankly, the day had been so full of emotions, I was feeling a bit stretched thin myself.

"I'm sorry again–"

"Stop." The command was muffled through my clothes between long drags he pulled in, smelling me like he'd been too long under water, and I was the oxygen his lungs burned for.

"I need to settle Ben, and then–" Troy sighed, long and low, and then stood. He dragged his body up until his forehead pressed to mine, and Ben nestled between us.

"I'll make us dinner. You settle our son." I could feel the pain still screaming from his fingertips as he walked away. But all I could hear was the echo in my chest: our son.

An hour and a half; that's how long we moved without words while I tried to think of ways to help him feel centered again.

I bathed Ben and fed him his bottle.

He prepared food and set the table.

He took Ben to finish feeding him while I ate.

I put Ben to bed, and Troy grabbed the baby monitor, then took my hand.

Leading me across the hall to his former bedroom, he closed the door behind us.

This was where I would restore his peace.

"Today...was unacceptable." His voice was so low I had to strain to hear him. "I never should have taken my eyes from you." He placed the monitor on the floor by the door, and grazed his fingers up my body as he spun me to face away from him, and stood behind me. "But you should never have wandered so far from me."

"I know. I didn't–" His hand slipped up the front of my body until his fingers wrapped around my neck and silenced my words.

There was no pressure, no grip, but the ownership rippled through me.

"Your phone was discarded. You weren't in my line of sight. Not in any direction." Content with my silence, Troy's hand slid down to the edge of my shirt, lifting it over my head. "Do you know what that did to me?"

The cool air sent goosebumps shivering across my skin, even as his warm chest pressed behind me–his shirt discarded too.

"I'm so sorry." I whimpered, watching as his hands slipped around my waist to unfasten my jeans. "I was just–"

His hand returned to my throat in a move so fast I barely registered it.

"You *never* apologize to me." Even as he spoke, hand at my throat and breath on my neck, I felt so unbelievably cherished. It made no sense that an act so aggressive could be so loving, and yet that is how I felt. "Tell me. You understand."

He released me only when I nodded on a sigh.

"I called for you." He returned his attention to my pants, sliding them to the floor. Standing, I felt his pants whisper to a heap behind me.

"I searched aisle after aisle." His hard length was pressed against my back, radiating heat and calling to the heat in me. "Imagining all the ways you might've left me." His hand on the middle of my back, Troy nudged me to the bed. "Imagining all the ways you were very nearly taken from me."

I crawled on all fours to the middle, then spun around. Facing, for the first time, the gut-wrenching pain in his eyes. I wanted to apologize, to beg his forgiveness, but he didn't want words. Leaning to the side, he reached into a drawer, all while I sat perched, naked in the bed.

I began to understand when he stood holding three neckties.

"I need you to know how sorry I am for losing track of you." He lifted my wrists, placing them together, palms up, and putting a kiss in each palm. "I was careless. Had something happened to you, I don't know what I would have done." He made a point to show me the ties, watching my eyes until I glanced at them and then back to him. "I need to secure you again...to me." He made a point to show me the ties, watching as my eyes flicked to them and then back to him. "I need this...if you will allow it."

Not a command, but a choice.

I answered with a single nod and a faint whisper. "I trust you."

He moved in quick, smooth motions. Securing my wrists together with one of his ties. He worked the material into a knot firm enough that I was secure, then planted another kiss in each palm. It may as well have been napalm for all the heat that exploded inside me.

"I need you to believe me when I say I am not angry with you." The second tie was slowly lifted to my mouth. He waited at the edge of my lips until I opened for him. His smile sent my heart galloping as he secured the tie around my head, careful not to pull my hair with the knot.

"But believe me when I tell you I will never lose you like that again." Troy pressed me back into the bed, then nestled his shoulders between my thighs and devoured me.

Arching and writhing, I was instantly catapulted into an orgasm before his fingers gently breached my entrance. Stretching me with one, then two, then three digits, he massaged that secret spot deep inside and shattered me again. Troy feasted until I was a trembling heap, and just as I was about to beg for mercy, he climbed up my body, and the third tie flashed before my eyes.

"A single tug at your wrist and you are free. Nod, if you understand." He waited as I panted a time or two, searching the desperate need in his pupil-blown eyes. I nodded in agreement with my entire soul. This was how I could fix him.

"Need the tie removed from your mouth? Pull it free. Nod, if you understand." His body was screaming for peace, a need to claim born not from control but fear. Nodding again, tears spilled from the corners of my eyes in an apology I couldn't voice.

Then the third tie was placed over my eyes, and the room went dark.

I knew I was safe with Troy; without doubt or failing, he wouldn't hurt me. But the instant the lights dimmed to darkness, adrenaline flooded my body, and I was flying. Shaking, writhing, panting, and feeling everything so heightened, I thought I might explode as the bed shifted under his weight and his knees propped up under my thighs.

"My siren," He lifted my hips and positioned the head of his cock at my entrance. "Grab the headboard."

Giving all my control and power over, I obeyed.

Thrusting into me, root to tip, repeatedly with wild abandon, Troy found peace. Fucking me into a fourth orgasm. My breath was ragged, gasping between slams of his cock so deep I felt my body give to them out of sheer force of will, and still he didn't slow. Another climax coiled inside of me, and my hands slipped from the headboard. I was instantly pinned again, his body falling on mine with all the force of a bull charging through my body with unhinged desire.

"You belong to me." Holding my hands above my head, his body hovered over mine, his breath hot in my ear. "You will never be taken from me."

I wanted to shout his name, my agreement, anything, but all I could do was yield.

My body...for his peace.

The next orgasm that took me under was too much, too deep, and I sobbed his name around his tie as he slammed his cock to the hilt with a roar, spilling himself inside me.

I shuddered and sobbed in the blindfolded darkness as my pussy clenched around him in rhythmic waves of ecstasy, and he mumbled the sweetest words in my ears.

"I will always protect you." He removed the tie from my eyes, kissing away the tears that flowed still as I sobbed through my aftershocks. "I will never let anything or anyone hurt you." He removed the tie from my hands, kissing each wrist. "You are loved. You...are mine." He slipped the tie loose from my mouth as I gasped his name like a prayer, wrapping my arms around him even as he twitched inside of me.

"I love you." I whimpered as he peppered kisses across my cheeks, and I felt him finally relax.

I was his.

As true as his promise, I vowed the same.

I would always protect him. I would never let anything or anyone hurt this beautiful, wonderful, broken man.

He was mine.

36

TROY

I SLEPT, BUT THE day's chaos looped behind my eyelids—the what-ifs, the ways I could have lost her. I wanted her tethered, wrapped in my arms, tied to the bed, tied to this life. Locked doors weren't enough. My skin wasn't enough. She was with me, holding my hand, my arms wrapped around her, and it wasn't enough. I feared I'd lose her if I showed the complete chaos inside of me. I had to be careful, even as something inside of me screamed to mark her.

Claim her.

I would have cuffed her to the bed, immovable underneath my weight to take the worship I wanted to give her. But I had to be careful. Gia deserved to be treasured, and cuffs held a darker note.

She deserved lighter songs.

Bound in my ties, physically gifted and surrendered to me, that beautiful creature nodded her tear-filled eyes, willing her body to me in a silent gift I hadn't earned. I ate her, licked her, fucked her until my cum painted the inside of her walls, and all thoughts stopped racing except one, singular, throbbing truth.

Mine...mine....mine.

Holding her all night, my ties no longer necessary, we were bound by something more profound. I imagined the ring I'd buy for her. I envisioned the one I'd tattoo for her–ink never fades.

The morning came with birdsong and another text from my Captain.

> Captain: A clue as to when your girl's making a statement might be nice.

I very nearly threw my phone into the abyss at reality's intrusion, but my beautiful siren stretched awake just as Ben smiled–my world.

"Good morning, love." I gazed into her sleepy eyes, still half-closed. "I have a bit of shopping to finish up and coffee to make."

She rolled my way, smiling at the two of us.

"How long has he been awake?" She sat up, tucking the sheet around her breasts and reaching for him.

"A few minutes. I pulled him in about an hour ago, and he dozed."

"An hour?"

"Mm-hmm. I needed him with us." I pressed a kiss to her head and strode to the door. "I'll start the coffee and his bottle."

Donning my phone in one hand, I finished the few shopping carts I'd started the day before, including a quick screenshot of one item for my brothers. Their immediate agreement was a bigger relief than expected. By the time Gia came out, I'd shifted to my laptop, where I was pursuing another clothing store for her.

"I'd welcome your input on a few things. I already have some things coming, but there are a few areas I'd like to know your tastes." She peered over my shoulder, and her eyes went wide.

"You don't need to buy me a diaper bag that costs–"

"Woman. You'll be carrying around items for Ben, plus your own things, and I'll not have you trudging about with a shabby backpack full of bad memories." She looked again at the screen, and I bit my tongue before I blurted something about the next baby she'd carry. "Select a color or I will."

I tabbed to a page of soft athletic wear.

"Yoga pants?" Her eyebrows hit her hairline with a smirk. "I'm not much of a gym girl."

"No. But you're a mom, and jeans aren't as comfortable as I hear my sisters lament." I paused, smirking. "And I wouldn't hate watching you walk away in those."

That got me a smile—and three colors in the cart.

"That's more than enough." She scolded, sliding Ben into his bouncy chair with a teething toy. "I've got eons of options, and you've paid for more than–" she yelped when I scooped her up, tossing her over my shoulder with a swift smack to her backside.

"Troy!"

"Was I not clear?" I had to give Sam his due; this power position was gratifying. "I plan to provide what you need."

"Yes, but I don't–" Another smack of her ass halted her again.

"And I've more than proven I rather enjoy spoiling you. Yes?" My palm twitched for another spanking, but the goal was to ease her in, not toss her in the deep end.

"Yes. Yes. Okay, it's just that–" I cut her off this time with a quick jab to her ribs, narrowly missing a kick to my nose by flailing feet as she howled with laughter. It was music to my ears. "Okay, Okay. I give. You win!" Setting her on her feet, breathless, the sparkle in her eyes made the world melt away.

"You should do that more often." She pulled me down, nuzzling my cheek with her nose.

"Toss you around like a caveman?"

"Laugh." Pulling back, I looked down into her eyes and realized she was right. I had been laughing. "You have a great laugh. And I get the impression you don't let it show very much."

The rest of the day, I vowed to laugh for her, if only to make her happy in the blissful cocoon we'd created—watching movies, caring for Ben, and never letting go of each other.

Until reality charged again.

> Captain: Get your ass in the station or I'm sending a Uni to haul you in!

My dousing bucket of cold, hard truth had arrived as scheduled. I had ignored my captain too long, declining calls and texts, even though I'd been keeping tabs on the gunman's progress on my laptop. From the cabin to the hospital, then into a cell once his foot was determined to be a grazing wound. He'd not bothered to plead for his innocence, a sign that he had some brains, but he had made a single phone call for his lawyer.

A firm in Manhattan that had yet to heed the call.

I wondered whether he had hoped to have Brinks represent him, and, if so, whether that meant he was unaware of Brinks' death? Or were there other attorneys to contend with? That thought haunted me whenever I checked for progress on my laptop, considering every possible path forward. The pressure grew to be a thing with legs when it collided precariously close to hurting the very creature I longed to save.

37

TROY

THE NEXT DAY, AS Gia finished making breakfast, the boxes began to arrive.

"What's all this?" She watched as I organized the first of three deliveries that day. "Surely the items I picked aren't arriving this quickly."

"I confess, I may have gone a little overboard a few nights back." I didn't try to hide my smile as she flicked a finger at the box on top of the stack, and I nodded for her to open it. "In my defense, I was trying to consider immediate needs, but future as well." I watched as she sliced open the first box and pulled back the packaging.

"Is all of this for Ben?" Her blue eyes were radiant as she lifted the first outfit for inspection. "You know he's completely happy in footie pajamas or a onesie." Spinning the tiny hangar, she giggled at the puppy dog embroidered on the backside of the tiny 9-12-month-old pants. "When did you..."

She lifted out a matching t-shirt and little socks with tiny puppy ears. Digging deeper, tears shone in her eyes when she reached the bibs, pacifiers, and teething rings.

"If there is something here you don't like, we can return it." I brushed a thumb across her cheek, digging my other hand deeper into the box to reveal my favorite selection. "But I insist we keep this."

"A tiny policeman outfit?" Her words fell on a laugh, and my heart clenched to hear it. She found the stuffed police bear and the new blue shield diaper bag. "I'm sensing a theme."

"A man must be properly dressed when he goes out." I opened the second box, lifting out a soft newsboy cap and matching bow tie. "If we can keep him from gnawing on them, he'll be a dapper man on the playground."

The third box was still unopened, but I knew it held basics in various sizes.

The boy would grow.

I'd be ready

"And you thought he'd like to try hiking?" Gia lifted the impulse hiking boots that would not be necessary for at least a year or two.

"I suppose I did go a little crazy when–" Her arms wrapped around my neck, stopping my words with her own.

"It's so perfect...and so much. I can't - ".

"Indulge me this...without protest," I added, waiting until I had her full attention, "because it is my joy." It took her but a moment to sigh before nodding agreement.

I'd won.

Her indulgence lasted through the afternoon's second delivery of clothes for her, and on into our evening, prepping dinner in the kitchen.

I loved sharing Nonna's sauce recipe, especially when she joked, 'I have the family recipe...guess I'm stuck with you now.'

At least she was on the same page.

The third delivery came via courier. I signed for the three small boxes, as she eyed me from the couch.

"A gift," I offered, peeking in the delivery box. "I'll present it to you at dinner."

"I think you've showered Ben and me with so much that whatever is in that box could hardly be called a gift as much as an indulgence." She smiled, fingers teasing the edge of the box.

"Then spoil you I shall." Pulling the box away, I kissed her hand, then swatted her backside. It was fast becoming my favorite thing.

Hosting my family with Gia was as easy as breathing. She moved, I moved, a delicate dance as if she'd been in my life for years. But lifetimes had been shared in our short time...hadn't they? It certainly felt like it as I silenced a call from my captain, knowing I was on borrowed time before the world would pull me away from her.

Unlike previous meals, I didn't give the girls a moment to sequester Gia for a grilling, not wanting her to think about the stress from recent days. I wanted her present...with me...until I could present my final gift. As we neared the end of the meal, I handed each of my brothers one of the three gift boxes. I suspected they'd told their wives ahead of time, their faces showing no sign of surprise, but for Gia, this would be new. She sensed the shift in the room, as each woman gave her box and her husband their full attention. I reached over and grabbed her chair leg, tugging it towards me until we were knee to knee. The glimpse of a smile she gave while moving immediately dropped, as did her jaw, when she eyed the velvet box in my hand.

"I know what it looks like." I kept my voice soft and low. "It's not that kind of jewelry." Dropping to a whisper just for her, I added, "Yet." I slid to my knees, removed her shoes, and lifted one foot to rest in the middle of my chest as I rolled the edge of her jeans up, revealing her delicate ankle.

"We've each experienced losing one of you at one point." I felt, more than I saw, that my brothers shared a knowing glance. "A few days ago, I witnessed firsthand the moment I thought I'd lost you." Squeezing Gia's leg, I couldn't help but kiss her knee, pausing just a moment to breathe in her scent.

"Troy," My name was an exhale from her lips, and I opened my eyes to see her blushing, eyes darting around the room. "I'm so sorry that I–"

"This gift, this anklet," I said, opening the box and lifting out the delicate gold chain with a single circular charm. "Holds a GPS tracker inside."

"Each of them is linked to our phones." Sam picked up the explanation. "They won't buzz...won't flash...no one will know they're sending a signal."

Lila and Moira exchanged glances full of meaning, then nodded in understanding. Gia's eyes, however, were still wide with an emotion I could only name as surprise...or apprehension.

"You won't even feel it," I reassured, pulling her focus back to me as I gently clasped the chain around her ankle. "But I will. I'll know you're safe, even when you're not in arm's reach." Gia leaned forward, her fingers brushing the edge of the chain as her eyes searched mine. "Until I can make it safe, for good."

I lifted my hand, showing her the braided leather bracelet I wore, which held a matching circular charm; Chase and Sam did the same.

"I don't give this to you as a leash, but as a tether. Both ways. You will always know where I am, and I will always know where you are." Gia's foot dropped, and she leaned forward a little more, tugging my wrist close enough to inspect the bracelet.

"You need this?" Her request was quiet as she considered the gift.

"You...need this." Letting my words say less than my eyes and my tone, I silently commanded, begged her to accept this. Her hand cupped my jaw, and the sheen of tears in her eyes made me long to scoop her up and haul her to our bedroom. "This," I whispered, needing to hear the words. "Will keep you safer." She considered me for a heartbeat longer, torturing me as I placed a kiss in her palms, willing my body to still, my heart to steady, waiting for an eternity.

"And when the danger is done?" She asked the question to me, but I caught her glance at my family as if confirming their feelings on the matter.

I needed to tread carefully.

I would not be the monster her father had been, but I also couldn't lie and ignore my true nature. As I tried to find the words to convey what I needed, in a way that didn't sound crazy or over-whelming, it was Chase who came to my rescue.

"For now. This is needed and good." He glanced at his wife, who nodded. "And we can reevaluate everything...when it's finally done."

The room felt electrified as they all, one by one, agreed.

Only after did I look up at my beautiful siren, still kneeling at her goddess-feet, the beast in me all but howling for her total submission to this small trinket that would keep her in my grasp.

"Please, Gia," I begged, eyes closing in prayer. "I can't lose you again."

"Okay." I snapped my eyes to hers, reveling in the slight curl in her lips. "Yes, Troy. I will wear this–for you."

Air whooshed out of my lungs as my hands slipped around her waist and I crawled between her knees until my head was in her lap. Blood was pumping so loudly in my ears that I almost couldn't hear Lila's murmured question.

"Did we just witness a hostage proposal?"

"With jewelry," Moira whispered. "That tracks."

Wilder Bro's Group Chat

Me: I need an assist.

Chase: Name it.

Me: I have to go to the station.

Chase: PTO tapped out?

Me: Paperwork on the perp who attacked Gia.

Sam: How you spinning it?

Me: No idea.

Chase: Where do you need us?

Me: Gia wants to get out of the cabin. I'd rather she be with one of you.

Chase: Copy that. Moira will be thrilled.

Sam: You two set a date yet?

Me: Date?

Chase: He means that epic proposal you pulled.

Sam: Don't play dumb, Grandpa.

Chase: You got on one knee and swore a lifetime of fealty.

Sam: And she said yes!

Me: I hardly have words.

Chase: Tread carefully, TJ. She looked half-spooked for a minute there.

Sam: Should've seen her the night they went shopping. #DeerInHeadlights

Me: Gia is fine.

Chase: You're acting like she'll get snatched out of thin air.

Me: Enough.

Sam: We get it—shit's tense.

Me: I said... enough.

Chase: Bro. We've got your back.

Sam: Like you've always had ours.

Me: Have you forgotten her father RUNS Apex?

Me: The same Apex that tried to kill Moira and Lila.

Chase: Fuck, dude. We get it.

Sam: We're with you, TJ. Jesus.

Me: I won't lose her.

Chase: You're not doing this alone!

38

TROY

R EALITY HAD BEEN CHARGING at me for days, my captain at the helm. His messages had grown fever-pitched, and his fourth message landed like an anvil.

> **Captain: Get your ass in the station or I'm sending a Uni to haul you in!**

I'd been keeping tabs on the gunman's progress on my laptop. From the cabin to the hospital, then into a cell once his foot was determined to be a grazing wound. He'd not bothered to plead for his innocence, but he had made a single phone call for his lawyer. A firm in Manhattan that had yet to heed the call.

I wondered whether he had hoped to have Brinks represent him, and, if so, whether that meant he was unaware of Brinks' death? Or were there other high-paid attorneys to contend with? That thought plagued all night, holding a boneless Gia sleeping in my arms as I considered every possible path forward. Preparing for work the next morning was as familiar as it was uncomfortable. My routine of shower, dress, gun and badge on, coffee to go, suddenly felt like an ill-fitting pair of shoes.

My head knew I had to go, my body screamed to stay.

I called to see if Lila had found anything yet, and she lamented the slowness of her ability to hack the shipping records to find container contents and travel plans. Gia was happy to spend a day with Moira and the girls. Pleased as I was to see her comfort with my family, I was a little jealous that today's smiles wouldn't be for me. Leaving her and Ben with a kiss, I could hear Chase's warning in my ear from our text. 'Tread carefully, TJ.'

He was right–I was obsessing.

Entering the station, I was bombarded with familiar smells and sounds as I waved through the metal detector and badged into the back offices. Entering the primary bullpen of desks, a fellow officer, Sgt. Jake teased my absentee status before launching into his regular lamenting of his wife of 30 years for her honey-do list, which he so loathed—mundane and droll. I'd give anything for such a list from Gia. I was near-relieved when my name was bellowed across the room.

"Wilder!" My Captain's voice beckoned impatiently from his office. "Get your ass in here."

Jake whistled low under raised eyebrows as I closed the door to the captain's office.

"Jesus Christ, Wilder. In all my years, I don't think I've ever seen you drop the ball on a case like this."

"My apologies for not coming sooner." I began, banking on my reputation to buy me the time I needed. "I was keeping tabs on things, I just–"

"Can it!" The captain held up a thick finger in emphasis as he commanded, "I'm giving you exactly one opportunity to come clean about what the hell went on at your cabin and why I've had fuck-all to show for it with reports unfiled by my best goddamn detective." He set his hand down and looked me square in the eyes and added, "And it better be good, cause this morning, the shit show leveled up."

I watched as his eyes darted to a lidded bankers' box marked 'evidence' while deciding what to share and what not to share.

"Of course," I breathed, centering myself and slipping my mask in place. "The man appeared on the trail behind my cabin with a gun. I subdued him. Intent unknown. I hoped we'd get more on him at interrogation."

"And why were you at one of your rental cabins?" The captain cocked an eyebrow as his go-to questioning tone took center stage.

He was interrogating...me.

"I have been staying at the cabin to be closer to my brother's and their family. Both Chase and Sam are building houses, and given our real estate work, proximity makes it–"

"And the woman?" I had to draw in a slow breath to hold my restraint in place as my hackles rose at the mere mention of my siren. "Who's the woman with no last name on the report?"

"Someone I've been seeing." I forced a thin smile, willing nonchalance and confidence into my words. "The encounter understandably rattled her, but she is fine." I needed to side-step this as quickly as possible, so I regained control by standing. "I can interrogate the perp now, see what I can get out of him, and then finish up the paperwork. This mess will be off your desk by the end of–"

"Perps dead." My blood ran cold.

"Dead?" I'd checked the system just yesterday before dinner; there was no mention of the perp being ill or at any risk. "How is that possible?" My first thoughts went to Jensen and how Brinks somehow managed to have him declared dead when he wasn't.

"Happened in the night. Guards found him this morning. M.E.'s first guess is coronary. He'll rush an autopsy for me and get the results stat." He reached for the lidded banker's box and slid it to me. "Here's all we had on the guy. Some low-level criminal. Rap sheet for GTA, B&E, and a few assaults. He was screaming for his lawyer, but refused to talk, so we had nothing else."

My relief that the man hadn't given up Gia's identity fell flat as I saw his belongings bagged and tagged for evidence, including his cell phone. Rummaging through the box, finding nothing else of worth, I wondered if there were other mentions of her on his phone record or a connecting thread back to her father. If there was, how could I get my hands on it?

"No next of kin?" I asked, still white-knuckling my outer calm even as my inner shit began to unravel.

What if this guy wrote a text about Gia's whereabouts?

What if the trip to the store were just one careless way I'd put her at risk?

What if her father was lying in wait for me to leave her...Like I had this morning?

Fool. Fool!

"Not that I could find...But I wouldn't look like you would, ammiright?" I glanced at the box, dying to get started. "Perp's cell is dead, but since you're here, find a charger and see if you can find anything on it, will ya?" I nodded, dropping the lid on the box and hoping he didn't see my shaking hands.

I had to get to Gia.

I needed to call and make sure they were okay.

My brothers would want to know.

"I'll start right away." Turning to leave, the Captain stopped me halfway out the door.

"Autopsy notwithstanding, this was damn sloppy work, Wilder." He ran his hands over his face. "And the first time I've seen you leave shit incomplete. I'm gonna go out on a limb and guess this woman isn't some casual date." I stared blankly, not wanting to offer any more details than I had to. "And you aren't just staying at the cabin for the sake of your brother's and their families either." I prepared to lie like a cheap rug if that's what it took to shield Gia and Ben. "Eh...You deserve a little happiness, ya tight-lipped bastard." My relief...was a thing with wings. "When the dust settles on this, bring her around. I'd love to meet her."

With a disbelieving nod, I walked to my desk, set the box down, and immediately lifted my phone to call Gia. To my relief, my phone already had a picture waiting from her and Moira. Full selfie mode, on the floor, surrounded by babies, toys, and what appeared to be mimosas. The ease of seeing her was temporary as I plugged in the perp's phone, setting it aside while dialing my girl.

"You've not been gone an hour, Sergeant Wilder." Her voice was fluid and smiling, her happiness damn near sparkling through the phone.

"I was," I hesitated as the perp's phone lit up, coming online. "Calling to check in. Your picture made it seem like a good time is being had."

As the screen came on, I immediately navigated to the text messages, finding all the threats he'd continued sending to Gia. I wanted to resurrect the man and kill him again for the filthy words he used near the end.

"Yes! We have snacks, and a billion pillows on the floor, and Moira is showing off some of her yoga poses...badly." She snickered a laugh, muffled as if her hand was over her mouth. I hated to rip this moment from her, but their safety was paramount. "Her balance is terrible cause her girls are tugging her hair." She laughed again, and one of the twins squealed in the background as I navigated to the only other text chain saved in the phone—messages between my dead perp and another unknown number.

> Unknown: Have you found the girl yet?

> Unknown: What about the books and the baby?

> Unknown: Your silence is problematic. Report.

> Unknown: I expect a response within 24 hours; otherwise, your contract will be terminated.

All four messages were unread; the most recent one was sent two days ago.

The 24 hours would have been up at 8 pm last night.

"Did you need something?" Gia's voice pulled me back to our chat. My mind split between needing to exist in her space and this nagging thought burning through my brain: Was 'contract terminated' code for dead?

We knew that Brinks was able to fake Jensen's death. His ability to manipulate system paperwork aside, I had no idea what other shadow agents were placed around town. Could someone have snuck in and terminated this perp's contract? Would the M.E. find poison, or some other nefarious means of a heart attack? If so, was it an officer, a visitor, or some other as yet discovered threat that I was ill-prepared for, and if so, who else was in town searching for my family?

It was all too much–Too many threads to pull, and I was unraveling by the second.

I was running out of time and resources to get everything done.

"Not at all, love. I merely needed to hear your voice."

"I know you didn't want to go in today. But we're okay." Gia was a balm, caressing the edges of me as if she'd reached right through the phone. "And I know you'll be back as soon as you can." Such beautiful, blind trust she'd given in those few words.

She felt safe, and she trusted me to return.

More than that, she was happy and laughing.

I had no reason, beyond paralyzing fear, to remove that peace from her.

"Be good," I commanded, knowing my brothers would help me. "Send more pictures." I wanted to see her happy. I needed her reporting in.

"Aye, Aye, Boss Man."

Immediately, I fired up my laptop, clicking through the system to see any preliminary reports on the perp's death. With nothing on record yet, I tossed everything into the box, grabbed my phone, and began texting my brothers.

"Not so fast, Wilder." My captain's interruption set my teeth on edge, and my frustration grew in my chest. "I need you back in the office this weekend. There's schmoozing to be done."

"My PTO is through-"

"Save it." He lifted a hand, silencing my protest. "The mayor's in a tizzy about the new library opening. Expects the full dog and pony. We'll have Uni's there but need plain clothes on the scene for extra security."

"A library re-opening hardly needs extra security?" I protested, trying to keep my voice level despite the clanging alarm bells as I gripped the file box to the point of crumpling.

"There'll be media. It'll be a chaotic mess." The captain waved it off casually, but blood was rushing in my head. "The mayor controls the budget...and you volunteered for that damn committee." It was all I could do not to quit on the spot; to flee my old life and run home to rescue Gia and Ben so they would never be in harm's way again.

I had no time for duties.

I had no way of escaping them.

My vast lack of fucks was stifling as I stormed out of the station, even as my better reasoning reminded me, my position on the force still provided the best insights into Apex's movements. And I could hardly provide for Gia and Ben if I were unemployed.

Glancing at my phone, I saw my brother's frantic response to my earlier text.

> Me: Headed to the Morgue.

> Chase: What?

> Sam: Who died!?

I climbed in, fired up my truck, and fired off an answer that I knew would blow their world up like it had mine.

> Me: The perp who was stalking Gia.

> Sam: Jesus Fuck.

> Chase: On my way.

> Sam: Be there in 10.

39

TROY

C HASE AND SAM MET me at the morgue. Flashing my badge, the attendant buzzed us through the secure doors, where the sterile antiseptic smell of cold, dead air assaulted us. Sam led the way to a small room, where a wall of coolers stood watch over a single metal gurney.

"Morning, gentlemen." The medical examiner peered over the edge of his magnifying specs, scalpel in hand. "I was unaware I'd have an audience for the autopsy."

"Hey, Lou," I answered, working to keep my voice professional. "I was hoping to close the case quickly, before the mayor's big weekend shindig." The M.E. tipped his head in acknowledgement. "Is this the perp from lock-up?"

"Mr. Robert Smythe, age 34. I was just about to make the first cut, but I can wait a beat if you need to," He gave my brothers a questioning glance. "Discuss the case?"

"Do you have an official cause of death?" Sam asked.

"Initial lividity is more pronounced here," he waved a hand around the edges of the torso. "And up near the face. Both indicators of blood flow disruption common to myocardial infarction. I'd say Mr. Smythe barely felt it when his heart all but stopped."

"So...big ass heart-attack." Sam translated, handing over a pair of dry nitrile gloves to both Chase and me.

"We need to discuss a few details, Lou," I confirmed. "If I could have a moment," I waved the case file in my hand as Lou dropped the scalpel onto the metal tray with a clang.

"No problem, officer. I need to catch up on a little charting anyway. Just tap the window on your way out." His shoes squeaked on the linoleum as he exited cold storage and headed to his office, which had a large glass window.

Circling the table, I pulled the sheet down to expose the bruised face of the man whom I'd last seen bleeding at my feet.

"What do we know about him?" Chase asked.

"Almost nothing. I set the file on the sheeted body, opening to the small rap sheet. "Small time, a few Grand Thefts and a B&E back in New York. No known next of kin."

"Connection to Apex?" Sam began lifting the fingers, inspecting them with rapt attention.

"None. Made a single call to a Manhattan law firm that went unanswered." I watched as Sam rounded the table to inspect the other hand.

"Did he identify Gia?" Chase was now flipping through the file. "I don't see her name."

"From what I can tell, he hadn't spoken to anyone." I watched as Sam continued his inspection down the body. "If he were answering directly to her father, he'd have left her name out until instructed otherwise. It's just a guess, though."

"I don't see any signs of injections under the nails or between the digits." Sam stood at last. "Most common spots for an injectable-induced cardiac event."

"So you think it's natural causes?" Chase's raised eyebrows matched my own.

"Autopsy would say for sure." Coming to stand by my side, Sam sighed. "But Lila found something." I leaned forward, knuckles on the edge of the exam table. "I called her on my way here. Told her what was up." Sam gave me a quick, complicated glance. "She's bringing her gun to Moira's house. Figured you'd wanna know." I nodded. "She's still working on that ledger Gia stole, but the few shipping containers she identified were found in criminal cases."

"Shocker." Chase huffed.

"Two were stopped at the Mexico border, full of guns." He crossed his arms, dragging in a breath. "Third hit a Midwest Canadian border full of Opioids."

"Drugs and guns." I sighed. The new information fit into everything I suspected.

Gia's father, a sitting senator, was the head of an organization that paraded itself as humanitarian but pulled favors and votes by moving cargo loads of drugs and guns. I knew he'd been cruel to her, too. She hadn't given me details yet, but she ran out of the very thought Ben could grow up in the shadow of that. My fists clenched and unclenched, imagining all the possible ways she'd been hurt, and what Ben's placement could have meant.

"Jesus Christ." Chase's words echoed around the otherwise silent room. "What are the chances the other shipments are the same?"

"Or worse," I mumbled, head still bowed, as the worst of the possibilities played through my head—visions of Moira in that fire after being kidnapped and assaulted multiple times by a low-level Apex lackey.

"Or what?"

"OR WORSE!" I snapped, instantly pacing while my brothers' eyes bore down on me. "Lila witnessed the murder of two cops, her family, and she'd been honing in on a string of dead women no one would claim."

Drugs, guns, and women. My heart all but stopped as I sucked in air, and Sam and Chase's eyes on me told me they were connecting dots too.

"Gia ran because her father was gonna ship her into an arranged marriage to someone, anyone, including the same evil mother fucker who killed Lila's family!" I could feel Sam bristle at my words, even as he cast eyes on the windowed office. "And he took Ben, MY BEN, to farm him out to strangers for what?!"

"Hey, Troy, man," Chase was at my side, his big body blocking me from the M.E.'s window.

"WHY WOULDN'T THAT BASTARD BE TRAFFICKING WOMEN AND CHILDREN if it gets him what he wants!"

"Alright. TJ. We hear you, man." Sam flanked me, both blocking my view of the medical examiner. "We get it. It's bad. But let's take a beat."

"I can't take-"

"You can." Chase cut me short. "You have to. You can't lose your shit right here." He stepped closer, nodding at Sam. "We're taking a walk."

Without another word, Chase's big hands had my bicep in his grip, and we exited, Sam following behind with the file in hand. Whatever he mumbled to the M.E. on his way out was lost, throbbing in my brain as my heart galloped catastrophically forward towards every possible bloody ruined ending.

Gia, one in a sea of faceless victims.

Ben, another nameless asset, pawned around.

"Take a breath." Sam's voice filtered in. Somehow, we were at my truck.

I didn't remember walking.

Just the roaring in my skull.

"Take a goddamn breath, Troy!" Sam was loud, commanding, and I wanted to punch his fucking lights out.

Didn't he see how Gia and Ben needed me? Both utterly helpless in the hands of a political power so immense that we barely scratched the surface of, and now both mine to somehow disentangle and shield, and I'd already failed her once.

"Come on, Grandpa, we need you here." Sam sounded distant and steady. "They need you."

They needed me here.

I wanted blood.

"We need your brain, man." Chase was in front of me now, crouching in front of me with his big ass muscles. "No one knows the law on this more than you."

"Deep breath." Sam's hand on my wrist finally pulled me out of myself enough to realize they were right. "She's okay. Everyone you love is okay. But you need to take a step back. We don't know he's trafficking humans. Just drugs and guns."

"The law can't help us," I gasped, my cognitive processes finally firing. "Unless we find a connection from Apex to Gia's father or even something concrete on him, the law is impotent...I'm impotent here." Standing, I lifted my hands over my head and began pacing again. "Only Gia seems to know that Apex belongs to her father. We have only her word and nothing more. Even if she testified, shared everything she'd ever seen or heard, it'd be hearsay." My lungs burned. I'd been gasping for how long?

"Okay...the law is out." Sam crossed his arms, casting a worried glance I couldn't think about to Chase. "What else can we do? Did you get anything from Smythe before he died?"

"Only a cell phone." I waved a hand at my truck. "I was hoping Lila could dig into it, maybe trace the account or any calls/text messages."

"She's good. She'll find it." Chase reassured. "Do we need to move the girls?"

"From what I could tell, Smythe hadn't had a chance to disclose anything on Gia's whereabouts." Calm returning, a rush of embarrassment began closing in...I'd lost my shit.

"So the girls are safe," Sam parroted. "No one knows where Gia and Ben are. We are all staying in unlisted cabins, not in our direct names, and Jensen, Brinks, and this Smythe guy are all dead." I couldn't help the small huff of laughter as I saw him line up the punchline. "Oorah."

"Oorah." Chase lifted a fist, our old Marine shout-out still our mantra when something went our way in bloody fashion.

"Oorah," I answered with a knuckle-bump, knowing they were right.

For now, Gia and Ben, my family, my world, were safe.

"Let's get back to the house." Sam, the apparent voice of reason, now that mine had fled. "Let's get the phone to Lila, update everyone, and we'll discuss next steps."

40

GIA

THE CARAVAN OF BROTHERS pulled into the driveway like a cavalry, busting through the front door in a cloud of testosterone-soaked tension. Troy found me immediately, beelining to hug me and check on Ben with an odd sense of urgency. Moira, Lila, and I exchanged knowing looks as their husbands did the same.

Whatever they'd discovered at the morgue had them all rattled.

Lila had already shared that the man who hunted me, attacked me, and nearly shot Troy...was now dead. I felt terrible for being relieved, but reading the additional messages he'd tried to send to my old phone squelched that guilt pretty quickly. The man's descriptive threats painted a grim picture of what he wanted to do to me.

The immediate threat was gone, and Lila was holding the man's cell phone for tracking, but Troy still carried a low simmering agitation. He wasn't clinging to me, constantly pulling me to him, but I could see the restraint in how he moved. Hands that had just pulled back from white-knuckle gripping the steering wheel, and flexing jaw muscles of gritted teeth between words spoken with a forced calm that was palpable. He was lost in his phone and laptop, searching...for something. I tried to ask what he had focused on, and he told me a kind lie as he angled his laptop out of my view; 'It's nothing important: I need to catch up on paperwork from the office.'

I tried to let the matter go, but his silence was making me nervous. I thought about it all night, until I got Ben to sleep, worrying myself into knots until I finally decided enough was enough. Troy had told me time and again that I could trust him, lean on him, and never needed to apologize for my wants or needs.

Surely, I could extend that same courtesy to him.

Slipping into the bathroom, I freshened up my hair, glossed my lips, and donned the slinky black nightgown with the high thigh slit and teeny spaghetti straps. Looking at myself in the mirror, I barely recognized the woman trying her hand at seduction. Gone was the naive, sheltered girl, though my continual tug between lowering the slit and raising my top belied that my confidence could still use some work. I hated how uncomfortable I felt and worried that I was missing sexy and landing somewhere in the land of cheap. Still, I was determined, so with another flip and fluff of my hair, I told myself the thin silk fabric was armor and ventured forth.

At the hallway's edge, I leaned against the framing and watched as Troy stared intently at his laptop again. His brow was drawn low, jaw clenched, as he scrolled past images or articles or whatever it was that had his entire body coiled for battle.

So much stress and worry because of me.

Because of my father and what I took from him.

Because Troy chose to hide me...to help me.

Thinking through my short time with Troy, I couldn't help but remember all he'd given and how he treated my body with reverence. That was what finally had my feet moving, even before my courage fully showed up at the party. Troy deserved nothing less than the same reverence he'd offered, and if my body soothed him before, maybe I could give him this again.

"We need to talk." I forced my voice to steadiness, grabbing a throw cushion from the couch as I slipped past it.

"A moment more, Love." His eyes were glued to the laptop even as his hand reached out mindlessly in my direction. Swallowing my nerves, I tried again, willing an edge into my tone.

I could do this. I could be bold and demand what I wanted.

"No." I stepped into his open hand, his fingers grasping the thin silk just as his eyes snapped away from his laptop, and to me. "Now, please."

Troy blindly closed the computer with his free hand, turning in his chair to face me in a full manspread. His eyes grazed down the black nightgown, his hands sliding from thigh to waist before tugging me closer.

"I wondered when I'd get to see this."

His voice had shifted back from the edge of strained cordiality and slipped into a low, husky tone I loved so much. But it wasn't quite the tone I was looking for.

"I was saving it for something special." I ignored the blush in my cheeks and focused on his hands tugging me between his spread knees. "But you seemed to need it tonight." He slid his hands around my waist, burying his face into my belly and squeezing into me.

"I am sorry. I don't mean—"

"You. *Don't*. Apologize." It was beyond, over the top, bold for me to cut him off. Even my voice didn't sound like my own. But I'd started this seduction, and his apology risked derailing me into a spiral of self-pity or doubt. I blame the nightgown's silky armor for what I said next. "Tonight, I want to learn how to please you." Troy pulled back, eyes locked on mine like he wasn't sure if he'd heard me right.

I stepped back and dropped the pillow to the floor in front of me.

"You've done nothing but give to me." I slowly lowered to my knees. "You have given your home," I settled back on my feet, "and you're family," I let my hands trail up his thighs, loving how his jaw dropped and his pupils blew wide. "You've provided me with every comfort I could ask for." I found his belt, tugging at the polished leather. "You've cared for me in every way imaginable." Lost in my actions, I fought a smile as I found the button to his pants. "And you've shown me, body and soul, how cherished I am to you."

"You don't need to—" His hands halted me, his expression a mixture of worry and lust.

"I want to do this," I flipped his tie over his shoulder, and tugged his pants open, channeling all my nerves into the steady slide of his zipper. "I need you to teach me how you like it."

"Gia." He sighed, my hand around his length—I had him.

A full-body shiver rolled through me, part nerves, part want, when he shifted his hips until he was bared to me. I knew Troy was blessed in size. Every surface of this house—walls, tables, beds—was a memory burned into my skin of a time he'd stretched me with the sheer mass of him. But seeing his cock this close, thick, veined, and hard as steel, was awe-inspiring.

"Do I stroke you like this?" I squeezed his shaft, tugging down to the base, then lifting to the tip. At his groan, I leaned forward to taste the bead of precum glistening at the tip.

Salt...and desire.

"Okay, Siren."

There it was.

That commanding timbre I was waiting for.

"Seeing as you're so determined," he wrapped his hand around mine, adding more pressure and driving our combined grip down and up. Arousal dripped down my inner walls, making my core ache as he tangled his other hand in the hair at the back of my head, the bite of pain sending me soaring. "Open for me." I did as he asked, swirling my tongue around the tip before lowering my head into his lap. "Start slow...squeeze me with your hand as you go."

The feel of him in my mouth was incredibly arousing. He was hard, but smooth, and my tongue reveled at the feel of the ridge where his flared head met the shaft. I lingered there a time or two, loving the moans I was rewarded with. Troy slid down in the chair, leaning further back, which gave me better access. I pushed lower, testing my limit. The second his head hit the back of my throat, my shoulders jolted—my inexperience showing as I struggled to hold composure.

"Now," He threaded his other hand into my hair, fashioning a makeshift ponytail. "Look at me."

I lifted my eyes as he gently wiped away a tear. He was magnificent. Commanding. Loving. Everything I never knew I'd always wanted, and I lived to please him.

"Relax your jaw...and suck that cock."

I had only a moment to breathe before Troy shoved my mouth back down.

My hand was the only thing saving me from completely choking, guided up and down his length at an ever-increasing speed. Mouth watering, he grew harder as I worked, savoring each little groan and grunt he offered to prove he was enjoying me. My core clenched around nothing as I felt the tug of my hair, and I squeezed my thighs together for any friction.

I wanted him, wanted to feel him touch me.

"Fuck, Gia...your mouth," His voice was growling, desperate even, as I licked and sucked, swallowed and gagged, my way around his cock. "So hot...so...fuck." The head of his cock began to swell as his words grew more ragged. He gripped my hair tightly, and his thighs flexed and tightened. "Goddamnit, Siren."

Gripping my head in his hands, his hips lifted.

I gladly handed him the control he needed.

"I'm gonna cum," he growled, hips lifting with raw, relentless force—fucking my mouth with abandon. "You don't spill a drop, you hear me?"

He punctuated each word with a thrust—

"Not."

"One."

"Fucking."

"Drop."

His rhythm grew frantic, taking me deeper and deeper as I desperately gasped for breath between his uneven and unyielding thrusts before–

"Giaaaaah!"

Hot spurts of spicy, thick liquid shot into my mouth, and I heeded his command to swallow every...last...drop. Greedily, loving his taste almost as much as I needed his touch on my swollen and needy clit, I licked and sucked him clean until Troy yanked me off the floor, laid me across the table like a beast unleashed, and devoured me within an inch of my life.

Wilder Sisters Group Chat

Moira: OMG—Carol just texted me a flyer about the library event. There'll be a petting zoo and face painting!

Me: Really?

Lila: Sam's working the first aid station.

Moira: Chase too. The fire station's doing a "touch-a-truck" with one of their rigs.

Me: Aw, that sounds so cute.

Moira: Since Troy's working it too... I say we make it a family outing.

Lila: I hear the food truck selection will be on point.

Me: Nausea is finally letting up?

Lila: Feed me. Feed me now.

Moira: YAY! We can meet at your place, Gia. Troy can load Ben's car seat in my SUV before he leaves, and we'll all carpool over.

Me: I need to check with Troy... but it sounds fantastic.

Moira: Remind him your bad guy is pushing daisies now.

Lila: And that the cell showed no signs of anyone knowing where you are.

Me: It'd be so great to take Ben to see the animals.

Moira: I wanna introduce my girls to the library crew!

Lila: So... 9 a.m. at Gia's?

Moira: Yes! This is gonna be great!

41

GIA

FOR THE FIRST TIME in my life...I felt like I could breathe.

As much as Mr. Smythe's body had rattled Troy, I absorbed the news differently. Knowing that my father's last known communication hadn't given anything away about my whereabouts brought light to my world. We'd made it. I was okay...Ben was okay. We were free.

By some miracle of fate or destiny, we'd landed in the arms of a wonderful man. We were safe and provided for and ... loved. Of that, I had no doubt. Troy loved me. He loved me, flaws and insecurities, and he'd asked nothing in return in his deep, abiding care for me and Ben.

I'd never been so cherished.

I knew I'd never find such love ever again.

I never wanted to try.

Along with Troy, I'd been gifted a family too, and Moira & Lila's group chat was a constant source of happiness for me, right down to its title, 'Wilder Sisters Chat'. They considered me a sister and treated me accordingly, and I loved them almost as fiercely as I did Troy. So their text about the library event was blissfully normal and represented a turning point; an end of my sequestering.

"You seem extra happy." Troy leaned in to kiss the top of Ben's head, even as I bobbed and weaved with the spoon, attempting to introduce a vegetable. "Does this mean little man is enjoying peas?" Ben's well-timed raspberry answered for me.

"He enjoys turning my shirt into a Jackson Pollack." I tossed the spoon and bowl onto the table and grabbed the wipes to clean us both off. "But I'm not sure much actual food is making it in his mouth." Ben smiled, sliding his hands back and forth across the tray with glee, finger-painting in green. "Moira and Lila were texting about the library's grand opening this weekend."

Troy's audible groan was expected, as he'd done almost nothing but lament his time on the committee, but I had a plan.

"Oh...don't be grumpy. Look!" I held my phone out so he could see the group chat between the girls and me. "There's going to be a petting zoo! Wouldn't that be amazing for Ben?" I pointed out Lila's comment about the food truck. "And I know you and all the guys are working, but maybe I could bring you something for lunch and—"

"Wait." He gripped my hand, pulling the phone closer. "You three are planning to go?"

"Well...yes." He flinched like my words held all the weight of an emotional wrecking ball. "The man, Smythe, is gone." I quickly reassured, prepared for Troy's apprehension.

"It's not a good idea." His tone was smooth and even, but the feathering of his jaw muscle was singing a different song. He was controlling his anxiety.

284

"And remember, Lila told us the cell phone had no connections to me." Goosebumps covered my arms as an old familiar sensation settled in my chest at Troy's visible agitation. "I understand your worries. But I'm okay." I motioned to my body, willing him to see how happy and healthy I was...because of him. "We've gone out before, remember? Just to the store. It was fine."

I knew the moment the words left my mouth that I'd made a mistake.

"Losing you there? Yes, *that* I remember!" Troy tossed a hand towards the back deck as his voice lashed out, whip sharp. "Having a man rip you from my arms at gunpoint as we hiked? Yes, Gia. *That*...I remember."

Hurt stung my eyes as the memories collapsed the small bubble of sunshine I had naively surrounded myself with. I was excited, and Troy was ruining it with his worry and gruffness, and the last feeling I wanted from him was suffocation in the name of protection.

"Your father," He softened his voice, and it was at once irritating and placating as his words slammed my life before into the emotions of the moment.

"Is still in New York!" I hardly recognized the sharpness in my voice as the words flew out, unbidden. "He can't find me here, we've proven that, right?"

Troy blinked at me, as surprised by my outburst as I was. Seconds, lifetimes, of emotions flicked past his gaze as he took me in. The scrutiny was unbearable.

"We can't be sure until he's apprehended...Love, I *have* to keep you *safe*."

"You mean keep me *hidden*?" A weight bottomed out in my gut as the cabin walls grew thicker, and before I realized what I was doing, I

285

had Ben unbuckled from his highchair. "Guess the conversation's done then."

"Please...Gia." Troy stepped towards me, hands outstretched, as I stepped towards the bedroom. "I am sorry...I was too curt with you."

Bile, hot and thick, bubbled up as my father's words rang through Troy's voice. *'I was, perhaps, too curt with you.'* Papa dressed up control as love, and I'd been so saturated in it I couldn't see it for what it was. And here was Troy, parading as protection.

"Let me explain."

Surely not the fire from the frying pan. Please God, not that.

"Ben needs a bath," I mumbled, leaving Troy in the crackling silence behind me as I reimagined the gilded bars I'd left behind...as cabin walls.

WILDER FAMILY GROUP CHAT

-3-

Me: I made a mistake.

Moira: ?

Me: Earlier today…Gia was excited about the library event.

Me: I said no.

Chase: Oh shit.

Sam: the fuck, dude?

Me: It caught me off guard…I overreacted. She's been avoiding me ever since.

Lila: So you're why she went radio silent?

Me: We haven't caught her father or Apex yet. Her safety is everything.

Moira: Safety isn't a CAGE, Troy.

Chase: Dude, no one gets this more than we do.

Sam: We wouldn't let our wives go if we didn't think it was safe.

Moira: We'll LITERALLY all be with her.

Lila: Remember me - the ex-cop with killer aim and shiny new gun?

Me: I can't lose her and Ben.

Chase: You can't lock her up, TJ. Not even for the right reasons.

Me: I'm not trying to cage her.

Moira: So she survived that monster and signed on as your prisoner.

Me: SHE'S NOT A PRISONER!

Sam: You sure she knows that?

Me: She won't even look at me.

Lila: If she pulled back, it's because she thinks SHE messed up—

Lila: —when really, YOU did.

Moira: Suffocation. Isn't. Protection.

Me: What do I do?

Sam: Apologize

Chase: A lot...maybe beg.

Moira: Lila and I will be there at 10 tomorrow.

Lila: And you'll put Ben's car seat in Moira's car.

Moira: The girls will love the baby goats.

Lila: I'm getting little Ben's face painted.

Me: You…seriously still mean to go?

Chase: They're SERIOUSLY supporting Gia.

Lila: You should fucking try it.

42

TROY

I POSITIONED MYSELF IN Gia's line of sight all that night. Not to press, but let her know I was here for her. I hoped she'd reach out to me...to bring us back to where I was her peace. She was still, always, my center.

It was foolish–I hadn't earned it.

That fact hit hard when I secured the cabin for the night and found her asleep, curled into a ball, one gorgeous leg slipped gracefully outside the covers, and my pillow...missing. It wasn't on the floor. She wasn't hugging it. My chest burned as I seethed across the hall and found it on the guest bed—her silent stand.

My siren had summarily removed me.

Me...who'd sheltered her.

Me...worshipped her.

Me...who loved her and...who'd hurt her?

My jaw locked around the ugly truth. Grabbing my pillow, I slunk back to our bedroom, kissing Ben. His little purring breaths only barely soothed the ache in my chest. Settling into the chair, I admired Gia's raven locks sprayed out behind her, taking up the space I once called mine.

Tonight, I had the chair. My words, delivered carelessly, had stripped away the security I'd given her. The beast in me gnashed at the renewed boundary, but if my protection felt like suffocation, then I deserved the chair.

The morning came with quiet tension.

She handled breakfast for her and Ben, and I had to admit a particular pride in her surprising temper. She smiled when I found the coffee pot empty, even leveling me with a look over the rim of her mug before returning her attention to Ben. Such beautiful defiance.

She hadn't lost her voice.

My family arrived in a flurry as I donned my holster and unlocked my guns. It was earlier than anticipated—but clearly by design—as Moira strolled past my scowl, a baby on each hip, and snarked:

"Smile, Sergeant. It's not Gia's job to make you feel better while you work out your issues."

I opened my mouth to argue, but Sam halted me with a slap on my shoulder.

"If you hadn't fixed it by now, it'll have to wait. We gotta help set up, right?" Gia had honed in on the twins, actively using my family as human shields, which chafed at my need to wrap her in my arms.

"I'll move over the car seat," Chase sighed, his eyes glancing between me and my girl. "But that's all the time I'm giving you."

"Don't," Lila cut in, finger in my chest and eyes glaring daggers at me, "fuck it up."

This wasn't what I wanted. I needed time to put things right. Gia deserved more than a rushed conversation. But the house was full of people, half of whom were damn near pulling me out the door. Crossing to my siren, I reached for her hand.

"Please, before I go." I lifted a hand towards the back door. The deck was our only sliver of privacy left—even with its damn wall of windows. Sam lifted Ben from her arms, and Gia didn't resist as I led her into the cool morning air.

"I want us to–" She slipped her fingers from mine. Took two steps back. Arms crossed. Shoulders squared, but looking me dead in my eyes; a scathing message.

I shouldn't start with what I wanted.

"Yesterday, I messed up." My confession had to lead. "I reacted badly. I was careless with my words." I took a step towards her, and she didn't retreat. "I know I can be intense. That is my problem, not yours." Another step closer, each one a victory. "But I swear to you," I reached out, my fingers grazing the edge of her arm. "I never meant to hurt or anger you."

Touching her was everything. And still—she made me earn every inch.

"My need to protect you, to love you, is only ever born from a place of devotion, and there is still so much going on that we can't see." I put a hand on my chest, willing her to feel everything I couldn't say. "So much I can't fight cause I can't find it, and that kills me."

There, a flicker of softness, born from the shine of tears she was fighting, but there nonetheless, I wrapped one hand around her arm, tugging her into me as I cupped her jaw.

"My god, Gia," forehead to forehead at last, I could breathe in everything I'd been denied in the lifetime apart from her. "I close my eyes and see the worst possible outcomes to threats I'm all but shadowboxing, and the idea of you walking out that door feels–" She tensed, and I couldn't help but grip her tighter. "I am not sorry for wanting you safe. I'll never regret doing anything necessary to protect you - even angering you if need be, but please." I slid my hand behind her waist and neck, gripping her hair. "I am deeply sorry for making you feel anything less than cherished, loved...and free."

A heartbeat.

Two.

Three.

The moment her body softened, hands unfurling to slide up my forearms, I was alive again.

Lifting her head, she gave me her mouth and returned to me. My tongue begged entrance to her lips, and when she opened, I delved into the only thing I had left to show my devotion to her.

"I am so sorry I caused you pain, or made you feel scared or caged or–" She nodded, retaking my mouth and melting her body into mine.

A whimper...my God...a single sound that blew all my pretty words out of the water.

"Yo, Troy man," Chase's voice slashed the moment apart. "It's hard to see if y'all made up with the windows all steamed, but we gotta go." The door closed again as my frustration came roaring back.

"I'm going to kill him," I growled, eliciting a small huff of laughter from my love. Opening my eyes, I finally brushed a thumb across the trail of tears in my name. "I know it's not enough. Not by half." I tucked a lock of her hair behind her ear, whispering there. "We'll finish this conversation tonight."

She only nodded as I turned and left my whole heart on that god-damn deck.

43

TROY

S AM DROPPED CHASE AT the fire station and me at the library before heading to the first aid tent. I hated this volunteer job, but the tactical advantage was undeniable. With Chase and Sam choosing their perches and me front and center, we had eyes on everything.

The girls would never be out of sight.

Until Captain showed, I was the senior officer on duty. I briefed the assigned uniforms, stationed them at potential choke points, then oversaw stage setup. The stage was dressed up like a goddamn wedding—nauseating white roses, an acrylic podium, and arrogance.

Overkill for a ribbon-cutting.

I almost texted the girls about the flowers—white roses held bad memories for them all—but Gia let me go without saying a word, and I didn't know if she'd see my text as care or control.

Anger would've been easier than silence.

A vendor approached with folding chairs, and I directed him to the clipboard layout. I glanced over the park: booths and tents were aligned to spec. I was a pointless figurehead.

Tracker app showed Gia—ten minutes out, maybe less.

I pocketed my phone, adjusted my holster, and tapped the mic in my cuff.

"Girls are 10 out."

"Copy," Sam and Chase chimed.

Clear. Tight. Like old times.

The custom tactical-grade surveillance earpieces were something we'd used in our time in the Marines. Securing the private ops channel now seemed more than reasonable given the various kidnappings, fires, and attempted murders our wives had endured. A task easily done during my early nights spent patrolling the cabin.

The weight of everything was staggering.

A man in a gray suit flanked by library staff approached the stage. Probably the VIP my captain had mentioned. I gave him a nod, noting his overly slick suit, and returned my eyes to the crowd. He wasn't my concern today.

"Wilder." My captain tapped my shoulder, all clipped command. "You've got this covered?"

"Yes, sir." I held up the clipboard. "Stage is set. Florals done. Vendor grid holding steady."

"Great." He tipped his head toward the gray suit. "Let the AV team get the mic check in for Mr. Garrison." I followed his glance to the two AV kids standing awkwardly beside the suit, juggling cables and laptops, and shooting nervous glances at me and the gun on my hip. "Perhaps the brooding man with a visible gun could move stage left, Wilder?" The captain whispered his last part, but his expression made it clear he wasn't asking.

I was an idiot. I was up here by duty, and wholly checked out as I scanned outward. And the poor kids from the high school AV club didn't know how to tell the giant, armed man they needed him to move.

"Apologies, Captain," I nodded to the kids and then to the grey suit. "Mr. Garrison, is it?" I extended a hand to the man, who smiled back as if he'd won a prize at the fair.

"Nonsense, Officer." Mr. Garrison stepped in as if he owned the place. "Just here for the press optics. Glad to have your support." I barely registered his words, irritated at his presumption of support, and leaned into my captain's ear.

"Sir, I'd like to do a perimeter sweep. With you here now," I swept an arm towards the parking lot. "I could–"

"Not so fast, Wilder." His hand on my arm might as well have been a gun for all the adrenaline it released. "Mr. Garrison is here for the soundcheck before his boss arrives. I need you here." I nodded, but my stomach clenched.

This was way too much pomp & circumstance.

Since when did I need to supervise the soundcheck?

Unless something was off.

I glanced at my phone and froze–the girls' tracker was blank.

"Besides...perimeter sweep?" My captain screwed his face up as he half shrugged, and my blood ran cold. "Not sure a library re-opening needs presidential-level security."

He slapped my shoulder, tipped his head to the corner of the stage where he expected me to stand, and laughed as he returned to the grey suit.

I could only stare at the screen, circling their last known location.

"The app. It's dark." I squeezed the mic in my cuff. "Do you have eyes on –"

"I got 'em." Chase came through quickly, barely staving off my stage leap into the crowd. "Stroller loading took a beat. They're headed Sam's way."

Just then, the app returned online, and I had to remind my legs to hold steady as I figured out a way to white-knuckle my way through this god-forsaken-event.

44

SAM

JESUS, TROY WAS WOUND tight as a spring. A momentary blip on the GPS and he looked ready to crowd surf his way to us. Thank god I'd set up the first-aid booth to be equidistant from Troy and Chase. I had a clean, triangulated view of the petting zoo and a wedge of artisan booths.

The layout was Chase's idea. We texted it out a few nights back and planned to communicate the girl's movements during the day. We all wanted our family to be safe, but after last night and this morning, I got the vibe we'd be more likely to keep Troy from flying off the rails. Thank God for Chase's quick response, or we'd be peeling Troy off the goddamn walls.

"Hey, Baby," Lila leaned in for a kiss, Moira and Gia behind her with their strollers. "Figured we better check in with ya big bunch of worrywarts early on."

"Not a bad call," I murmured, her eyes following mine to the podium where Troy stood, fists clenched, peering across the crowd to where we stood. "He looks like someone yelled bomb."

"Give him a break, Lumberjack." Lila tipped her head back, nuzzling my beard with her nose. "If I recall, you were once a rabid dog." I couldn't resist the growl in her ear that gave me her giggling smile.

"You feeding my baby, yet?" Resting a hand on her belly, I nodded back towards the food trucks.

"Oh, she already had one snack on the way over," Moira chimed in.

"We're gonna try and let them visit the petting zoo before it got crowded." Gia finished, her eyes glancing briefly at Troy.

She seemed settled. That was good. She and Troy would work this out. This morning's brief tension was just that, brief. Troy was an intense motherfucker on a good day. It stood to reason it would take him time to equalize all this newness in his life. But my brother loved as hard as he protected. Love would win out. Troy would apologize, and Gia would be my new sister...making that adorable little boy my new nephew.

"Better head over." I smacked my wife's ass, tapping the mic hidden in my shirt collar. "Girls are hitting the petting zoo before it gets crowded."

"Copy." Troy's voice was so clipped that the word sounded choked.

"Was that Gia and little Ben?" said a voice to my left. I turned to find a young guy, maybe mid-thirties. His blazer covered the logo on his hospital polo.

"You are?" I cocked an eyebrow down at the guy who wasn't quite as tall as me, and not half as muscled.

"Oh, sorry." He extended a hand. "Dr. Alex Freeman."

"Sam Wilder, EMT." I returned his handshake. "Are you my second in the tent today?"

"Yep. Assigned by county ER." He held up his lanyard emblazoned with his face, title, and hospital credentials. "I saw those two at the pediatric urgent care a while back." He returned to Gia and Ben, pointing to where the girls pulled babies out of the strollers to enter the pen. "I think he had an earache, wasn't it?"

"Oh yeah," I turned half facing him, half watching Lila guide River's hands across the back of a bunny. Her smile was huge, as were the belly laughs my niece was throwing out. I couldn't wait to see her doing that with our baby soon. "He shook it off in a day or so. I'm surprised you remembered that."

This guy's attention to detail was unsettling.

"He was a cute kid. And his dad...it was Troy, right?" Dr. Freeman glanced around casually, then pointed to the stage. "Yeah, there he is." My hand slunk up towards the mic in my collar, half wanting to confirm this guy's identity with Troy. I hesitated. Troy was a breath away from getting fired just to hold Ben in a goat pen, and his tension was making me jumpy.

Looking back at the girls, I felt an unsettling sense of exposure. The crowd was growing, my line of sight was interrupted, and we had hours to go.

"Yeah, so," I pulled Freeman's attention away from my family, gauging his focus. "I've organized basic first aid supplies here in sets for all the usual things, sunburns, cuts, scrapes, etc." He observed, eyes never returning to Gia and Ben. "Additional supplies are under the table."

"Alrighty." Clapping his hands, Dr. Freeman smiled out at the crowd. "Looks like the weather is gonna be perfect," he huffed with a smile. "Here's hoping for a boring day, ammiright?" I nodded, but my gut stayed tight.

Lately, boring wasn't in the cards for the Wilders.

45

CHASE

I spent a good hour organizing all the hand-outs and swag at the fire station while a probie polished up one of our newer rigs. Then we donned our gear and rolled it into position for the Touch-A-Truck feature at the location I chose, nearest the bathroom trailers and the face-painting booths. Both short structures that, if I climbed to the top of my rig, I could easily see over. I would also have the high ground to see Troy, Sam, and anything else I needed to, in case something went awry. It shouldn't, but... history demanded diligence.

The night Troy thought he'd lost Gia in the store, I heard about it from Sam, but I felt it down to my bones. I'd lost Moira the day Jensen snatched her off the damn city bus. I was forced to listen to him drool all over her while Sam and I tried to find her in time and–

"Yo, Wilder. Ease up on that grip, wouldja?" I looked down at my white-knuckle grip, pausing to shake out my arms from the hoses we pulled to let kids fire off water out back.

The group chat was pretty hard on Troy, and I agreed that he'd maybe been too harsh with Gia. She was fragile, and we didn't fully know what all she'd been through before joining us. I suspected Moira and Lila probably knew more, but Gia wasn't built like them. Troy was a hard guy to communicate with sometimes, and if he admitted he'd messed up...I knew it had to be bad. Still, knowing what I know about how hard Jensen worked to scam my wife and that he was the bottom of the Apex food chain, I was more than half on team-Troy during today's events.

This place was wide open and public, and families wanting to get a head start were already beginning to crowd in. We'd done all we could to secure things, but the reality was that Apex and Gia's dad were still a threat. After my girls came to see me, all the firehands taking turns gushing over my daughters, I sent them to Uncle Sam and the petting zoo. I hated that I couldn't be there with them, but I knew Sam would keep watch, and Moira would take a shit-ton of pictures, then walk me through the day like I'd been there.

She loved retelling her day with them for me.

I loved seeing our life through her eyes.

My wife was such a great mother.

I watched my family stroll away, Lila and Gia tagging along with little Ben. Man, that kid was cute. He looked just like his mother, or rather, his sister? That situation was a clusterfuck of epic proportions. I didn't envy Troy's situation. I also didn't envy his stress level today, given that I was already feeling the pressure from the crowds.

Half the county must have had the same idea as my family, since the stroller brigade was out in force. Well beyond what we'd initially anticipated crowd-wise. I was inundated with squirming faces bouncing in line to climb around the truck. The more we tried to keep the crowd moving, keep the kids engaged and learning about fire safety, the less

I was able to watch my wife and daughters. At one point, I heard the familiar lift of my wife's laughter float above the noise, and I glanced her way, but some asshat wearing a suit that looked totally out of place blocked my view.

Black pinstriped and way too much gel slicked through black hair; the guy looked more Godfather than Main Street. A too-crisp suit like Brinks, all polish and menace. Even thinking his name dragged up the memory of Moira, shaking and fierce, holding a smoking gun.

Shadows of bad things never really left, did they?

Shaking it off, I sneered at the suited jerk, craning to see around him before he slipped offside in time to see River give her biggest smile to the bunny her aunt Lila helped hold for her. My girls smiled just like their mama. Big and full, they'd never once know a day of hurt in their lives if I had a say in the matter.

I wanted this for Troy. I wanted him settled, all that loving control channeled into its proper place. I wanted him grounded by something other than his damn sense of duty, and I wanted to see him utterly whipped by a sweet smile, and that little boy's tiny hand gripping his big ass fingers.

Troy deserved joy.

We just needed to get him past Apex — without losing Gia and Ben.

46

GIA

AFTER TROY SLEPT IN the chair the night of our fight, my anger lingered into the morning—served with a salty side of 'I drank all your coffee.' Petty? Maybe. But I couldn't shake the frustration over how easily he'd shattered the thin veil of happiness he'd given me. His smirk at my defiant act felt monumental, though. I could be angry, and Troy wouldn't hate me for it.

His apology didn't just placate—it asked for trust.

As much as I hated how he'd hurt me, I respected that my safety truly was his only motivation. He wasn't sorry for wanting to keep me sheltered and protected. He would have happily locked me in a different kind of cage if it meant keeping me safe, and telling me as much was a risky move on his part. But then he let me go, and that distinction was everything.

He didn't like my anger, or my hurt...didn't like that I wanted to do something counter to his wishes. Still, he surrounded me with family who supported me, then backed off to let me have a day I desperately needed.

For the first time in my life, I was at a fair!

Okay, it was a library reopening. Not an actual fair and certainly not at any level compared to Manhattan-based festivals I'd seen my father attend, but I was here. I laughed with Moira and Lila, and we played with the kids. I was inundated with sights, sounds, and smells so delicious that it was almost overwhelming, and I had never been happier. Silently, over the smiles of Ben, laying his hand on the giant firetruck in the arms of Chase...his Uncle Chase...I thanked Troy for giving me a chance to reclaim a sliver of the childhood I'd been denied.

Today was a good, new day, and I was living all of it through Ben's eyes.

I had seen Troy's stance on the platform, stiff and unyielding. His sunglasses hid his eyes from me, but I could see the tension in his whole body as he continually scanned the crowd. If he spotted me, he never let on. There was no text message from him on my phone, and there was no request for me to bring Ben to him. Then again, hadn't I all but silently demanded he let me be? I told myself that Ben and I would be front and center when it came time for the library ribbon-cutting, so he could see us safe and happy, and maybe some of it would rub off on him.

Ben at the petting zoo was officially my new favorite memory. He was little and would never remember it, but I felt incredibly blessed to see his face as we gently explored the fluffy bunnies and scruffy baby goats. I held his chubby hand in mine, and we petted and gently held ducklings and even a micro-pig, which grunted and squirmed, making Ben let loose a belly laugh of pure baby glee. I wanted to stay there a little longer, but the line was growing quickly, and even I couldn't ignore the pull of the delicious-smelling food trucks.

"Can we talk about the Kielbasa on a stick?" Lila groaned, "Cause fetal lumberjack here is a meat-eater and I'm dying a little."

"Should we make a play to see Sam and Troy first?" Moira nodded towards the first-aid station, where Sam gave Lila a wink before returning his attention to a little girl with a scraped knee.

"If I don't eat soon, I'm not responsible for what falls out of my mouth." Lila deadpanned, then fired off a text message. Sam lifted his phone to glance at it with a smile as if on cue, then nodded his head towards the food trucks. "He knows we'll be back around soon."

"Then baby gets Kielbasa," Moira laughed.

"Should I text Troy?" I glanced up at the stage, hating how still he was. The first pang of regret tugged at me for forcing his hand. "Or I can go wait there and–"

"Oh no, you don't." Lila scooped Ben from my hands, clipped him into his carrier, and stowed him in the stroller. "You deserve this day, and Grandpa up there deserves to squirm a little."

Grabbing my free hand, she guided Ben and me to the picnic tables, which were circled by five different food trucks.

"The WBPS is well-meaning, but intense." Moira smiled, settling her stroller next to Ben. "At times we've each had to put them in their place about their overbearing–"

"Caveman level–" Lila interrupted

"Tendencies." Moira finished, laughing as I looked back for Troy but could barely see him across the sea of faces. "If you need to go to him," she took my hand, her face softening. "We can watch Ben so you two can have a moment."

I was tempted, but I shook my head.

"Let's eat, then see about a little face paint," I said, not wanting to detract from their happy moment with fears and regrets. "Besides, I can't wait to see his face when he sees Ben in his new outfit."

Looking down, Ben happily gnawed on a teething toy, drool soaking the upper edge of the adorable navy onesie emblazoned with a bright yellow police badge and the title 'Officer Adorable' embroidered on the teeny chest pocket.

"Did you wanna grab some food first?" Moira hooked a thumb over her shoulder to the funnel-cake and fried Oreos truck. "'Cause mama's craving something sweet."

"I need to get Ben's bottle ready. Leave the girls and I'll watch them while you're in line."

Moira left, and I angled the two strollers until all the babies faced me. Seeing their tiny, happy faces all staring up at me felt surreal. Little Ben, who looked just like me...and River and Blue, who looked just like Moira, and whom I was finally starting to be able to tell apart. I narrated Ben's bottle-making process, smiling at each of them as we discussed the adorable animals we'd seen and the face painting we'd do next.

"Well, aren't you a picture?" I looked towards the familiar voice to find the happy peds clinic receptionist with grey wispy hair and soft crinkled eyes. "And I see your little one is happy and healthy too."

"Oh, hello." My voice was a touch too high as I pulled my surprise away from the edge of panic. "Yes...he's doing very well, thank you."

"I knew he would," The sweet grandmotherly woman leaned over, not touching Ben but giving him a jovial smile. I appreciated the respectful distance.

"And are these two beauties yours as well?"

"Those are my nieces," the title rolled off my tongue with ease as I gestured to Chase at the giant fire truck station. "Their father is working the touch-a-truck."

"Oh, I brought my grandson here for exactly that. He adores anything with wheels and the bigger the better!"

I looked around her but saw no little boy. My question must have shown in my eyes because she glanced behind her and then gave a little laugh.

"Oh, he's there now with my daughter. She asked me to go scope out the petting zoo line."

"It was growing quite long when we left there." I nodded my head towards Sam. "It's over in front of the big first-aid tent."

"Even better!" She clapped her hands with a sigh. "I was gonna see if they needed volunteers to help out. Last I heard, they were struggling to find doctors willing to volunteer."

Her words tripped a memory of the night we'd taken Ben in, and the doctor who helped us. I was so nervous then and...I was Jane, then. Cold panic rolled through me, realizing she might call me Jane—or worse, hear someone call me Gia—and the whole fragile truth I'd built would go off like a grenade.

I gaped at Sam's tent, hoping to catch his eye, but he was busy. Looking back at the food truck line, I saw that Lila had joined Moira, and they were waiting for their food, neither looking my way.

"Well, dear, it's been lovely catching up. You two enjoy your day."

Just like that...all the air left my lungs in a huge sigh of relief.

Ben gurgled happily, and I forced a smile.

We were fine. We were finally okay.

I deserved to hold on to that.

47

TROY

I STALKED MY RAVEN-HAIRED beauty from my post, watching her
glisten in the sunlight as she strolled from booth to booth. Gia and
Ben had hit every station—Chase's firetruck, the petting zoo, and half
a dozen vendors. I breathed easier when Ben was in her arms, even if
I struggled to hold my position. I wanted to see her smile when Ben
discovered the animals.

She'd settled at a picnic table, strollers all around her, blocking half
her body from view. Then, a woman stepped before her, and my girl
was gone. Fear choked me as I struggled to hold steady. Up and to the
right, I could see Moira and Lila at the food trucks. They surely were
watching out for Gia. They wouldn't leave River and Blue at risk. Still,
the woman's backside blocking my view began to grate, so I pinched the
mic in my cuff.

"Eyes on my girl?" I waited for a response, hearing a second of static
before Chase answered.

"Seated at the food trucks. Talking with an older lady."

They were okay.

They were okay.

The woman finally turned to leave, her profile ringing familiar as I worked to place her face. Unable to resist, I picked up my phone and typed out a text to Gia.

> Me: Who was that?

Hesitating, I deleted and retyped, then deleted again. I hated the distance still between us. I hated that my careless words and our hurried morning had left me unable to freely text her a simple question for fear that she'd think me controlling. Typing and deleting the message a third time, I pocketed my phone in a huff.

"Unclench, dude." Sam's voice buzzed through the comms. "I can hear your molars grinding from here."

"Moira and Lila are back with her. I've got eyes on them." Chase added, and I could only nod.

I had no choice but to see this awful day through. Tonight, I would put everything to rest between us, but for now, this torture was my penance. To my left, the grey-suited man smiled and laughed with the head librarian, glancing at his phone, before his smarmy voice drifted over the crowd.

"Looks like the senator will be delayed. I may be giving the opening notes myself."

Blood pounded in my head as the word registered: 'senator.'

Replaying the events of earlier, it finally clicked that the grey-suited ass wasn't the focus; he was the advance team to a bigwig so crucial that all this damn pomp & circumstance slid into place like oily, black, vile puzzle pieces.

The flowers, white roses, Apex's calling card, for a senator.

A gut punch of realization.

Jumping off the stage, I began pushing through the crowd as I glanced at the tracker app on my phone. Gia was still here...that was good. Pushing forward, I was instantly overwhelmed and overwrought by the sheer number of bodies in my way. Shoulder to shoulder, I couldn't get a clean line to move without bobbing and weaving in and out of adults and children alike. My trajectory not only shifted, but slowed, as I watched out for small bodies of toddlers squealing by with sticky hands and cotton-candy highs.

A sudden tug at my holster snapped me sideways—Just a toddler—sticky hands.

A mother scolding.

Not the mother I needed.

Not the baby I loved.

My comms were garbage down here. Static hissed every time I tried. I was blind. Deaf. Cornered by sunshine and bodies, Vendors and patrons laughing, parents yelling at children, and in the distance, my captain shouting my name.

I ignored him.

I ignored them all.

At the petting zoo, the earthy scent of animals and hay coated my nose and mouth as I was waylaid by the crowd of kids and strollers waiting their turns. Much as I tried to push through, no force was more immovable than a toddler screaming to see baby cows. Shoved off course again, I ended up at the first aid tent, and Sam's smirk.

"Your captain finally realize you're no good up there?"

"The speaker!" Sam's eyes snapped to attention at my words, his glance flicking to the platform behind me before focusing back on me.

"What's going on?" He glanced across at Chase, but the crowd formed a wall of colors and shapes, with face-painted children and balloons filling the theatre between us.

"Oh, Officer." A chipper voice sliced through the air, and Sam and I both turned to the woman who'd been blocking my view from before. "You might not remember me, I'm Dolores. I worked the night you and your wife brought your little boy in."

"Delores." The name came out clipped, but I couldn't help it. I was all but frozen as I replayed the night of Ben's illness and her face, and then her blocking my view of Gia today.

"I just saw them both over at the picnic tables. The little guy has grown so much, hasn't he?" Sam intervened as if knowing I was at a complete loss for words.

"He really has." Sam shoved his hand out to the woman. "Sam Wilder, I'm the little guys' uncle."

"Big as he is, those big blue eyes still slayed me, though." She turned back to me, her face happily oblivious to my internal meltdown, pressing the comms mic repeatedly and getting static. "He gets those from his mama...well, and his grandpa, I suppose?"

Time...stopped.

"Grandpa?" I vibrated, every fiber of my being coiled to pounce, as icy claws dug into my bones.

"Well, yes," The woman gestured over her shoulder. "Or I assumed it was his grandpa. Older gentleman, well dressed, same dark hair as your wife, and those handsome eyes." Turning back to us, her words trailed off slowly as she took in my face. "He was looking for them. I pointed to where–"

I ran.

48

GIA

"OH NO!" BEN'S CHUBBY hand darted out, snagging my fork so fast it launched a heaping bite of nachos across both of us—splatters of sour cream, beef, and lettuce everywhere. His little foot kicked the rest to my lap in a flailing moment of glee. My reaction, his giggle-fodder.

"Little man's got lightning reflexes." Lila laughed, reaching for Ben, as Moira handed over some baby wipes.

"How is he so fast?" I wiped the guacamole that rebounded to my face, then turned to wipe Ben's hands and toes free from taco grease that thankfully wasn't hot. "How are you so fast, son!"

Setting aside the rest of my food, I stood, brushing lettuce onto the ground.

"Guess I was done eating."

"Want me to clean him up while you reorder?" Moira asked, even though her hands were full of her food and what she was feeding her girls.

"No. I got enough, I think." Lifting Ben from Lila's arms, I snuggled a kiss into his cheek and hugged him to me, noticing his soggy bottom. "I'll change his diaper, and we can head over to face painting?" The girls nodded in agreement as I grabbed Ben's stroller and bag and walked towards the bathrooms.

The crowd was dense as we worked our way past the food trucks, and I opted to go back behind them all to avoid the line wrapping around Chase's station. Ben was too young to enjoy the festivities this year, but I smiled at the thought that he'd get to grow up in a town like this...with uncles and aunts and a community. There would be other events, and we'd go to each one. It was more privilege than I'd been afforded, and everything I ever hoped for.

The bathrooms were another bank of impressive rolling trailers that the town brought in. On the outside, they didn't appear much larger than the food trucks, but the interior featured pristine laminate floors and sleek, modern surfaces. Each trailer had a small central hallway with exits at both ends, and a single large bathroom on each side. The bathroom itself held a nice vanity area with a countertop and an extra-large changing station complete with a wide, smooth surface and safety buckles to help contain wiggling babies. The thing was large enough to hold me, Ben, and his stroller easily and still have room to walk around.

"Okay, little man, let's get you cleaned up." I laid out the changing table, giving it a cursory wipe down before laying out the changing pad. Once Ben was buckled in, I started changing him, stopping when my phone vibrated with an incoming call in my pocket. One hand on Ben's belly, I slipped the phone out, disappointed to see an unknown caller instead of Troy's face. Ignoring the call, I pocketed my phone and returned my attention to Ben, who was particularly squirmy and needed both hands to keep him steady.

A knock at the door added to my hurry.

"Just a minute." Discarding the old diaper, I refastened Ben's onesie and slid up his soft little pants, smiling at the idea that Troy would reach to hold Ben and smell nachos. My phone pinged with a text alert, and I pulled it out of my pocket after settling Ben into his stroller once more.

> Unknown: Answer the phone, my Gia.

My...Gia.

That's what Father used to call me when I disappointed him—right before the punishment came. My phone rang again, the same unknown number as before, just as someone knocked on the bathroom door again.

"Just a minute!" I yelled, as old instincts surfaced: obey first, question never, hesitate at your peril.

Ignoring my father's direct command felt impossible...But Troy. Surely if I called Troy, he'd be here in a flash. I had to take that chance. Ignoring the call again, I swiped over to the contacts and tapped Troy's name just as another text message came in, with no words...only a single picture; Moira, Lila, and the twins. They were laughing and happy, oblivious to being watched at the picnic tables outside the food trucks.

> Unknown: Answer, my Gia. I won't ask again.

My father's message was clear. If I didn't obey, they were in danger....because of me.

Another knock rattled the door like a gunshot. I jerked so hard I nearly dropped my phone—and Ben startled.

"I said just a minute!" The words came on a half-sob as I looked at Ben, smiling around his teething ring, and then at the photo in my text messages. I had to do something, TRY something, but I could lose everything if I weren't careful.

The knock...the door!

I could use that person. I could answer my father's call and some-how alert the person in the hallway to get help. Troy was too far away on the stage, but Chase was close by; they could get Chase, and we'd be okay.

Ben would be okay.

Slowly, my hands trembled so badly I nearly dropped the phone, sliding the icon across the screen and accepting the call.

"Hello, daughter." My father's voice had my stomach instantly sour, terror coursing through me in violent waves.

"H-How did you..." I tried to speak, tried to think, as I looked around and realized I had nothing to write a note with, no way to alert someone in the hall save for a desperate prayer they could read my lips or the panic on my face.

"We'll discuss that when we get home." Father's voice held no hint of irritation, but his calmness offered no safety. I pushed Ben's stroller to the far corner, out of view as I sidestepped toward the door. "First, we'll retrieve the documents you stole. Then, you'll tell me every person you spoke to so I can erase them. After that, you'll marry whom I assign you. Only then will you ensure that the boy...Ben, was it?"

Erase them all?!

My feet turned to lead, my heart galloping, as my father laid his plans in a bold move that showed, with that flat tone of confidence I'd heard so many times, he held all the cards.

"Ben's safety will be assured only when you do these things."

"Please...Papa...don't do this," I begged, hoping to buy time as I opened the bathroom door.

"Dignity, Gia," I swear I could hear his smile in the words. "I'm waiting outside. Come now."

The phone disconnected, and in a moment of terror, I lunged for the bathroom door, ripping it open in a desperate plea to have anyone on the other side. I had to get a message to Chase and Troy while I stalled.

Whoever was outside was now my only hope.

"Hello, Ms. Bianchi." In front of me was the doctor from the urgent care clinic.

"Doctor, thank God, I need you to..." I let my words trail off, connections in my brain moving too slowly as red flags and alarms screamed in my brain. "You...called me..."

The doctor smiled, his face as gentle and kind as the night he cared for Ben.

"Dr. Freeman." He reached a hand toward me in introduction, like we were meeting for coffee—calm, pleasant, practiced. My stomach flipped. "I assume you remember me from–"

I slammed the door shut, locking it and leaning against it as I looked around the bathroom in a panic, my brain clicking details into place that made no sense. The doctor called me Ms. Bianchi. He could only know that if he knew my father, which meant he had to be in league with my father.

The doctor's voice came muffled through the door as my world began to spin out of control.

"I am armed. Come quietly, and things will go smoothly, Ms. Bianchi."

Another text message pinged; another photo from my father of Troy near the petting zoo.

> Unknown: Don't be stupid. Bring your phone.
> Things can always get worse for you.

A sobbing, half-hysterical laugh escaped at the absurdity of his message.

Worse...worse!

What could be worse than being trapped in a bathroom by a father who has all but admitted he'll kill everyone I love, including the child he'd so hatefully abandoned, if I didn't willingly hand us both over? Another text had me clenching my teeth as I lifted the screen and saw it was Moira.

> Moira: Everything okay in there?

I wanted to cry, to hurl my phone across the room and shatter it into a billion pieces. The door knocked again, and the whole world began to spin, gasping into a tunnel of black that felt like the very walls were closing in on me. I was trapped and could see no way out. If I alerted Moira, she'd surely send up the alarm, and that could put Ben and me both at risk. But I couldn't, no matter what happened to me, I couldn't hand Ben back into the Jaws of these monsters.

"Ms. Bianchi." The man in the hallway sounded as if he were pressed against the door. "He doesn't enjoy waiting. Open the door. We'll go get the baby without making a scene. I'll tell your father how compliant you were, and we'll all start on a good footing."

Go. Get. The. Baby.

My heart shattered and reformed in the seconds it took my brain to realize the meaning of those words. He'd somehow not seen Ben earlier. He didn't know Ben was with me! A plan began to shape with the thinnest of threads. Replying to my father's last message, I fired off the carrot I hoped would take him away from here the fastest.

> Me: I don't have your documents with me. They're at the cabin.

> Unknown: You'll take me there before we leave. Now, Gia.

Then, I opened a text to Lila privately, knowing that if I did something in the group chat, one of the guys could come busting in here and get shot on the spot. I prayed that Lila would be the quickest to get to Ben and that she'd react to that first as I typed words I hoped would be enough to alert her that something was wrong without tipping off my father about my deception.

> Me: Tell Troy I love him…and I'm sorry…and please care for Ben.

Before I hit send, I leaned down and kissed Ben on the forehead, tears soaking his soft, downy hair as he gripped and tugged at my locks, curtaining his sweet face.

"They'll love you, little man… and you'll save him."

I yanked off the anklet Troy had given me and slid it beneath Ben's body—the last vestige of safety I could offer him in the hopes his life would be better than mine. Then I secured his safety buckle, praying Lila would reach him quickly, and fired off her text.

Then, with every fiber of my being screaming, I eased the door open... and walked willingly into hell to save them all.

49

TROY

"TROY, HOLD UP!"

Sam's voice chased me as I bolted into the crowd, knowing everything was deeply wrong.

"Something's up." His voice came through the comms mic in my ear.

"Headed to the girls." Chase's reply didn't question.

I couldn't have answered if he had. I had nothing beyond a bone-deep knowing that Gia's father, the senator, had found her.

The man whose dark hair and blue eyes matched her own—matched my Ben.

Every step felt too slow. Mired in the sea of inconsequential faces and noise. A curly red-headed teen bumped my shoulder. A beer-gutted man spilled his drink on my shoes. Seconds crawled, my ears hearing only comms static and my heavy breathing as I pushed towards the picnic area, scanning the island of tables until I found Moira and Lila sitting with the girls.

"Where is she?" I bellowed. The greasy stench of fried food turned my stomach. "Gia!"

"It's okay. She went to change his diaper," Moira said, waving toward the bathrooms.

"All good," Lila added, though both of them looked at me with raised brows and matching concern.

"What did Delores say?" Sam panted behind me. "You took off like she'd set off a bomb."

"What's going on!" Chase arrived, drawing the eyes of passersby as I opened the tracking app and saw her location was still in the bathroom. "He's here," I started—but the words choked off. "Her father, *Gia's* father, is here."

The air crackled as my family stiffened. Moira and Chase secured their girls in their stroller as Lila stood, scanning the crowd.

"The senator?" Her hand ghosted to her back pocket. "How do you know?"

"I just know!" I barked, hardly having the capacity to explain the dots connecting in my brain.

"Dude." Sam's tone was protective, knowing I was on edge, but warning me not to snap at his wife. "The tracker shows her in the bathroom. She's good."

"And I don't see her dad anywhere. Are you sure?" Chase added, scanning the crowd from his advantage, being a head taller than the rest of us.

"The man in the grey suit, he's the advance team for a senator." I barked, looking again at the tracker app. "How long has she been gone?"

"Troy, we're all here with you." Moira soothed. "Why don't Lila and I go back and—"

"No." Lila's voice was sharp. "No!"

She tapped her phone screen and thrust it to me as she bolted towards the bathroom.

"Baby, wait!" Sam chased her as my brain registered the words I read.

> Gia: Tell Troy I love him...and I'm sorry...and please care for Ben.

Cold dread soaked into my marrow as the beast inside me howled.

"Gia!" She wouldn't leave me, not willingly. Something was deeply wrong. "Gia!" I mowed through the crowd, no longer caring if anyone noticed. Let them notice; let a crowd be drawn. Maybe it would slow her down or buy me time to get to her. I saw Sam's back in the hallway of a bathroom trailer, shoulders rising and falling as he blocked a doorway. "Gia!" I knew she was angry with me. But we were okay. She wouldn't just leave—not unless she had been forced to.

Right?!

My heart thundered up into my throat as anxiety and fear choked my breathing. Reaching Sam, I grabbed his shoulder, throwing him aside as I slammed into the bathroom to where Gia was.

"No." It wasn't Gia. "No, no, no."

It was Lila, holding a crying Ben.

"She wouldn't leave him here alone." She sobbed at me, eyes shining with tears as she tried to walk and bounce my boy. "She wouldn't leave him, Troy." Lila's voice cracked. "Not like this. Not unless..."

I reached for Ben, needing to soothe him with the rhythmic patting he liked.

Needing to soothe the beast.

"Find her," I whispered, handing Sam my phone. "Track her. Now." My muscles and energy channeled into a calmness I couldn't claim as

I slowly checked over Ben for any injuries, not knowing how long he'd been alone.

"It says she's here," Sam said, showing the screen to Chase, who'd joined us in the hallway. "How is that possible?"

"Oh fuck." Lila's voice broke. She stepped to the stroller, reached in—then froze. "Troy..."

She turned.

Dangling from her fingers, delicate and damning, was Gia's anklet. The GPS.

Hidden beneath Ben, a message burned in silence: And my world was ashes.

Sam cursed softly, reaching for his crying wife, as Lila whispered, "She hid it under Ben."

Ben.

I had Ben.

I didn't have her...

But I had Ben.

I pulled him back just far enough to see his face—fat tears rolling down his cheeks, those angelic blue eyes blinking up at me and begging me to make his world safe again.

The crowd swirled.

Uniforms buzzed.

My sisters cried.

My brothers cursed.

And with every shallow breath, I died a little as my soul split into two. Half in my hands with the son who needed me, and half gone with his mother.

I would get her back.

With blood.

And pain.
Gia would be mine again.
But fuckall if I knew how.

50

TROY

I CHECKED THE TRACKER app three more times before my brothers took my phone. Sam silently drove us back to the cabin, with Chase and the girls behind us. I focused on Ben to keep my mind from fracturing. I focused on his routine.

He needed dinner.

This was my job.

She'd entrusted him to me.

Lila dug into her laptop immediately, trying to track Gia's cell signal, which was shut off just south of town. Lila informed me, in whispers and side glances, that we could only wait for the phone to be activated again before we could track her. I nodded my understanding, ignoring the eggshells they all tiptoed around.

Ben needed a bath.

I pulled him into the shower with me.

Gia liked it when I did that.

I cradled him, gently washing away the petting zoo I'd missed sharing with them because I was working. I bet it was her first petting zoo, too. And I was the bastard who held myself back to give her space; instead, she was taken.

The anger was suffocating.

Ben was tired.

I dried and lotioned his little body, losing myself in the trust this tiny thing gave me. Just like his mother had trusted me with Ben, she'd undoubtedly left him behind to shield him from her father. She was so brave. She'd left her tracker with him, ensuring I would find and protect Ben. She was so smart.

But she'd left...me.

Dressing Ben in his pajamas, I turned towards his crib and saw the chair. Gia sat in that chair her first night here, her injured hand wrapped, and a baby in her arms. It was the first safe space she'd known, the chair. I lowered myself to the floor, groveling to be near my queen. I'd sat sentry in that chair as they slept. Slaying demons in her dreams even before she knew I served.

She left me.

I'd sat in that chair again the last night we'd spoken, when I opened my fool mouth, choosing foolish words attached to foolhardy sentiments that were fucking right! I was right. I was fucking right. And the next morning, she only listened as I tried to mend things between us before forcing myself to step away despite everything in me knowing it was wrong.

Going was wrong.

The event was wrong.

Taking Ben there was wrong.

Leaving me was all…wrong…and now here I stood, needing to put Ben to bed as he had already slept in my arms. Instead, I was frozen in place, staring at the goddamn chair that mocked me in the corner of a room that was ours to love in just days before.

It would stand sentry now, it mocked.

An upholstered homage to a time when she was mine.

I was alone and my Gia was gone and this chair….this goddamn chair–

"If you would, please." Stepping outside the bedroom, I motioned for Lila to take Ben from me. "I need a moment." I handed over the sleeping infant, ignoring my brothers' worried looks as I turned back around, closed the door to the bedroom, and stared down my opponent.

Stepping up to the chair, I leaned in and gripped the loose cushion. Pulling it close, I dug my fingers into the seams and inhaled its stale scent, wishing I could pick up notes of my Gia.

The bastard denied me, and I was a beast, unleashed.

Pulling with all my might, I ripped the cushion clean, sending cotton tufts of shredded despair raining down around my feet. It wasn't enough. It wouldn't bring her back. Balling my fists, I set loose the first volley.

Whomp.

Backed into a corner, all it could do was take as I poured my wrath into each killing blow, loving the first crack of weakness squeaking into the room. I pounded into the seat until it groaned as if it missed her like I did.

Whomp.

It didn't deserve to miss her.

Whomp.

I didn't deserve her.

Whomp.

Reaching for the arms, I lifted the chair over my head, hurling it across the room and reveling in its wobbling legs as they screeched across the hardwood floors.

Yes. Scream for me, bastard.

Crossing to the toppled throne, I planted my foot into its side until I was buried in the inner workings. It tried to fight back, to bite back, drawing blood along my ankle as I pulled myself from its sucking wound. I wouldn't yield.

Whomp.

I kept going, climbing onto its legs, gripping the arm in both hands, and pulling until I heard the pop of its bone give from its socket. I tossed the arm aside, focusing on the half-dead carcass at my feet.

Hurt for me.

Lifting the remains over my head, I hurled again, rage blooming fresh when it slid into Ben's crib, slamming into the wall and violating the last safe place that baby had. All I asked, all I wanted, was my Gia back, and if it couldn't give me that, the least it could do was die with dignity.

Whomp.

Pulling the last arm free, all that was left were the legs held together by guts of thread and twine and splintered springs. It wasn't enough to cover the miles that grew between me and my life, stolen away. I raised the last piece of the chair over my head and slammed it, crashing down. The chair screamed, a wild and feral sound of fear and hurt, but I kept slamming it down, reveling in my blood that flowed in penance to all my lifetime of failures.

Again.

Scream Again.

Bleeding Again.

My brothers entered, drawn to the bleating sound of the dying. They were too late. She was gone. My siren was gone. I had no way to track her, no way to save her, and no way to protect her. I raised and lowered my fists, slamming the stabbing splinters into the ground, slamming my fists into the ground, slamming myself...screaming...into the ground.

Arms surrounded me, pulling me up.

Voices I knew and loved called to me as the red haze lifted.

The room was gone.

My Gia...was gone.

There was nothing left.

Not of the chair.

Not of me.

Just blood and tears, as I shattered.

51

GIA

M Y LIMBS MOVED LIKE they'd been packed in wet sand.

My tongue was dry-stuck to the roof of my mouth.

A bitter, chemical film lined the back of my throat.

It tasted of perfume and metal.

The cloying smell of imported roses built a pressure behind my eyes so tense that the room pulsed as I tried to focus my senses.

I wasn't dreaming.

I'd been taken.

Slowly, I sat up. Images swirling behind my clenched eyelids as flashes of Ben's smile, the doctor's hand, and a sharp sting in my neck all sifted like sand through my fingers. Gleaming like a trophy, the gilded bars of my childhood bedroom beckoned me home with ironed linens, floor polish, and sterile air. Sheets with an ungodly thread count—luxury weaponized—down pillows and all the trappings to frame abuse with privilege. A cage padded in opulence, but crafted by a devil who called cruelty devotion. So far from the man who loved me with a gentle strength that built a life...and would burn the world to find me.

Stretching my neck, the pain was acute and sharp, and brought with it the flash of memory.

I'd left the bathroom with the doctor. My father wanted the books and Ben. A commotion at the trailers caught our attention, and a crowd had gathered behind us. Troy called for me. I opened my mouth to answer, but something stabbed into my neck, the world keeled sideways–drugged.

This wasn't my home anymore. This...was my battlefield.

My opponent, my father, had not fought fairly. But Ben was safe. Troy was safe. I now had to make sure they both stayed that way.

Standing on shaky legs, I let fresh, warm blood circulate into my fingers and toes, marveling that the room was unchanged from the last time I saw it. Part of me expected wreckage of rage, but that kind of devotion required love. Michael Bianchi hadn't loved anything or anyone enough to rage in its absence.

I used the bathroom, brushed my teeth, and stepped into the hallway; Shoulders back, head high. I hadn't been summoned, but I tread the black marble runway to my doom, nonetheless. I would not wait for fate to find me. I found my father perched at his desk. I stepped into the lion's den with all the authority I could muster despite the vast ocean of unknowns before me.

I was always an excellent improv artist.

"The prodigal daughter returns." Father smiled at the tumbler in his hand, ice clinking as he swirled his scotch in the old-world cut crystal he so cherished. "I hope you rested well, mia caro." I didn't bother speaking, merely crossed to sit in the chair across from him–stuffed with pockets full of Lila-grade audacity; Her courage, Moira's wit, my new arsenal.

"I don't recall that story starting with a needle in the neck." My tone was flat as I leaned back and steepled my fingers in front of my chest. I held the cards now.

"You've grown bold in your time away."

"Grown a spine, you mean." Too fast. Boldness would end me if I overplayed it. "Shall we get to it then?" I sighed, regrounding on an exhale.

My father's smile didn't reach his eyes.

"Where is the ledger?" There it was—the thing that would save or damn me.

"I told your lackey I didn't have them." I inspected my nails, flicking away invisible lint as I slowed to buy time. "I would've told you, too, had you left me conscious."

"So they're upstate." I nodded at his statement—a small acquiescence to placate. I had nothing to lose, but that didn't mean he couldn't make things painful. "Where?"

He drew his line.

He wanted obedience, but anything I gave him put Troy and his family at risk.

"Cause your Canadian border access demands container tracking?" It was a long shot, a big one, but I was banking on him not knowing what I'd overheard the night I left. I was also banking on him thinking I didn't understand what I'd taken. "Because surely the guns and drugs you traffic would be easier to move through there than Mexico, right?"

My father ignored my bait, smirking as he emptied his scotch and rose to pour another.

"You have no leverage here, Gia." A confident statement with his back turned, and no one keeping me from running. He knew I was helpless. "But I will be lenient if you do as you're told."

"You mean, like picking which handcuffs Brinks could use when we wed?"

A millisecond passed as his head cocked ever-so-slightly, and the ice I walked on grew thin.

"That's why you ran?" An edge of violence laced his words.

"You thought a Plaza wedding to that madman was lenient?"

"I offered you other options." He answered, his hackles soothing again as his shoulders relaxed.

"One less now, though. Since Brinks is dead." I lobbed the bomb in the hopes of causing him another pause. Surely if he began to think of me as more than a mindless share to trade, he'd negotiate more. I needed to buy time. Stay alive. Outthink the devil.

The words repeated in my mind as he spun with a madman's smile.

"You think I raised you to be smarter than me?" He prowled back, leaning on the front edge of his desk and looming over me with a cold dread I could taste. "Let me remind you that with one call." He lifted a single finger. "I'll ruin them all."

"You're bluffing."

"Upstanding small town police officer found with kidnapped infant son of Presidential hopeful, Senator Michael Bianchi!" He flashed a wide, menacing smile, throwing his hands out in a flash of pizzazz. "Ooooh, the headline practically writes itself."

My stomach clenched at the truth in his words. Ben was his biological son, and Troy had him without proper cause. I handed him a kidnapped child, and without me there, Troy was vulnerable.

"Heartbroken father makes public plea for his safe return." He held a hand over his heart, sighing wistfully. "Imagine the sympathy votes." My father had played a heavy hand with Ben's freedom, but I still had the books.

Buy time. Stay alive. Outthink the devil.

"You won't do that." I postured. "You promised him to someone for campaign support."

"You think I haven't already?" He leaned closer, the scotch mixing with his pungent aftershave. "One call, Gia, and I'll wipe 'em all out."

My heart pounded as I willed my face and voice to remain steady.

"If they go down," I gulped. "Or anything happens to Ben...your ledger goes public. Shipping containers, contents, recipients...all of it." He squeezed his scotch glass, knuckles white and hands near shaking in a rage I could feel down to my toes. This slight advantage was all I had. "Every political vote you ever bought goes public, and they all go down - you at the helm." Then, in a final plea to try and appease the devil, I made the only offer I could think of. "Let Ben go, and I'll give the books back."

My father grew violently still, his eyes narrowing as he considered my words for long seconds.

It was all I could do to hold my head steady, as my stomach twisted and knotted in my gut with the very real fear of knowing that if I missed my mark, I was as good as dead.

"You have no leverage." He said at last, relaxing back and waving away my promise like a gnat.

"Then prove me wrong." I pushed. "Give me my phone. I'll make the call." I waited a heartbeat, then added. "Or don't...and prove me right."

The stand-off took a lifetime.

He stared again, stone-faced and impassive, as he weighed my words. I felt myself unmade and made anew in the gap. My lifetime of trained obedience shattering at my feet as the scaffolding of a life built in love and family shored up my courage. Ben would have that life, even if it cost me my own. I clung to those people, my family, with bloodied fingertips as I prayed the cliff's edge I stood on didn't end with all of them at the bottom of the abyss.

My father tipped his glass back, rounded his desk, and sat in his chair. Reaching into a side drawer, he pulled out my phone, turned it on, then slid it across the desk like a detonator.

"You have 5 minutes."

52

TROY

M Y BROTHERS THREW ME into a cold shower where I crumbled to nothing.

Afterwards, Sam tended to my wounds, Chase cleaned out the chair debris, and their wives turned the guest bedroom into a makeshift nursery with portable cribs for the twins.

None of them was leaving tonight.

I was surprised when I stepped out to find Fire Chief Brandt and his wife, Carol, standing around the kitchen table. Chase's chief had always been in our corner, even bringing the first traces of Apex's malice to our attention. But it was the bag at his feet and the words he delivered that ripped through me.

"Phil sends his regards," Brandt said, kicking the heavy duffel to my feet with a thunk.

I knelt and unzipped the bag to find a cache of weapons I recognized from past raids. Chase whistled as he lifted a stack of high-volume mags. Carol gently set down a second, smaller bag.

"Your captain's been following your work on Apex through his wife." She smiled softly, unzipping the bag to show three sets of Kevlar. "Our bunco nights always did spill the best tea." She gave Lila a wink. "Maybe no one gets shot this time."

"He had to keep his nose clean for plausible deniability." Brandt lifted a sawed-off shotgun and a box of buckshot, handing them to Sam. "Figured off-books gear won't be tied to the department and can be written off later as gang-related violence."

"I... don't know what to say." I rasped past a grief-raw throat. "He knows about today?"

I was hauled out of the event so fast that I hadn't even considered speaking to my boss or any of the uniforms alerted by the commotion. I hadn't even thought to ask for their help or inform them.

"He's a smart guy, Phil. And he's damn tired of Apex turning our town upside down." Chief crossed to his wife Carol, wrapping an arm around her even as she held hands with Lila. "And so you know, I plan to stay here when the time comes. Protect the girls and all the kids."

He nodded to Chase, who returned the nod in kind.

I thought my Captain's support stopped when he turned a blind eye while I ran an off-books investigation into Apex. But when he shut me down, and I worried about Internal Affairs infiltration, he planned for plausible deniability.

I had underestimated the man.

I had underestimated them all.

Hours ticked by as I sat at the kitchen table with bandaged knuckles, making plans upon plans with my family. Lila scoured every file and every document we'd ever collected on Apex and Gia's senator father. Our best guess was that Gia had been taken back to Manhattan. So we focused on real estate holdings for a list of potential addresses.

The addresses spread across half of New York and up into Canada.

The cell phone was untraceable in its current state, but as Lila explained, she'd need only a few minutes to narrow the search field the second it was activated. She had set the tracking station to ready, compiled a list of potential addresses, and... we waited.

I ate something I couldn't taste.

Sam forced Lila into a nap.

Chase and Moira did the same.

Chief stayed up with me, staring at the bank of cell phones and laptops like they held the answer to all life's mysteries. I couldn't stop moving. I checked my gear, then double-checked it. Still, the phone sat cold. Ben woke twice; His world was undone, too. Holding him grounded me, so I kept him on my chest.

Time was immeasurable...until 11:36 pm, when my cell phone rang and a flurry of activity exploded. Carol lifted Ben from my arms, Sam darted to wake Lila, Chase and his chief circled me, holding a hand over my phone until Lila was in position.

The phone rang again.

"30 seconds and I have a zip code," she breathed, "Longer is better."

"Assume the call is being monitored," Chase warned, my knuckles aching as I clenched them.

A third ring came before my wrist was released, and I swiped to accept the call.

"Gia."

"Troy!" The seas parted, stars were born, and I came to life at her siren call.

"Where are you?" I slumped into the chair, knees unable to hold my weight.

There was a shuffling noise, and a new voice entered the call.

"Now, now, Officer Wilder. Let's not get ahead of ourselves." The devil incarnate.

Chase's hand clenched on my shoulder, and Sam moved into my line of sight, mouthing a silent message: stay cool.

"I assume you have a list of demands, Senator." My molars vibrated as I clamped on the rage rattling to break free.

"Don't waste my time by being small." His voice was smooth and precise. If not for the threat in his words, you might have mistaken the tone for business-like. "You have nothing to negotiate with." Lila motioned that she had the zip code, but gestured for me to buy more time.

I had to keep him talking and stay cool.

"Then why call at all?" I lowered my mask, stoic and calm. "If I have nothing you want?"

"You know, I did a little looking into you, Troy James Wilder. You're a helluva guy."

Chase and Sam exchange quizzical expressions at the sudden shift in tone. The man sounded almost jovial.

"A small-town cop, moving up in rank at an unprecedented rate. That's a climb I might've appreciated under better circumstances." His tone dripped with arrogance, but he was talking, and that was the goal.

"Is this the part where you try to recruit me like Dean Jensen?" I couldn't help the jab I fired off after.

"Oh-ho-ho, and the boy came to play!" I swear I heard him clap his hands with glee. This bastard was enjoying this. "A former Marine like you should understand...every army needs fodder on the front lines."

Chase and Sam shifted on their feet to match the shift in his tone. He'd looked well into my background. Lila's thumbs-up told me I no longer needed to placate the piece of shit.

"Don't waste my time being small, Michael." I mimicked his tone while spitting his words back at him.

"I want the documents Gia stole from me." He commanded. "Bring them to me, alone, and I'll hand over Ben's birth Certificate and a notarized document that signs over all my rights."

"And Gia?"

"Take the deal," Gia shouted from the background. "I'll be fine."

"No Gia...no books." I barked, desperate to hear her call out again. "That's the deal."

"You think you have the power to tell me what to do, boy?" The coldness in his voice was nearly as jarring as the volume he'd reached, and it sounded like he paced around the phone as his voice went round and round. "You think you can outdo me when I have your entire backwater town in my goddamn pocket?" His muffled steps clicked under the rising volume of his words. "That event today...that was mine: every permit, every face. I plucked Gia like low-hanging fruit. You think I can't end her just as fast?"

"You won't touch her!" The Beast snapped, unfurling its claws for a fight'

'Troy, stop–' Gia's distant plea was cut short by a hard slap...and a yelp of pain.

"NO!" I stood so fast my chair slammed back, but there was nothing to do, nowhere to run, nothing to hit. "I'll end you, Bianchi. I swear to God if a single hair on her head is harmed, I'll—"

Chief Brandt rested a hand on my shoulder, trying to stop me even as Gia's father broke into a huff of dry laughter.

"Oh my, my, my." The Senator's tone shifted into something cruel. "She let you touch her."

My heart stuttered; I'd given away too much.

"Did she let you in, Officer Wilder?"

'Troy...No...Papa, please!' Another slap cracked through the line, sending Lila and Moira hiding in Chief Brandt's arms.

"That explains your sudden boldness, daughter." He spoke, low and soft, in a growl dripping with the intensity of a monster stalking its next meal. "You opened your legs for a cheap badge and a warm bed." His roar came with another yelp, and shuffling sounds that painted violent details I'd never recover from. "Preening with all the confidence of a well-laid whore...like your mother, I suppose."

"You bastard!" I screamed as glass shattered somewhere near her.

"Get her out of my face!" He hollered to a third party as Gia's call to me drifted away.

'Troy, please. Just take Ben and...'

I was a fool.

I'd given him my love here, and it was her ruin.

"Seeing as you've fallen for my daughter's big cow eyes and sob story, you've lost your balls, so let me tell you how this'll go."

Lila leaned over, pale and sobbing, as Carol and Sam tried to help her.

"The books....where?" I growled, another distant cry from Gia cracking across my chest.

"Get in the car. Start driving to the city." The Senator's earlier levity was gone. "I'll call you in 2 hours with the address. Come alone, items unboxed in one hand and my son in the other."

"No." Moira clamped a hand over her mouth, her slip as unintended as mine had been.

"Love's made you stupid, officer." A slight singsong in his voice belied the malice in Bianchi's words. "You have no move here. I know your whole family. I have your town on a wire and my finger on the trigger." He laughed...actually laughed...before adding. "So you'll do the smart thing, or I'll burn your world."

"I'll come. I'll bring what you asked for. But Gia–"

"Only lives if you obey." A small huff was sighed over the line. "And that's only if I decide she's worth the effort to clean off your smeared fingerprints."

The call was disconnected.

Lila threw up.

Moira collapsed in Chase's arms.

I finalized plans for Michael Bianchi's death.

He used my love as a weakness–He would bleed for it.

53

GIA

I BARELY REGISTERED THE pain of being pulled from my father's office by my hair, as the sound of my screams echoed off cold marble floors. I'd tried to save Ben and Troy, and I had hoped that my father's need for his ledgers was enough. He wanted votes and power without consequences, and I thought I could return his leverage and save my family. I'd miscalculated how much my father could still barter me off. I had stupidly assumed that because I'd rebelled, I'd be tainted goods.

But I forgot... my father's favorite pastime was always taking away what I loved.

I saw the switch flip in my father's eyes when Troy's heart bled through the line.

My father was no longer human enough to want to use and discard me. He'd keep me here to punish, to make me serve, or otherwise discard me like my mother.

"Ms. Bianchi, if you would please." The doctor from the clinic half-dragged me down the hall until we reached the kitchen, and I was summarily flung through the swinging doors. The cold marble floor slammed into my knees as I struggled to protect my face and head from the sprawl I was thrown into. "Your father seems none too happy with you." He slid a kitchen chair around, gliding his hand towards the seat with a gentile calm that belied all the violence he'd been a part of.

His silence was even worse as he watched me–brows lifted in anticipation.

I crawled into the chair, a dog heeling to a command.

"I don't believe we've been properly introduced." He unbuttoned his sports coat, pulled a chair before me, and sat knee to knee. "I'm Dr. Alex Freeman."

I promptly spat on his extended hand.

"What did he promise you?" Dr. Freeman smiled as he pulled a handkerchief from his pocket, wiping his hands before answering.

"I genuinely believe your father will improve the world." The calm, almost cordial way he spoke was chilling and echoed a near familiarity in his ease. No anger, no manipulation. Just stoic politeness that grated on the nerves. I steadied myself, bolstering my courage in the protection of an otherwise empty room. No servants, but no father either. Using his own technique against him, I sat still, eyes wide, waiting for him to answer my question even as he shook his finger and smiled at me.

"You're a smart girl, Ms. Bianchi." I lifted my brows again...here boy... "Surgeon General in his presidential cabinet."

"So a pretty wife, a pretty title, but no soul." I snarked.

"Oh, I have no wife *yet*." His inflection on the word yet had my skin prickling. "Though I suspect that'll be remedied soon. His campaign kicks off next year. With an easy win, my role will be shaping federal policy and—"

My father entered the kitchen in an explosion of red-faced, disheveled rage. He paced the island like a race circuit, slowly removing his suit jacket. He folded it methodically, then set it aside. He never looked at me or Dr. Freeman as he turned his eyes to his shirt cuffs, and my heart all but stopped.

First sleeve, unbuttoned. Rolled three times to the elbow as he steadied his breathing.

Taking the air I no longer needed as my lungs forgot their function.

Second sleeve, unbuttoned. Rolled three times to the elbow.

My legs begged to run even as my brain screamed to make myself small.

His breathing slowed, my father removed his tie, tugging it to one side and the other before it was loose enough to slip free. He then paused all movement, rolling the tie from tip to tip in an orderly fashion.

He stacked the tie neatly on top of his folded jacket.

Cold skittered down my spine.

He rounded the island to where I sat, only looking into my eyes at the last step.

Only to show me how hollow his eyes were.

Then he hit me so hard, I flew.

The darkness flickered but couldn't hold me. I floated above it in spurts, feeling my body lifted off the ground, tasting the blood in my mouth. My father's face waved in front of me as he took a seat, watching someone else clean his mess.

Darkness came again.

The sharp burn of ammonia in my nose yanked me into the cold scrutiny of my father's scathing gaze.

"You disappoint me, daughter." He was calm now, like the man at the desk with the glass of scotch.

"Sorry," I slurred, my head lolling to the side of the kitchen chair I was still somehow sitting in. "I was trained to be a wife...not take a punch."

"You were trained to be untouched." He tilted sideways before Dr. Freeman waved a stick of something sharp and pungent under my nose.

The jerk of my head back to center pounded in waves.

"Sorry, Papa." I bit back a smile at the ridiculousness of our conversation. "Guess I was a lousy student." My father stood, and the flinch that jerked my face to the side had my cheek throbbing in memory of the last hit I'd taken. But he didn't strike.

"You mistake my disappointment for a loss, my Gia." My father nodded over my shoulder as hands gripped me under my arms, lifting me to my feet and half-dragging me to the kitchen table.

"What?" I tried to sit up, but was laid back to the table with a shove, my head throbbing as it bounced off the wood. "What are you..."

Adrenaline cut through my fog as I watched my father round to stand above my head, while slowly removing his belt.

"I don't suppose you wanna tell me how long you were fucking that man, daughter." He slipped his belt loose from his pants, rolling each end around his fists into a tight grip as my stomach coiled. "Did you use protection, or did you breed yourself out like a broodmare?" In a blur, the belt was around my neck. "'Cause your man's coming here, and I'd love a little surprise leverage if he finds out there's a baby on board."

I grasped at the belt against my neck as it dragged me to the edge of the table until my head hung off the edge, and the belt tightened in my father's grip.

"Worth a mention, sir." Dr. Freeman's voice rang through with all the vanilla politeness of a 1950s milkman. "A blood test can take a while to get results. A pelvic exam and urine test are faster, though they require...cooperation."

"Thank you, Doctor." My father sat in a chair near my head, applying just enough pressure with the belt to hold me in place, but not to suffocate me into unconsciousness while I thrashed and kicked my legs. "What's it gonna be, mia caro?" Leaning down, he whispered in my ear. "You gonna cooperate for a pregnancy test, or do I need to tighten this belt until you take a nap and then have the good doctor find out firsthand?"

Sick, psychotic, evil, vile...

I opened my mouth, trying to speak, but unable to breathe enough for words.

Flailing my legs, I let my fingertips slip loose from where the belt dug into my neck, and I swung wildly towards my father's face until the pressure lessened just enough to get a lungful of air.

My father released the belt and stood with a smirk.

He'd made his point.

Cooperation came easily after that.

54

TROY

O F ALL THE ADDRESSES we'd linked to Bianchi and Apex, only one was a historic Manhattan penthouse. Lucky us, Lila knew that the old penthouses were subject to regulations from the Landmarks Preservation Commission (LPC) when undergoing renovations. According to her, 'the one percenters were known to renovate for every major holiday,' letting her hack blueprints.

Chase drove the first hour, while Sam finalized his portion of the plan over the phone with Lila. We had a ledger, a few documents, and even a flash drive, but there were holes. Lila reasoned there had to be more documents to connect it all, and so, while I was focused on Gia, Sam would work his way into Bianchi's office to search for more.

Once we were about 40 minutes out of Manhattan, we pulled off to gear up and switched me to the driver's seat so Chase could discuss his plan with Moira and his Chief. According to Brandt, the NYFD gained access to most penthouses through strategic access points using

Key Boxes and/or Data Terminals that required Mobile Access Codes. Chase wouldn't know which until he was on-site. Key boxes were easy, but mobile access codes could change daily. As Chase was the muscle to get Gia out if I became incapacitated, he was also our escape route and thus crucial. It sickened me to think he might be delayed—or blocked entirely.

Another grey area I couldn't afford to focus on as 1:56 am rolled around and a text from Gia's father arrived.

"Confirmed the penthouse address," I announced. "Ten minutes out."

I circled the building, dropping Sam and Chase off a block away, then rounded to the front and parked.

'Comms Check.' Lila's voice in my ear was all business.

The comms system we used at the library event was short-range, and we needed both Chief and Lila here for this to work. As such, we cobbled together a system using dummy burner phones and a VPN that routed directly into Lila's workstation. She and Chief worked from a speakerphone at the cabin, while Chase, Sam, and I had encrypted Bluetooth earpieces.

'Boyscout's at the outer door,' Chase confirmed. *'Key box here... no sweat.'*

'Time to work those legs, kiddo.' His Chief responded. *'You've got about 40 flights to climb.'*

'Oorah,' Sam replied. *'Samoa's at rear sanitation entrance. I think I'm about to dumpster-dive this bitch to get in.'*

'Trash chutes,' your best bet,' Lila answered. *'Bring her home, baby.'*

"Oorah," I answered, reaching for the files I'd brought from the cabin before exiting the car.

Rounding it, I glanced inside the windowed lobby to find a single security guard behind the desk. "One guard at the desk." Leaning into the passenger seat of Sam's SUV, I unbuckled my tiny bundle wrapped in blue.

Everything about this made me sick.

But I had to save Gia.

I hoisted Ben's diaper bag on one shoulder, tucked the files up under my arm, and headed into the lobby with a battle cry in my ear.

'Go get her, TJ.'

55

GIA

MY HANDS STRUGGLED TO hold the package as the foil wrapper surrounding the pregnancy test slowed my progress. I'd been dragged back to my childhood bedroom, to the ensuite within it, to determine what my new value to my father would be.

Thankfully, my father didn't come with me, and I was given privacy to do this alone.

That's all I could find to be thankful for now: Privacy to pee.

Taking the test out, I didn't bother to read the instructions as Dr. Freeman barked them to me when he shoved the box in my hands. 'Pee on the stick, cap it, and set it on the counter for me.' I completed it, set it aside, and washed my hands. Drying, I tipped the box off the edge, and a second test emerged. 'Bonus 2 for 1' read the foil label. I tossed it back in the box, then threw it in the trash.

I took a moment of quiet with my mirrored reflection.

Troy's love lingered in a million quiet ways—fuller curves, brighter skin, jeans that now hugged my hips. How long would it take to undo it all? Even the circles under my eyes were all but gone, save for the new bloom of color courtesy of my father.

I hated how my hands shook when I grazed the print on my cheek and the violent red mottling around my neck. I was unprepared for the belt. My father had never been so vicious, and yet tonight he pinned me to the table as easily as reading the morning paper.

How would he respond if I were pregnant?

How would he respond if I weren't?

One answered as I glanced at the pregnancy test, saturated with a dark blue control line and...

A faint second line?

Lifting the test closer, I squinted my eyes, tilting the stick back and forth in the light, hardly able to believe what I saw, as that shadow of a second line grew unmistakable.

I was pregnant.

I remembered Troy's face, launching into climax and swearing I'd always be his while we promised nothing would be between us. Then I imagined Troy's shock and fear when my father used this baby as leverage to torment him. Love twisted into fear, then sank into desolate terror as the knowledge of my father's cruelty poured into this new development in a violent gut-wrenching sickness that had me dry heaving.

Who would my father sell my baby to?

"Ms. Bianchi?" Dr. Freeman knocked at the door.

"Just a minute!" I shouted between painfully silent heaves, "I'll be out in a second." Tears ran hot down my nose, and when I reached for a tissue, I saw the box with the second test inside.

An idea took shape.

"You get one minute, then I'm coming in." Spurred into action, I quickly opened the second test, flushing the toilet to hide the noise, then dipped the second test into the remnants of the flushing toilet, hoping it held enough urine to activate the control line, but not enough to show a positive result.

I rewashed my hands, watching as the liquid moved across the test window and activated the control line. Success had me gasping in relief, so I waited to see if a second line would appear again.

"Ms. Bianchi." Freeman knocked at the door again, and I grabbed the first test and shoved it into the outer edge of my bra. Not even a minute had passed on the second test, but the jiggling door handle told me I was out of time.

"Fine, here!" I spun as the door opened, thrusting the fake test into Dr. Freeman's chest. "Guess I'm not even allowed to have a moment to pee alone." He palmed the test, noting its results with a nod before pocketing it and smiling back with the unnerving calm I was growing to hate.

"Your father has asked that you remain here for now. I'll report the results of your test and will return shortly." Turning on his heels, the smiling madman left.

The last thing I heard for hours was the sound of my door lock and receding footsteps.

I scoured my room, looking for anything that I could use. My in-house phone to the servants' quarters went unanswered, as expected. Father always sent them home when corrections were needed. I went through my closet and drawers, finding nothing of use. My small desk in the corner held nothing of value, except pens and papers, but I could write notes to no one of consequence.

My windows up here didn't open.

I could get no note out.

At some point, I must have drifted off, because the next thing I felt was the gentle caress of a hand petting my hair. Smooth, relaxing strokes, as if combing my locks with his fingers while softly whispering my name.

"Gia." He murmured, leaning to smell my hair.

It had been a dream.

A terrible dream.

"Gia," Troy's voice sounded lighter, higher, somehow, and I worked to pull myself closer to him even as remnants of the drugs used to knock me out earlier still lingered in my tissues. "Come, darling. We have a quick meeting, then we can go home." I lifted my head, my neck aching from its stiff position, but my brain tried to focus on the thing in his words that felt off. "I know, that needle was just awful." This wasn't Troy's usual cadence. This voice was too passive...too... "But it'll heal soon, and we won't need those in the future, will we, darling?"

Darling!?

With sudden awareness, I bolted up, shaking the last of the fog away as I spun to find Dr. Freeman standing next to my chair. This wasn't a terrible dream...but a living nightmare.

"Take your hands off me." I spat, stomach curdling at the echo of him sniffing and petting me like a dog.

"Your father is waiting." He ignored my reaction and again expected cool obedience. "And I think you'll want to hear what he has to say." Taking in his unruffled demeanor and the simpleton smile he lifted across his sycophant face, I considered my options and realized I had none.

Straightening, I pinned him with an icy glare, then brushed his shoulder with mine as I passed between him and my desk to exit the room, secretly pocketing an ink pen. I didn't know where I could use it, but I felt armed for battle as I walked the silent corridor between my room and my father's office.

Freeman's slimy countenance became more unnerving by the second. He was never without a smile, never without the pinnacle of well-bred manners, and yet he happily obeyed my father, petting me and calling me darling. I didn't have time to think about it as we approached my father's office. Before stepping through the door, I let my hand drift to my shoulder, feeling the slight pressure from the pregnancy test hidden in my bra.

I'd saved Troy, spared Ben, but now there was so much more at stake and only I knew it.

"Took you long enough." My father snipped, giving only half his attention as he scanned his laptop.

"The ketamine lingers. She was napping." Dr. Freeman answered for me, pulling around a chair and offering the seat to me along with a bottle of water. I hated this attentive shift from the man, but I couldn't ignore that my mouth was dry.

I took the water, swigging it half down in one gulp.

"Who the fuck owns this account!" My father bellowed into his phone, slamming his hand on his desk. "They posted again. Over a million hits in an hour." Whoever my father was yelling at clearly didn't have an answer he liked. "I don't care about goddamn tweets. I care about the email I just got about donors backing out!"

My father seethed and noticed for the first time his untucked shirt and hair so rumpled it appeared he'd spent the last hour pulling at it with both hands.

"Don't I pay you to handle this shit? Don't ask me if it's true—just kill that goddamn hashtag!" Slamming the phone on his desk, my father leaned back and chugged the last of his scotch before crossing to the bar for another.

"Congratulate me, daughter." He spun, glass in hand, as he sneered. "I'm trending." He tossed back two fingers of scotch in a gulp, then sat once more at his desk. "I don't know how you did it, but I'll confess... it's a masterclass in underhanded fuckery."

I had no clue what he was talking about, but every instinct screamed to act like I did.

"I learned at the feet of the master now, didn't I?" I kept my tone calm, my face stoic, desperately hoping to hide all emotion.

"They posted since you've been here." My father spun his laptop towards me, and Dr. Freeman pulled it closer so we could see a social media feed open on the screen. "So it can't be from you."

> @InsiderFromBianchiOffice: How does Senator' traditional values' sleep at night! Staffer quoted as saying, 'If she so much as says a cross word, he threatens her. She's not sheltered - she's imprisoned!' #SetHerFree
>
> @InsiderFromBianchiOffice: Look at this screenshot someone sent of her holding a baby. She looks too thin and exhausted. Is this why her father kept her out of college? The people want to know. #SetHerFree
>
> @InsiderFrom BianchiOffice: Just In! New screenshots from a former donor claim they were told their son would be promised to Senator Daddy's dear daughter for the right price. Is he trafficking his daughter for votes?!? #SetHerFree

The photos were all blurry or off-center, so the proof wasn't as straightforward as one would hope. However, the truly staggering part was the comments flying in faster than I could read.

Comment: Hard to preach family values when your daughter is blinking 'help me' off camera.

Comment: Maybe dear ol' dad is really Daddy Dearest. #nowire-hangars

Comment: Has anyone seen her recently?

Comment: Time for a welfare check at the 1-percenters.

Each post shared the same hashtag, #SetHerFree, and each one contained insider knowledge, screenshots, promises, and quotes all about me, my life, and my whereabouts. One even had a side shot of me holding Ben, his face obscured, but I could tell it was from when I was barely leaving the rental house the night Troy found me. I could only guess that Lila lifted it off the original attacker's phone. I looked like a deer in headlights.

"This doesn't matter." Father's voice was velvet-wrapped venom, laced with the promise of retribution. I'd heard the tone only once before, the night I'd been slapped to the ground with a newborn in my arms. "This is a nuisance, but it doesn't change my plans."

"If I may, sir?" Freeman cleared his throat, waiting for his master's dismissive wave to go on before he picked up where my father left off. "You see, darling, the smear campaign was clearly launched by someone aiming to discredit your father and somehow protect you in the light of temporary fame."

"Like I didn't coin the phrase, 'fall into a bucket of shit, step out smelling like a rose.'" My father's sneer was a little slurred, and it was clear he'd been drinking more than usual.

"Masterful, you are," Freeman fanboyed. "And what better way to spin some unfortunate posts about broken family values than a happy wedding and a baby to bolster voter confidence?"

"But I'm not pregnant." I blurted.

"Oh, we'll remedy that." The doctor smiled, lifting the lid on a small box containing a collection of syringes, needles, and pill bottles. "Did you know that, medically speaking, there are a multitude of drugs considered safe for women during early pregnancy and/or when trying to conceive?" He lifted each bottle, lining them across the desk, turning the labels towards me.

Haloperidol, Benadryl...the names were long and ominous.

"Depending on the need, they can be slipped in water, injected, or swallowed."

Seroquel, Lorazepam...it all seemed like something I should react to, but I was just so damn tired of the mental gymnastics.

"The effects can be instant, or long build over time, and a dull, shaky countenance can be explained as anemia or hormonal fatigue."

My head felt tingly as I reevaluated my half-drank water bottle.

"Nothing swings the image of a tyrant father like a doting grandfather swooning over his new son-in-law and their baby boy." My father's voice was the purr of a predator. "I can't kill you for leaving me, but I can marry you off to a man who'll keep you compliant."

Vomit - I wanted to vomit. Why couldn't I vomit?

"You're feeling the Benadryl now." Dr. Freeman leaned in, sliding my chair closer to him as a single tear slipped down my cheek. "That'll keep you groggy while we work out the license and get little Ben re-settled."

Ben...no...not Ben!

"After we kill the Wilders, I'll start you on a round of meds to help you enjoy our wedding night, and before long, all this nonsense will be forgotten."

"Weddings at the Plaza and Grandbabies look great on a campaign trail." My father laughed...laughed...as I clamored to think of any way to avoid being chemically erased. "And the best part is, thanks to your little dalliance with one slightly unhinged officer in upstate New York... I'll get to write off all this media as the work of a jealous suitor who couldn't take no for an answer."

The room spun as my father maniacally triumphed over all my best plans.

Footsteps in the hall—heavy and urgent.

Freeman glanced toward the door.

My father stood, fixing his shirt.

Something had shifted...arrived.

My someone.

"Troy," I whimpered, trying to stand, to run to him. Dr. Freeman snaked around my waist as he cooed in my ear.

"Don't worry, darling. I won't let him hurt you."

56

TROY

T HE ELEVATOR RIDE TO the penthouse was slow, and with
comms muted by the elevator's walls, I could hear the full roar
of all my darkest thoughts.

I'd lost her.

Failed her.

Let her go.

The mantra spun on repeat like a highlight reel of failures. My
siren deserved so much more than I'd given her. I'd let her down.
Had it not been for the opening of the elevator doors, I might have
lain down and died under the weight of it all.

'I Repeat...Clear your throat when you're off the elevator,' Lila
commanded softly in my comms.

I did as she asked, stepping into a vacant marbled corridor, dark
save for the glow of light coming from an open door at the halfway
point.

'Hashtag's paying off.' Moira's voice came through. *'Lila's fakes are solid enough that the smear campaign grew legs instantly.'* Moira devised the idea to build extra protection to keep Gia from being moved, or worse. By her logic, if the whole world were looking at her father, he'd have his hands tied and not be as free to work around the system. *'Hashtag SetHerFree's been picked up by two major network outlets already, and his opponent has knocked it into the stratosphere with their own theories trending.'*

'Daddy's Dearest's gonna be pissed.' Lila's gleeful sarcasm dripped through the line.

Muddled voices grew clear as I neared the door that opened into an office, but one voice in particular had my beast clanging against the bars of his cell.

"Troy." That was her.

Rounding the corner, I locked eyes with my girl and the dead-man-walking coiled up behind her, whispering in her ear. She seemed pale and shaky, but I couldn't tell if it was fatigue or fear with how her hair half-hung in front of her face.

I wanted to brush it back.

"Ah, the man of the hour." Senator Bianchi straightened his tie as he rounded the desk and stood beside his daughter. I scanned and saw no overt weapons. "I see you brought the baby and the files." He spoke with all the bravado of a bullfighter wearing a red cape. "If you were any more obedient, I'd need to monogram your leash."

I would make him eat those words.

'This fucker has a death wish.' Sam commented.

'Yeah, he does.' Chase added.

'Focus, Kid.' Chief Brandt, the reasonable CO amidst the haze in my bloodthirsty head. *'Get her outta there.'*

"Gia." I kept my voice level, knowing my audience was two-fold. "What have they done to you?"

I stepped forward, noting the shards of glass under my feet as I scanned her body for signs of cuts. Still, I didn't smell gunpowder. Surely they didn't invite me here without arming themselves.

Surely this couldn't be that easy.

"Troy, no...not Ben." Her words were slurred, halted by the man who tightened his grip around her waist. A water bottle hung limp in one of her hands.

Sedated?

"My fiancé is a little tired at present." The voice was familiar, and I had to squint to make out his features as he half hid behind my siren's raven mane. "She'll feel much better when you hand over our son."

My rage was a living thing.

She wasn't his fiancée; she was mine. And Ben was never their son, but ours. Mine and Gia's. They were my family, that was my girl. I focused on the details I could see of the man as I cataloged the litany of ways I could flay the skin from his bones, then recognition dawned.

"You're the doctor from the urgent care clinic." The pieces clicked into place. "How long have you known my Gia and my Ben?" I glared at his fingers digging into her belly, like she was his to lose.

'Dr. Alex Freeman?' Sam's question rang through the comms. *'He was at the Fair, too.'*

'I'm running his file.' Lila chimed in. *'One second.'*

"Dr. Freeman, isn't it?" I added the new knowledge, hoping to throw him off guard. "How long have you known *my* Gia and *my* Ben?" I gave the little blue bundle in my arms a lift, hoping to tap into his misplaced sense of propriety to buy time, to get him off my girl.

"Troy...no." Gia tried to speak, hands reaching up around her shirt collar, but shook her head, her eyes struggling to focus. She was definitely drugged.

"What did you give her?" I barked.

"My daughter was a little distressed." Her father answered, parading in front of her before patting Dr. Freeman on the back. "What with planning a wedding so quickly and all."

'Got him,' Lila whispered. *'New York MD. Legit credentials. But he just filled a fuck-ton of scripts. I'm texting the list to Sam.'*

It took Sam only seconds to respond.

'Goddamn...if he's put any of this in her, she's half-out of her mind.' Sam huffed. *'I can flush it out with IV bags I brought, but she's not walking out on her power.'*

'I'll get her down,' Chase answered.

They'll all bleed for this.

"I gotta hand it to you, officer." The senator strolled over to a stocked bar, pouring a generous serving of something brown. "Your little social media campaign was a surprise." He took a swig, then tipped the glass towards me. "Are you a Scotchman?"

I glared as he shrugged and swigged the rest. Then, he inexplicably sent the glass flying across the floor, shattering into an explosion of tiny, glittering shards; Landscape explained.

"You don't get to where I am without contingencies, boy!" His voice was raised, angry, and not stable.

'I'm on the level.' Sam chirped in my ear. *'Where am I going?'*

"I assume we aren't meeting in your office so you can break your arm patting your back." I did my best to convey a tone of nonchalance as I scanned the room, looking for weapons and calculating the safest way to get Gia out of the hands of a man who was all but holding her upright.

"You thought you had me, officer. Admit it." Gia's father preened, strutting back and forth between her and the bar like a prize peacock. "You thought you could take me down like my backups don't have backups."

'Let him talk, Troy,' Lila said. *'Arrogant Fucker'll hang himself with what I'm recording.'*

"But Apex can't lose!" Bianchi grabbed the front of Gia's shirt as he screamed. Gia flinched, eyes popping open, and I couldn't stop my step towards her.

"Look at me, love." Her eyes were glassy, but I had her. "I've got you."

I tried my best to convey all that I couldn't say with my eyes.

My brothers were here.

We had a plan.

It will all be okay.

But she struggled just to stay awake.

"Even still?" Her father released her with a disgusted sneer, "As she stands engaged in the arms of another man?" He asked the question as if she were somehow tainted goods. "Maybe the dog needs to smell another scent, eh, doc?"

The doctor tried to shuffle Gia forward, but she stumbled.

"You won't take her," I growled, preparing to empty my hands, release my gun, and shorten the guest list to this party by one.

"Oh, but I think I will." The doctor produced a syringe, pressing the tip against her neck as he slowly stalked past me. There...was the real weapon, and it threatened the one thing guaranteed to keep me frozen in my place. "I think I'll visit my fiancé's bedroom."

'Bedroom, got it...rerouting,' Sam whispered in my ear as the doctor glanced at the senator.

"One more hurrah under daddy's roof before I take my bride to her new life?"

He'd said one more...one more...my God, what had they done to her?

"Come, darling." Sleepy tears rolled down my girl's cheeks, her hands gripping her belly in terror or pain, I couldn't tell.

I would burn them all to the ground for this.

"Enjoy her, son." Impotent to stop them, I locked onto her eyes, willing her to hear my heart pounding.

He won't touch you again.

I will save you.

I will stop him.

"You can't have her," I growled.

'I'm on the level.' Chase huffed. *'Meet you in the bedroom, Sam.'*

'Focus, Troy.' Moira's voice, calm and smooth, feathered into my ears. *'Your brothers have her. Now help us stop her father.'*

57

GIA

"I THINK THAT WENT well, don't you, darling?" Freeman's voice vibrated my hair, making my skin prickle with revulsion.

Why was he touching me?

The hallway was dimly lit, making it harder for my eyes to focus as I was half-shoved, half-dragged to my room. I stumbled, sending my eyes open in flutters of light and tears as the tiny wave of adrenaline burned through the drugs pulling me down. Everything felt heavy, my limbs, my thoughts, but I knew with pristine clarity that I had to fight. I pulled at the hands around me, straining to uncurl the fingers that dug into my sides.

"Come, darling." His voice was velvet rot, and I wished I could throw up on him. "Let's make our coupling official for the sake of your father's wishes."

He tossed me forward.

I prepared to hit the floor, but landed on something mercifully soft. I rolled to my back, lifting on my elbows and muscling my eyelids open to face Dr. Freeman.

"Why are you–" Fingers tugged at my ankles, dragging me down before my waist began to jerk back and forth. My hands grabbed for my jeans, only to find other hands.

No.

No, no, no, no.

I grappled for purchase against fingers that moved so fast they blurred in my watery eyes. I bent my knees, landing one good, solid kick to Dr. Freeman's gut before–

"No, you fucking don't!"

There, that voice, I knew that voice.

It wasn't Troy.

A bang.

A whomp.

Someone grunted.

"I got this asshat, check Gia." Someone else now.

I was surrounded.

To move.

To run.

I had to open my eyes.

"Whoa, little sister." A soft, familiar voice hovered. Hands, arms, held mine as a bright flash grazed my eyes. "She's barely here." He spoke to the man whomping something in the background. "Gia...can you hear me? It's Sam."

"Sam?" crashing in the distance. A lamp? "Freeman...he's" I tried to warn them; My brain couldn't connect.

"Chase's taking the trash out. Can you focus on me?"

I opened my eyes. Sam was there, swirling in the dark edges.

"Troy...tell him..."

I needed to tell him about the baby.

I lifted my hand to the test in my bra, but Sam held my wrist.

"Pulse is steady, but weak." Why wouldn't he let me get the test? "Gia, do you know what they gave you?"

He flashed the light again.

It hurt.

"Come on, Gia. Stay with me." Knuckles dug into my sternum, jolting me. "She's taken a hit or two. Maybe a concussion."

In the background, someone growled a slur, and the whomping picked up again.

"Benadryl." I slurred. "Bastard..."

I pointed weakly toward a blur of Freeman flying across the room like garbage.

"Okay. Benadryl hits hard, but it'll burn off quick."

Sam was commanding and clear.

How was he so clear?

"Baby," at last. I made words. "The baby."

"Ben's safe." Sam moved around me, wrapping me in something warm. "Moira and Lila, they're all waiting for you."

"No." I lifted my hand again, tugging at the test wedged in my bra. "Tell him..."

It was at the edge of my...

I barely grabbed....

fingers wouldn't...

too stuck...

The test slipped clear as the voices grew dim.

"Oh shit, dude." Sam's voice was all I could hear.

Arms scooped me up.

"Don't jostle her head. Keep her up in case she hurls."

I was shifted.

Strong arms.

"I gotcha, Gia."

Darkness.

Floating.

Silence.

58

TROY

Troy *'Focus, Troy.'* Moira's voice, calm and smooth, feathered into my ears. *'Your brothers have her. Now help us stop her father.'*

'She's right, bro.' Sam's hushed voice followed. *'Going dark until Gia's out.'*

No!

I knew what it meant: he'd muted his comms.

It was the right call to keep me focused.

I could have bloodied Sam for it.

"Now that it's just the two of us," Gia's father rounded his desk, plopping into his chair with a smug grin of triumph while I stood frozen, remembering how Dr. Freeman touched...held her. My jaw ached under the pressure of my imagination. "Shall we dispense with the pleasantries?" His arrogance hung in the air—oily and thick, coating everything in the room, expecting me to do his bidding.

But he was right.

I had to wait until my girl was safe.

I had to wait while my brothers got her out.

I had to wait.

I had to make him wait.

I had to buy... more... time.

"You surprise me, Senator Bianchi." Having no other ideas, I decided to stroke the man's ego and hope all the broken glass meant he was drunk enough to get confessional.

"How so?"

"A single security guard in the lobby. No weapons check. No one is in the elevator. And now," I gave the room a cursory once-over, noting the audacious chandelier that hung mid-room like it fell out of a castle. "Not a single member of security guarding you or your daughter."

"Oh, you American-made men, always so hands-on." Bianchi broke into a blustery laugh that seemed to bubble up from his guts. "You learn quick in the Stidda; you control an opponent best when you control their mind."

'Stidda.' Lila was still in my ear. *'Digging now. Keep him talking.'*

"Not you, though," I tipped my head once to the side as if considering. "You like to bully little girls?"

"You think I came up working logistics out of Palermo...turning shipping brokers for blood and bodies...just to bully my daughter?" A flash of irritation simmered beneath the cocky smile plastered across his face. "I broke off on my own when I found a stateside power with much more commercial appeal and a far greater reach." He spread his hands wide, waving around the room as if it held an audience hanging on his every word.

"And still, here you sit. Short man in a cheap suit surrounded by yes-men with no real power." It was a direct dig at his pride, and my aim landed true.

"I HAVE ALL THE POWER, BOY!" He slammed a fist to the desk, standing to pace as he ranted. "Who else could take a local skin trade up through the cartel ranks and spin that mother fucker into good ol' American red, white, and blue votes?!" He crossed to the bar, emptying the last of the brown liquor into a glass. "Who else could foresee the value of international logistics routes going to our great neighbor in the north instead of through Mexico? I fucking did that!"

He tipped the glass, giving it an irritated sneer before slamming it to the bar in a panting huff, like he couldn't tell the difference between fury and pride.

"So...you didn't come to Lake Placid for the scenery?" I goaded, making my voice as blasé as possible, but needing to know how he'd ended up in my family's world.

"No one knows the value of those long-abandoned Logging routes like a shipping man." He gave a broad smile, flaring his fingers in a showy gesture of pride.

'Got it!' Lila said. *'Stidda was a Cosa Nostra spin-off that floundered back in the 80s. But their roots run deep.'* I listened intently, sifting for whatever I could use. *'Jesus, Bianchi's father was a Vieri by blood. They were known as the white wolves across Tuscany, Lombardy, and Sicily. He's old mafia money.'*

"And so the great white wolf landed here and decided to spread his pack." I let the revelation drop coolly, watching Bianchi's dead eyes freeze above his empty smile.

"Marcus warned me about you." He sneered, momentary surprise stifled. "When his recruitment experiment failed to launch, but garnered the attention of an unhinged fireman with brothers...he told me you'd be a problem." He faced me head-on as if squaring up for a fight, and I couldn't stop my smirk at the idea of pounding this waste of skin into the ground. "But he didn't tell me you'd be so dumb as to bring up my roots."

I was right.

Bianchi came here to spread his father's mafia contacts.

"Brinks' was an idiot who died pissing himself." I took another jab, beginning to feel the tingle of time passing as my brothers remained silent.

"Marcus understood legacy." His retort was sharp; I'd struck another nerve.

"Legacy?" I cocked an eyebrow at the blue bundle sitting quietly in my arms.

"Organized Crime can only get you so far without going legit." Bianchi stalked back to his desk. "And there's no better syndicate, no better global power broker, than public office." He slunk into his chair. "Gia's mother was convenient and pretty and connected, but my daughter held the most value with my timeline." He pointed limply to my arms. "That little guy will secure my votes with a republican senate majority leader. But Gia was to end up with a future Supreme Court judge before she spread her whore legs for you."

"Can't control your family but expect to run a nation?" I tsk'd, channeling my murderous impulses into my only weapon of use; words. "What would Hashtag SetHerFree say about that?"

"You think a goddamn social media campaign can undo me, boy?!" He was red-faced and spitting, exactly where I wanted him. "I have other senators. I can make other sons and–"

"But you can't get there on your own merit?"

"I'm returning the purpose of men!" He slammed a fist on the desk, a vein pulsing in his neck. "Ask yourself, how does a man get to my position? Huh? How does a kid with old country ties make it to the presidential ticket unless he's put there by people who believe in him?! I gave broken men purpose by serving their needs in the quickest way possible."

"A little blow?" I teased

"No one parties like the Italians!"

That's drugs. Lila marked.

"Some guns?" I let him linger in the moment

"God bless the 2nd amendment, baby!"

That's weapons.

"And a little human trafficking across the border?" It was the piece I'd guessed, but we hadn't confirmed.

"Every president likes a warm bed for his foreign allies!"

Mother Fucker. Lila spit in my ear. *I got it all.*

"And all for the price of a little... emphatic assertion?"

Oh, the delicious rage that flashed through that man's eyes.

"Marcus floated that experiment to see if he could recruit some muscle for the dirty work." Bianchi's voice grew deadly calm, and as a fellow predator in the wings, I understood how very close he was to tipping into the kind of madness where mistakes were made. "Power requires grunts."

"You mean your right-hand man, Marcus Brinks, who you directed to kill the two NYPD Cops, Rivera and Rivera, but lost the third one? The one who hustled his way into a failed Internal Affairs position to corrupt the state of New York's police processes, and then lost control of a misogynistic arsonist, Dean Jensen, before attacking two women who ended up shooting him dead?" I smirked, giving that wild-eyed bastard the coldest stare down in history as he rapidly ticked off all the things I just told him we had proof of. "Or did your power not reach that far?"

The snap was nearly audible.

"POWER BELONGS TO THOSE WHO TAKE IT!" He stretched a handout to me, spitting as he screamed. "NOW GIVE ME MY GODDAMN FILES OR I'LL KILL THE BITCH AND HAVE HER HEAD MOUNTED LIKE A FUCKING DEER!"

'We got her, Troy.' Sam, in my ears, fed me the words I desperately needed. *'She's out of it, but okay. Chase's is getting her down. I'm heading to you.'*

"Thank you," I said for my family's benefit, even as I stepped slowly to the desk of US Senator Michael Bianchi.

He looked enraged, mad, and impatiently confused.

My footfalls were a measured cadence as I uncaged the beast.

Bianchi's eyes darted to my face, to my hands, unaware of the way I counted his breaths...backwards.

I slipped the ledger and files out from under my arm.

10, 9, his final breaths looked so good.

I stretched my arm slowly, hanging the files just above his hand.

6, 5, he glared, still unyielding in his desire for me to bend to his will.

The smile that split my face was unmistakable. Arrogant bastard missed it as he grasped for the files, flipping through them, brows pinching as the red, angry cheeks began to glisten with a sheen of sweat.

"What's this?" He flipped frantically through empty pages, blank ledgers, and files that held nothing. "What's...This?!"

3, 2, The dawning of realization was a work of art.

He looked to me, anger spinning to confusion as I slowly unwrapped the cradled blue bundle in my arms.

Not Ben.

Never, my Ben.

A perfectly wrapped and cradled nylon rope, coiled into a tight figure-eight formation.

The senator's mouth opened–to demand or beg–I didn't care.

I couldn't hear.

The Beast was snarling too loudly.

Gripping the end of the coil, I swung with all my might, backhanding the good senator right out of his glossy, leather chair. The sound of skull hitting marble was all I'd ever longed for. I let the rope unwind as I rounded to where the man clambered up his desk, reaching for a drawer that might have held a gun.

I didn't know.

I didn't check.

I cinched the rope around his neck like a collar on a rabid dog, yanking him back. His hands grasped his neck, the lovely purple color blushing his cheeks with such vigor. I dragged him across the room as Sam entered.

"The place is empty, Chase's working lookout. I wiped down her room for prints." He announced, smirking as the dog reached towards him. "Have fun, bro." He continued to the senator's desk, sat in the chair, put on a new pair of nitrile gloves, and opened the laptop. "Okay, babe. I'm at the desk. Guide me."

I tuned out Lila's instructions, giving the rope a little swing into a make-shift loop around the senator's neck, tightening it to the point of pain before stomping the edges down to the ground with my boot, driving Biachi's bloated face into the pretty glass shards.

'What's Troy doing?' Chase's voice interrupted Lila and Sam's discussion.

'Remember that chair?' Sam answered as I admired the angry weals blooming beneath Bianchi's jaw. *'The good senator wishes he were that chair.'*

One loop. Two. Three. I imagined each loop was named for some atrocity that deserved a swift and certain death.

Gia's life.

Ben's sale.

Gia's mother's death.

Bianchi flailed his legs and arms wildly, reaching for my pants as I paused my work. I lifted my foot only a hair's breadth, the purple receding as he gasped.

One in.

One out.

Foot down.

I let him watch as I braided the rope, loving the copper penny tang of blood that fed the beast who wanted a more violent end. The glass would have to do. As the noose took shape, I dropped it in front of Bianchi's face, the dull thud splashing the pool of spit and tears he'd grown in the absence of words.

'Files are downloading.' Lila's voice held an edge. *'Gimme five minutes.'*

Sam stood, coming to my side and watching as I reached for the senator, lifting him to his feet as he gagged and sputtered at false oxygen that wouldn't spare him.

"Let's make...a deal." He croaked. "I can give...anything...name it."

He grated...like a gnat at a picnic.

"Sam," I shoved the senator to my brother, who held the man by his elbows, pulling his arms back until his head bobbed forward. "How tall would you say this room is?" Sam glanced up, considering the height.

"Looks like 30...35 feet to me." I leaned down, pushing my gloved fist into the glass shards along the floor.

"If a great white wolf fell from that height," I pulled myself back to standing, meeting Sam's eyes just beyond Bianchi's shoulder and eyeing the glittering spikes adorning my weapon. "Would its jaw break?"

"I dunno. It'd have to be a massive wolf."

"I can make you police captain." The gnat bartered. "Money? I'm fucking loaded."

I balled my fist, swinging with all my might, planting the shards of glass in my knuckles into the jaw of US Senator Michael Bianchi. The singular click of his teeth wasn't nearly as satisfying as I'd hoped, but the echoing left-handed punch cracked his jaw. That wet thud bounced through the room like a thunderstorm.

I enjoyed that part more.

His head lolled sideways; a sob escaped in the drooling blood that leaked from his foul mouth.

"Guess he was a big wolf, after all." Sam shifted, steadying the imbalanced gnat who finally gave up words but puddled into sounds like a wounded animal.

Guttural, unformed syllables, and the plinking music of a dropped tooth on the tile when he leaned forward.

"Thank you, Senator." I smiled, lifting the tooth and shoving it back into his mouth with all my might. "But I will have to decline your bribes."

Turning, I lifted the length of rope off the floor, looping it once around my arm until I had enough weight to sling it up toward the ceiling. As it descended, it hooked around the chandelier's gilded rungs with a graceful, perfect arc.

First try.

Once the rope was secured, I gave it a good, hefty tug.

The ceiling wobbled, dust and sheetrock flaking to the ground. The old beams in that ceiling didn't look like they'd hold a hanging man the size of Senator Bianchi, whose sounds became rhythmic begging noises.

I would do this well...or not at all...so I let him have a moment to take it all in.

Two heartbeats, three.

Just enough so he'd figure out what was coming.

Grabbing the rope, I pulled again, flecks of paint joined the rain as I channeled all my weight into yanking against the reinforced support structures meant to hold the pompous, ostentatious light fixture in place.

At last, I felt it give, just a little, and then I stopped.

I turned to Sam, who nodded, shoving the senator forward until I grabbed him with a single-handed grip around his broken jaw.

His pain was exquisite.

Tears and snot and bloody drool oozed from every lying orifice of the man who'd made my girl's life a living hell. I squeezed only a little to make sure his eyes widened and stayed fixed on me as I memorized every detail on his face. I wanted to remember placing the noose around his neck as he begged, and oh, how deliciously he begged. Even as I put the rope around his neck, tightening it until it turned his skin red, then yanking it around to burn the skin so it dangled off the back of his body.

Tears.

Begging.

It was a beautiful moment for Senator Bianchi.

I wanted to feel, smell, this moment for Gia, who couldn't fight for herself.

I did this for every brutalized, trafficked, abused, and abandoned woman that this man and every other man like him had used and discarded like chattel. Here was the moment I redeemed the monster I'd become by killing all the monsters who'd made me this way.

Pulling the wasting sack of skin closer, I leaned my face down until I was right in his ear. I drew in the smell of sweat and blood, and let the exhale drop like an anvil.

"Power belongs to those who take it."

His eyes widened as I violently snapped his head to the side; Shattered teeth, a broken neck, then nothing.

I dropped him to the bloody glass-covered floor, then pulled the chandelier down on top of him with a shattering crash. He gurgled his last beneath shattered glass, unused rope, and the weight of his crumbling house of cards.

Press Release

BREAKING NEWS: Senator Michael Bianchi Found Dead in Manhattan Penthouse
By: Caroline Marks | Political Correspondent, The New York Ledger

Manhattan, NY: Political heavyweight U.S. Senator Michael Bianchi (R-NY) was found dead early this morning in his private Manhattan penthouse. Sources within NYPD confirm the scene appears to be a suicide, though details remain tightly controlled.

Bianchi's body was discovered in the early morning hours by his housekeeper. He was found beneath the wreckage of a shattered chandelier, with early reports suggesting the structure collapsed under the weight of a hanging body—though forensic confirmation is still pending. This, of course, just hours after a series of explosive anonymous social media posts began circulating under the hashtag SetHerFree, accusing the senator of gross abuse, family imprisonment, and even connections to a global crime syndicate.

"We're treating this as a developing investigation," said a spokesperson for NYPD Commissioner Niall. "Preliminary forensics indicate suicide by hanging, but the medical examiner will determine the official cause of death after an autopsy is completed."

The #SetHerFree campaign gained traction after posts claimed the senator's adult daughter, Gia Bianchi, had been held against her will. Screenshots, leaked correspondence, and images of a woman holding a baby in distress prompted two prominent campaign donors to withdraw their support publicly late yesterday afternoon, with others casting doubt on the senator's long-touted family values platform.

Bianchi's office had not yet responded before the news of his death broke, and is remaining silent now as even more heat hits his political affiliations, which are undergoing a federal audit. One auditor anonymously commented to this news outlet that the senator is linked to a criminal network funneling money and drugs through an alleged trafficking ring with international reach.

Federal agencies have not commented on these allegations. However, a sealed federal indictment, previously thought unrelated, has now been reopened, implicating a growing list of high-profile political figures on both sides of the aisle. The U.S. Senate is expected to convene an emergency ethics committee next week to address growing speculation around Bianchi's connections, his charitable organization APEX, and the fallout of his sudden death.

Multiple state and federal investigations are reportedly underway.

Bianchi is survived by his daughter, Gia Bianchi, who has not made a public statement. Sources close to the investigation report she is under protective medical care following an undisclosed incident earlier this week.

Developing Story. Check back for updates.

59

TROY

I WAS BORN AGAIN when I lifted my beautiful girl into my arms.

I cradled her in the backseat, and Chase drove, as Sam filled me in on her rescue while monitoring the IV fluids she needed to flush the drugs from her system. They'd made it to her in time, but we were all too late to spare her from whatever violence caused the visible bruises and likely concussion.

In our ears, Moira kept us apprised of the shift on social media as Lila's media bomb began to roll out, but honestly, all I could do was hold my siren.

Begging her to wake up.

Begging her to forgive me.

She did both when her eyes flickered open, searching my face as tears flooded those crystalline blue eyes, and she whispered.

"Ben?" Her voice was broken, no doubt from the swelling to match the strap of purple bruise that made me wish I could resurrect her father just to kill him again.

"Safe." I gripped her tighter, pulling her into me for fear that if she slipped even a moment, she'd flit away like a dream. I let my one free hand tuck her hair behind her ears, freeing me to see the colors blooming on her cheek. Each shade, a deeper well of regret, as I catalogued her injuries as personal failures.

"Forgive me, love. I did not keep you safer." Gia grabbed my hand, slowly shaking her head into my palm as a tear burned through me.

"You came for me...saved me." A fresh sob made the words sound pained, and my heart cracked in two.

"Hush." I pressed my lips to her forehead, careful not to jostle her or add too much pressure. Tugging my palm, Gia looked at the cuts and scrapes across my knuckles. Sam had cleaned them, but I refused bandages as they would block me from feeling my girl's skin.

"Are you okay?" She flicked her eyes to Sam next, then to the front seat. "Are you all–"

"Aces." Sam leaned in. "This was a walk in the park."

Chase's 'oorah' from the front seat gave my girl a small smile as she relaxed back into my arms.

"And the baby?" The drugs were still not entirely out of her system, and I shot a look at Sam, wondering how long before the confusion would clear.

"Ben's okay, Love," I repeated. "We found him in seconds. He's been with Moira and Lila this whole time."

"She means, the other baby." Sam smiled and handed over a small blue-and-white stick with two blue lines.

"Congrats, Dad." Chase beamed through the rearview.

Gaping in wonder, in disbelief, I looked at the test and then to my siren.

Pregnant.

She was pregnant.

"Oh...my heart." I gasped, breathing in the scent of my girl, my world, as I held both her and our baby in my arms, and cried. "How can I ever thank you for such a gift?"

"Tell me," She pulled at my shirt, burying her face in my neck. "Tell me he's gone."

"He is dead. I killed him for you." I saw Sam's eyes go wide with my admission, but I never hesitated. If anyone deserved to know their monster had been slain, it was Gia. "He will never hurt you, never hunt you, ever again."

I would never share the gritty details with her, but this she deserved.

Her father, her tormentor, was forever gone.

She dozed after that, in and out of consciousness. I asked about taking her to a hospital, pushed even once I knew she was pregnant, but Sam and Lila both agreed the heat was too intense and the scrutiny would shine a light on Ben. Brandt, his reason reigning supreme, reminded us all that until his parentage was confirmed, CPS could be called. Sam personally promised close monitoring, so I relented to cooler heads.

Our homecoming came with tears.

I carried my love over the threshold to the smiles and cheers of our entire family.

Moira and Lila, tear-streaked, exhausted, and achingly relieved, were beaming to hug their husbands, and then Gia, though my arms made that a challenge.

I couldn't let her go.

Chief Brandt and his wife, Carol, watching over the children and fussing over us all like doting grandparents, prepared a feast of a breakfast, which I was happy to see Gia able to partake in. Unsure of the full weight of what she'd endured, no one was quick to pepper her with questions, save Sam, who, medically, insisted on a better exam.

My brave girl told us everything.

Through tears, she shared each moment of her time away from me with everyone at some point. From her decision to spare Ben with the tracker, to her father's vile treatment of her when he found out she'd fallen in love with me. She paused her story at that point, resting a hand on my jaw until I unclenched, whispering reminders of how she was here...with me...and safe.

I should have killed him harder.

Continuing, she shared how Moira's clever campaign had shifted her father's plans, and how he'd tried to pivot into an arranged marriage with Dr. Freeman, who, sadistically or not, was at least gentle with her. I tipped my head at Chase, having heard how he'd thrown the man to the ground like the deadweight he was–bouncing once before staying down.

That poor man took an unfortunate tumble down 40 flights of stairs.

When fatigue crept into her eyes, I called the sharing circle to a close, carrying her to the bedroom where she looked longingly at the bathroom. With a nod, I brought her to the shower, starting the water to warm as I carefully perched her at the edge of the counter and began undressing us both.

She was blessedly free of other injuries save the bruises to her neck and face.

Those were still too many.

Then, wrapping her around me, I bathed my queen, worshipping her body with lathered hands, washing away every ounce of the evil that hinted across the canvas of her body. I gently washed her hair, soaking in her groans of satisfaction like rewards. Kneeling at her feet, I carefully shaved every inch of her long, creamy legs before lingering on the floor and pressing my face into the home of our child.

My tears fell with the shower's grace.

Afterwards, I dried us both and carried her to the bed, noting the way her eyes scanned over where the crib once stood.

"The room across the hall has been made into a make-shift nursery," I stated, sliding my girl into the middle of the bed, lowering myself gently behind her. "We can move Ben back in after a day or two has passed if you wish. You need time to rest and heal." Gia nodded, a slight hum of approval leading the way to her only question. "But...where's the chair?"

EPILOGUE

MOIRA

I UTILIZED ALL THE skills at my disposal to launch the viral #SetHer-Free campaign.

But what started as my desperate cry for help became something far bigger than me. #SetHerFree didn't just shine a light on Gia's captors; it set a blaze aimed at The Apex Society. Survivors came forward in waves—women from towns like ours, women from countries I'd only read about, women walking into U.S. embassies with trembling hands and borrowed courage. When their stories hit the feed, they were met with an army.

Women everywhere took the torch and ran.

Men everywhere rose to stand behind them.

And for once, people in power had no choice but to follow through.

I still can't believe I lived to see it.

Once my family was settled into our new home, on the massive plot of land that my husband and his brothers had long secured in the Wilder lands, I began planning Troy and Gia's wedding. She insisted she didn't need anything big or fancy. Troy grumbled that he would elope if I didn't hurry.

Lila and I needed just six weeks, and the entire town came.

Not a single member of emergency services missed a moment. Troy's Captain delivered him in full color guard, and the town put on a parade-worthy procession that carried straight into the after-party, which raged long after the happy couple disappeared for their honeymoon. They deserved that joy—every second of it.

And now, when River and Blue climb into bed, I tell them my favorite story—the one I earned.

"Once upon a time," I whisper, "your mommy slayed a giant."

I tell my girls about the day their daddy was a hero, pulling me from a fire when I was scared and alone. Then I share all the big and small ways that he and their uncles saved me, and their aunts, and the town, and how we all banded together to save the whole world.

Our girls will only ever know such bold bravery.

Our new home was done about 2 weeks after that fateful night that I stood over a burner phone, listening to my husband and his brothers rescue my new sister. The fear, the pride, was almost too much to carry had it not been for Lila, Carol, and the Chief by my side. All branches of the family that welcomed me with open arms and stitched themselves into my heart.

We didn't just survive—we built something that mattered.

And when Chase wraps his arms around me at night, I some-times think of that girl I used to be—the one slamming her palm against a burning window, believing her life was over.

But I'm not ashamed of her anymore.

The fire that almost stole everything now fuels everything good: passion, purpose, faith, and family.

My story ends where I always dreamed it would—loud, messy, rooted, fierce, and whole.

Epilogue

CHASE

SENATOR BIANCHI DIED LIKE a coward, buried beneath the evil he spent decades cultivating. While the media raced to cover the scandal, my family and I stayed rooted where healing could take hold.

So much healing was needed.

My wife's brilliant plan sparked a series of Senate hearings that lasted for months. I was proud of what she accomplished—and even more grateful to be free of it. I hated how much Gia had to endure, but Troy had her back, which left me free to settle my family into our new home.

I built this place from the ground up with Moira and the girls in mind. It sits high on a ridge, tucked near the woods but just a quick blacktop drive down the mountain to the station. Coming home to find them all playing makes my soul happy. My girls are growing so fast–lungs like a banshee and their mama's steel in their spines.

I never knew a man could be so damn happy and still so tired.

It made finally saying yes to the promotion a lot easier.

Chief Jacobs is retiring at the end of the year, and I'll be stepping in as Battalion Chief. Took me a while to accept that I don't have to be the one charging into the fire to protect people. Sometimes you protect more by leading and training the next wave.

By going home at night in one piece.

Spaghetti night is louder now—highchairs, teething rings, and sippy cups next to beer bottles. Lila grunts every time Sam brings up wanting more kids. I think she and Moira are planning a covert trip for injectable birth control to keep Sam from repeating history.

Though I wouldn't mind a little brother or sister for my girls.

Chief and Carol wouldn't hate a few more grands either.

The family we fought for, the one we damn near died for, is bigger than ever, and I still sit in slack-jawed amazement that I get to have this. That a man like me—quiet, flawed, terrible with words—gets this kind of love.

It humbles me every damn day.

I'm whole.

Family. Purpose. Peace. Fire-tested and still standing.

Life is so...so good, but if the world ever came to claim any of them again, with fire or blood, we'd be the ones standing between them all.

My brothers and I.

Wilder iron.

Forged.

Oorah.

EPILOGUE

LILA: 4 MONTHS LATER

I ONCE HURLED MYSELF into a booze-soaked, kamikaze mission of vengeance—uncaring if I survived, as long as Marcus Brinks didn't. But my world grew. Healed. And it was no longer enough to stop a single cog in a wheel that would keep turning. Justice for my family came in a new way. We learned who the true villains were and we smashed the wheel to pieces.

I'd never been more proud of my husband than when he'd ridden into battle beside Troy. Doing for his brother what they'd once done for me. Behind the scenes, Moira and I made sure no rat escaped into the darkest corners of Apex's world. The additional files I leaked to the press became the backbone of a sweeping FBI investigation, leading to the indictment of dozens of Apex affiliates. It was a media wildfire, and in the ashes, Apex began eating itself alive. And us...we were still standing.

Looking forward felt good.

Troy and Gia needed a little time to heal and recover, so Moira jumped in to help plan their wedding. I was roped in, like it or not, and between the two of us, it was a whopping 6 weeks before the entire town celebrated the wedding of the newest Mr. and Mrs. Wilder. We all celebrated like we'd earned it, and no one deserved the way the town turned out like Gia and Troy did. I was so glad I'd stopped puking when I shoveled in my third slice of cake.

My burst of second-trimester energy ushered in a new passion, too—for repurposing the Scaled Back bar. Apex's crumbling empire left the property in limbo, allowing me to buy it for a song. Using the funds from my father's and brother's life insurance, I repurposed the space into a multi-use halfway house for women looking to reboot their lives from abuse, neglect, and other such atrocities.

By the time the smoke had lifted, the Rivera House was born.

It filled a need I saw when the victims of Apex began pouring out. I could think of no better way to honor my father and brother than to use their name to help others find footing again after escaping the worst life could offer. We provided shelter, education, healthcare, and therapy to women from all walks of life. My work kept me engaged in rooting out and supporting the countless women affected by Apex, but more than that, it gave me an outlet for all my technical skills.

Building on our mission, The Rivera House brought in teachers to provide continuing education classes to the women in our care. My 12-week course, called the Reboot Lab, was one I designed. A month of beginner skills on PC literacy, digital hygiene, and navigating the eWorld via email and online resources. The second month dialed up the personal power tools: online banking, job search strategies, and advanced digital privacy. The final month was a tactical sprint, involving basic coding, digital design, and guided support to launch them into safe networking and ongoing job security.

I adored empowering these women to fix their own damn lives.

I even enjoyed coordinating local high schoolers who needed volunteer hours to come in and teach my curriculum when my pregnancy advanced so far that I was officially waddling. I swear my daughter was learning Krav Maga in the womb, judging by the way she was kicking my ribs. My new director at Rivera House teased me about it relentlessly as she polished her trusty bat, figuring I deserved a little rib-kicking payback for all the brawls I'd started in her bar.

Turns out Marge hated Florida.

Sam took the lead on our home construction while I worked, fussing at me daily to rest, sit, and otherwise die a slow death of boredom as he cooed nightly to my baby bump. I went into labor less than 48 hours after the last box was unloaded into our new home, and Jesse Delilah Wilder arrived like a freight train. My labor hit so fast that Moira and Carol supported my back while Sam delivered her—just as the EMTs skidded into our driveway.

My Lumberjack was beyond thrilled.

My brand-new couch... not so much.

Who cares?

There was a time I didn't think I'd live long enough to have this. A husband who treated me like royalty, sisters who were my sparring partners in almost every way imaginable, brothers who shielded us all like warriors, and a daughter who looked like my mother and had a telescope perched in her nursery, courtesy of her uncles.

I'm not a cop.

Not a hacker.

Still a fighter.

Free...and wildly loved.

EPILOGUE

SAM: 6 MONTHS LATER

W E WILDER MEN DID our part the night we brought Gia home. But the real work began for the women after that. Moira and Lila both rallied to support Gia through investigative interviews. Chase and I could only watch and be a listening ear when the firestorm got too intense for Troy. And it was brutal for him, not being able to shield Gia from the fallout of her father's crimes. She went through hell before, and all the heat after was a new kind of torture.

He never wavered for her.

We never wavered for him.

The 6-week wait for the wedding might have been harder, though. I swear that big stoic grandpa was such a softy for Gia. She soothed something in him I don't think any of us knew was there, and I loved that for him.

I was happy to warm the sidelines while my wife grew into her new role as head of Rivera House - and head of our new house. She was so Lila-focused on the revamp of Scaled Back that I had to make the decisions on our new home construction. So, I made sure we had enough rooms for a few extra kiddos down the line.

Especially with how damn sexy she looked—big, round, and glowing with our daughter.

I tried to get my wife to rest more, to take it easy, but she fought me every step of the way. At least until I got Marge back. Then we only bickered about baby names, with me drawing the line at anything that sounded like a stripper or a hurricane. In the end, my wife chose the perfect moniker for my daughter.

My Jessie-girl.

Ten fingers, ten toes, a head full of wild dark hair, and lungs that proved she was her mama through and through. Catching her as she entered this world will forever be a core memory–the moment everything in my world just...clicked.

Life is now messy, sleepless, and loud, just the way I always wanted it. A far cry from the perma-bachelor life I'd endured before my wife blew onto the scene.

I am so damned content.

My wife is next to me in our bed, my daughter is on my chest, and I am planning all the things I can try to convince Lila to try for baby number two. She tells me it'll never happen, that she's content to be one-and-done, but seeing the softness in her as she cares for our baby is mesmerizing. She has this radiant peace that makes it so clear she was meant for this.

I'll convince her.

Why the hell else did I build all these extra rooms?

I'm still running EMS shifts and driving the guys crazy with all my new-dad stories and entirely too many baby pictures—but mostly, I love being home. Spaghetti nights are a fucking circus. Ben, River, and Blue are into everything, and now my Jesse-girl is adding her vocals to the mix. Gia is due any day now, and in no time flat, the Wilder cousins are gonna rule this little town of ours.

God help anyone who gets in their way.

My brothers and I are raising 'em tough, but frankly, their mamas are instilling pure steel in their spines.

We've earned it–Troy, Chase, and I.

Three orphaned boys who fell into a home full of love...and who have now created a space where three strong women could have been cut from Nonna's cloth. She would have loved them all so much.

She fought for this legacy.

We fought for this peace.

And now...we get to keep it.

Oorah.

EPILOGUE

GIA: 8 MONTHS LATER

C AGED NO LONGER, THE freedom I found with Troy was immeasurable and multifaceted.

The media frenzy I endured in the wake of my father's death was stressful, but it passed. Troy's steadfast nature kept him by my side through it all, shadowing me at every interview and supporting me through every emotional meltdown.

So many tears.

The media stopped looking at me as soon as the Senate hearings began, and I was able to move forward...as Mrs. Gia Wilder. Changing my name was the easiest decision I've ever made, seconded only by formally adopting Ben as my son. A process that went flawlessly, as his only known living relative. Troy and I kept the adoption records closed and agreed only to disclose his true parentage if and when the time felt right in Ben's early adult years.

His entry into the world was soaked in sorrow and terror.

I meant to give him a life free of it.

Small-town living took some getting used to. I'd never had so much attention or affection shared by so many. It took about a month of walking Main Street with my husband for me to stop flinching when people spoke to me. It was overwhelming in the best way, and by the time my belly grew round enough to enter a room before I did, I understood why Troy and his brothers loved it so.

Even Carol Brandt took me under her wing, teaching me prenatal yoga alongside Lila, and accompanying me to visit the gravesite of my mother—something Troy discovered during his work with the authorities.

That moment was hard.

Carol was unflinching.

My energy during the second trimester was incredible, and Troy encouraged me to take the lead with the contractors as we finalized our new home. I found myself surprisingly decisive, and we had it done nearly the same time as Sam and Lila's. I was a little sad to see the work end, which spurred my new sisters to propose a career path for me. I was hesitant at first, but with Troy's quiet enthusiasm at my back, I secured my realtor's license and became the official face of NB Realty.

I'd never experienced a life with such forward-facing joy.

I never wanted to go back into the shadows again.

Helping families find or build their homes became a quiet pleasure—an indulgence I never expected. Like each front door opened, chipped away at everything my father had done to tear down the idea of family. It was a silent defiance I reveled in, and somehow, Moira and Lila knew I needed that little flag to fly.

No home touched my heart more than the one I built for us; with the nursery I designed behind locked doors as a surprise for my Boss Man.

A surprise finished just in time.

Me: Hey, boss man?

Bossman: Yes, my love?

Me: Got that hospital bag ready?

Bossman: What?!?!?

Epilogue

Troy: 8 Months & 15 Minutes Later

T HE WAR INSIDE ME was won the moment my family was whole again. Gia hadn't just saved herself, but Ben and our unborn child in a blaze of courage that astounded me.

Then she buried Apex in the ashes.

My need for control stilled...I only needed her. A feeling that roared through me as the uniformed officer drove me to the hospital in record time, finding my family gathered around my wife at the Labor & Delivery intake desk.

"My water broke about 40 minutes ago." My siren sighed.

"Gia!" I slid to a stop at her side. "40 minutes? You only told me 15 ago! Why did you not–"

"Hey, hey, Boss Man." Her hand rested on my cheek as I knelt beside her, my hand on her belly as I scanned her up and down. "I needed a shower. Then I called Carol to sit with Ben. Moira drove me here."

Even now, as we prepared to launch into the unknown, she was thinking of our son—the raucous 1-year-old who was cruising, talking, and getting into everything.

Such a wonderful mother.

"Labor takes time." Moira smiled, snuggling into Chase's chest.

"Unless you're Jessie, and you arrive on mommy's new couch." Lila and Sam smiled down at their infant daughter, unbothered by the need to replace furniture upon her arrival.

"What do we do now?" I looked at the nurse, who seemed decidedly bored despite my world exploding around me.

"Now you say goodbye to the entourage, Dad, and we'll get Mama back into a room." She focused on my family next. "The waiting room for labor and delivery is—"

"Just around the corner." They answered in unison. "We know."

Hugs were shared all around, with both my brothers whispering last-minute tips in my ears before I heard my girl give a sucking hiss of discomfort.

Labor...was brutal.

My Gia was a goddess, pure and powerful, breathing and rocking and swaying through 4 hours of pain as if she'd prepared her whole life for the moment. But watching her hurt, seeing her pant and cling, ripped my heart in two.

I was privileged to do anything she needed.

I hated that I couldn't do it all.

Her strength, her voice, calmed me as I watched in awe—a voyeur to a display of power I would never match. I held her through each contraction, reminding her with all I could how loved and cherished she was. As she breathed between her work, I fanned her head, slid ice across her lips, trying to keep her calm, and stalking the beeping monitors that reported mysterious data from the variety of belts strapped around my world.

Then she'd grip my hand, and we'd go again.

When Dr. Burner arrived, Gia begged to push, and he conducted the final exam before taking command of the room with practiced precision. Nurses wheeled in a variety of beds, tables, and everything our little one might need.

But I only had eyes for my warrior.

"Ready to unwrap this gift, mama?" He gave her a knowing wink, and Gia nodded, smiling through sobs. "Dad, help her sit forward. We'll try this position first unless she tells us she needs to move."

"She tells us?" I couldn't hide my shock as the slumbering beast in me lifted its head.

"Laboring is hard work." He answered. "I find it goes better if we stay out of the way and let the moms tell us what they need." Gia gripped my hand, and I pulled her forward as she held her chin to her chest through the first of six earth-shattering pushes.

Speechless, I could only watch in stunned awe as Gia bled and roared and gave life...to our son.

A boy.

Dr. Burner plopped him onto Gia's chest as we both sobbed at the tiny, squalling miracle. I let my tears fall into my siren's hair and worshiped at the altar of the woman who'd made me a father...again.

"Ready to cut the cord, Dad?" I pulled back, wishing I had words to convey the deep respect and pride I had for my wife. She was always so strong, so capable, and never had that been more on display than in this moment. Holding our son to her as I leaned down with one hand and snipped between the clamps, I returned to kiss her forehead, her nose, and then I watched as she spoke her first words to our son.

"Welcome to the world, little man." His crying quieted, and his face turned towards her in a way I felt in my bones.

We would all, always, listen for her voice.

The world slipped away; nurses still moved, Dr. Burner still at his post between my wife's feet, but my world narrowed to just Gia — and my boy.

"You knew," I confirmed, realizing why she'd hidden the nursery. "You knew we were having a boy."

Gia looked at me as if to speak, but sucked in another sharp breath.

"She's not done, Dad." He nodded to a nurse. "It's time to move, here." A nurse whisked our son away, delivering him to a warming table which blessedly stayed in my line of sight–my heart split in two.

"What's happening?" I asked, as Gia pulled herself forward using my arms again for leverage, chin to chest, once more to deliver ... another son.

Twins.

TWINS!

I had three boys.

My bride had held a gift so precious for me and let their birth blow the roof off my happiness. I learned later that the nursery at home was finished and decorated, with a matching pair of cribs, dual car seats, and pairs of infant care gear, all staged and ready.

Benji, Bryant, and Bolten–My boys.

Gia steadied, stilled, and healed me in ways beyond my comprehension. Gifting me a future full of loud and wild and everything I never knew I'd always wanted. Pure love, screaming in stereo, and not a single piece of the past left to haunt us.

My family.

My entire world.

Safe, in my arms, forever.

Safe, as they would remain, in my protection.

Oorah.

ACKNOWLEDGEMENTS

THE WILDER FAMILY'S JOURNEY to the page has been anything BUT solitary. The team of people who have helped bring my vision to life, are nothing short of amazing.

Thank you to Jonathan House and the Candlelight Creative team. The artwork for Gaslight, Matchstrike, and Burn gave my little broken box of crayons and word pictures absolute wings.

To Laura at The Writers Life, LLC, stay amazing and don't ever leave me or my pet ellipsis...clearly...we'll forever need you and your unique brand of encouragement and critiques.

Finally, to Aimee Ravichandran at Abundantly Social. Rapid release has been brutal but you've gone the extra mile to make sure my stories have reached as many hands as possible. You rock.

This trilogy is all mine, but each of you helped deliver it to the world. Thank you all.

About the Author

R HONE ATLESHEN IS A multi-award-winning, and Amazon best-selling author writing under a new name to explore the darker corners of the thriller world. After more than fifteen years crafting stories across genres, Rhone launched this brand to focus on what truly haunts the page: domestic danger, emotional reckoning, and villains you love to hate.

Known for strong voice, cinematic pacing, and deeply flawed characters, Rhone's work delivers adrenaline-soaked tension with explosive payoffs—and sometimes a little spice. Whether writing psychological thrillers, romantic suspense, or twisted moral dilemmas, the common thread is always this: the bad guys burn in the end.

Read more Rhone

The Apex Society Trilogy
Gaslight (Book One)
Matchstrike (Book Two)
Burn (Book Three) — You're holding it.
COMING SOON — Another thriller in the works. For sneak peeks, or
bonus scenes from Rhone works you already love, visit rhoneatleshen.
com or follow
@RhoneAtleshen on socials for updates.

One Last Thing

A SMALL REQUEST...

I F BURN, OR ANY OF the Apex Society Trilogy, made you lose sleep, cheer for the characters, or throw the book across the room (in the best way) — please leave a review.

It doesn't have to be long or fancy. Even a one-liner like 'Super hated that villain1' or *'Makes a great doorstop!'* can help other readers discover this story, and me keep creating villains you'll love to hate. Truly, even the smallest of rating and honest reviews make's a difference.

So share the love, then share the book with a friend. Your words matter more than you know. Thank you for being part of my journey.

—Rhone